KT-475-223

'A splendid success . . . the remarkable achievement of this book is to bring the classical detective story up to date' Julian Symons, *Times Literary Supplement*

'The science is neat. The characters are permitted to be complicated. Ambitions and disappointments in an institutional snakepit are superbly manipulated. The pathological sex is just right. And the writing is fine.' *New York Times*

'Beautifully written . . . She has a great descriptive gift' Peta Fordham, *Kaleidoscope, BBC Radio 4*

'I put her fair and square among the best living novelists' *Books & Bookmen*

Also by P. D. James in Sphere Books

THE BLACK TOWER
UNNATURAL CAUSES
COVER HER FACE
SHROUD FOR A NIGHTINGALE
AN UNSUITABLE JOB FOR A WOMAN
INNOCENT BLOOD

Death of an Expert Witness

P. D. JAMES

SPHERE BOOKS LIMITED
30/32 Gray's Inn Road, London WC1X 8JL

First published in Great Britain
by Faber and Faber Limited 1977

Copyright © P. D. James 1977
First Sphere Books Edition 1978
Reprinted 1978 (twice), 1979, 1980 (twice), 1981, 1983

TRADE
MARK

This book is sold subject to the condition that
it shall not, by way of trade or otherwise, be lent,
re-sold, hired out or otherwise circulated without
the publisher's prior consent in any form of
binding or cover other than that in which it is
published and without a similar condition
including this condition being imposed on the
subsequent purchaser

Set in Linotype Baskerville

Printed and bound in Great Britain by
Collins, Glasgow

CONTENTS

Author's Note

There is no official forensic science laboratory in East Anglia and, even if there were, it is in the highest degree improbable that it would have anything in common with Hoggatt's Laboratory, whose staff, like all other characters in this story – even the most unpleasant – are purely imaginary and bear no resemblance to any person living or dead.

BOOK ONE

A CALL TO MURDER

1

The call had come at 6.12 precisely. It was second nature to him now to note the time by the illuminated dial of his electric bedside clock before he had switched on his lamp, a second after he had felt for and silenced the raucous insistence of the telephone. It seldom had to ring more than once, but every time he dreaded that the peal might have woken Nell. The caller was familiar, the summons expected. It was Detective-Inspector Doyle. The voice, with its softly intimidating suggestion of Irish burr, came to him strong and confident, as if Doyle's great bulk loomed over the bed.

'Doc Kerrison?' The interrogation was surely unnecessary. Who else in this half-empty, echoing house would be answering at 6.12 in the morning? He made no reply and the voice went on.

'We've got a body. On the wasteland – a clunch field – a mile north-east of Muddington. A girl. Strangulation by the look of it. It's probably pretty straightforward but as it's close . . .'

'All right, I'll come.'

The voice expressed neither relief nor gratitude. Why should it? Didn't he always come when summoned? He was paid well enough for his availability, but that wasn't the only reason why he was so obsessively conscientious. Doyle, he suspected, would have respected him more if he had occasionally been less accommodating. He would have respected himself more.

'It's the first turn off the A142 after you leave Gibbet's Cross. I'll have a man posted.'

He replaced the receiver, swung his legs out of bed and, reaching for his pencil and pad, noted the details while they were still fresh in his mind. In a clunch field. That probably meant mud, particularly after yesterday's rain. The window was slightly open at the bottom. He pushed it open, wincing at the rasp of the wood, and put out his head. The rich loamy smell of the fen autumn night washed over his face; strong, yet fresh. The rain had stopped and the sky was a tumult of grey clouds through which the moon, now almost full, reeled like a pale demented ghost. His mind stretched out over the deserted fields and the desolate dykes to the wide moon-bleached sands of the Wash and the creeping fringes of the North Sea. He could fancy that he smelt its medicinal tang in the rain-washed air. Somewhere out there in the darkness, surrounded by the paraphernalia of violent death, was a body. His mind recalled the familiar ambience of his trade; men moving like black shadows behind the glare of the arc-lights, the police cars tidily parked; the flap of the screens, desultory voices conferring as they watched for the first lights of his approaching car. Already they would be consulting their watches, calculating how long it would be before he could make it.

Shutting the window with careful hands, he tugged trousers over his pyjamas and pulled a polo-necked sweater over his head. Then he picked up his torch, switched off the bedside light and made his way downstairs, treading warily and keeping close to the wall to avoid the creaking treads. But there was no sound from Eleanor's room. He let his mind wander down the twenty yards of landing and the three stairs to the back bedroom where his sixteen-year-old daughter lay. She was always a light sleeper, uncannily sensitive even in sleep to the ring of the telephone. But she couldn't possibly have heard. He had no need to worry about three-year-old William. Once asleep, he never woke before morning.

Actions as well as thought were patterned. His

routine never varied. He went first to the small washroom near the back door where his wellington boots, the thick red socks protruding like a pair of amputated feet, stood ready at the door. Pushing up his sleeves over the elbow, he swilled cold water over his hands and arms, then bent down and sluiced the whole of his head. He performed this act of almost ceremonial cleansing before and after every case. He had long ago ceased to ask himself why. It had become as comforting and necessary as a religious ritual, the brief preliminary washing which was like a dedication, the final ablution which was both a necessary chore and an absolution, as if by wiping the smell of his job from his body he could cleanse it from his mind. The water splashed heavily against the glass, and rising to fumble for a towel, he saw his face distorted, the mouth hanging, the heavily-lidded eyes half hidden by glistening weeds of black hair like the surfacing visage of a drowned man. The melancholy of the early hours took hold of him. He thought:

'I'm forty-five next week and what have I achieved? This house, two children, a failed marriage, and a job which I'm frightened of losing because it's the only thing I've made a success of.' The Old Rectory, inherited from his father, was unmortgaged, unencumbered. This wasn't true, he thought, of anything else in his anxiety-ridden life. Love, the lack of it, the growing need, the sudden terrifying hope of it, was only a burden. Even his job, the territory where he moved with most assurance, was hedged with anxiety.

As he dried his hands carefully, finger by finger, the old familiar worry returned, heavy as a morbid growth. He hadn't yet been appointed as Home Office Pathologist in succession to old Dr. Stoddard and he very much wanted to be. The official appointment wouldn't give him more money. The police already employed him on an item of service basis, and paid generously enough for each case. That and the fees for coroner's post-mortems provided an income which was one of the reasons why his professional colleagues in the pathology department of the district general hospital both envied and resented his unpredictable absences on police work, the long days in court, the inevitable publicity.

Yes, the appointment was important to him. If the Home Office looked elsewhere it would be difficult to justify to the Area Health Authority a continuing private arrangement with the local Force. He wasn't even sure that they would want him. He knew himself to be a good forensic pathologist, reliable, more than competent professionally, almost obsessively thorough and painstaking, a convincing and unflappable witness. The Force knew that their meticulously erected edifices of proof wouldn't fall to pieces under cross-examination when he was in the witness box, although he sometimes suspected that they found him too scrupulous for complete comfort. But he hadn't the easy masculine camaraderie, the blend of cynicism and *machismo* which had bound old Doc Stoddard so strongly to the Force. If they had to do without him he wouldn't be greatly missed, and he doubted whether they would put themselves out to keep him.

The garage light was blinding. The overhead door swung up easily to his touch and the light splayed out over the gravel of the drive and the unkempt verges of silvered grass. But at least the light wouldn't wake Nell. Her bedroom was at the back of the house. Before switching on the engine he studied his maps. Muddington. It was a town on the edge of his area, about seventeen miles to the north-west, less than half an hour's drive each way if he were lucky. If the laboratory scientists were there already – and Lorrimer, the Senior Biologist, never missed a homicide if he could help it – then there mightn't be much for him to do. Allow, say, an hour at the scene, and with luck he would be home again before Nell woke and she need never know that he had been away. He switched off the garage light. Carefully, as if the gentleness of his touch could somehow silence the engine, he turned on the ignition. The Rover moved slowly into the night.

2

Standing motionless behind the curtains on the front landing, her right hand cupped round the pale flicker of her night-light, Eleanor Kerrison watched the sudden red blaze of the Rover's rear lights as the car stopped at the gate before turning left and accelerating out of sight. She waited until the glare of the headlights had finally faded from view. Then she turned and made her way along the corridor to William's room. She knew that he wouldn't have woken. His sleep was a sensuous gluttony of oblivion. And while he slept she knew that he was safe, that she could be free of anxiety. To watch him then was such a mingled joy of yearning and pity that sometimes, frightened of her waking thoughts but more afraid of the nightmares of sleep, she would carry her night-light into his bedroom and crouch by the cot for an hour or more, her eyes fixed on his sleeping face, her restlessness soothed by his peace.

Although she knew that he wouldn't wake, she turned the handle of the door as carefully as if expecting it to explode. The night-light, burning steadily in its saucer, was unnecessary, its yellow gleam extinguished by the moonlight which streamed through the uncurtained windows. William, bagged in his grubby sleeping suit, lay as always on his back, both arms flung above his head. His head had flopped to one side and the thin neck, stretched so still that she could see the pulse beat, looked too fragile to bear the weight of his head. His lips were slightly parted, and she could neither see nor hear the thin whisper of breath. As she watched he suddenly opened sightless eyes, rolled them upwards, then closed them with a sigh and fell again into his little semblance of death.

She closed the door softly behind her and went back to her own room next door. Dragging the eiderdown from her bed, she wrapped it round her shoulders and shuffled her way down the landing to the top of the stairs. The heavily studded oak banister curved down into the darkness of the hall from which the tick of the grandfather clock sounded as unnaturally loud and ominous as a time bomb. The atmosphere of the house came up to her nostrils, sour as a stale vacuum flask, redolent with the sad effluent of stodgy clerical dinners. Placing the night-light against the wall she sat down on the top stair, humping the eiderdown high over her shoulders and gazing into the darkness. The stair-carpet was gritty to her bare soles. Miss Willard never vacuumed it, pleading that her heart couldn't stand the strain of lugging the cleaner from step to step, and her father never appeared to notice the drabness or dirtiness of his house. He was, after all, so seldom there. Sitting rigid in the darkness she thought of her father. Perhaps he was already at the scene of crime. It depended how far he had to drive. If it were on the very fringe of his area he might not be back until lunch-time.

But what she hoped was that he would return before breakfast so that he would find her here, crouched lonely and exhausted on the top stair, waiting for him, frightened because he had left her alone. He would put away the car quietly, leaving the garage open in case the thud of the door woke her, then sneak in like a thief at the back door. She would hear the swirl of water from the downstairs washroom, his footsteps on the tessellated floor of the hall. Then he would look up and see her. He would come running up the stairs, torn between anxiety for her

14

and fear of disturbing Miss Willard, his face suddenly old with weariness and concern as he put his arms round her trembling shoulders.

'Nell, darling, how long have you been here? You shouldn't be out of bed. You'll get cold. Come on, old girl, there's nothing to be frightened of now. I'm back. Look, I'll take you back to bed again and you try to get some sleep. I'll see to the breakfast. Suppose I bring it up on a tray in about half an hour. How would you like that?'

And he would guide her back to her room, cajoling, murmuring reassurance, trying to pretend that he wasn't frightened, frightened that she would start to cry for her mother, that Miss Willard would appear, censorious and whining, complaining that she had to get her sleep, that the precarious little household would fall apart and he would be parted from William. It was William he loved, William couldn't bear to lose. And he could only keep William and stop the court from giving Mummy custody if she were at home to help care for her brother.

She thought about the day ahead. It was Wednesday, a grey day. Not a black day when she wouldn't see her father at all, but not a yellow day like Sunday, when, unless on call, he might be there most of the time. In the morning, immediately after breakfast, he would be at the public mortuary doing the post-mortem. There would be other autopsies too, those who had died in hospital, the old, the suicides, the accident victims. But the body he was probably examining now would be first on the mortuary table. Murder has priority. Wasn't that what they always said at the Lab? She mused, but without real curiosity, on what he might be doing at this very moment to that unknown cadaver, young or old, male or female. Whatever he was doing, the body wouldn't feel it, wouldn't know about it. The dead had nothing to be frightened of any more, and there was nothing

15

to fear from them. It was the living who held the power to hurt. And suddenly two shadows moved in the darkness of the hall, and she heard her mother's voice, pitched high, frighteningly unfamiliar, a strained, cracked, alien voice.

'Always your job! Your bloody job! And my God, no wonder you're good at it. You haven't the guts to be a real doctor. You made one wrong diagnosis early on and that was the end, wasn't it? You couldn't take responsibility for living bodies, blood that can flow, nerves that can actually feel. All you're fit for is messing about with the dead. It makes you feel good, doesn't it, the way they defer to you? The phone calls at all hours of the day and night, the police escort. Never mind that I'm buried alive here in this bloody fen with your children. You don't even see me any more. I'd be more interesting to you if I were dead and lain out on your slab. At least you'd be forced to take some notice of me.'

Then the low defensive mumble of her father's voice, dispirited, abject. She had listened in the darkness and wanted to call out to him:

'Don't answer her like that! Don't sound so defeated! Can't you understand that it only makes her despise you more?'

His words had come to her in snatches, barely audible.

'It's my job. It's what I do best. It's all that I can do.' And then, more clearly. 'It's what keeps us.'

'Not me. Not any longer.'

And then the slam of the door.

The memory was so vivid that for a second she thought she heard the echo of the slam. She stumbled to her feet, clutching the eiderdown around her, and opened her mouth to call to them. But then she saw that the hall was empty. There was nothing but the faint image of the stained glass in the front door where the moonlight streamed through, the ticking of the

16

clock, the bundle of coats hanging from the hallstand. She sank back again on to the stair.

And then she remembered. There was something she had to do. Slipping her hand into her dressing-gown pocket she felt the cold slippery plasticine of her model of Dr. Lorrimer. Carefully she drew it out through the folds of the eiderdown and held it close to the flame of the nightlight. The model was a little mis-shapen, the face furred with fluff from her pocket, but it was still intact. She straightened the long limbs and pressed the strands of black cotton she had used for hair more firmly into the scalp. The white coat, cut from an old handkerchief, was particularly successful, she thought. It was a pity that she hadn't been able to use one of his handkerchiefs, a strand of his hair. The model represented more than Dr. Lorrimer who had been unkind to her and William, who had practically thrown them out of the laboratory. It stood for the whole of Hoggatt's Lab.

And now to kill it. Gently she knocked the head against the baluster. But the plasticine merely flattened, the head lost its identity. She remodelled it with careful fingers, then held it close to the flame. But the smell was disagreeable and she was afraid that the white linen would burst into flame. She dug the nail of her little finger deeply in behind the left ear. The cut was clean and sharp, right through to the brain. That was better. She sighed, satisfied. Holding the dead creature in her right palm she squeezed the pink plasticine, the white coat, the cotton hair into one amorphous lump. Then, huddling deep into the eiderdown, she sat and waited for the dawn.

3

The car, a green Morris Minor, had been toppled over the edge of a shallow depression in the wasteland, and had lurched to rest on a grassy plateau about ten feet from the ridge like a clumsy animal going to earth. It must have been there for years, abandoned to the plunderers, an illicit plaything for the local children, a welcome shelter for the occasional vagrant like the seventy-year-old alcoholic who had stumbled on the body. The two front wheels had been removed, and the rusted back wheels with their rotting tyres were firmly embedded in the chalky earth, the paintwork was battered and scratched, the interior stripped of instruments and steering wheel. Two mounted arc-lights, one directed downwards from the top of the bank and the other precariously planted on the edge of the plateau, illuminated its stark decrepitude. Thus brightly lit it looked, thought Kerrison, like some grotesque and pretentious modern sculpture, symbolically poised on the brink of chaos. The back seat, its padding springing from the slashed plastic, had been ripped out and hurled to one side.

In the front seat rested the body of a girl. Her legs were decorously planted together, the glazed eyes were slyly half open, the mouth, devoid of lipstick, was fixed in a drool elongated by two small trickles of blood. They gave a face which must have been pretty, or at least childishly vulnerable, the vacuous look of an adult clown. The thin coat, too thin surely for a night in early November, was pulled waist high. She was wearing stockings; and the suspender clips bit into plump white thighs.

Drawing close to the body, under the watchful eyes of Lorrimer and Doyle, he thought, as he often did at such a scene, that it looked unreal, an anomaly, so singularly and ridiculously out of place that he had to stifle a nervous impulse to laugh. He didn't feel this so strongly when a corpse was far advanced in decay. It was then as if the rotting maggot-infested flesh, or the tags of matted clothing, had already become part of the earth which clung to and enclosed them, no more unnatural or frightening than a clump of compost or a drift of decaying leaves. But here, colours and outlines intensified in the glare, the body, still outwardly so human, looked an absurd burlesque, the skin of the pallid cheek as artificial as the stained plastic of the car against which it rested. It seemed ridiculous that she should be beyond help. As always he had to fight the impulse to fasten his mouth over hers and begin resuscitation, to plunge a needle into the still warm heart.

He had been surprised to find Maxim Howarth, newly appointed director of the Forensic Science Laboratory, at the scene, until he remembered that Howarth had said something about following through the next murder case. He supposed that he was expected to instruct. Withdrawing his head from the open door he said:

'It's almost certainly a case of manual throttling. The slight bleeding from the mouth is caused by the tongue being caught between the teeth. Manual strangulation is invariably homicidal. She couldn't have done this herself.'

Howarth's voice was carefully controlled.

'I should have expected more bruising of the neck.'

'That's usual, certainly. There's always some damage to the tissues, although the extent of the bruised area depends on the position of the assailant and victim, the way in which the neck is grasped as well as the degree of pressure. I'd expect to find deep-seated internal bruising, but it's possible to get this without many superficial signs. This happens when the murderer has maintained pressure until death; the vessels have been emptied of blood and the heart stops beating before the hands are removed. The cause of death is asphyxia, and one expects to find the usual signs of this. What is so interesting here is the cadaveric spasm. You'll see that she's clutching the bamboo handle of her bag. The muscles are absolutely rigid, proof that the grasp occurred at or about the moment of death. I've never before seen cadaveric spasm in a case of homicidal manual throttling, and it's interesting. She must have died extraordinarily quickly. But you'll get a clearer idea of what exactly happened when you watch the post-mortem.'

Of course, thought Howarth, the post-mortem. He wondered how early Kerrison would expect to get down to that job. He wasn't afraid that his nerve would fail him, only his stomach, but he wished he hadn't said he would be there. There was no privacy for the dead: the most one could hope for was a certain reverence. It now seemed to him monstrous that tomorrow he, a stranger, would be looking unrebuked at her nakedness. But for the present he had seen enough. He could step aside now without loss of face. Turning up the collar of his Burberry against the chill morning air, he climbed up the slope to the rim of the hollow and stood looking down at the car. This must be what shooting a film was like: the brightly lit scene, the ennui of waiting for the chief actors to appear, the brief moments of activity, the concentrated attention to detail. The body could easily be that of an actress simulating death. He half expected one of the police to dart forward and rearrange her hair.

The night was nearly over. Behind him the eastern sky was already brightening, and the wasteland, which had been a formless void of darkness above the lumpy earth, was assuming an identity and a shape. To the west he could see the outline of houses, probably a

council estate, a trim row of identical roofs and square
slabs of darkness broken by patterned squares of
yellow as the early risers switched on their lights. The
track along which his car had bumped, rock-strewn and
silver, alien as a moonscape in the glare of the headlights, took shape and direction, became ordinary.
Nothing was left mysterious. The place was an arid
scrubland between the two ends of the town, litter-
strewn and edged with sparse trees above a ditch. He
knew that the ditch would be dank with nettles and
sour with rotting rubbish, the trees wounded by van-
dals, the trunks carved with initials, the low branches
hanging torn from the boughs. Here was an urban no-
man's-land, fit territory for murder.

It was a mistake to have come, of course, he should
have realised that the rôle of voyeur was always ig-
noble. Few things were more demoralising than to
stand uselessly by while other men demonstrated their
professional competence; Kerrison, that connoisseur
of death, literally sniffing at the body; the photographers, taciturn, preoccupied with lighting and
angles; Inspector Doyle, in charge of a murder case at
last, impresario of death, tense with the suppressed
excitement of a child at Christmas gloating over a new
toy. Once, while waiting for Kerrison to arrive, Doyle
had actually laughed, a hearty guffaw, filling the
hollow. And Lorrimer? Before touching the body he
had briefly crossed himself. It was so small and precise
a gesture that Howarth could have missed it, except
that nothing Lorrimer did escaped him. The others
seemed unsurprised at the eccentricity. Perhaps they
were used to it. Domenica hadn't told him that Lorrimer was religious. But then his sister hadn't told
him anything about her lover. She hadn't even told
him that the affair was over. But he had needed only
to look at Lorrimer's face during the past month to
know that. Lorrimer's face, Lorrimer's hands. Odd
that he hadn't noticed how long the fingers were or

with what apparent gentleness they had taped the plastic bags over the girl's hand to preserve, as he had tonelessly explained, conscientious in his rôle of instructor, any evidence under the fingernails. He had taken a sample of blood from the plump flaccid arm, feeling for the vein as carefully as if she could still flinch at the needle's prick.

Lorrimer's hands. Howarth thrust the tormenting, brutally explicit images out of his mind. He had never before resented one of Domenica's lovers. He hadn't even been jealous of her dead husband. It had seemed to him perfectly reasonable that she should eventually wish to marry, just as she might choose, in a fit of boredom or acquisitiveness, to buy herself a fur coat or a new item of jewellery. He had even quite liked Charles Schofield. Why was it then that, even from the first moment, the thought of Lorrimer in his sister's bed had been intolerable. Not that he could ever have been in her bed, at least not at Leamings. He wondered yet again where they had managed to meet, how Domenica had contrived to take a new lover without the whole laboratory and the whole village knowing. How could they have met and where?

It had begun, of course, at that disastrous dinner party twelve months ago. At the time it had seemed both natural and civilised to celebrate the taking up of his directorship with a small private party at his house for the senior staff. They had, he remembered, eaten melon, followed by *boeuf stroganoff* and a salad. He and Domenica liked good food and, occasionally, she enjoyed cooking it. He had opened the 1961 claret for them because that was the wine he and Dom had chosen to drink and it hadn't occurred to him to offer his guests less. He and Dom had changed because that was their habit. It amused them to dine in some style, formally separating the working day from their evenings together. It hadn't been his fault that Bill Morgan, the vehicle examiner, had chosen to come in

22

open-necked shirt and corduroys; neither he nor Dom had cared a damn what their guests chose to wear. If Bill Morgan felt awkward about these unimportant shibboleths of taste, he should learn either to change his clothes or to develop more social confidence in his sartorial eccentricities.

It had never occurred to Howarth that the six senior staff sitting awkwardly around his table in the candlelight, unmellowed even by the wine, would see the whole occasion as an elaborate gastronomic charade designed to demonstrate his social and intellectual superiority. At least Paul Middlemass, the Principal Scientific Officer Document Examiner, had appreciated the wine, drawing the bottle across the table towards him and refilling his glass, his lazy ironic eyes watching his host. And Lorrimer? Lorrimer had eaten practically nothing, had drunk less, pushing his glass almost petulantly aside and fixing his great smouldering eyes on Domenica as if he had never before seen a woman. And that, presumably, had been the beginning of it. How it had progressed, when and how they had continued to meet, how it had ended, Domenica hadn't confided.

The dinner party had been a private and public fiasco. But what, he wondered, had the senior staff expected? An evening of solid drinking in the private snug in the Moonraker? A free-for-all jollification in the village hall for the whole laboratory including the cleaner, Mrs Bidwell, and old Scobie, the Laboratory attendant? 'Knees Up Mother Brown' in the public bar? Perhaps they had thought that the first move should have come from their side. But that was to admit that there were two sides. The conventional sophistry was that the Laboratory worked as a team harnessed by a common purpose, reins lightly but firmly in the director's hands. That had worked well enough at Bruche. But there he had directed a research laboratory with a common discipline. How could you direct a team when your staff practised half a dozen different scientific disciplines, used their own methods, were responsible for their own results, stood finally alone to justify and defend them in the only place where the quality of a forensic scientist's work could properly be judged, the witness box of a court of law? It was one of the loneliest places on earth, and he had never stood there.

Old Dr. Mac, his predecessor, had, he knew, taken the occasional case, to keep his hand in as he would say, trotting out to a scene of crime like an old blood-hound happily sniffing after half-forgotten scents, doing the analysis himself, and finally appearing, like a resurrected Old Testament prophet in the witness-box, greeted by the judge with dry judicial compliments, and boisterously welcomed in the bar by counsel like a long-missed old reprobate drinking comrade happily restored to them. But that could never be his way. He had been appointed to manage the Laboratory and he would manage it in his own style. He wondered, morbidly introspective in the cold light of dawn, whether his decision to see the next murder case through from the call to the scene of crime to the trial had really arisen from a desire to learn or merely from a craven wish to impress or, worse, to propitiate, his staff, to show them that he valued their skills, that he wanted to be one of the team. If so, it had been one more error of judgment to add to the bleak arithmetic of failure since he had taken up his new job.

It looked as if they had nearly finished. The girl's rigid fingers had been prised from her handbag and Doyle's hands, gloved, were spreading out its few contents on a plastic sheet laid on the bonnet of the car. Howarth could just make out the shape of what looked like a small purse, a lipstick, a folded sheet of paper. A love letter probably, poor little wretch. Had Lorrimer written letters to Domenica? he wondered. He was always first at the door when the post arrived, and usually brought his sister her letters. Perhaps Lorrimer had known that. But he must have written. There must have been assignations. Lorrimer would hardly have risked telephoning from the Laboratory or from home in the evenings when he, Howarth, might have taken the call.

They were moving the body now. The mortuary van had moved closer to the rim of the hollow and the stretcher was being manoeuvred into place. The police were dragging out the screens from their van, ready to enclose the scene of crime. Soon there would be the little clutch of spectators, the curious children shooed away by the adults, the Press photographers. He could see Lorrimer and Kerrison conferring together a little way apart, their backs turned, the two dark heads close together. Doyle was closing his notebook and supervising the removal of the body as if it were a precious exhibit which he was frightened someone would break. The light was strengthening.

He waited while Kerrison climbed up beside him and together they walked towards the parked cars. Howarth's foot struck a beer-can. It clattered across the path and bounced against what looked like the battered frame of an old pram, with a bang like a pistol shot. The noise startled him. He said pettishly:

'What a place to die! Where in God's name are we exactly? I just followed the police cars.'

'It's called the clunch field. That's the local name for the soft chalk they mined here from the Middle Ages onwards. There isn't any hard building stone hereabouts, so they used clunch for most domestic building and even for some church interiors. There's an example in the Lady Chapel at Ely. Most villages had their clunch pits. They're overgrown now. Some are quite pretty in the spring and summer, little oases of wild flowers.'

He gave the information almost tonelessly, like a dutiful guide repeating by rote the official spiel. Suddenly he swayed and reached for the support of his car door. Howarth wondered if he were ill or whether this was the extremity of tiredness. Then the pathologist straightened himself and said, with an attempt at briskness:

'I'll do the P.M. at nine o'clock tomorrow at St Luke's. The hall porter will direct you. I'll leave a message.'

He nodded a goodbye, forced a smile, then eased himself into his car and slammed the door. The Rover bumped slowly towards the road.

Howarth was aware that Doyle and Lorrimer were beside him. Doyle's excitement was almost palpable. He turned to look across the clunch field to the distant row of houses, their yellow brick walls and mean square windows now plainly visible.

'He's over there somewhere. In bed probably. That is, if he doesn't live alone. It wouldn't do to be up and about too early, would it? No, he'll be lying there wondering how to act ordinary, waiting for the anonymous car, the ring at the door. If he's on his own, it'll be different, of course. He'll be creeping about in the half-dark wondering if he ought to burn his suit, scraping the mud off his shoes. Only he won't be able to get it all off. Not every trace. And he won't have a boiler big enough for the suit. And even if he had, what will he say when we ask for it? So maybe he'll be doing nothing. Just lying there and waiting. He won't be asleep. He didn't sleep last night. And he won't be sleeping again for quite a time.'

Howarth felt slightly sick. He had eaten a small and early dinner and knew himself to be hungry. The sensation of nausea on an empty stomach was peculiarly unpleasant. He controlled his voice, betraying nothing but a casual interest.

'You think it's relatively straightforward then?'

'Domestic murder usually is. And I reckon that this is a domestic murder. Married kid, torn stump of a

26

ticket for the local Oddfellows' hop, letter in her bag threatening her if she doesn't leave another bloke alone. A stranger wouldn't have known about this place. And she wouldn't have come here with him even if he had. By the look of her, they were sitting there cosily together before he got his hands on her throat. It's just a question of whether the two of them set off home together or whether he left early and waited for her.'

'Do you know yet who she is?'

'Not yet. There's no diary in the bag. That kind don't keep diaries. But I shall know in about half an hour.'

He turned to Lorrimer.

'The exhibits should be at the Lab by nine or there-abouts. You'll give this priority?'

Lorrimer's voice was harsh.

'Murder gets priority. You know that.'

Doyle's exultant, self-satisfied bellow jangled Howarth's nerves.

'Thank God something does! You're taking your time over the Gutteridge case. I was in the Biology Department yesterday and Bradley said the report wasn't ready; he was working on a case for the defence. We all know the great fiction that the Lab is independent of the police and I'm happy to go along with it most of the time. But old Hoggatt founded the place as a police lab, and when the chips are down that's what it's all about. So do me a favour. Get moving with this one for me. I want to get chummy and get him quickly.'

He was rocking gently on his heels, his smiling face uplifted to the dawn like a happy dog sniffing at the air, euphoric with the exhilaration of the hunt. It was odd, thought Howarth, that he didn't recognise the cold menace in Lorrimer's voice.

'Hoggatt's does an occasional examination for the defence if they ask us and if the exhibit is packed and submitted in the approved way. That's departmental policy. We're not yet a police lab even if you do walk in and out of the place as if it's your own kitchen. And I decide priorities in my Laboratory. You'll get your report as soon as it's ready. In the meantime, if you want to ask questions, come to me, not to my junior staff. And, unless you're invited, keep out of my Laboratory.'

Without waiting for an answer, he walked over to his car. Doyle looked after him in a kind of angry bewilderment.

'Bloody hell! His Lab! What's wrong with him? Lately he's been as touchy as a bitch on heat. He'll find himself on a brain-shrinker's couch or in the bin if he doesn't get a hold of himself.'

Howarth said coldly:

'He's right, of course. Any enquiry about the work should be made to him, not to a member of his staff. And it's usual to ask permission before walking into a laboratory.'

The rebuke stung. Doyle frowned. His face hardened. Howarth had a disconcerting glimpse of the barely controlled aggression beneath the mask of casual good humour. Doyle said:

'Old Dr Mac used to welcome the police in his lab. He had this odd idea, you see, that helping the police was what it was all about. But if we're not wanted, you'd better talk to the chief. No doubt he'll issue his instructions.'

He turned on his heel and made off towards his car without waiting for a reply. Howarth thought:

'Damn Lorrimer! Everything he touches goes wrong for me.' He felt a spasm of hatred so intense, so physical that it made him retch. If only Lorrimer's body were sprawled at the bottom of the clunch pit. If only it were Lorrimer's cadaver which would be cradled in porcelain on the post-mortem table next day, laid out for ritual evisceration. He knew what

28

was wrong with him. The diagnosis was as simple as it was humiliating: that self-infecting fever of the blood which could lie deceptively dormant, then flare now, into torment. Jealousy, he thought was as physical as fear; the same dryness of the mouth, the thudding heart, the restlessness which destroyed appetite and peace. And he knew now that, this time, the sickness was incurable. It made no difference that the affair was over, that Lorrimer, too, was suffering. Reason couldn't cure it, nor, he suspected, could distance, nor time. It could be ended only by death; Lorrimer's or his own.

4

At half-past-six, in the front bedroom of 2 Acacia Close, Chevisham, Susan Bradley, wife of the Higher Scientific Officer in the Biology Department of Hoggatt's Laboratory, was welcomed by the faint, plaintive wail of her two-month-old baby, hungry for her first feed of the day. Susan switched on the bedside lamp, a pink glow under its frilled shade, and reaching for her dressing-gown, shuffled sleepily to the bathroom next door, and then to the nursery. It was a small back room at the back of the house, little more than a box, but when she pressed down the switch of the low-voltage nursery light she felt again a glow of maternal, proprietorial pride. Even in her sleepy morning daze the first sight of the nursery lifted her heart; the nursing chair with its back decorated with rabbits; the matching changing table fitted with drawers for the baby's things; the wicker cot in its stand which she had lined with a pink, blue and white flowered cotton to match the curtains; the bright fringe of nursery-rhyme characters which Clifford had pasted round the wall.

With the sound of her footsteps the cries became

stronger. She picked up the warm, milky-smelling cocoon and crooned reassurance. Immediately the cries ceased and Debbie's moist mouth, opening and shutting like a fish, sought her breast, the small wrinkled fists freed from the blanket, unfurled to clutch against her crumpled nightdress. The books said to change baby first, but she could never bear to make Debbie wait. And there was another reason. The walls of the modern house were thin, and she didn't want the sound of crying to wake Cliff.

But suddenly he was at the door, swaying slightly, his pyjama jacket gaping open. Her heart sank. She made her voice sound bright, matter-of-fact.

'I hoped she hadn't woken you, darling. But it's after half-past six. She slept over seven hours. Getting better.'

'I was awake already.'

'Go back to bed, Cliff. You can get in another hour's sleep.'

'I can't sleep.'

He looked round the little nursery with a puzzled frown, as if disconcerted not to find a chair. Susan said:

'Bring in the stool from the bathroom. And put on your dressing-gown. You'll catch cold.'

He placed the stool against the wall and crouched there in sullen misery. Susan raised her cheek from resting against the soft furriness of the baby's head. The small, snub-nosed leech latched on to her breast, fingers splayed in an ecstasy of content. Susan told herself that she must keep calm, mustn't let nerves and muscles knot themselves into the familiar ache of worry. Everyone said that it was bad for the milk. She said quietly:

'What's wrong, darling?'

But she knew what was wrong. She knew what he would say. She felt a new and frightening sense of resentment that she couldn't even feed Debbie in peace.

And she wished he would do up his pyjamas. Sitting like that, slumped and half-naked, he looked almost dissolute. She wondered what was happening to her. She had never felt like this about Cliff before Debbie was born.

'I can't go on. I can't go into the Lab today.'

'Are you ill?'

But she knew that he wasn't ill, at least not yet. But he would be ill if something wasn't done about Edwin Lorrimer. The old misery descended on her. People wrote in books about a black weight of worry, and they were right, that was just how it felt, a perpetual physical burden which dragged at the shoulders and the heart, denying joy, even destroying, she thought bitterly, their pleasure in Debbie. Perhaps in the end it would destroy even love. She didn't speak but settled her small, warm burden more comfortably against her arm.

'I've got to give up the job. It's no use, Sue. I can't go on. He's got me in such a state that I'm as useless as he says I am.'

'But Cliff, you know that isn't true. You're a good worker. There were never complaints about you at your last lab.'

'I wasn't an H.S.O. then. Lorrimer thinks I ought never to have been promoted. He's right.'

'He isn't right. Darling, you mustn't let him sap your confidence. That's fatal. You're a conscientious, reliable forensic biologist. You mustn't worry if you're not as quick as the others. That isn't important. Dr. Mac always said it's accuracy that counts. What does it matter if you take your time? You get the answer right in the end.'

'Not any longer. I can't even do a simple peroxidase test now without fumbling. If he comes within two feet of me my hands start shaking. And he's begun checking all my results. I've just finished examining the stains on the mallet from the suspected Pascoe

31

murder. But he'll work late tonight doing it again. And he'll make sure that the whole biology department knows why.'

Cliff couldn't, she knew, stand up to bullying or sarcasm. Perhaps it was because of his father. The old man was paralysed now after a stroke and she supposed that she ought to feel sorry for him lying there in his hospital bed, useless as a felled tree, mouth slavering, only the angry eyes moving in impotent fury from face to watching face. But from what Cliff had let slip he had been a poor father, an unpopular and unsuccessful schoolmaster yet with unreasonable ambitions for his only son. Cliff had been terrified of him. What Cliff needed was encouragement and affection. Who cared if he never rose any higher than H.S.O.? He was kind and loving. He looked after her and Debbie. He was her husband and she loved him. But he mustn't resign. What other job could he get? What else was he suited for? Unemployment was as bad in East Anglia as it was elsewhere. There was the mortgage to pay and the electricity bill for the central heating – they couldn't economise there because of Debbie needing warmth – and the hire-purchase on the bedroom suite to find. Even the nursery furniture wasn't paid for yet. She had wanted everything nice and new for Debbie, but it had taken all their remaining savings. She said:

'Couldn't you apply to Establishment Department for a transfer?'

The despair in his voice tore at her heart.

'No-one will want me if Lorrimer says I'm no good. He's probably the best forensic biologist in the service. If he thinks I'm useless, then I'm useless.'

It was this, too, which she was beginning to find irritating, the obsequious respect of the victim for his oppressor. Sometimes, appalled by her disloyalty, she could begin to understand Dr. Lorrimer's contempt. She said:

32

'Why not have a word with the director?'

'I might have done if Dr. Mac was still there. But Howarth wouldn't care. He's new. He doesn't want any trouble with the senior staff, particularly now when we're getting ready to move into the new Lab.'

And then she thought of Mr. Middlemass. He was the Principal Scientific Officer Document Examiner, and she had worked for him as a young S.O. before her marriage. It was at Hoggatt's Laboratory that she had met Cliff. Perhaps he could do something, could speak to Howarth for them, could use his influence with Estabs. She wasn't sure how she expected him to help, but the need to confide in someone was over-whelming. They couldn't go on like this. Cliff would have a breakdown. And how would she manage with the baby and Cliff ill and the future uncertain? But surely Mr. Middlemass could do something. She believed in him because she needed to believe. She looked across at Cliff.

'Don't worry, darling, it's going to be all right. We're going to think of something. You go in today and we'll talk about it in the evening.'

'How can we? Your mother's coming to supper.'

'After supper then. She'll be catching the quarter to eight bus. We'll talk then.'

'I can't go on like this, Sue.'

'You won't have to. I'll think of something. It's going to be all right. I promise you, darling. It's going to be all right.'

5

'Mum, did you know that every human being is unique?'

'Of course I did. It stands to reason, doesn't it? There's only one of every person. You're you. I'm me.

Pass your Dad the marmalade and keep your sleeves out of that butter.'

Brenda Pridmore, recently appointed Clerical Officer/receptionist at Hoggatt's Laboratory, pushed the marmalade across the breakfast table and began methodically slicing thin strips from the white of her fried egg, postponing, as she had from early childhood, that cataclysmic moment when she would plunge the fork into the glistening yellow dome. But indulgence in this small personal ritual was almost automatic. Her mind was preoccupied with the excitements and discoveries of her wonderful first job.

'I mean biologically unique. Inspector Blakelock, he's the Assistant Police Liaison Officer, told me that every human being has a unique fingerprint and no two types of blood are exactly the same. If the scientists had enough systems they could distinguish them all, the blood types I mean. He thinks that day may come in time. The forensic serologist will be able to say with certainty where the blood came from, even with a dried stain. It's dried blood that's difficult. If that blood is fresh we can do far more with it.'

'Funny job you've got yourself.' Mrs. Pridmore refilled the teapot from the kettle on the Aga hob and eased herself back into her chair. The farmhouse kitchen, its flowered cretonne curtains still undrawn, was warm and cosily domestic, smelling of toast, fried bacon and hot strong tea.

'I don't know that I like the idea of you checking in bits of body and bloodstained clothes. I hope you wash your hands properly before you come home.'

'Oh Mum, it's not like that! The exhibits all arrive in plastic bags with identifying tags. We have to be ever so particular that all of them are labelled and properly entered in the book. It's a question of continuity of evidence, what Inspector Blakelock calls the integrity of the sample. And we don't get bits of body.'

Remembering suddenly the sealed bottles of stomach contents, the carefully dissected pieces of liver and intestines, looking when you came to think of it, no more frightening than exhibits in the science laboratory at school, she said quickly:

'Well, not in the way you mean. Dr. Kerrison does all the cutting up. He's a forensic pathologist attached to the Laboratory. Of course, some of the organs come to us for analysis.'

Inspector Blakelock, she remembered, had told her that the Laboratory refrigerator had once held a whole head. But that wasn't the kind of thing to tell Mum. She rather wished that the Inspector hadn't told her. The refrigerator, squat and gleaming like a surgical sarcophagus, had held a sinister fascination for her ever since. But Mrs. Pridmore had seized gratefully on a familiar name.

'I know who Dr. Kerrison is, I should hope. Lives at the Old Rectory at Chevisham alongside the church, doesn't he? His wife ran off with one of the doctors at the hospital, left him and the two kids, that odd-looking daughter and the small boy, poor little fellow. You remember all the talk there was at the time, Arthur?'

Her husband didn't reply, nor did she expect him to. It was an understood convention that Arthur Pridmore left breakfast conversation to his women. Brenda went happily on:

'Forensic science isn't just helping the police to discover who's guilty. We help clear the innocent too. People sometimes forget that. We had a case last month – of course, I can't mention names – when a sixteen-year-old choir girl accused her vicar of rape. Well, he was innocent.'

'So I should hope! Rape indeed!'

'But it looked very black against him. Only he was lucky. He was a secreter.'

'A what, for goodness sake?'

'He secreted his blood group in all his body fluids. Not everyone does. So the biologist was able to examine his saliva and compare his blood group with the stains on the victim's . . .'

'Not at breakfast, Brenda, if you don't mind.'

Brenda, her eyes suddenly alighting on a round milk stain on the table cloth, herself thought that breakfast wasn't perhaps the most suitable time for a display of her recently acquired information about the investigation of rape. She went on to a safer subject.

'Dr. Lorrimer – he's the Principal Scientific Officer in charge of the Biology Department – says that I ought to work for an A-level subject and try for a job as an Assistant Scientific Officer. He thinks that I could do better than just a clerical job. And once I got my A.S.O. I'd be on a scientific grade and could work myself up. Some of the most famous forensic scientists have started that way, he said. He's offered to give me a reading list, and he says he doesn't see why I shouldn't use some of the laboratory equipment for my practical work.'

'I didn't know that you worked in the Biology Department.'

'I don't. I'm mainly on Reception with Inspector Blakelock, and sometimes I help out in the general office. But we got talking when I had to spend an afternoon in his laboratory checking reports for courts with his staff, and he was ever so nice. A lot of people don't like him. They say he's too strict; but I think he's just shy. He might have been Director if the Home Office hadn't passed him over and appointed Dr. Howarth.'

'He seems to be taking quite an interest in you, this Mr. Lorrimer.'

'Dr. Lorrimer, Mum.'

'Dr. Lorrimer, then. Though why he wants to call

himself a doctor beats me. You don't have any patients at the lab.'

'He's a Ph.D., Mum. Doctor of Philosophy.'

'Oh, is he? I thought he was supposed to be a scientist. Anyway, you'd better watch your step.'

'Oh Mum, don't be daft. He's old. He must be forty or more. Mum, did you know that our Lab is the oldest forensic science lab in the country? There are regional labs covering the whole country but ours was the first. Colonel Hoggatt started it in Chevisham Manor when he was Chief Constable in 1860, then left the manor house to his force when he died. Forensic science was in its infancy then, Inspector Blakelock says, and Colonel Hoggatt was one of the first Chief Constables to see its possibilities. We've got his portrait in the hall. We're the only lab with its founder's name. That's why the Home Office has agreed that the new Laboratory will still be called Hoggatt's. Other police forces send their exhibits to their regional laboratory, North-East or the Metropolitan and so on. But in East Anglia they say "Better send it to Hoggatt's".'

'You'd better send yourself to Hoggatt's if you want to get there by eight-thirty. And I don't want you taking any short cuts through the new Lab. It isn't safe, only half-built, especially these dark mornings. Like as not you'd fall into the foundations or get a brick down on your head. They're not safe, building sites aren't. Look what happened to your Uncle Will.'

'All right, Mum. We're not supposed to go through the new Lab anyway. Besides, I'm going by bike. Are these my sandwiches or Dad's?'

'Yours, of course. You know your Dad's home to dinner on Wednesdays. Cheese and tomato this morning, and I've put you in a boiled egg.'

When Brenda had waved goodbye, Mrs. Pridmore sat down for her second cup of tea and looked across at her husband.

'I suppose it's all right, this job she's found for her-self.'

Arthur Pridmore, when he did condescend to talk at breakfast, talked with the magisterial authority of head of his family, Mr. Bowlem's bailiff and People's warden at the village church. He laid down his fork.

'It's a good job, and she was lucky to get it. Plenty of girls from the grammar school after it, weren't they? An established civil servant, isn't she? And look what they're paying her. More than the pigman gets at the farm. Pensionable too. She's a sensible girl and she'll be all right. There aren't many opportunities left loc-ally for girls with good O-levels. And you didn't want her to take a job in London.'

No indeed, Mrs. Pridmore hadn't wanted Brenda to go to London, a prey to muggers, I.R.A. terrorists and what the Press mysteriously called 'the drug scene'. None of her infrequent, but uneventful and pleasant, visits to the capital on Women's Institute theatre ex-cursions or rare shopping trips had failed to shake her conviction that Liverpool Street was the cavernous en-try to an urban jungle, where predators armed with bombs and syringes lurked in every Underground sta-tion, and seducers laid their snares for innocent pro-vincials in every office. Brenda, thought her mother, was a very pretty girl. Well, no point in denying it, she took after her mother's side of the family for looks even if she had her dad's brains, and Mrs. Pridmore had no intention of exposing her to the temptations of London. Brenda was walking out with Gerald Bow-lem, younger son of her father's boss, and if that came off there's no denying it would be a very satisfactory marriage. He wouldn't get the main farm, of course, but there was a very nice little property over at Wis-bech which would come to him. Mrs. Pridmore couldn't see the sense of more examinations and all this talking about a career. This job at the lab would do Brenda very well until she married. But it was a pity that there was all this emphasis on blood.

As if reading her thoughts, her husband said:

'Of course it's exciting for her. It's all new. But I daresay it's no different from other jobs, pretty dull most of the time. I don't reckon anything really frightening will happen to our Brenda at Hoggatt's Lab.'

This conversation about their only child's first job was one they'd had before, a comforting reiteration of mutual reassurance. In imagination Mrs. Pridmore followed her daughter as she pedalled vigorously on her way; bumping down the rough farm track between Mr. Bowlem's flat fields to Tenpenny Road, past old Mrs. Button's cottage where, as a child, she had been given rice-cake and home-made lemonade, by Tenpenny Dyke where she still picked cowslips in summer, then a right turn into Chevisham Road and the straight two miles skirting Captain Massey's land and into Chevisham village. Every yard of it was familiar, reassuring, unmenacing. And even Hoggatt's Laboratory, blood or no blood, had been part of the village for over seventy years, while Chevisham Manor had stood for nearly three times as long. Arthur was right. Nothing frightening could happen to their Brenda at Hoggatt's. Mrs. Pridmore, comforted, drew back the curtains and settled down to enjoy her third cup of tea.

6

At ten minutes to nine the post van stopped outside Sprogg's Cottage on the outskirts of Chevisham to deliver a single letter. It was addressed to Miss Stella Mawson, Lavender Cottage, Chevisham, but the postman was a local man and the difference in name caused him no confusion. There had been Sproggs living in the cottage for four generations, and the small triangle of green in front of the gate had been Sprogg's Green for almost as long. The present owner, having improved the cottage by the addition of a small brick garage and a modern bathroom and kitchen, had decided to celebrate the metamorphosis by planting a lavender hedge and renaming the property. But the villagers regarded the new name as no more than a foreigner's eccentric fancy which they were under no obligation either to use or recognise. The lavender hedge, as if in sympathy with their views, failed to survive the first fen winter and Sprogg's Cottage remained Sprogg's.

Angela Foley, the twenty-seven-year-old personal secretary to the Director of Hoggatt's Laboratory, picked up the envelope and guessed at once by the quality of the paper, the expertly typed address and the London postmark what it must be. It was a letter they had been expecting. She took it through to the kitchen where she and her friend were breakfasting and handed it over without speaking, then watched Stella's face as she read. After a minute she asked:

'Well?'

'It's what we feared. He can't wait any longer. He wants a quick sale, and there's a friend of his who thinks he might like it for a weekend cottage. As sitting tenants we get first refusal, but he must know by next Monday whether we're interested.'

She tossed the letter across the table. Angela said bitterly:

'Interested! Of course we're interested! He knows we are. We told him weeks ago that we were writing round trying to get a mortgage.'

'That's just lawyer's jargon. What his solicitor is asking is whether we're able to go ahead. And the answer is that we can't.'

The arithmetic was plain. Neither of them needed to discuss it. The owner wanted sixteen thousand pounds. None of the mortgage societies they had approached would advance them more than ten. Together they had a little over two thousand saved. Four thousand short. And, with no time left, it might just as well be forty.

Angela said:

'I suppose he wouldn't take less?'

'No. We've tried that. And why should he? It's a fully converted, reed-thatched seventeenth-century cottage. And we've improved it. We've made the garden. He'd be a fool to let it go for under sixteen even to a sitting tenant.'

'But, Star, we are sitting tenants! He's got to get us out first.'

'That's the only reason why he's given us as long as he has. He knows we could make it difficult for him. But I'm not prepared to stay on here under sufferance, knowing that we'd have to go in the end. I couldn't write under those conditions.'

'But we can't find four thousand in a week! And, with things as they are, we couldn't hope for a bank loan even if . . .'

'Even if I had a book coming out this year, which I haven't. And what I make from writing barely pays my part of the housekeeping. It was tactful of you not to say so.'

She hadn't been going to say it. Stella wasn't a conveyor-belt writer. You couldn't expect her novels to make money. What was it that last reviewer had said? Fastidious observation wedded to elegantly sensitive and oblique prose. Not surprisingly, Angela could quote all the reviews even if she sometimes wondered what exactly they were trying to say. Wasn't it she who pasted them with meticulous care into the cuttings-book which Stella so affected to despise! She watched while her friend began what they both called her tiger prowl, that compulsive pacing up and down, head lowered, hands sunk in her dressing-gown pockets. Then Stella said:

'It's a pity that cousin of yours is so disagreeable. Otherwise one might not have minded asking him for a loan. He wouldn't miss it.'

'But I've already asked him. Not about the cottage, of course. But I've asked him to lend me some money.'

It was ridiculous that this should be so difficult to say. After all, Edwin was her cousin. She had a right to ask him. And it was her grandmother's money after all. There was really no reason why Star should be cross. There were times when she didn't mind Star's anger, times even when she deliberately provoked it, waiting with half-shameful excitement for the extraordinary outburst of bitterness and despair of which she herself was less a victim than a privileged spectator, relishing even more the inevitable remorse and self-incrimination, the sweetness of reconciliation. But now for the first time she recognised the chill of fear.

'When?'

There was nothing for it now but to go on.

'Last Tuesday evening. It was after you decided that we'd have to cancel our bookings for Venice next March because of the exchange rate. I wanted it to be a birthday present, Venice I mean.'

She had pictured the scene. Herself handing over the tickets and the hotel reservations tucked into one of those extra-large birthday cards. Star trying to hide her surprise and pleasure. Both of them poring over maps and guide books, planning the itinerary of every marvellous day. To see for the first time and together that incomparable view of San Marco from the western end of the Piazza. Star had read to her Ruskin's description. 'A multitude of pillars and white domes, clustered into a long low pyramid of coloured light.' To stand together on the Piazzetta in the early morning and look across the shimmering water to San Giorgio Maggiore. It was a dream, as insubstantial as the crumbling city. But the hope of it had been worth steeling herself to ask Edwin for that loan.

'And what did he say?'

There was no chance now of softening that brutal negative, of erasing the whole humiliating episode from her memory.

'He said no.'

'I suppose you told him why you wanted it. It didn't occur to you that we go away from here to be private, that our holidays are our own affair, that it might humiliate me to have Edwin Lorrimer know that I can't afford to take you to Venice, even on a ten-day package tour.'

'I didn't.' She cried out in vehement protest, horrified to hear the crack in her voice, and feel the first hot, gritty tears. It was odd, she thought, that it was she who could cry. Star was the emotional, the vehement one. And yet Star never cried.

'I didn't tell him anything, except that I needed the money.'

'How much?'

She hesitated, wondering whether to lie. But she never lied to Star.

'Five hundred pounds. I thought we might as well do it properly. I just told him that I badly needed five hundred pounds.'

'So, not surprisingly, faced with that irrefutable argument, he declined to hand out. What exactly did he say?'

'Only that grandmother had made her intentions perfectly plain in her will and that he had no intention of upsetting them. Then I said that most of the money would come to me after his death, anyway – I mean, that's what he told me when the will was read – and it would be too late then. I'd be an old lady. I might die first. It was now that was important. But I didn't tell him why I wanted it. I swear that.'

'Swear? Don't be dramatic. You're not in a court of law. And then what did he say?'

If only Star would stop that agitated pacing, would only turn and look at her instead of questioning her in that cold, inquisitorial voice. And the new bit was even harder to tell. She couldn't explain to herself why it should be, but it was something which she had tried to put out of her mind, for the present anyway. One day she would tell Star, the moment when it was right to tell. She had never imagined being forced into confidence with such brutal suddenness.

'He said that I shouldn't rely on getting anything in his will. He said that he might acquire new obligations. Obligations was the word he used. And if he did, the will would no longer stand.'

And now Star swung round and faced her.

'New obligations. Marriage! No, that's too ridiculous. Marriage, that desiccated, pedantic, self-satisfied prude. I doubt whether he ever deliberately touches a human body except his own. Solitary, masochistic, surreptitious vice, that's all he understands. No, not vice, the word's too strong. But marriage! Wouldn't you have thought . . .'

She broke off. Angela said:

'He didn't mention marriage.'

'Why should he? But what else would automatically set aside an existing will unless he made a new one? Marriage cancels a will. Didn't you know that?'

'You mean that as soon as he married I should be disinherited?'

'Yes.'

'But that isn't fair!'

'Since when has life been noted for its fairness? It wasn't fair that your grandmother left her fortune to him instead of sharing it with you just because he's a man and she had an old-fashioned prejudice that women shouldn't own money. It isn't fair that you're only a secretary at Hoggatt's because no-one bothered

44

to educate you for anything else. It isn't fair, come to that, that you should have to support me.'

'I don't support you. In every way except the unimportant one, you support me.'

'It's humiliating to be worth more dead than alive. If my heart gave out tonight, then you'd be all right. You could use the life assurance money to buy the place and stay on. The bank would advance the money once they knew you were my legatee.'

'Without you I shouldn't want to stay on.'

'Well, if you do have to leave here, at least it will give you an excuse to live on your own, if that's what you want.'

Angela cried out in vehement protest:

'I shall never live with anyone else but you. I don't want to live anywhere but here, in this cottage. You know that. It's our home.'

It was their home. It was the only real home she'd ever known. She didn't need to look around her to fix with startling clarity each familiar loved possession. She could lie in bed at night and in imagination move confidently around the cottage touching them in a happy exploration of shared memories and reassurance. The two Victorian lustre plant pots on their matching pedestals, found in The Lanes at Brighton one summer weekend. The eighteenth-century oil of Wicken Fen by an artist whose indecipherable signature, peered at through a microscope, had provided so many shared moments of happy conjecture. The French sword in its decorated scabbard, found in a country sale room and now hanging above their fireplace. It wasn't just that their possessions, wood and porcelain, paint and linen, symbolised their joint life. The cottage, their belongings, were their joint life, adorned and gave reality to it just as the bushes and flowers they had planted in the garden staked out their territory of trust.

She had a sudden and terrifying memory of a recurrent nightmare. They were standing facing each other in an empty attic room, bare walls squared with the pale imprints of discarded pictures, floorboards harsh to the feet, two naked strangers in a void, herself trying to reach out her hands to touch Stella's fingers, but unable to lift the heavy monstrous bolsters of flesh that had become her arms. She shivered and then was recalled to the reality of the cold autumn morning by the sound of her friend's voice.

'How much did your grandmother leave? You did tell me, but I've forgotten.'

'About thirty thousand, I think.'

'And he can't have spent any of it, living with his old father in that poky cottage. He hasn't even renovated the windmill. His salary alone must be more than enough for the two of them, apart from the old man's pension. Lorrimer's a senior scientist, isn't he? What does he get?'

'He's a Principal Scientific Officer. The scale goes up to eight thousand.'

'God! More in a year than I could earn from four novels. I suppose if he jibbed at five hundred he'd hardly part with four thousand, not at a rate of interest we could afford. But it wouldn't hurt him. I've a good mind to ask him for it after all.'

Stella was only teasing, of course; but she recognised this too late to control the panic in her voice.

'No, please, Star! No, you mustn't!'

'You really hate him, don't you?'

'Not hate. Indifference. I just don't want to be under an obligation to him.'

'Nor, come to that, do I. And you shan't be.'

Angela went out to the hall and came back pulling on her coat. She said:

'I'll be late at the Lab if I don't hurry. The casserole is in the oven. Try to remember to switch on at half-past five. And don't touch the regulator. I'll turn down the heat when I get back.'

46

'I think I can just about manage that.'

'I'm taking sandwiches for lunch, so I shan't be back. There's the cold ham and salad in the fridge. Will that be enough, Star?'

'No doubt I'll survive.'

'Yesterday evening's typing is in the folder, but I haven't read it through.'

'How remiss of you.'

Stella followed her friend out to the hall. At the door she said:

'I expect they think at the Lab that I exploit you.'

'They know nothing about you at the Lab. And I don't care what they think.'

'Is that what Edwin Lorrimer thinks, too, that I exploit you? Or what does he think?'

'I don't want to talk about him.'

She folded her scarf over her blonde hair. In the antique mirror with its frame of carved shells she saw both their faces distorted by a defect in the glass; the brown and green of Stella's huge luminous eyes smeared like wet paint into the deep clefts between nostrils and mouth; her own wide brow bulging like that of a hydrocephalic child. She said:

'I wonder what I'd feel if Edwin died this week; a heart attack, a car accident, a brain haemorrhage.'

'Life isn't as convenient as that.'

'Death isn't. Star, shall you reply today to that solicitor?'

'He doesn't expect an answer until Monday. I can ring him at the London office on Monday morning. That's another five days. Anything can happen in five days.'

7

'But they're just like mine! The panties I mean. I've got a pair like that! I bought them from Marks and

Spencer's in Cambridge with my first salary cheque.'

It was 10.35 and Brenda Pridmore, at the reception desk at the rear of the main hall of Hoggatt's Laboratory, watched wide-eyed while Inspector Blakelock drew towards him the first labelled bag of exhibits from the clunch pit murder. She put out a finger and tentatively slid it over the thin plastic through which the knickers, crumpled and stained round the crotch, were clearly visible. The detective-constable who had brought in the exhibits had said that the girl had been to a dance. Funny, thought Brenda, that she hadn't bothered to put on clean underclothes. Perhaps she wasn't fastidious. Or perhaps she had been in too much of a hurry to change. And now the intimate clothes which she had put on so unthinkingly on the day of her death would be smoothed out by strange hands, scrutinised under ultra-violet light, perhaps be handed up, neatly docketed, to the judge and jury in the Crown Court.

Brenda knew that she would never again be able to wear her own panties, their prettiness contaminated for ever by the memory of this dead unknown girl. Perhaps they had even bought them together in the same store, on the same day. She could recall the excitement of spending for the first time money she had actually earned. It had been a Saturday afternoon and there had been a crush round the lingerie counter, eager hands rummaging among the panties. She had liked the pair with the sprays of pink machine-embroidered flowers across the front. So, too, had this unknown girl. Perhaps their hands had touched. She cried:

'Inspector. Isn't death terrible?'

'Murder is. Death isn't; at least, no more than birth is. You couldn't have one without the other or there'd be no room for us all. I reckon I won't worry overmuch when my times comes.'

'But that policeman who brought in the exhibits said that she was only eighteen. That's my age.'

He was making out the folder for the new case, meticulously transferring details from the police form to the file. And his head, with the cropped dry hair which reminded her so of corn-stubble, was bent low over the page so that she could not see his face. Suddenly she remembered being told that he had lost an only daughter, killed by a hit-and-run driver, and she wished the words unsaid. Her face flared and she turned her eyes away. But when he replied his voice was perfectly steady.

'Aye, poor lass. Led him on, I daresay. They never learn. What's that you've got?'

'It's the bag of male clothes, suit, shoes and underwear. Do you think these belong to the chief suspect?'

'They'll be the husband's, likely as not.'

'But what can they prove? She was strangled, wasn't she?'

'No telling for certain until we get Dr. Kerrison's report. But they usually examine the chief suspect's clothes. There might be a trace of blood, a grain of sand or earth, paint, minute fibres from the victim's clothes, a trace of her saliva even. Or she could have been raped. All that bundle will go into the Biology Search Room with the victim's clothes.'

'But the policeman didn't say anything about rape! I thought you said this bundle belongs to the husband.'

'You don't want to let it worry you. You have to learn to be like a doctor or a nurse, detached, isn't it?'

'Is that how forensic scientists feel?'

'Likely as not. It's their job. They don't think about victims or suspects. That's for the police. They're only concerned with scientific facts.'

He was right, thought Brenda. She remembered the time only three days previously when the Senior Scientific Officer of the instrument section had let her look

49

into the giant scanning electron microscope and watch the image of a minute pill of putty burst instantaneously into an exotic incandescent flower. He had explained:

'It's a coccolith, magnified six thousand times.'

'A what?'

'The skeleton of a micro-organism which lived in the ancient seas from which the chalk in the putty was deposited. They're different, depending on where the chalk was quarried. That's how you can differentiate one sample of putty from another.'

She had exclaimed:

'But it's so lovely!'

He had taken her place at the eyepiece of the instrument.

'Yes, nice, isn't it?'

But she had known that, while she looked back in wonder across a million years, his mind on the minute scrape of putty from the heel of the suspect's shoe, the trace which might prove a man was a rapist or a murderer. And yet, she had thought, he doesn't really mind. All he cares about is getting the answer right. It would have been no use asking him whether he thought there was a unifying purpose in life, whether it could really be chance that an animal so small that it couldn't be seen by the naked eye could die millions of years ago in the depths of the sea and be resurrected by science to prove a man innocent or guilty. It was odd, she thought, that scientists so often weren't religious when their work revealed a world so variously marvellous and yet so mysteriously unified and at one. Dr. Lorrimer seemed to be the only member of Hoggatt's who was known to go regularly to church. She wondered if she dared ask him about the coccolith and God. He had been very kind this morning about the murder. He had arrived at the Laboratory over an hour late, at ten o'clock, looking terribly tired because he had been up that night at the scene of crime, and had come over to the reception desk to collect his personal post. He had said:

'You'll be getting exhibits from your first murder case this morning. Don't let them worry you, Brenda. There's only one death we need to be frightened of, and that's our own.'

It was a strange thing to have said, an odd way to reassure her. But he was right. She was suddenly glad that Inspector Blakelock had done the documentation on the clunch pit murder. Now, with care, the owner of those stained panties would remain, for her, unknown, anonymous, a number in the biology series on a manila folder. Inspector Blakelock's voice broke into her thoughts:

'Have you got those court reports we checked yesterday ready for the post?'

'Yes, they've been entered in the book. I meant to ask you. Why do all the court statements have "Criminal Justice Act 1967 sections 2 and 9" printed on them?'

'That's the statutory authority for written evidence to be tendered at committal proceedings and the Crown Court. You can look up the sections in the library. Before the 1967 Act the labs had a hard time of it, I can tell you, when all scientific evidence had to be given orally. Mind you, the court-going officers still have to spend a fair amount of time attending trials. The defence doesn't always accept the scientific findings. That's the difficult part of the job, not the analysis but standing alone in the witness-box to defend it under cross-examination. If a man's no good in the box, then all the careful work he does here goes for nothing.'

Brenda suddenly remembered something else that Mrs. Mallett had told her, that the motorist who had killed his daughter had been acquitted because the scientist had crumbled under the cross-examination; something to do with the analysis of chips of paint found on the road which matched the suspect's car. It must be terrible to lose an only child; to lose any child. Perhaps that was the worst thing that could happen to a human being. No wonder Inspector Blakelock was often so quiet; that when the police officers came in with their hearty banter he answered only with that slow, gentle smile.

She glanced across at the Laboratory clock. Ten-forty-five. Any minute now the Scene of Crime course would be arriving for their lecture on the collection and preservation of scientific evidence, and this brief spell of quiet would be over. She wondered what Colonel Hoggatt would think if he could visit his laboratory now. Her eyes were drawn, as they so often were, to his portrait hanging just outside the Director's office. Even from her place at the desk she could read the gold lettering on the frame.

Colonel William Makepeace Hoggatt V.C.
Chief Constable 1894–1912
Founder of Hoggatt's Forensic Science Laboratory.

He was standing in the room which was still used as a library, his ruddy face stern and bewhiskered under the sprouting plumes of his hat, his braided, be-medalled tunic fastened with a row of gilt buttons. One proprietorial hand was laid, light as a priestly blessing, on an old-fashioned microscope in gleaming brass. But the minatory eyes weren't fixed on this latest scientific wonder; they were fixed on Brenda. Under his accusing gaze, recalled to duty, she bent again to her work.

8

By twelve o'clock the meeting of senior scientists in the Director's office to discuss the furniture and equipment for the new Laboratory was over, and Howarth rang for his secretary to clear the conference table. He watched her as she emptied and polished the ashtray (he didn't smoke and the smell of ash offended him), collected together the copies of the Laboratory plans and gathered up the strewn discarded papers. Even from his desk Howarth could see Middlemass's complex geometrical doodles, and the crumpled agenda, ringed with coffee stains, of the Senior Vehicle Examiner, Bill Morgan.

He watched the girl as she moved with quiet competence about the table wondering, as always, what, if anything, was going on behind that extraordinarily wide brow, those slanted enigmatic eyes. He missed his old personal assistant, Marjory Faraker, more than he had expected. It had, he thought ruefully, been good for his self-conceit to find that her devotion didn't, after all, extend to leaving London where, surprisingly, she had been discovered to have a life of her own, to join him in the fens. Like all good secretaries she had acquired, or at least known how to simulate, some of the idealised attributes of wife, mother, mistress, confidante, servant and friend without being, or indeed expecting to be, any of these. She had flattered his self-esteem, protected him from the minor irritations of life, preserved his privacy with maternal pugnacity, had ensured, with infinite tact, that he knew all he needed to know about what was going on in his Laboratory.

He couldn't complain about Angela Foley. She was a more than competent shorthand typist and an efficient secretary. Nothing was left undone. It was just that for her, he felt that he hardly existed, that his authority, meekly deferred to, was nevertheless a charade. The fact that she was Lorrimer's cousin was irrelevant. He had never heard her mention his name. He wondered from time to time what sort of a life she led in that remote cottage with her writer friend, how far it had satisfied her. But she told him nothing, not even about the Laboratory. He knew that Hoggatt's had a heartbeat — all institutions did — but the pulse eluded him. He said:

'The Foreign and Commonwealth Office want us to take a Danish biologist for two or three days next month. He's visiting England to look at the service. Fit him in, will you, when I'm free to give him some time. You'd better consult Dr. Lorrimer about his diary commitments. Then let the F.C.O. know what days we can offer.'

'Yes, Dr. Howarth.'

At least the autopsy was over. It had been worse than he had expected, but he had seen it through and without disgrace. He hadn't expected that the colours of the human body would be so vivid, so exotically beautiful. Now he saw again Kerrison's gloved fingers, sleek as eels, busying themselves at the body's orifices. Explaining, demonstrating, discarding. Presumably he had become as immune to disgust as he obviously was to the sweet-sour smell of his mortuary. And to all the experts in violent death, faced daily with the final disintegration of the personality, pity would be as irrelevant as disgust.

Miss Foley was ready to go now and had come up to the desk to clear his out tray. He said:

'Has Inspector Blakelock worked out last month's average turn-round figures yet?'

'Yes, sir. The average for all exhibits is down to twelve days, and the blood alcohol has fallen to 1.2

days. But the figure for crimes against the person is up again. I'm just typing the figures now.'

'Let me have them as soon as they're ready, please.'

There were memories which, he suspected, would be even more insistent than Kerrison marking out with his cartilage knife on the milk-white body the long line of the primary incision. Doyle, that great black bull, grinning at him in the washroom afterwards as, side by side, they washed their hands. And why, he wondered, had he felt it necessary to wash. His hands hadn't been contaminated.

'The performance was well up to standard. Neat, quick and thorough, that's Doc Kerrison. Sorry we shan't be able to call for you when we're ready to make the arrest. Not allowed. You'll have to imagine that bit. But there'll be the trial to attend, with any luck.'

Angela Foley was standing in front of the desk, looking at him strangely, he thought.

'Yes?'

'Scobie has had to go home, Dr. Howarth. He's not at all well. He thinks it may be this two-day 'flu that's going about. And he says that the incinerator has broken down.'

'Presumably he telephoned for the mechanic before he left.'

'Yes, sir. He says it was all right yesterday morning when Inspector Doyle came with the court orders authorising the destruction of the cannabis exhibits. It was working then.'

Howarth was irritated. This was one of those minor administrative details which Miss Faraker would never have dreamed of troubling him with. Miss Foley was, he guessed, expecting him to say something sympathetic about Scobie, to enquire whether the old man had been fit to cycle home. Dr. MacIntyre had, no doubt, bleated like an anxious sheep when any of the staff were ill. He bent his head over his papers.

But Miss Foley was at the door. It had to be now. He made himself say:

'Ask Dr. Lorrimer to come down for a few minutes, will you please?'

He could, perfectly casually, have asked Lorrimer to stay on after the meeting; why hadn't he? Probably because there might have been an echo of the headmaster in so public a request. Perhaps because this was an interview he had been glad to postpone, even temporarily.

Lorrimer came in and stood in front of the desk. Howarth took out Bradley's personal file from his right-hand drawer and said:

'Sit down will you, please. This annual report on Bradley. You've given him an adverse marking. Have you told him?'

Lorrimer remained standing. He said:

'I'm required by the reporting rules to tell him. I saw him in my office at ten-thirty, as soon as I got back from the P.M.'

'It seems a bit hard. According to his file, it's the first adverse report he's had. We took him on probation eighteen months ago. Why hasn't he made out?'

'I should have thought that was obvious from my detailed markings. He's been promoted above his capacity.'

'In other words, the Board made a mistake?'

'That's not so unusual. Boards occasionally do. And not only when it comes to promotions.'

The allusion was blatant, a deliberate provocation, yet Howarth decided to ignore it. With an effort he kept his voice level.

'I'm not prepared to countersign this report as it stands. It's too early to judge him fairly.'

'I made that excuse for him last year when he'd been with us six months. But if you disagree with my assessment you'll presumably say so. There's a space provided.'

56

'I intend to use it. And I suggest that you try the effect of giving the boy some support and encouragement. There are two reasons for an inadequate performance. Some people are capable of doing better and will if judiciously kicked into it. Others aren't. To kick them is not only pointless, it destroys what confidence they have. You run an efficient department. But it might be more efficient and happier if you learned how to understand people. Management is largely a matter of personal relationships.'

He made himself look up. Lorrimer said through lips so stiff that the words sounded cracked:

'I hadn't realised that your family were noted for success in their personal relationships.'

'The fact that you can't take criticism without becoming as personal and spiteful as a neurotic girl is an example of what I mean.'

He never knew what Lorrimer was about to reply. The door opened and his sister came in. She was dressed in slacks and a sheepskin jacket, her blonde hair bound with a scarf. She looked at them both without embarrassment and said easily:

'Sorry, I didn't realise you were engaged. I ought to have asked Inspector Blakelock to ring.'

Without a word, Lorrimer, deathly pale, turned on his heels, walked past her and was gone. Domenica looked after him, smiled and shrugged. She said:

'Sorry if I interrupted something. It's just to say that I'm going to Norwich for a couple of hours to buy some materials. Is there anything you want?'

'Nothing, thank you.'

'I'll be back before dinner, but I think I'll give the village concert a miss. Without Claire Easterbrook the Mozart will be pretty insupportable. Oh, and I'm thinking of going up to London for the best part of next week.'

Her brother didn't reply. She looked at him and said:

57

'What's wrong?'

'How did Lorrimer know about Gina?'

He didn't need to ask her if it was she who had
told him. Whatever else she may have confided, it
would not have been that. She went across, ostensibly
to study the Stanley Spencer set in the overmantel of
the fireplace, and asked lightly:

'Why? He didn't mention your divorce, did he?'

'Not directly, but the allusion was intended.'

She turned to face him.

'He probably took the trouble to find out as much
as possible about you when he knew that you were a
candidate for the job here. It isn't such a large service
after all.'

'But I came from outside it.'

'Even so, there would be contacts, gossip. A failed
marriage is one of those unconsidered trifles he might
expect to sniff out. And what of it? After all, it's not
unusual. I thought forensic scientists were particularly
at risk. All those late hours at scenes of crime and the
unpredictable court attendances. They ought to be
used to marital break-ups.'

He said, knowing that he sounded as petulant as an
obstinate child:

'I don't want him in my Lab.'

'Your Lab? It isn't quite as simple as that, is it? I
don't think the Stanley Spencer is right over the fireplace. It looks incongruous. It's strange that Father
bought it. Not at all his kind of picture I should have
said. Did you put it here to shock?'

Miraculously, his anger and misery were assuaged.
But then she had always been able to do that for him.

'Merely to disconcert and confuse. It's intended to
suggest that I may be a more complex character than
they assume.'

'Oh, but you are! I've never needed "Assumption at
Cookham" to prove it. Why not the Greuze? It would
look good with that carved overmantel.'

58

'Too pretty.'

She laughed, and was gone. He picked up Clifford Bradley's report and, in the space provided, wrote:

'Mr. Bradley's performance has been disappointing, but not all the difficulties are of his making. He lacks confidence and would benefit from more active encouragement and support than he has received. I have corrected the final marking to what I consider a more just assessment and have spoken to the senior biologist about the personnel management in his department.'

If he did finally decide, after all, this wasn't the job for him, that snide comment should go some way to ensure that Lorrimer stood no chance of succeeding him as Director of Hoggatt's.

9

At one-forty-eight precisely Paul Middlemass, the Document Examiner, opened his file on the clunch pit murder. The Document Examination Room, which occupied the whole of the front of the building immediately under the roof, smelled like a stationer's shop, a pungent amalgam of paper and ink, sharpened by the tang of chemicals. Middlemass breathed it as his native air. He was a tall, rangy, large-featured man with a mobile, wide-mouthed face of agreeable ugliness and iron-grey hair which fell in heavy swathes over parchment-coloured skin. Easy-going and seemingly indolent, he was in fact a prodigious worker with an obsession for his job. Paper in all its manifestations was his passion. Few men, in or outside the forensic science service, knew so much about it. He handled it with joy and with a kind of reverence, gloated over it, knew its provenance almost by its smell. Identification of the sizing and loading of a specimen by spectrographic or X-ray crystallography merely confirmed what touch and sight had already pronounced. The satisfaction of watching the emergence of an obscure water-mark under soft X-rays never palled, and the final pattern was as fascinating to his unsurprised eyes as the expected potter's mark to a collector of porcelain.

His father, long dead, had been a dentist, and his son had taken for his own use the old man's inordinately large store of self-designed surgical overalls. They were old-fashioned in cut, waisted and full-skirted as the coat of a Regency buck, and with crested metal buttons fastening high to the side of the throat. Although they were too short in the arm so that his lean wrists protruded like those of an overgrown schoolboy, he wore them with a certain panache, as if this unorthodox working garb, so different from the regulation white coats of the rest of the Laboratory staff, symbolised that unique blend of scientific skill, experience and flair which distinguishes the good Document Examiner.

He had just finished telephoning his wife, having remembered rather belatedly that he was due to help out that evening with the village concert. He liked women, and before his marriage had enjoyed a succession of casual, satisfactory and uncommitted affairs. He had married late, a buxom research scientist from Cambridge twenty years his junior, and drove back to their modern flat on the outskirts of the city each night in his Jaguar – his chief extravagance – frequently late, but seldom too late to bear her off to their local pub. Secure in his job, with a growing international reputation, and uxoriously contented with his comely Sophie, he knew himself to be successful and suspected himself to be happy.

The Document Examination Laboratory with its cabinets and range of monorail cameras took up what some of his colleagues, notably Edwin Lorrimer, regarded as more than its share of room. But the Laboratory, lit by rows of fluorescent lights and with its low ceiling, was stuffy and ill-ventilated, and this afternoon the central heating, unreliable at the best of times, had concentrated all its efforts on the top of the building. Usually he was oblivious of his working conditions, but a sub-tropical temperature was difficult to ignore. He opened the door to the passage. Opposite and a little to the right were the male and female lavatories, and he could hear the occasional feet, light or heavy, hurried or dilatory, of passing members of staff, and hear the swing of the two doors. The sounds didn't worry him. He applied himself to his task.

But the specimen he was now poring over held little mystery. If the crime had been other than murder he would have left it to his Scientific Officer assistant, not yet returned from a belated lunch. But murder invariably meant a court appearance and cross-examination – the defence seldom let the scientific evidence go unchallenged in this, the gravest of charges – and a court appearance put document examination in general, and Hoggatt's Laboratory in particular, on public trial. He made it a matter of principle always to take the murder cases himself. They were seldom the most interesting. What he most enjoyed were the historical investigations, the satisfaction of demonstrating, as he had only last month, that a document dated 1872 was printed on paper containing chemical wood-pulp which was first used in 1874, a discovery which had initiated a fascinating unravelling of complicated documentary fraud. There was nothing complicated and little of interest about the present job. Yet, only a few years ago, a man's neck could have depended upon his opinion. He seldom thought of the half-dozen men who had been hanged during the twenty years of his forensic experience, primarily because of his evidence, and when he did, it was not the strained but oddly anonymous faces in the dock which

61

he remembered, or their names; but paper and ink, the thickened downward stroke, the peculiar formation of a letter. Now he spread out on his table the note taken from the dead girl's handbag, placing on each side the two specimens of the husband's handwriting which the police had been able to obtain. One was a letter to the suspect's mother written on holiday at Southend – how, he wondered, had they managed to extract that from her? The other was a brief telephoned message about a football match. The note taken from the victim's purse was even briefer.

'You've got your own chap so lay off Barry Taylor or you'll be sorry. It would be a pity to spoil a nice face like yours. Acid isn't pretty. Watch it. A Well-wisher.'

The style, he decided, was derived from a recent television thriller, the writing was obviously disguised. It was possible that the police would be able to provide him with some more samples of the suspect's handwriting when they visited the lad's place of work, but he didn't really need them. The similarities between the threatening note and the samples were unmistakable. The writer had tried to alter the slant of his hand and had changed the shape of the small r. But the lifts of the pen came regularly at every fourth letter – Middlemass had never found a forger who remembered to vary the interval at which he lifted pen from paper – and the dot above the i, high and slightly to the left, and the over-emphatic apostrophe were almost a trade-mark. He would analyse the paper sample, photograph and enlarge each individual letter and then mount them on a comparison chart, and the jury would pass it solemnly from hand to hand and wonder why it needed a highly-paid expert to come and explain what anyone could see with his own eyes.

The telephone rang. Middlemass stretched out a long arm and held the instrument to his left ear. Susan Bradley's voice, at first apologetic then conspiratorial and finally close to tears, squeaked into his ear in a long monologue of complaint and desperation. He listened, made soft encouraging noises, held the receiver an inch or two from his ear, and meanwhile noted that the writer, poor bastard, hadn't even thought of altering the distinctive cross-bar of his small letter t. Not that it would have done any good. And he couldn't have known, poor devil, that his effort would feature as an exhibit in his trial for murder.

'All right,' he said. 'Don't worry. Leave it to me.'

'And you won't let him know that I phoned you?'

'Of course not, Susan. Relax. I'll settle it.'

The voice crackled on.

'Then tell him not to be a fool, for God's sake. Hasn't he noticed that we've got one and a half million unemployed? Lorrimer can't sack him. Tell Clifford to hang on to his job and stop being a bloody fool. I'll deal with Lorrimer.'

He replaced the receiver. He had liked Susan Moffat who, for two years, had worked for him as his S.O. She had both more brains and more guts than her husband, and he had wondered, without greatly caring, why she had married Bradley. Pity probably, and an over-developed maternal instinct. There were some women who simply had to take the unfortunate literally to their breast. Or perhaps it was just lack of choice, the need for a home of her own and a child. Well, it was too late to try and stop the marriage now, and it certainly hadn't occurred to him to try at the time. And at least she had the home and the kid. She had brought the baby to the Lab to see him only a fortnight ago. The visit of the prune-faced yelling bundle had done nothing to change his own resolution not to produce a child, but certainly Susan herself had seemed happy enough. And she would probably be happy again if something could be done about Lorrimer.

He thought that the time had perhaps come to do something about Lorrimer. And he had, after all, his own private reason for taking on the job. It was a small personal obligation, and to date it hadn't particularly fretted what he supposed other people called conscience. But Susan Bradley's call had reminded him. He listened. The footsteps were familiar. Well, it was a coincidence, but better now than later. Moving to the door he called at the retreating back:

'Lorrimer. I want a word with you.'

Lorrimer came and stood inside the door, tall, unsmiling in his carefully buttoned white coat, and regarded Middlemass with his dark, wary eyes. Middlemass made himself look into them, and then turned his glance away. The irises had seemed to dilate into black pools of despair. It was not an emotion he felt competent to deal with, and he felt discomforted. What on earth was eating the poor devil? He said, carefully casual:

'Look, Lorrimer, lay off Bradley will you? I know he's not exactly God's gift to forensic science, but he's a conscientious plodder and you're not going to stimulate either his brain or his speed by bullying the poor little beast. So cut it out.'

'Are you telling me how to manage my staff?'

Lorrimer's voice was perfectly controlled, but the pulse at the side of his temple had begun to beat visibly. Middlemass found it difficult not to fix his eyes on it.

'That's right, mate. This member of your staff anyway. I know damn well what you're up to and I don't like it. So stow it.'

'Is this meant to be some kind of a threat?'

'More a friendly warning, reasonably friendly anyway. I don't pretend to like you, and I wouldn't have served under you if the Home Office had been daft enough to appoint you Director of this Lab. But I admit that what you do in your own department isn't normally my business, only this happens to be an exception. I know what's going on, I don't like it, and I'm making it my business to see that it stops.'

'I didn't realise that you had this tender regard for Bradley. But of course, Susan Bradley must have phoned you. He wouldn't have the guts to speak for himself. Did she telephone you, Middlemass?'

Middlemass ignored the question. He said:

'I haven't any particular regard for Bradley. But I did have a certain regard for Peter Ennalls, if you can remember him.'

'Ennalls drowned himself because his fiancée threw him over and he'd had a mental breakdown. He left a note explaining his action and it was read out at the inquest. Both things happened months after he'd left the Southern Laboratory; neither had anything to do with me.'

'What happened while he was at the Lab had a hell of a lot to do with you. He was a pleasant, rather ordinary lad with two good A-levels and an unaccountable wish to become a forensic biologist when he had the bad luck to begin to work under you. As it happens, he was my wife's cousin. I was the one who recommended him to try for the job. So I have a certain interest, you could say a certain responsibility.'

Lorrimer said:

'He never said that he was related to your wife. But I can't see what difference it makes. He was totally unsuited for the job. A forensic biologist who can't work accurately under pressure is no use to me or the Service and he'd better get out. We've no room for passengers. That's what I propose to tell Bradley.'

'Then you'd better have second thoughts.'

'And how are you going to make me?'

It was extraordinary that lips so tight could produce any sound, that Lorrimer's voice, high and distorted, could have forced itself through the vocal cords without splitting them.

'I shall make it plain to Howarth that you and I can't serve in the same Lab. He won't exactly welcome that. Trouble between senior staff is the last complication he wants just now. So he'll suggest to Establishment Department that one of us gets a transfer before we have the added complication of moving into a new Lab. I'm banking on Howarth – and Estabs come to that – concluding that it's easier to find a forensic biologist than a Document Examiner.'

Middlemass surprised himself. None of this rigmarole had occurred to him before he spoke. Not that it was unreasonable. There wasn't another Document Examiner of his calibre in the Service and Howarth knew it. If he categorically refused to work in the same Laboratory as Lorrimer, one of them would have to go. The quarrel wouldn't do either of them any good with the Establishment Department, but he thought he knew which one it would harm most.

Lorrimer said:

'You helped stop me getting the directorship, now you want to drive me out of the Lab.'

'Personally I don't care a damn whether you're here or not. But just lay off bullying Bradley.'

'If I were prepared to take advice about the way I run my Department from anyone, it wouldn't be a third-rate paper fetishist with a second-rate degree, who doesn't know the difference between scientific proof and intuition.'

The taunt was too absurd to puncture Middlemass's secure self-esteem. But at least it warranted a retort. He found that he was getting angry. And suddenly he saw light. He said:

'Look, mate, if you can't make it in bed, if she isn't finding you quite up to the mark, don't take your frustration out on the rest of us. Remember Chesterfield's advice. The expense is exorbitant, the position ridiculous, and the pleasure transitory.'

The result astounded him. Lorrimer gave a

strangled cry and lunged out. Middlemass's reaction was both instinctive and deeply satisfying. He shot out his right arm and landed a punch on Lorrimer's nose. There was a second's astonished silence in which the two men regarded each other. Then the blood spurted and Lorrimer tottered and fell forward. Middlemass caught him by the shoulders and felt the weight of his head against his chest. He thought: 'My God, he's going to faint.' He was aware of a tangle of emotion, surprise at himself, boyish gratification, pity and an impulse to laugh. He said:

'Are you all right?'

Lorrimer tore himself from his grasp and stood upright. He fumbled for his handkerchief and held it to his nose. The red stain grew. Looking down, Middlemass saw Lorrimer's blood spreading on his white overall, decorative as a rose. He said:

'Since we're engaging in histrionics, I believe your response ought now to be "By God, you swine, you'll pay for this".'

He was astounded by the sudden blaze of hate in the black eyes. Lorrimer's voice came to him muffled by the handkerchief.

'You will pay for it.' And then he was gone.

Middlemass was suddenly aware of Mrs. Bidwell, the Laboratory cleaner, standing by the door, eyes large and excited behind her ridiculous upswept diamanté spectacles.

'Nice goings on, I don't think. Senior staff fighting each other. You ought to be ashamed of yourselves.'

'Oh we are, Mrs. Bidwell. We are.' Slowly Middlemass eased his long arms from his overall. He handed it to her.

'Drop this in the soiled linen, will you.'

'Now you knew very well, Mr. Middlemass, that I don't go into the gents' cloakroom, not in working hours. You put it in the basket yourself. And if you want a clean one now, you know where to find it. I'm putting out no more clean linen until tomorrow. Fighting, indeed. I might have known that Dr. Lorrimer would be mixed up in it. But he's not a gentleman you'd expect to find using his fists. Wouldn't have the guts, that would be my view. But he's been odd in his manner these last few days, no doubt about that. You heard about that spot of bother in the front hall yesterday, I suppose? He practically pushed those kids of Dr. Kerrison's out of the door. All they were doing was waiting for their Dad. No harm in that, I suppose. There's a very nasty atmosphere in this Lab recently, and if a certain gentlemen doesn't take a hold of himself there'll be a mischief done, you mark my words.'

10

It was nearly five o'clock and dark before Detective-Inspector Doyle got back to his home in the village four miles to the north of Cambridge. He had tried to telephone his wife once, but without success: the line was engaged. Another of her interminable, secretive and expensive telephone calls to one of her old nursing friends, he thought, and, duly satisfied, made no further attempt. The wrought iron gate, as usual, was open and he parked in front of the house. It wasn't worth garaging the car for a couple of hours, which was all the time he could allow himself.

Scoope House hardly looked its best in the late afternoon of a dark November evening. No wonder that the agents hadn't recently sent anyone to view. It was a bad time of the year. The house was, he thought, a monument to miscalculation. He had bought it for less than seventeen thousand and had spent five thousand on it to date, expecting to sell it for at least forty. But that was before the recession had upset the calculations of more expert speculators than he. Now, with the property market sluggish, there was nothing to do but wait. He could afford to hang on to the house until the market quickened. He wasn't sure that he would be given a chance to hold on to his wife. He wasn't even sure that he wanted to. The marriage, too, had been a miscalculation, but given the circumstances of the time, an understandable one. He wasted no time on regrets.

The two tall oblongs of light from the first-floor drawing-room window should have been a welcoming promise of warmth and comfort. Instead they were vaguely menacing; Maureen was at home. But where else, she would have argued, was there for her to go in this dreary East Anglian village on a dull November evening?

She had finished tea, and the tray was still at her side. The milk bottle, with its crushed top pressed back, a single mug, sliced bread spilling out of its wrapper, a slab of butter on a greasy dish, a bought fruit cake in its unopened carton. He felt the customary surge of irritation, but said nothing. Once when he had remonstrated at her sluttishness she had shrugged :

'Who sees, who cares?'

He saw and he cared, but it had been many months since he had counted with her. He said :

'I'm taking a couple of hours' kip. Wake me at seven, will you?'

'You mean we aren't going to the Chevisham concert?'

'For God's sake, Maureen, you were yelling yesterday that you couldn't be bothered with it. Kids' stuff. Remember?'

'It's not exactly The Talk of the Town, but at least we were going out. Out! Out of this dump. Together for a change. It was something to dress up for. And you said we'd have dinner afterwards at the Chinese restaurant at Ely.'

'Sorry. I couldn't know I'd be on a murder case.'

'When will you be back? If there's any point in asking?'

'God knows. I'm picking up Sergeant Beale. There are still one or two people we've got to see who were at the Muddington dance, notably a lad called Barry Taylor who has some explaining to do. Depending on what we get out of him, I may want to drop in on the husband again.'

'That'll please you, won't it, keeping him in a muck sweat. Is that why you became a cop – because you like frightening people?'

'That's about as stupid as saying you became a nurse because you get a kick out of emptying bedpans.'

He flung himself in a chair and closed his eyes, giving way to sleep. He saw again the boy's terrified face, smelt again the sweat of fear. But he'd stood up well to that first interview, hindered rather than helped by the presence of his solicitor, who had never seen his client before and had made it painfully apparent that he would prefer never to see him again. He had stuck to his story, that they'd quarrelled at the dance and he had left early. That she hadn't arrived home by one o'clock. That he'd gone out to look for her on the road and across the clunch pit field, returning alone half an hour later. That he'd seen no-one and hadn't been anywhere near the clunch pit or the derelict car. It was a good story, simple, unelaborated, possibly even true except in that one essential. But, with luck, the Lab report on her blood and the stain on his jacket cuff, the minute traces of sandy soil and dust from the car on his shoes, would be ready by Friday. If Lorrimer worked late tonight – and he usually did – the blood analysis might even be available by tomorrow. And then would come the elaborations, the inconsistencies, and finally the truth. She said:

'Who else was at the scene?'

It was something, he thought, that she had bothered to ask. He said sleepily:

'Lorrimer, of course. He never misses a murder scene. Doesn't trust any of us to know our jobs, I suppose. We had the usual half-hour hanging about for Kerrison. That maddened Lorrimer, of course. He's done all the work at the scene – all anyone can do – and then he has to cool his heels with the rest of us, waiting for God's gift to forensic pathology to come screaming up with a police escort and break the news to us that what we all thought was a corpse is – surprise, surprise – indeed a corpse, and that we can safely move the body.'

'The forensic pathologist does more than that.'

'Of course he does. But not all that much more, not at the actual scene. His job comes later.'

He added:

'Sorry I couldn't ring. I did try but you were engaged.'

'I expect that was Daddy. His offer still stands, the job of Security Officer in the Organisation. But he can't wait much longer. If you don't accept by the end of the month, then he'll advertise.'

Oh God, he thought, not that again.

'I wish your dear Daddy wouldn't talk about the Organisation. It makes the family business sound like the Mafia. If it were, I might be tempted to join. What Daddy's got are three cheap, shabby shops selling cheap, shabby suits to cheap shabby fools who wouldn't recognise a decent cloth if it were shoved down their throats. I might've considered coming into the business if dear Daddy hadn't already got Big Brother as a co-director, ready to take over from him, and if he didn't make it so plain that he only tolerates me because I'm your hubsand. But I'm damned if I'm going to fart around like a pansy floor-walker watching that no poor sod nicks the Y-fronts, even if

71

I am dignified with the name security officer. I'm staying here.'

'Where you've got such useful contacts.'

And what exactly, he wondered, did she mean by that? He'd been careful not to tell her anything, but she wasn't altogether a fool. She could have guessed. He said:

'Where I've got a job. You know what you were taking on when you married me.'

But no-one ever does know that, he thought. Not really.

'Don't expect me to be here when you get back.'

That was an old threat. He said easily:

'Suit yourself. But if you're thinking of driving, forget it. I'm taking the Cortina, the clutch is playing up on the Renault. So if you're planning on running home to Mummy before tomorrow morning, you'll have to phone Daddy to call for you, or take a taxi.'

She was speaking, but her voice, peevishly insistent, was coming from far away, no longer coherent words but waves of sound beating against his brain. Two hours. Whether or not she bothered to rouse him, he knew that he would wake almost to the minute. He closed his eyes and slept.

BOOK TWO

DEATH IN A WHITE COAT

1

It was very peaceful in the front hall of Hoggatt's at eight-forty in the morning. Brenda often thought that this was the part of the working day she liked best, the hour before the staff arrived and the work of the Lab got really under way, when she and Inspector Blakelock worked together in the quiet emptiness of the hall, still and solemn as a church, making up a supply of manila folders ready to register the day's new cases, repacking exhibits for collection by the police, making a final check of the Laboratory reports to courts to ensure that the examination was complete, that no relevant detail had been omitted. Immediately on arrival she would put on her white coat, and at once she felt different, no longer young and uncertain, but a professional woman, almost like a scientist, a recognised member of the Lab staff. Then she would go into the kitchen at the back of the house and make tea. After the dignification of the white coat this domestic chore was something of a let-down, and she didn't really need a drink so soon after breakfast. But Inspector Blakelock, who motored from Ely every day, was always ready for his tea, and she didn't mind making it.

'That's the stuff to give the troops,' he would invariably say, curving back moist lips to the mug's brim and gulping the hot liquid down as if his throat were asbestos. 'You make a nice cup of tea, Brenda, I'll say that for you.' And she would reply:

'Mum says the secret is always to warm the pot and let the tea brew for just five minutes.'

This small ritual exchange, so invariable that she could silently mouth his words and had to resist an impulse to giggle, the familiar domestic aroma of the tea, the gradual warmth as she curved her hands around the thick mug, constituted a reassuring and comforting beginning to the working day.

She liked Inspector Blakelock. He spoke seldom, but he was never impatient with her, always kind, a companionable father figure. Even her mother, when she visited the Lab before Brenda took up her post, had been happy about her working alone with him. Brenda's cheeks still burned with shame when she remembered her mother's insistence that she should visit Hoggatt's to see where her daughter was going to work, although Chief Inspector Martin, the Senior Police Liaison Officer, had apparently thought it perfectly reasonable. He had explained to her mother how it was an innovation for Hoggatt's having a clerical officer on the desk instead of a junior police officer. If she made a success of the job it would mean a permanent saving in police manpower as well as a useful training for her. As Chief Inspector Martin had told her mother: 'The reception desk is the heart of the Laboratory.' At present he was with a party of police officers visiting the United States and Inspector Blakelock was totally in charge doing the two jobs, not only receiving the exhibits, making out the register of court attendances and preparing the statistics, but discussing the cases with the detective in charge, explaining what the Laboratory could hope to do, rejecting those cases where the scientists couldn't help, and checking that the final statements for the court were complete. Brenda guessed that it was a big responsibility for him and was determined not to let him down.

Already, when she had been making the tea, the first exhibit of the day had arrived, brought in no doubt by a detective constable working on the case. It was another plastic bag of clothes from the clunch pit murder. As Inspector Blakelock turned it over in his large hands, she glimpsed through the plastic a pair of dark blue trousers with a greasy waistband, a wide-lapelled striped jacket, and a pair of black shoes with pointed toes and ornate buckles. Inspector Blakelock was studying the police report. He said:

'These belong to the boy-friend she was messing about with at the dance. You'll need a new file for the report, but register it to Biology under the Muddington reference with a sub-group number. Then attach one of the red Immediate slips. Murder gets priority.'

'But we might have two or three murders at the same time. Who decides the priority then?'

'The head of the department concerned. It's his job to allocate the work to his staff. After murder and rape, it's usual to give priority to those cases where the accused hasn't been bailed.'

Brenda said:

'I hope you don't mind my asking so many questions. Only I do want to learn. Dr. Lorrimer told me that I ought to find out all I can and not just look on this job as routine.'

'You ask away, lass, I don't mind. Only you don't want to listen too much to Dr. Lorrimer. He isn't the director here, even if he thinks he is. When you've registered that clobber, the bundle goes on the Biology shelf.'

Brenda entered the exhibit number carefully in the day-book and moved the plastic-shrouded bundle to the shelf of exhibits waiting to go into the Biology Search Room. It was good to be up to date with the entering. She glanced up at the clock. It was nearly eight-fifty. Soon the day's post would be delivered and the desk would be heaped with padded envelopes containing yesterday's blood samples from the drink and driving cases. Then the police cars would start arriving. Uniformed or plain-clothes policemen would bring in large envelopes of documents for Mr. Middlemass, the Document Examiner; specially prepared kits issued by the Laboratory for the collection of saliva, blood and semen stains; unwieldy bags of stained and dirty bed linen and blankets; the ubiquitous blunt instruments; blood-stained knives carefully taped into their boxes.

And at any moment now the first members of staff would be arriving. Mrs. Bidwell, the cleaner, should have been with them twenty minutes ago. Perhaps she had caught Scobie's influenza. The first of the scientific staff to arrive would probably be Clifford Bradley, the Higher Scientific Officer in the Biology Department, scurrying through the hall as if he had no right to be there, with his anxious hunted eyes and that stupid, drooping moustache, so preoccupied that he hardly noticed their greeting. Then Miss Foley, the Director's secretary, calm and self-possessed, wearing always that secret smile. Miss Foley reminded Brenda of Mona Rigby at school, who was always chosen to play the Madonna in the Christmas nativity play. She had never liked Mona Rigby – who wouldn't have been chosen twice for the coveted rôle if the staff had known as much about her as did Brenda – and she wasn't sure that she really liked Miss Foley. Then someone she did like, Mr. Middlemass, the Document Examiner, with his jacket slung over his shoulders, leaping up the stairs three steps at a time and calling out a greeting to the desk. After that they would come in almost any order. The hall would become alive with people, rather like a railway terminus, and at the heart of the seeming chaos, controlling and directing, helping and explaining, were the staff of the reception desk.

As if to signal that the working day was about to begin, the telephone rang. Inspector Blakelock's hand enveloped the receiver. He listened in silence for what seemed a longer period than normal, then she heard him speak.

'I don't think he's here, Mr. Lorrimer. You say he never came home last night?'

Another silence. Inspector Blakelock half turned away from her and bent his head conspiratorially over the mouthpiece as if listening to a confidence. Then he rested the receiver on the counter and turned to Brenda:

'It's Dr. Lorrimer's old dad. He's worried. Apparently Dr. Lorrimer didn't take him his early tea this morning and it looks as if he didn't come home last night. His bed hasn't been slept in.'

'Well, he can't be here. I mean, we found the front door locked when we arrived.'

There could be no doubt about that. As she had come round the corner of the house from putting her bicycle in the old stable block, Inspector Blakelock had been standing at the front door almost as if he were waiting for her. Then, when she had joined him, he had shone his torch on the locks and inserted the three keys, first the Yale, and then the Ingersoll, and lastly the security lock which disconnected the electronic warning system from Guy's Marsh police station. Then they had stepped together into the unlighted hall. She had gone to the cloakroom at the back of the building to put on her white coat and he had gone to the box in Chief Inspector Martin's office to switch off the system which protected the inner doors of the main Laboratory rooms.

She giggled and said:

'Mrs. Bidwell hasn't turned up to start the cleaning and now Dr. Lorrimer's missing. Perhaps they've run away together. The great Hoggatt scandal.'

It wasn't a very funny joke, and she wasn't surprised when Inspector Blakelock didn't laugh. He said:

'The locked door doesn't necessarily signify. Dr. Lorrimer has his own keys. And if he did make his bed and then come in extra early this morning, like as not he'd have relocked the door and set the internal alarms.'

'But how would he have got into the Biology Lab, then?'

'He'd have had to have opened the door and then left it open when he reset the alarms. It doesn't seem likely. When he's here alone he usually relies on the Yale.'

He put the receiver again to his ear and said:

'Hold on a moment will you, Mr. Lorrimer. I don't think he's here, but I'll just check.'

'I'll go,' said Brenda, anxious to demonstrate helpfulness. Without waiting to lift the flap she slipped under the counter. As she turned she saw him with startling clarity, brightly instantaneous as a camera flash. Inspector Blakelock, with his mouth half-open in remonstrance, his arm flung out towards her in a gesture, stiff and histrionic, of protection or restraint. But now, uncomprehending, she laughed and ran up the wide stairs. The Biology Laboratory was at the back of the first floor, running with its adjoining search room almost the whole length of the building. The door was shut. She turned the knob and pushed it open, feeling along the wall for the light switch. Her fingers found it and she pressed it down. The two long fluorescent tubes suspended from the ceiling blinked, then glimmered, then glowed into steady light.

She saw the body immediately. He was lying in the space between the two large central examination tables, face downwards, his left hand seeming to claw at the floor, his right arm hunched beneath him. His legs were straight. She gave a curious little sound between a cry and a moan and knelt beside him. The hair above his left ear was matted and spiked like her kitten's fur after he had washed, but she couldn't see the blood against the dark hair. But she knew that it was blood. Already it had blackened on the collar of his white coat and a small pool had separated and congealed on the Lab floor. Only his left eye was visible,

80

fixed and dull and retracted, like the eye of a dead calf. Tentatively she felt his cheek. It was cold. But she had known as soon as she had seen the glazed eye that this was death.

She had no memory of closing the Lab door or coming down the stairs. Inspector Blakelock was still behind the counter, rigid as a statue, the telephone receiver in his hand. She wanted to laugh at the sight of his face, he looked so funny. She tried to speak to him, but the words wouldn't come. Her jaw jabbered uncontrollably and her teeth clattered together. She made some kind of gesture. He said something that she couldn't catch, dropped the receiver on the counter and raced upstairs.

She staggered to the heavy Victorian armchair against the wall outside Chief Inspector Martin's office, Colonel Hoggatt's chair. The portrait looked down at her. As she watched, the left eye seemed to grow larger, the lips twisted to a leer.

Her whole body was seized with a terrible cold. Her heart seemed to have grown immense, thudding against the rib-cage. She was breathing in great gulps, but still there wasn't enough air. Then she became aware of the crackling from the telephone. Rising slowly like an automaton, she made her way over to the counter and picked up the receiver. Mr. Lorrimer's voice, frail and querulous, was bleating at the other end. She tried to say the accustomed words 'Hoggatt's Laboratory here. Reception speaking.' But the words wouldn't come. She replaced the receiver in its cradle and walked back to her chair.

She had no memory of hearing the long peal of the doorbell, of moving stiffly across the hall to answer it. Suddenly the door crashed open and the hall was full of people, loud with voices. The light seemed to have brightened, which was odd, and she saw them all like actors on a stage, brightly lit, faces made grotesque and heightened by make-up, every word clear and comprehensible as if she were in the front row of the stalls. Mrs. Bidwell, the cleaner, in her mackintosh with the imitation fur collar, her eyes bright with indignation, her voice pitched high.

'What the hell's going on here! Some bloody fool phoned my old man and told him that I needn't come in today, that Mrs. Schofield wanted me. Who's playing silly buggers?'

Inspector Blakelock was coming down the stairs, slowly and deliberately, the protagonist making his entrance. They stood in a small circle and looked up at him, Dr. Howarth, Clifford Bradley, Miss Foley, Mrs. Bidwell. The Director stepped forward. He looked as if he were going to faint. He said:

'Well, Blakelock?'

'It's Dr. Lorrimer, sir. He's dead. Murdered.'

Surely they couldn't all have repeated that word in unison, turning their faces towards each other, like a Greek chorus. But it seemed to echo in the quiet of the hall, becoming meaningless, a sonorous groan of a word. Murder. Murder. Murder.

She saw Dr. Howarth run towards the stairs. Inspector Blakelock turned to accompany him, but the director said:

'No, you stay here. See that no-one gets any further than the hall. Phone the Chief Constable and Dr. Kerrison. Then get me the Home Office.'

Suddenly they seemed to notice Brenda for the first time. Mrs. Bidwell came towards her. She said:

'Did you find him then? You poor little bugger!'

And suddenly it wasn't a play any more. The lights went out. The faces became amorphous, ordinary. Brenda gave a little gasp. She felt Mrs. Bidwell's arms go round her shoulders. The smell of the mackintosh was pressed into her face. The fur was as soft as her kitten's paw. And, blessedly, Brenda began to cry.

82

2

In a London teaching hospital close by the river, from which he could in his more masochistic moments glimpse the window of his own office, Dr. Charles Freeborn, Controller of the Forensic Science Service, all six foot four of him, lay rigidly in his narrow bed, his nose peaked high above the methodical fold of the sheet, his white hair a haze against the whiter pillow. The bed was too short for him, an inconvenience to which he had accommodated himself by neatly sticking out his toes over the foot board. His bedside locker held the conglomerate of offerings, necessities and minor diversions considered indispensable to a brief spell in hospital. They included a vase of official-looking roses, scentless but florid, through whose funereal and unnatural blooms Commander Adam Dalgliesh glimpsed a face so immobile, upturned eyes fixed on the ceiling, that he was momentarily startled by the illusion that he was visiting the dead. Recalling that Freeborn was recovering from nothing more serious than a successful operation for varicose veins, he approached the bed and said tentatively:

'Hello!'

Freeborn, galvanised from his torpor, sprang up like a jack-in-the box, scattering from his bedside locker a packet of tissues, two copies of the *Journal of the Forensic Science Society* and an open box of chocolates. He shot out a lean speckled arm encircled by the hospital identity bracelet and crushed Dalgliesh's hand.

'Adam! Don't creep up on me like that, damn you! God, am I glad to see you! The only good news I've had this morning is that you'll be in charge. I thought that you might have already left. How long can you spare? How are you getting there?'

Dalgliesh answered the questions in order.

'Ten minutes. By chopper from the Battersea heliport. I'm on my way now. How are you, Charles? Am I being a nuisance?'

'I'm the nuisance. This couldn't have happened at a worse time. And the maddening part of it is that it's my own fault. The op could have waited. Only the pain was getting rather tedious and Meg insisted that I had it done now before I retired, on the theory I suppose, that better in the Government's time than my own.'

Recalling what he knew of the ardours and achievements of Freeborn's forty odd years in the Forensic Science Service, the difficult war years, the delayed retirement, the last five years when he had exchanged his directorship for the frustrations of bureaucracy, Dalgliesh said:

'Sensible of her. And there's nothing you could have done at Chevisham.'

'I know. It's ridiculous, this feeling of responsibility because one isn't actually in post when disaster strikes. They rang from the duty office to break the news to me just after nine. Better that than learning it from my visitors or this evening's paper, I suppose they thought. Decent of them. The Chief Constable must have called in the Yard within a few minutes of getting the news. How much do you know?'

'About as much as you, I imagine. I've spoken to the C.C. and to Howarth. They've given me the main facts. The skull smashed, apparently by a heavy mallet which Lorrimer had been examining. The Lab found properly locked when the Assistant Police Liaison Officer and the young C.O. arrived at eight-thirty this morning. Lorrimer's keys in his pocket. He often worked late and most of the Lab staff knew that he proposed to do so last night. No sign of a break-in.

Four sets of keys. Lorrimer had one set as the Senior P.S.O. and Deputy Security Officer. The Assistant Police Liaison Officer has the second. Lorrimer or one of the Police Liaison Officers were the only people authorised to lock and open up the building. The Director keeps the third set of keys in his security cupboard, and the fourth are in a safe at Guy's Marsh police station in case the alarm rings in the night.'

Freeborn said:

'So either Lorrimer let in his murderer or the murderer had a key.'

There were, thought Dalgliesh, other possibilities, but now was not the time to discuss them. He asked:

'Lorrimer would have let in anyone from the Lab, I suppose?'

'Why not? He'd probably have admitted any of the local police whom he personally knew, particularly if it were a detective concerned with a recent case. Otherwise, I'm not so sure. He may have admitted a friend or relative, although that's even more doubtful. He was a punctilious blighter and I can't see him using the Lab as a convenient place for a rendezvous. And, of course, he would have let in the forensic pathologist.'

'That's a local man, Henry Kerrison, they tell me. The C.C. said that they called him in to look at the body. Well, they could hardly do anything else. I didn't know you'd found a successor to Death-House Donald.'

'Nor have we. Kerrison is doing it on an item of service basis. He's well thought of and we'll probably appoint him if we can get the Area Health Authority to agree. There's the usual difficulty about his hospital responsibilities. I wish to hell we could get the forensic pathology service sorted out before I go. But that's one headache I'll have to leave to my successor.'

Dalgliesh thought without affection of Death-House Donald with his ghoulish schoolboy humour

'Not that cake-knife, my dear lady. I used it this morning on one of Slash Harry's victims and the edge is rather blunted' – his mania for self-advertisement and his intolerable bucolic laugh, and was grateful that at least he wouldn't be interrogating that redoubtable old phoney. He said:

'Tell me about Lorrimer. What was he like?'

This was the question which lay at the heart of every murder investigation; and yet he knew its absurdity before he asked it. It was the strangest part of a detective's job, this building up of a relationship with the dead, seen only as a crumpled corpse at the scene of crime or naked on the mortuary table. The victim was central to the mystery of his own death. He died because of what he was. Before the case was finished Dalgliesh would have received a dozen pictures of Lorrimer's personality, transferred like prints from other men's minds. From these amorphous and uncertain images he would create his own imaginings, superimposed and dominant, but essentially just as incomplete, just as distorted – as were the others – by his own preconceptions, his own personality. But the question had to be asked. And at least he could rely on Freeborn to answer it without initiating a philosophical discussion about the basis of the self. But their minds must for a moment have flowed together, for Freeborn said:

'It's odd how you always have to ask that question, that you'll only see him through other men's eyes. Aged about forty. Looks like John the Baptist without his beard and is about as uncompromising. Single. Lives with an elderly father in a cottage just outside the village. He is – was – an extremely competent forensic biologist, but I doubt whether he would have gone any higher. Obsessional, edgy, uncomfortable to be with. He applied for the job at Hoggatt's, of course, and was runner-up to Howarth.'

'How did he and the Lab take the new appointment?'

'Lorrimer took it pretty hard, I believe. The Lab wouldn't have welcomed his appointment. He was pretty unpopular with most of the senior staff. But there are always one or two who would have preferred a colleague to a stranger even if they hated his guts. And the Union made the expected noises about not appointing a forensic scientist.'

'Why did you appoint Howarth? I take it you were on the Board.'

'Oh yes. I accept a share of the responsibility. That's not to say that I think we made a mistake. Old Doc Mac was one of the really great forensic scientists – we started together – but there's no denying that he'd let the reins slip a bit in recent years. Howarth has already increased the work turnover by ten per cent. And then there's the commissioning of the new Lab. It was a calculated risk to take a man without forensic experience, but we were looking for a manager primarily. At least, most of the Board were and the rest of us were persuaded that it would be no bad thing, without, I confess, being precisely clear what we meant by that blessed word. Management. The new science. We all make obeisance to it. In the old days we got on with the job, jollied staff along if they needed it, kicked the sluggards in the backside, encouraged the unconfident and persuaded a reluctant and sceptical police force to use us. Oh, and sent in an occasional statistical return to the Home Office just to remind them that we were there. It seemed to work all right. The service didn't collapse. Have you ever considered what exactly is the difference between administration and management, Adam?'

'Keep it as a question to confound the candidate at your next Board. Howarth was at the Bruche Research Institute wasn't he? Why did he want to leave? He must have taken a cut in pay.'

'Not more than about six hundred a year, and that wouldn't worry him. His father was rich, and it all came to him and his half-sister.'

'But it's a bigger place surely? And he can't be getting the research at Hoggatt's.'

'He gets some, but essentially, of course, it's a service laboratory. That worried us a bit on the Board. But you can hardly set out to persuade your most promising applicant that he's downgrading himself. Scientifically and academically – he's a pure physicist – he was well ahead of the rest of the field. Actually we did press him a bit and he gave the usual reasons. He was getting stale, wanted a new sphere of activity, was anxious to get away from London. Gossip has it that his wife had recently left him and he wanted to make a clean break. That was probably the reason. Thank God he didn't use that blasted word 'challenge'. If I have to listen to one more candidate telling me he sees the job as a challenge I'll throw up over the boardroom table. Adam, I'm getting old.'

He nodded his head towards the window.

'They're in a bit of a twitch over there, I need hardly say.'

'I know. I've had an exceedingly brief but tactful interview. They're brilliant at implying more than they actually say. But obviously it's important to get it solved quickly. Apart from confidence in the service, you'll all want to get the Lab back to work.'

'What's happening now? To the staff, I mean.'

'The local C.I.D. have locked all the interior doors and they're keeping the staff in the library and the reception area until I arrive. They're occupying themselves writing out an account of their movements since Lorrimer was last seen alive and the local force are getting on with the preliminary checking of alibis. That should save some time. I'm taking one officer, John Massingham, with me. The Met Lab will take on any of the forensic work. They're sending a chap down from Public Relations Branch to handle the publicity, so I won't have that on my plate. It's obliging of that pop group to break up so spectacularly. That and the Government's troubles should keep us off the front page for a day or two.'

Freeborn was looking down at his big toes with mild distaste as if they were errant members whose deficiencies had only now become apparent to him. From time to time he wriggled them, whether in obedience to some medical instruction or for his own private satisfaction, it was impossible to say. After a moment he spoke.

'I started my career at Hoggatt's, you know. That was before the war. All any of us had then was wet chemistry, test tubes, beakers, solutions. And girls weren't employed because it wasn't decent for them to be concerned with sex cases. Hoggatt's was old fashioned even for the 1930 service. Not scientifically, though. We had a spectrograph when it was still the new wonder toy. The fens threw up some odd crimes. Do you remember the Mulligan case, old man who chopped up his brother and tied the remains to the Leamings sluice-gates? There was some nice forensic evidence there.'

'Some fifty bloodstains on the pig-sty wall, weren't there? And Mulligan swore it was sow's blood.'

Freeborn's voice grew reminiscent.

'I liked that old villain. And they still drag out those photographs I took of the splashes and use them to illustrate lectures on bloodstains. Odd, the attraction Hoggatt's had – still has for that matter. An unsuitable Palladian mansion in an unexciting East Anglian village on the edge of the black fens. Ten miles to Ely, and that's hardly a centre of riotous activity for the young. Winters to freeze your marrow and a spring wind – the fen blow they call it – which whips up the peat and chokes your lungs like smog. And yet the staff, if they didn't leave after the first month, stayed for ever. Did you know that Hoggatt's has got a small Wren chapel in the Lab grounds? Architecturally it's much superior to the house because old Hoggatt never messed it about. He was almost entirely without aesthetic taste, I believe. He used it as a chemical store once it had been deconsecrated or whatever it is they do to unused churches. Howarth has got a string quartet going at the Lab and they gave a concert there. Apparently he's a noted amateur violinist. At the moment he's probably wishing that he'd stuck to music. This isn't a propitious start for him, poor devil. And it was always such a happy Lab. I suppose it was the isolation that gave us such a feeling of camaraderie.'

Dalgliesh said grimly:

'I doubt whether that will survive an hour of my arrival.'

'No. You chaps usually bring as much trouble with you as you solve. You can't help it. Murder is like that, a contaminating crime. Oh, you'll solve it, I know. You always do. But I'm wondering at what cost.'

Dalgliesh did not answer. He was both too honest and too fond of Freeborn to make comforting and platitudinous promises. Of course, he would be tactful. That didn't need saying. But he would be at Hoggatt's to solve a murder, and all other considerations would go down before that overriding task. Murder was always solved at a cost, sometimes to himself, more often to others. And Freeborn was right. It was a crime which contaminated everyone whom it touched, innocent and guilty alike. He didn't grudge the ten minutes he had spent with Freeborn. The old man believed, with simple patriotism, that the Service to which he had given the whole of his working life was the best in the world. He had helped to shape it, and he was probably right. Dalgliesh had learned what he had come to learn. But as he shook hands and said goodbye he knew that he left no comfort behind him.

3

The library at Hoggatt's was at the rear of the ground floor. Its three tall windows gave a view of the stone terrace and the double flight of steps going down to what had once been a lawn and formal gardens, but which was now a half-acre of neglected grass, bounded to the west by the brick annexe of the Vehicle Examination Department, and to the east by the old stable block, now converted into garages. The room was one of the few in the house spared by its former owner's transforming zeal. The original bookcases of carved oak still lined the walls, although they now housed the Laboratory's not inconsiderable scientific library, while extra shelf-room for bound copies of national and international journals had been provided by two steel movable units which divided the room into three bays. Under each of the three windows was a working table with four chairs; one table was almost completely covered by a model of the new Laboratory.

It was in this somewhat inadequate space that the staff were congregated. A detective-sergeant from the local C.I.D. sat impassively near the door, a reminder of why they were so inconveniently incarcerated. They were allowed out to the ground-floor cloakroom under tactful escort, and had been told they could telephone home from the library. But the rest of the Laboratory was at present out of bounds.

They had all, on arrival, been asked to write a brief account of where they had been, and with whom, the previous evening and night. Patiently, they waited their turn at one of the three tables. The statements had been collected by the sergeant and handed out to his colleague on the reception desk, presumably so that the preliminary checking could begin. Those of the junior staff who could provide a satisfactory alibi were allowed home as soon as it had been checked; one by one and with some reluctance at missing the excitements to come they went their way. The less fortunate, together with those who had arrived first at the Laboratory that morning and all the senior scientists, had been told they must await the arrival of the team from Scotland Yard. The Director had put in only one brief appearance in the library. Earlier he had gone with Angela Foley to break the news of Lorrimer's death to his father. Since his return he had stayed in his own office with Detective-Superintendent Mercer of the local C.I.D. It was rumoured that Dr. Kerrison was with them.

The minutes dragged while they listened for the first hum of the approaching helicopter. Inhibited by the presence of the police, by prudence, delicacy or embarrassment from talking about the subject foremost in their minds, they spoke to each other with the wary politeness of uncongenial strangers stranded in an airport lounge. The women were, on the whole, better equipped for the tedium of the wait. Mrs. Mallett, the typist from the general office, had brought her knitting to work and fortified by an unshakeable alibi – she had sat between the postmistress and Mr. Mason from the general store at the village concert – and with something to occupy her hands, sat clicking away with understandable if irritating complacency until given the order of release. Mrs. Bidwell, the Laboratory cleaner, had insisted on visiting her broom cupboard, under escort, and had provided herself with a feather duster and a couple of rags with which she made a vigorous onslaught on the bookshelves. She was unusually silent, but the group of scientists at the tables could hear her muttering to herself as she punished the books at the end of one of the bays.

Brenda Pridmore had been allowed to collect the exhibits received book from the counter and, white-faced but outwardly composed, was checking the previous month's figures. The book took more than its share of the available table space; but at least she had a legitimate job. Claire Easterbrook, Senior Scientific Officer in the Biology Department and, with Lorrimer's death, the senior biologist, had taken from her briefcase a scientific paper she had prepared on recent advances in blood grouping and settled down to revise it with as little apparent concern as if murder at Hoggatt's were a routine inconvenience for which, prudently, she was always provided.

The rest of the staff passed the time each in his own way. Those who preferred the pretence of business immersed themselves in a book and, from time to time, made an ostentatious note. The two Vehicle Examiners, who were reputed to have no conversation except about cars, squatted side by side, their backs against the steel book racks, and talked cars together with desperate eagerness. Middlemass had finished *The Times* crossword by quarter to ten and had made the rest of the paper last as long as possible. But now even the deaths column was exhausted. He folded the paper and tossed it across the table to eagerly awaiting hands.

It was a relief when Stephen Copley, the Senior Chemist, arrived just before ten, bustling in as usual, his rubicund face with its tonsure and fringe of black curly hair glistening as if he had come in from the sun. Nothing was known to disconcert him, certainly not the death of a man he had disliked. But he was secure in his alibi, having spent the whole of the previous day in the Crown Court and the evening and night with friends at Norwich, only getting back to Chevisham in time for a late start that morning. His colleagues, relieved to find something to talk about, began questioning him about the case. They spoke rather too loudly to be natural. The rest of the company listened with simulated interest as if the conversation were a dramatic dialogue provided for their entertainment.

'Who did they call for the defence?' asked Middlemass.

'Charlie Pollard. He hung his great belly over the box and explained confidentially to the jury that they needn't be frightened of the so-called scientific expert witnesses because none of us, including himself of course, really know what we're talking about. They were immensely reassured, I need hardly say.'

'Juries hate scientific evidence.'

'They think they won't be able to understand it so naturally they can't understand it. As soon as you step into the box you see a curtain of obstinate incomprehension clanging down over their minds. What they want is certainty. Did this paint particle come from this car body? Answer Yes or No. None of those nasty mathematical probabilities we're so fond of.'

'If they hate scientific evidence they certainly hate arithmetic more. Give them a scientific opinion which depends on the ability to divide a factor by two-thirds and what do you get from counsel? "I'm afraid you'll have to explain yourself more simply, Mr. Middlemass. The jury and I haven't got a higher degree in mathematics, you know." Inference: you're an arrogant bastard and the jury would be well advised not to believe a word you say.'

It was the old argument. Brenda had heard it all before when she ate her lunch-time sandwiches in the room, halfway between a kitchen and a sitting-room, which was still called the junior Mess. But now it seemed terrible that they should be able to talk so naturally while Dr. Lorrimer lay there dead upstairs.

Suddenly she had a need to speak his name. She looked up and made herself say:

'Dr Lorrimer thought that the service would end up with about three immense laboratories doing the work for the whole country with exhibits coming in by air. He said that he thought all the scientific evidence ought to be agreed by both sides before the trial.'

Middlemass said easily:

'That's an old argument. The police want a local lab nice and handy, and who's to blame them? Besides, three-quarters of forensic scientific work doesn't require all this sophisticated instrumentation. There's more of a case for highly equipped regional laboratories with local out-stations. But who'd want to work in the small labs if the more exciting stuff went elsewhere?'

Miss Easterbrook had apparently finished her revision. She said:

'Lorrimer knew that this idea of the lab as a scientific arbiter wouldn't work, not with the British accusatorial system. Anyway, scientific evidence ought to be tested like any other evidence.'

'But how?' asked Middlemass. 'By an ordinary jury? Suppose you're an expert document examiner outside the service and they call you for the defence. You and I disagree. How can the jury judge between us? They'll probably choose to believe you because you're better looking.'

'Or you, more likely, because you're a man.'

'Or one of them – the crucial one – will reject me because I remind him of Uncle Ben and all the family know that Ben was the world's champion liar.'

'All right. All right.' Copley spread plump hands in a benediction of appeasement. 'It's the same as democracy. A fallible system but the best we've got.'

Middlemass said:

'It's extraordinary, though, how well it works. You

look at the jury, sitting there politely attentive, like children on their best behaviour because they're visitors in an alien country and don't want to make fools of themselves or offend the natives. Yet how often do they come up with a verdict that's manifestly perverse having regard to the evidence?'

Claire Easterbrook said dryly:

'Whether it's manifestly perverse having regard to the truth is another matter.'

'A criminal trial isn't a tribunal for eliciting the truth. At least we deal in facts. What about the emotion? Did you love your husband, Mrs. B.? How can the poor woman explain that, probably like the majority of wives, she loved him most of the time, when he didn't snore in her ear all night or shout at the kids or keep her short of Bingo money.'

Copley said:

'She can't. If she's got any sense and if her counsel has briefed her properly, she'll get out her handkerchief and sob "Oh yes, sir. A better husband never lived, as God's my witness." It's a game, isn't it? You win if you play by the rules.'

Claire Easterbrook shrugged:

'If you know them. Too often it's a game where the rules are known only to one side. Natural enough when that's the side which makes them up.'

Copley and Middlemass laughed.

Clifford Bradley had half hidden himself from the rest of the company behind the table holding the model of the new Laboratory. He had taken a book from the shelves at random but, for the last ten minutes, hadn't even bothered to turn the page.

They were laughing! They were actually laughing! Getting up from the table he groped his way down the furthest bay and replaced his book in the rack, leaning his forehead against the cold steel. Unobtrusively Middlemass strolled up beside him and, back

to the company, reached up to take a book from the shelf. He said:

'Are you all right?'

'I wish to God they'd come.'

'So do we all. But the chopper should be here any minute now.'

'How can they laugh like that? Don't they care?'

'Of course they care. Murder is beastly, embarrassing and inconvenient. But I doubt whether anyone is feeling a purely personal grief. And other people's tragedies, other people's danger, always provoke a certain euphoria as long as one is safe oneself.' He looked at Bradley and said softly:

'There's always manslaughter, you know. Or even justified homicide. Though, come to think of it, one could hardly plead that.'

'You think I killed him, don't you?'

'I don't think anything. Anyway, you've got an alibi. Wasn't your mother-in-law with you yesterday evening?'

'Not all the evening. She caught the seven-forty-five bus.'

'Well, with luck, there'll be evidence that he was dead by then.' And why, thought Middlemass, should Bradley assume that he wasn't? Bradley's dark and anxious eyes narrowed with suspicion.

'How did you know that Sue's mother was with us last night?'

'Susan told me. Actually, she telephoned me at the Lab just before two. It was about Lorrimer.' He thought and then said easily, 'She was wondering whether there was a chance he might ask for a transfer now that Howarth has been in post a year. She thought I might have heard something. When you get home, tell her that I don't propose to tell the police about the call unless she does first. Oh, and you'd better reassure her that I didn't bash in his head for him. I'd do a lot for Sue, but a man has to draw the line somewhere.'

Bradley said with a note of resentment:

'Why should you worry? There's nothing wrong with your alibi. Weren't you at the village concert?'

'Not all the evening. And there's a certain slight embarrassment about my alibi even when I was ostensibly there.'

Bradley turned to him and said with sudden vehemence:

'I didn't do it! Oh God, I can't stand this waiting!'

'You've got to stand it. Pull yourself together, Cliff! You won't help yourself or Susan by going to pieces. They're English policemen, remember. We're not expecting the K.G.B.'

It was then that they heard the long awaited sound, a distant grinding hum like that of an angry wasp. The desultory voices at the tables fell silent, heads were raised and, together, the company moved towards the windows. Mrs. Bidwell rushed for a place of vantage. The red and white helicopter rattled into sight over the top of the trees and hovered, a noisy gadfly, above the terraces. No one spoke. Then Middlemass said:

'The Yard's wonder boy, appropriately, descends from the clouds. Well, let's hope that he works quickly. I want to get into my lab. Someone should tell him that he's not the only one with a murder on his hands.'

4

Detective-Inspector the Honourable John Massingham disliked helicopters, which he regarded as noisy, cramped and frighteningly unsafe. Since his physical courage was beyond question either by himself or anyone else, he would normally have had no objection to saying so. But he knew his chief's dislike of unnecessary chat, and strapped as they were side by side in uncomfortably close proximity in the Enstrom F28, he decided that the Chevisham case would get off to the most propitious start by a policy of disciplined silence. He noted with interest that the cockpit instrument panel was remarkably similar to a car dashboard; even the airspeed was shown in miles per hour instead of knots. He was only sorry that there the resemblance ended. He adjusted his earphones more comfortably and settled down to soothe his nerves by a concentrated study of his maps.

The red-brown tentacles of London's suburbs had at last been shaken off, and the chequered autumn landscape, multi-textured as a cloth collage, unrolled before them in a changing pattern of brown, green and gold, leading them on to Cambridge. The fitful sunshine moved in broad swathes across the neat, segmented villages, the trim municipal parks and open fields. Miniature tin cars, beetle-bright in the sun, pursued each other busily along the roads.

Dalgliesh glanced at his companion, at the strong, pale face, the spatter of freckles over the craggy nose and wide forehead, and the thatch of red hair springing under the headphones, and thought how like the boy was to his father, that redoubtable, thrice-decorated peer, whose courage was equalled only by his obstinacy and naïveté. The marvel of the Massinghams was that a lineage going back five hundred years could have produced so many generations of amiable nonentities. He remembered when he had last seen Lord Dungannon. It had been a debate in the House of Lords on juvenile deliquency, a subject on which His Lordship considered himself an expert since he had, indubitably, once been a boy and had, briefly, helped organise a youth club on his grandfather's estate. His thoughts, when they finally came, had been uttered in all their simplistic banality, in no particular order of logic or relevance, and in a curiously gentle voice punctuated by long pauses in which he had gazed thoughtfully at the throne and appeared to commune happily with some inner presence. Meanwhile, like lemmings who have smelt the sea, the noble lords streamed out of their chamber in a body to appear, as if summoned by telepathy, when Dungannon's speech drew to its close. But if the family had contributed nothing to statesmanship and little to the arts, they had died with spectacular gallantry for orthodox causes in every generation.

And now Dungannon's heir had chosen this far from orthodox job. It would be interesting to see if, for the first time and in so unusual a field, the family achieved distinction. What had led Massingham to choose the police service instead of his family's usual career of the Army as an outlet for his natural combativeness and unfashionable patriotism Dalgliesh had not enquired, partly because he was a respecter of other men's privacy, and partly because he wasn't sure that he wanted to hear the answer. So far Massingham had done exceptionally well. The police were a tolerant body and took the view that a man couldn't help who his father was. They accepted that Massingham had gained his promotion on merit although they were not so naïve as to suppose that being the elder son of a peer did any man harm. They called Massingham the Honjohn behind his back and occasionally to his face, and bore no malice.

Although the family was now impoverished and the estate sold – Lord Dungannon was bringing up his considerable family in a modest villa in Bayswater – the boy had still gone to his father's school. No doubt, though the Dalgliesh, the old warrior was unaware that other schools existed; like every other class, the aristocracy, however poor, could always find the money for the things they really wanted. But he was an odd product of that establishment, having none of the

100

slightly *dégagé* elegance and ironic detachment which characterised its alumni. Dalgliesh, if he hadn't known his history, would have guessed that Massingham was the produce of a sound, upper-middle-class family – a doctor or a solicitor, perhaps – and of an old established grammar school. It was only the second time they had worked together. The first time, Dalgliesh had been impressed by Massingham's intelligence and enormous capacity for work, and by his admirable ability to keep his mouth shut and to sense when his chief wanted to be alone. He had also been struck by a streak of ruthlessness in the boy which, he thought, ought not to have surprised him since he knew that, as with all good detectives, it must be present.

And now the Enstrom was rattling above the towers and spires of Cambridge, and they could see the shining curve of the river, the bright autumnal avenues leading down through green lawns to miniature hump-backed bridges, King's College Chapel upturned and slowly rotating beside its great striped square of green. And, almost immediately, the city was behind them and they saw, like a crinkled ebony sea, the black earth of the fens. Below them were straight roads ridged above the fields, with villages strung along them as if clinging to the security of high ground; isolated farms with their roofs so low that they looked half submerged in the peat; an occasional church tower standing majestically apart from its village with the gravestones planted round it like crooked teeth. They must be getting close now; already Dalgliesh could see the soaring west tower and pinnacles of Ely Cathedral to the east.

Massingham looked up from his map-reading and peered down. His voice cracked through Dalgliesh's earphones:

'This is it, sir.'

Chevisham was spread beneath them. It lay on a narrow plateau above the fens, the houses strung along the northerly of two converging roads. The tower of the impressive cruciform church was immediately identifiable, as was Chevisham Manor and, behind it, sprawling over the scarred field and linking the two roads, the brick and concrete of the new Laboratory building. They rattled along the main street of what looked like a typical East Anglian village. Dalgliesh glimpsed the ornate red-brick front of the local chapel, one or two prosperous-looking houses with Dutch gables, a small close of recently built, semi-detached boxes with the developer's board still in place, and what looked like the village general store and post office. There were few people about, but the noise of the engines brought figures from shops and houses and pale faces, their eyes shielded, strained up at them.

And now they were turning towards Hoggatt's Laboratory, coming in low over what must be the Wren Chapel. It stood about a quarter of a mile from the house in a triple circle of beech trees, an isolated building so small and perfect that it looked like an architect's model precisely set in a fabricated landscape, or an elegant ecclesiastical folly, justifying itself only by its classical purity, as distanced from religion as it was from life. It was odd that it lay so far from the house. Dalgliesh thought that it had probably been built later, perhaps because the original owner of the mansion had quarrelled with the local parson and, in defiance, had decided to make his own arrangements for spiritual ministrations. Certainly the house hardly looked large enough to support a private chapel. For a few seconds as they descended, he had an unimpeded view through a gap in the trees of the west front of the chapel. He saw a single high arched window with two balancing niches, the four Corinthian pilasters separating the bays, the whole crowned with a large decorated pediment and topped with a hexagonal lantern. The helicopter seemed almost to be brushing the trees. The brittle autumn leaves, shaken by the rush

102

of air, flurried down like a shower of charred paper over the roof and the bright green of the grass.

And then, sickeningly, the helicopter soared, the chapel lurched out of sight and they were poised, engines rattling, ready to land on the wide terrace behind the house. Over its roof he could see the forecourt patterned with parking lots, the police cars tidily aligned and what looked like a mortuary van. A broad drive, bordered with straggling bushes and a few trees, led down to what the map showed as Stoney Piggott's Road. There was no gate to the driveway. Beyond it he could see the bright flag of a bus stop and the bus shelter. Then the helicopter began to descend and only the rear of the house was in view. From a ground-floor window he could see the smudges of watching faces.

There was a reception committee of three, their figures oddly fore-shortened, the necks straining upwards. The thrash of the rotor blades had tugged their hair into grotesque shapes, flurried the legs of their trousers and flattened their jackets against their chests. Now, with the stilling of the engines, the sudden silence was so absolute that he saw the three motionless figures as if they were a tableau of dummies in a silent world. He and Massingham unclasped their seat belts and clambered to earth. For about five seconds the two groups stood regarding each other. Then, with a single gesture, the three waiting figures smoothed back their hair and advanced warily to meet him. Simultaneously his ears unblocked and the world again became audible. He turned to thank and speak briefly to the pilot. Then he and Massingham walked forward.

Dalgliesh already knew Superintendent Mercer of the local C.I.D.; they had met at a number of police conferences. Even at sixty feet his ox-like shoulders, the round comedian's face with the wide upturned mouth, and the button bright eyes, had been instantly recognisable. Dalgliesh felt his hand crushed, and then Mercer made the introductions. Dr. Howarth; a tall fair man, almost as tall as Dalgliesh himself, with widely spaced eyes of a remarkably deep blue and the lashes so long that they might have looked effeminate on any face less arrogantly male. He could, Dalgliesh thought, have been judged an outstandingly handsome man were it not for a certain incongruity of feature, perhaps the contrast between the fineness of the skin stretched over the flat cheekbones and the strong jutting jaw and uncompromising mouth. Dalgliesh would have known that he was rich. The blue eyes regarded the world with the slightly cynical assurance of a man accustomed to getting what he wanted when he wanted it by the simplest of expedients, that of paying for it. Beside him, Dr. Henry Kerrison, although as tall, looked diminished. His creased, anxious face was bleached with weariness and there was a look in the dark, heavily-lidded eyes which was uncomfortably close to defeat. He grasped Dalgliesh's hand with a firm grip but didn't speak. Howarth said:

'There's no entrance now to the back of the house; we have to go round to the front. This is the easiest way.'

Carrying their scene-of-crime cases, Dalgliesh and Massingham followed him round the side of the house. The faces at the ground-floor window had disappeared and it was extraordinarily quiet. Trudging through the leaves which had drifted over the path, sniffing the keen autumnal air with its hint of smokiness, and feeling the sun on his face, Massingham felt a surge of animal well-being. It was good to be out of London. This promised to be the kind of job he most liked. The little group turned the corner of the house and Dalgliesh and Massingham had their first clear view of the façade of Hoggatt's Laboratory.

5

The house was an excellent example of late seven-teenth-century domestic architecture, a three-storey brick mansion with a hipped roof and four dormer windows, the centre three-bay projection surmounted by a pediment with a richly carved cornice and medal-lions. A flight of four wide, curved stone steps led to the doorway, imposing on its pilasters but solidly, un-ostentatiously, right. Dalgliesh paused momentarily to study the façade. Howarth said:

'Agreeable, isn't it? But wait till you see what the old man did to some of the interior.'

The front door, with its elegant but restrained brass door handle and knocker, was fitted with two security locks, a Chubb and an Ingersoll, in addition to the Yale. At a superficial glance there was no sign of forcing. It was opened almost before Howarth had lifted his hand to ring. The man who stood aside, un-smiling, for them to enter, although not in uniform, was immediately recognisable to Dalgliesh as a police officer. Howarth introduced him briefly as Inspector Blakelock, Assistant Police Liaison Officer. He added:

'All three locks were in order when Blakelock ar-rived this morning. The Chubb connects the elec-tronic warning system to Guy's Marsh police station. The internal protection system is controlled from a panel in the Police Liaison Officer's room.'

Dalgliesh turned to Blakelock.

'And that was in order?'

'Yes, sir.'

'There is no other exit?'

It was Howarth was answered.

'No. My predecessor had the back door and one side door permanently barred. It was too complicated coping with a system of security locks for three doors. Everyone comes in and goes out by the front.'

'Except possibly one person last night,' thought Dalgliesh.

They passed through the entrance hall which ran almost the whole length of the house, their feet suddenly loud on the marble tessellated floor. Dalgliesh was used to receiving impressions at a glance. The party did not pause on their way to the stairs, but he had a clear impression of the room, the high moulded ceiling, the two elegant pedimented doors to right and left, an oil painting of the Laboratory founder on the right-hand wall, the gleaming wood of the reception counter at the rear. A police officer with a sheaf of papers before him was using the desk telephone, presumably still checking alibis. He went on with his conversation without glancing up.

The staircase was remarkable. The balustrades were carved oak panels decorated with scrolls of acanthus foliage, each newel surmounted by a heavy oak pineapple. There was no carpet and the unpolished wood was heavily scarred. Dr. Kerrison and Superintendent Mercer mounted behind Dalgliesh in silence. Howarth, leading the way, seemed to feel the need to talk:

'The ground floor is occupied with Reception and the Exhibits Store, my office, my secretary's room, the general office and the Police Liaison Officer's room. That's all, apart from the domestic quarters at the rear. Chief Inspector Martin is the chief P.L.O. but he's in the U.S.A. at the moment and we only have Blakelock on duty. On this floor we have Biology at the back, Criminalistics at the front and the Instrument Section at the end of the corridor. But I've put a plan of the Lab in my office for you. I thought you might like to take that over if it's convenient. But I haven't moved any of my things until you've examined the room. This is the Biology Lab.'

106

He glanced at Superintendent Mercer, who took the key from his pocket and unlocked the door. It was a long room obviously converted from two smaller ones, possibly a sitting-room or small drawing-room. The ceiling carvings had been removed, perhaps because Colonel Hoggatt had thought them inappropriate to a working laboratory, but the scars of the desecration remained. The original windows had been replaced by two long windows occupying almost the whole of the end wall. There was a range of benches and sinks under the windows, and two islands of work benches in the middle of the room, one fitted with sinks, the other with a number of microscopes. To the left was a small glass-partitioned office, to the right a dark-room. Beside the door was an immense refrigerator.

But the most bizarre objects in the room were a pair of unclothed window-dressers' dummies, one male and one female, standing between the windows. They were unclothed and denuded of their wigs. The pose of the bald egg-shaped heads, the jointed arms stiffly flexed in a parody of benediction, the staring eyes and curved arrow-like lips gave them the hieratic look of a couple of painted deities. And at their feet, a white-clad sacrificial victim, was the body.

Howarth stared at the two dummies as if he had never seen them before. He seemed to think that they required explanation. For the first time he had lost some of his assurance. He said:

'That's Liz and Burton. The staff dress them in a suspect's clothes so that they can match up bloodstains or slashes.' He added: 'Do you want me here?'

'For the moment, yes,' answered Dalgliesh.

He knelt by the body. Kerrison moved to stand beside him. Howarth and Mercer stayed one each side of the door.

After two minutes Dalgliesh said:

'Cause of death obvious. It looks as if he was struck

by a single blow and died where he fell. There's surprisingly little bleeding.'

Kerrison said:

'That's not unusual. As you know, you can get serious intercranial injury from a simple fracture, particularly if there's extradural or subdural haemorrhage or actual laceration of the brain substance. I agree that he was probably killed by a single blow and that wooden mallet on the table seems the likely weapon. But Blain-Thomson will be able to tell you more when he gets him on the table. He'll be doing the P.M. this afternoon.'

'Rigor is almost complete. What sort of estimate did you make of the time of death?'

'I saw him just before nine and I thought then that he'd been dead about twelve hours, perhaps a little longer. Say between eight and nine p.m. The window is closed and the temperature pretty steady at sixty-five Fahrenheit. I usually estimate a fall in body temperature in these circumstances of about one-and-a-half degrees Fahrenheit an hour. I took it when I examined the body and, taken with the rigor which was almost fully established then, I'd say it was unlikely that he was alive much after nine p.m. But you know how unreliable these estimates can be. Better say between eight-thirty and midnight.'

Howarth said from the door:

'His father says that Lorrimer rang him at a quarter to nine. I went to see the old man this morning with Angela Foley to break the news to him. She's my secretary. Lorrimer was her cousin. But you'll be seeing the old man, of course. He seemed pretty confident about the time.'

Dalgliesh said to Kerrison:

'It looks as if the blood flowed fairly steadily, but without any preliminary splashing. Would you expect the assailant to be bloodstained?'

'Not necessarily, particularly if I'm right about the

108

mallet being the weapon. It was probably a single swinging blow delivered when Lorrimer had turned his back. The fact that the murderer struck above the left ear doesn't seem particularly significant. He could have been left-handed, but there's no reason to suppose he was.'

'And it wouldn't have required particular force. A child could probably have done it.'

Kerrison hesitated, disconcerted.

'Well, a woman, certainly.'

There was one question which Dalgliesh had formally to ask although, from the position of the body and the flow of the blood, the answer was in little doubt.

'Did he die almost immediately, or is there any possibility that he could have walked about for a time, even locked the door and set the alarms?'

'That's not altogether unknown, of course, but in this case I'd say it was highly unlikely, virtually impossible. I did have a man only a month ago with an axe injury, a seven-inch depressed fracture of the parietal bone and extensive extradural haemorrhage. He went off to a pub, spent half an hour with his mates, and then reported to the casualty department and was dead within a quarter of an hour. Head injuries can be unpredictable, but not this one, I think?'

Dalgliesh turned to Howarth.

'Who found him?'

'Our clerical officer, Brenda Pridmore. She starts work at eight-thirty with Blakelock. Old Mr. Lorrimer phoned to say that his son hadn't slept in his bed, so she went up to see if Lorrimer were here. I arrived almost immediately with the cleaner, Mrs. Bidwell. Some woman had telephoned her husband early this morning to ask her to come to my house to help my sister, instead of to the Lab. It was a false call. I thought that it was probably some stupid village prank, but that I'd better get in as soon as possible in case something odd was happening. So I put her bi-

109

cycle in the boot of my car and got here just after nine. My secretary, Angela Foley, and Clifford Bradley, the Higher Scientific Officer in the biology department, arrived at about the same time.'

'Who at any time has been alone with the body?'

'Brenda Pridmore, of course, but very briefly, I imagine. Then Inspector Blakelock came up on his own. Then I was here alone for no more than a few seconds. Then I locked the Laboratory door, kept all the staff in the main hall, and waited there until Dr. Kerrison arrived. He was here within five minutes and examined the body. I stood by the door. Superintendent Mercer arrived shortly afterwards and I handed over the key of the Biology Lab to him.'

Mercer said:

'Dr. Kerrison suggested that I call in Dr. Greene – he's the local police surgeon – to confirm his preliminary findings. Dr. Greene wasn't alone with the body. After he'd made a quick and fairly superficial examination I locked the door. It wasn't opened again until the photographers and the finger-print officers arrived. They've taken his dabs and examined the mallet, but we left it at that when we knew the Yard had been called in and you were on your way. The print boys are still here, in the police liaison officer's room, but I let the photographers go.'

Putting on his search gloves, Dalgliesh ran his hands over the body. Under his white coat Lorrimer was wearing grey slacks and a tweed jacket. In the inside pocket was a thin leather wallet containing six pound notes, his driving licence, a book of stamps, and two credit cards. The right outer pocket held a pouch with his car keys and three others, two Yale and a smaller intricate key, probably to a desk-top drawer. There were a couple of ballpoint pens clipped to the top left-hand pocket of his white coat. In the bottom right-hand pocket was a handkerchief, his bunch of Laboratory keys and, not on the bunch, a

110

single heavy key which looked fairly new. There was nothing else on the body.

He went over to study two exhibits lying on the central work bench, the mallet and a man's jacket. The mallet was an unusual weapon, obviously hand-made. The handle of crudely carved oak was about eighteen inches long and might, he thought, have once been part of a heavy walking stick. The head, which he judged to weigh just over two pounds, was blackened on one side with congealed blood from which one or two coarse grey hairs sprouted like whiskers. It was impossible to detect in the dried slough a darker hair which might have come from Lorrimer's head, or with the naked eye to distinguish his blood. That would be a job for the Metropolitan Police Laboratory when the mallet, carefully packed and with two identifying exhibit tags instead of one, reached the Biology Department later in the day.

He said to the Superintendent:

'No prints?'

'None, except for old Pascoe's. He's the owner of the mallet. They weren't wiped away, so it looks as if this chap wore gloves.'

That, thought Dalgliesh, would point to premeditation, or to the instinctive precaution of a knowledgeable expert. But if he came prepared to kill it was odd that he had relied on seizing the first convenient weapon; unless, of course, he knew that the mallet would be ready to hand.

He bent low to study the packet. It was the top half of a cheap mass-produced suit in a harsh shade of blue with a paler pinstripe, and with wide lapels. The sleeve had been carefully spread out and the cuff bore a trace of what could have been blood. It was apparent that Lorrimer had already begun the analysis. On the bench was the electrophoresis apparatus plugged into its power pack and with two columns of six paired small circles punched in the sheet of agar gel. Beside it was a test-tube holder with a series of blood samples. To the right lay a couple of buff-coloured laboratory files with biology registrations and, beside them, flat open on the bench, a quarto-sized loose-leaf notebook with a ring binding. The left-hand page, dated the previous day, was closely covered in hieroglyphics and formulae in a thin, black, upright hand. Although most of the scientific jottings meant little to him, Dalgliesh could see that the time at which Lorrimer had started and finished each analysis had been carefully noted. The right-hand page was blank.

He said to Howarth:

'Who is the Senior Biologist now that Lorrimer's dead?'

'Claire Easterbrook. Miss Easterbrook, but it's advisable to call her Ms.'

'Is she here?'

'With the others in the library. I believe she has a firm alibi for the whole of yesterday evening, but as she's a senior scientist she was asked to stay. And, of course, she'll want to get back to work as soon as the staff are allowed into the Laboratory. There was a murder two nights ago in a clunch pit at Muddington – that jacket is an exhibit – and she'll want to get on with that as well as coping with the usual heavy load.'

'I'd like to see her first, please, and here. Then Mrs. Bidwell. Is there a sheet we could use to cover him?'

Howarth said:

'I imagine there's a dust-sheet or something of the kind in the linen-cupboard. That's on the next floor.'

'I'd be grateful if you'd go with Inspector Massingham and show him. Then if you'd wait in the library or your own office I'll be down to have a word when I've finished here.'

For a second he thought that Howarth was about to demur. He frowned, and the handsome face clouded momentarily, petulant as a child's. But he left with Massingham without a word. Kerrison was still standing by the body, rigid as a guard of honour. He gave a little start as if recalling himself to reality and said:

'If you don't want me any longer I ought to be on my way to the hospital. You can contact me at St. Luke's at Ely or here at the Old Rectory. I've given the sergeant an account of my movements last night. I was at home all the evening. At nine o'clock, by arrangement, I rang one of my colleagues at the hospital, Dr. J. D. Underwood, about a matter which is coming up at the next medical committee. I think he's already confirmed that we did speak. He hadn't got the information I was waiting for but he rang me back at about a quarter to ten.'

There was as little reason to delay Kerrison as there was at present to suspect him. After he had left, Mercer said:

'I thought of leaving two sergeants, Reynolds and Underhill, and a couple of constables, Cox and Warren, if that will suit you. They're all sound, experienced officers. The Chief said to ask for anyone and anything you need. He's at a meeting in London this morning, but he'll be back tonight. I'll send up the chaps from the mortuary van if you're ready for them to take him away.'

'Yes, I've finished with him. I'll have a word with your men as soon as I've seen Miss Easterbrook. But ask one of the sergeants to come up in ten minutes to pack up the mallet for the Yard lab, will you? The chopper pilot will want to get back.'

They spoke a few more words about the liaison arrangements with the local force, then Mercer left to supervise the removal of the body. He would wait to introduce Dalgliesh to his seconded officers; after that, his responsibility would end. The case was in Dalgliesh's hands.

6

Two minutes later Claire Easterbrook was shown into the laboratory. She entered with an assurance which a less experienced investigator than Dalgliesh might have mistaken for arrogance or insensitivity. She was a thin, long-waisted girl of about thirty, with a bony, intelligent face and a cap of dark curling hair which had been layered by an obvious expert, and no doubt expensive, hand to lie in swathes across the forehead and to curl into the nape of her high-arched neck. She was wearing a chestnut-brown sweater in fine wool belted into a black skirt which swung calf length above high-heeled boots. Her hands, with the nails cut very short, were ringless and her only ornament was a necklace of large wooden beads strung on a silver chain. Even without her white coat the impression she gave – and no doubt intended – was of a slightly intimidating professional competence. Before Dalgliesh had a chance to speak she said, with a trace of belligerence:

'I'm afraid you'll be wasting your time with me. My lover and I dined last night in Cambridge at the Master's Lodge of his college. I was with five other people from eight-thirty until nearly midnight. I've already given their names to the constable in the library.'

Dalgliesh said mildly:

'I'm sorry, Ms. Easterbrook, that I had to ask you to come up before we were able to remove Dr. Lorrimer's body. And as it seems impertinent to invite you to sit down in your own laboratory, I won't. But this isn't going to take long.'

She flushed, as if he had caught her out in a social solecism. Glancing with reluctant distaste at the shrouded, lumpen shape on the floor, at the stiff protruding ankles, she said:

'He'd be more dignified if you'd left him uncovered. Like this he could be a sack of rubbish. It's a curious superstition, the universal instinct to cover up the recently dead. After all, we're the ones at a disadvantage.'

Massingham said lightly:

'Not, surely, with the Master and his wife to vouch for your alibi?'

Their eyes met, his coolly amused, hers dark with dislike.

Dalgliesh said:

'Dr. Howarth tells me you're the senior biologist now. Could you explain to me, please, what Dr. Lorrimer was doing here last night? Don't touch anything.'

She went at once over to the table and regarded the two exhibits, the files and the scientific paraphernalia. She said:

'Would you open this file, please?'

Dalgliesh's gloved hands slipped between the covers and flipped it open.

'He re-checked Clifford Bradley's result on the Pascoe case. The mallet belongs to a sixty-four-year-old fen labourer called Pascoe whose wife has disappeared. His story is that she's walked out on him, but there are one or two suspicious circumstances. The police sent in the mallet to see if the stains on it are human blood. They aren't. Pascoe says that he used it to put an injured dog out of his misery. Bradley found that the blood reacted to anti-dog serum and Dr. Lorrimer has duplicated his result. So the dog it was that died.'

Too mean to waste a bullet or send for a vet, thought Massingham savagely. It struck him as odd that the death of this unknown mongrel should, for a moment, anger him more than the killing of Lorrimer.

Miss Easterbrook moved over to the open notebook.

115

The two men waited. Then she frowned and said, obviously puzzled:

'That's odd. Edwin always noted the time he began and finished an analysis and the procedure he adopted. He's initialled Bradley's result on the Pascoe file, but there's nothing in the book. And it's obvious that he's made a start with the clunch pit murder; but that isn't noted either. The last reference is five-forty-five and the final note is unfinished. Someone must have torn out the right hand page.'

'Why do you suppose anyone should do that?'

She looked straight into Dalgliesh's eyes and said calmly:

'To destroy the evidence of what he'd been doing, or the result of his analysis, or the time he'd spent on it. The first and second would be rather pointless. It's obvious from the apparatus what he's been doing, and any competent biologist could duplicate the work. So it's probably the last.'

So the appearance of intelligence wasn't misleading. Dalgliesh asked:

'How long would he take checking the Pascoe result?'

'Not long. Actually, he'd started on that before six and I think he'd finished when I left at six-fifteen. I was the last to leave. The junior staff had gone. It isn't usual for them to work after six. I usually stay later, but I had to dress for the dinner party.'

'And the work he's done on the clunch pit case – how long would that have taken?'

'Difficult to say. I should have thought it would have kept him busy until nine or later. He was grouping a sample of the victim's blood and the blood from the dried stain by the ABO blood group system, and using electrophoresis to identify the haptoglobins and PGM, the enzyme phosphoglucomutase. Electrophoresis is a technique for identifying the protein and enzyme constituents of the blood by placing the

116

samples in a gel of starch or agar and applying an electric current. As you can see, he'd actually started the run.'

Dalgliesh was aware of the scientific principle of electrophoresis, but didn't think it necessary to mention the fact. He opened the clunch pit file, and said:

'There's nothing on the file.'

'He would write up the result on the file later. But he wouldn't have started the analysis without noting the details in his book.'

There were two pedal-bins against the wall. Massingham opened them. One, plastic-lined, was obviously for laboratory waste and broken glass. The other was for waste paper. He stirred the contents: paper tissues, a few torn envelopes, a discarded newspaper. There was nothing which resembled the missing page.

Dalgliesh said:

'Tell me about Lorrimer.'

'What do you want to know?'

'Anything which could throw light on why someone disliked him enough to smash in his skull.'

'I can't help you there, I'm afraid. I've no idea.'

'You liked him?'

'Not particularly. It's not a question I've given much thought to. I got on all right with him. He was a perfectionist who didn't suffer fools gladly. But he was all right to work with if you knew your job. I do.'

'So he wouldn't need to check your work. What about those who don't know their jobs?'

'You'd better ask them, Commander.'

'Was he popular with his staff?'

'What has popularity to do with it? I don't suppose I'm popular, but I don't go in fear of my life.'

She was silent for a moment, then said in a more conciliatory tone:

'I probably sound obstructive. I don't mean to be.

It's just that I can't help. I've no idea who could have killed him or why. I only know that I didn't.'

'Had you noticed any change in him recently?'

'Change? You mean, in his mood or behaviour? Not really. He gave the impression of a man under strain; but then, he was that kind of man, solitary, obsessional, overworked. One rather odd thing. He's been interesting himself in the new C.O., Brenda Pridmore. She's a pretty child, but hardly his intellectual level, I should have thought. I don't think there was anything serious, but it caused a certain amount of amusement in the Lab. I think he was probably trying to prove something to someone, or, perhaps, to himself.'

'You've heard about the telephone call to Mrs. Bidwell, of course?'

'I imagined the whole lab knows. It wasn't I who rang her, if that's what you're thinking. In any case, I should have known that it wouldn't work.'

'How do you mean, it wouldn't work?'

'It depended, surely, on old Lorrimer not being at home yesterday. After all, the caller couldn't rely on his not noticing that Edwin hadn't come home last night until he didn't get his early tea brought to him. As it happens, he went off to bed quite happily. But the hoaxer couldn't have known that. Normally, Edwin would have been missed much earlier.'

'Was there any reason to suppose that old Mr. Lorrimer wouldn't be at the cottage yesterday?'

'He was supposed to be admitted to Addenbrooke's hospital in the afternoon for treatment of a skin complaint. I think the whole Biology Lab knew. He used to telephone often enough, fretting about the arrangements and whether Edwin would get time off to drive him there. Yesterday, just after ten, he rang to say that the bed wouldn't be available for him after all.'

'Who took the call?'

'I did. It rang in his private office and I took it

118

there. Edwin hadn't returned from the clunch pit autopsy. I told him as soon as he arrived.'

'Who else did you tell?'

'When I came out of the office I think I said something casually about old Mr. Lorrimer not having to go into hospital after all. I'm not sure of the actual words. I don't think anyone made a comment or took much apparent notice.'

Suddenly she lost her composure. She flushed and hesitated, as if realizing for the first time where all this was leading. The two men waited. Then, angry with herself, she burst out, clumsily defensive:

'I'm sorry, but I can't remember. You'll have to ask them. It didn't seem important at the time and I was busy. We were all busy. I think everyone was there, but I can't be certain.'

'Thank you,' said Dalgliesh coolly. 'You've been remarkably helpful.'

7

Mrs. Bidwell arrived at the door as the two attendants from the mortuary van were carrying out the body. She seemed to regret its disappearance and looked at the chalk outline marked by Massingham on the floor as if this were a poor substitute for the real thing. Gazing after the covered metal container, she said:

'Poor devil! I never thought to see him carried out of his lab feet first. He were never popular, you know. Still, I don't suppose that's worrying him where he is now. Is that one of my dust-sheets you've had over him?'

She peered suspiciously at the sheet, now folded neatly at the end of one of the benches.

'It came from the laboratory linen-cupboard, yes.'

'Well, as long as it's put back where you found it. Come to that, it had better go straight into the soiled linen. But I don't want any of your chaps taking it away. Laundry disappears fast enough as it is.'

'Why wasn't he popular, Mrs. Bidwell?'

'Too particular by half. Mind you, you've got to be these days if you want to get any work done. But from what I hear he was too fussy for his own good. And he'd been getting worse, no doubt about that. And very odd he'd been lately, too. Nervy. You heard about the unpleasantness in the reception hall the day before yesterday, I suppose? Oh well, you will. Ask Inspector Blakelock. Just before lunch it was. Dr. Lorrimer had a real old tussle with that barmy daughter of Dr. Kerrison's. Nearly pushed her out of the door. Screeching like a banshee, she was. I came into the hall just in time to see it. Her dad isn't going to like that, I said to Inspector Blakelock. He's crazy about those kids. Mark my words, I said, if Dr. Lorrimer doesn't take a hold of himself there'll be murder done in this Lab. I said the same to Mr. Middlemass.'

'I want you to tell me about the telephone call this morning, Mrs. Bidwell. What time was it?'

'It was near enough seven o'clock. We was eating breakfast and I just filled the teapot for second cups. Had the kettle in me hand when it rang.'

'And who answered it?'

'Bidwell. Phone's in the hall and he got up and went out to it. Cursin' he was 'cos he'd just settled down to his kipper. He hates cold kipper, does Bidwell. We always has kippers on Thursday on account of Marshall's fish van coming from Ely Wednesday afternoons.'

'Does your husband usually answer the phone?'

'He always answers the phone. And if he's not in I lets it ring. I can't abide the dratted things. Never could. Wouldn't have it in the house if our Shirley hadn't paid to get it put in. She's married now and lives Mildenhall way and she likes to think we can ring her if we want her. Fat lot of use that is. I can't

120

never hear what anyone says. And the ring is enough to put the fear of God in a soul. Telegrams and phone rings. I hate 'em both.'

'Who at the Lab would know that your husband always answered the phone?'

'Best part of them, more than likely. They knows I won't touch the thing. There's no secret about that. We're all as the good Lord made us and some of us a sight worse. Nothing to be ashamed of.'

'Of course not. Your husband's at work now, I expect?'

'That's right. Yeoman's Farm, Captain Massey's place. Tractor work mostly. Been there twenty years, near enough.'

Dalgliesh nodded almost imperceptibly to Massingham and the Inspector slipped out to have a quiet word with Sergeant Underhill. It would be as well to check with Mr. Bidwell while his memory of the call was fresh. Dalgliesh went on:

'What happened then?'

'Bidwell came back. Said that I wasn't to go to the Lab this morning because Mrs. Schofield wanted me over at Leamings particular. I was to bike there and she'd run me and the bike home afterwards. Sticking out of the back of that red Jaguar she's got, I suppose. I thought it was a bit of a cheek seeing as I'm due here mornings but I've nothing against Mrs. Schofield and if she wanted me I wasn't above obliging. The Lab would just have to wait, I said to Bidwell. I can't be in two places at once, I said. What don't get done today will get done tomorrow.'

'You work here every morning?'

'Except weekends. Gets here as near eight-thirty as makes no odds, and works till about ten. Then back at twelve in case any of the gentlemen wants their lunch cooking. The girls mostly manage for themselves. Afterwards I washes up for them. I reckons to get away by two-thirty most days. Mind you, it's light

121

work. Scobie – he's the Lab attendant – and I sees to the working labs but all the heavy cleaning is supposed to be done by the contractors. They comes on Mondays and Fridays only, from seven until nine, a whole van full of them from Ely, and does the main hall, the stairs and all the heavy polishing. Inspector Blakelock gets here early those mornings to let them in and Scobie keeps an eye on them. Not that you'd know they'd been most days. No personal interest, you see. Not like the old days when me and two women from the village did the lot.'

'So what would you normally have done as soon as you arrived if this had been an ordinary Thursday? I want you to think carefully, Mrs. Bidwell. This may be very important.'

'No need to think. I'd do the same as I does every day.'

'Which is?'

'Take off me hat and coat in the downstairs cloakroom. Put on me overalls. Get cleaning bucket and powder and disinfectant from the broom cupboard. Clean the toilets, male and female. Then check dirty laundry and get it bagged up. Put out clean white coats where wanted. Then dust and tidy Director's office and general office.'

'Right,' said Dalgliesh. 'Let's do the rounds then, shall we?'

Three mintes later a curious little procession made its way up the stairs. Mrs. Bidwell, clad now in a navy-blue working overall and carrying a plastic bucket in one hand and a mop in the other, led the way. Dalgliesh and Massingham followed. The two lavatories were on the second floor at the rear opposite the Document Examination Laboratory. They had obviously been converted from what had once been an elegant bedroom. But now a narrow passage leading to the single barred window had been constructed down the middle of the room. A mean-looking door gave entry to the women's cloakroom on the left, and, a few yards down, a similar door led to the men's washroom on the right. Mrs. Bidwell led the way into the left-hand room. It was larger than Dalgliesh had expected, but poorly lit from a single round window with pivoting opaque glass set about four feet from the floor. The window was open. There were three lavatory cubicles. The outer room contained two wash-hand basins with a paper towel dispenser and, to the left of the door, a long Formica-covered counter with a glass above it which apparently served as a dressing-table. To the right was a wall-mounted gas-fired incinerator, a row of clothes-hooks, a large wicker laundry-basket and two rather battered cane chairs.

Dalgliesh said to Mrs. Bidwell:

'Is this how you would expect to find it?'

Mrs. Bidwell's sharp little eyes peered round. The doors to the three lavatories were open and she gave them a quick inspection.

'No better nor no worse. They're pretty good about the toilets, I'll say that for them.'

'And that window is usually kept open?'

'Winter and summer, except it's bitter cold. That's the only ventilation you see.'

'The incinerator is off. Is that usual?'

'That's right. Last girl to leave turns it off at night, then I puts it on next morning.'

Dalgliesh looked inside. The incinerator was empty except for a trace of carbon ash. He went over to the window. Rain had obviously driven in some time during the night and the dried splashes were clearly visible on the tiled floor. But even the inside pane, where no rain could have splashed, was remarkably clean and there was no discernible dust around the sill. He said:

'Did you clean the window yesterday, Mrs. Bidwell?'

'Of course I did. It's like I told you. I cleans the

lavatories every morning. And when I cleans, I cleans. Shall I get on with it now?'

'I'm afraid there'll be no cleaning done today. We'll pretend you've finished in here. Now what happens? What about the laundry?'

The laundry-basket contained only one overall, marked with the initials C.M.E. Mrs. Bidwell said:

'I wouldn't expect many dirty coats, not on a Thursday. They usually manages to make them last a week and drop them in here on Friday before they go home. Monday's the busy day for laundry and putting out the new coats. Looks as though Miss Easterbrook spilt her tea yesterday. That's not like her. But she's particular is Miss Easterbrook. You wouldn't find her going round with a dirty coat, no matter what day of the week.'

So there was at least one member of the Biology Department, thought Dalgliesh, who knew that Mrs. Bidwell would make an early visit to the lab to put out a clean white coat. It would be interesting to learn who had been present when the fastidious Miss Easterbrook had had her accident with the tea.

The male washroom, apart from the urinal stalls, differed very little from the women's. There was the same round open window, the same absence of any marks on the panes or sill. Dalgliesh carried over one of the chairs and, carefully avoiding any contact with the window or the sill, looked out. There was a drop of about six feet to the top of the window beneath, and an equal drop to that on the first floor. Below them both a paved terrace ran right up to the wall. The absence of soft earth, the rain in the night and Mrs. Bidwell's efficient cleaning meant that they would be lucky to find any evidence of a climb. But a reasonably slim and sure-footed man or woman with enough nerve and a head for heights could certainly have got out this way. But if the murderer were a member of the Lab staff, why should he risk his neck when he must have known that the keys were on Lorrimer? And if the murderer were an outsider, then how account for the locked front door, the intact alarm system, and the fact that Lorrimer must have let him in?

He turned his attention to the wash-basins. None was particularly dirty, but near the rim of the one nearest the door there was a smear of porridge-like mucus. He bent his head over the basin and sniffed. His sense of smell was extremely acute and, from the plug-hole, he detected the faint but unmistakably disagreeable smell of human vomit.

Mrs. Bidwell, meanwhile, had thrown open the lid of the laundry-basket. She gave an exclamation.

'That's funny. It's empty.'

Dalgliesh and Massingham turned. Dalgliesh asked:

'What were you expecting to find, Mrs. Bidwell?'

'Mr. Middlemass's white coat, that's what.'

She darted out of the room. Dalgliesh and Massingham followed. She flung open the door of the Document Examination room and glanced inside. Then she closed the door again and stood with her back against it. She said:

'It's gone! It's not hanging on the peg. So where is it? Where's Mr. Middlemass's white coat?'

Dalgliesh asked:

'Why did you expect to find it in the laundry-basket?'

Mrs. Bidwell's black eyes grew immense. She slewed her eyes furtively from side to side and then said with awed relish:

'Because it had blood on it, that's why. Lorrimer's blood!'

8

Lastly they went down the main staircase to the Director's office. From the library there was a broken mur-
mur of voices, subdued and spasmodic as a funeral
gathering. A detective-constable was standing at the
front door with the detached watchfulness of a man
paid to endure boredom but ready to leap into action
should, unaccountably, the boredom end.

Howarth had left his office unlocked and the key in
the door. Dalgliesh was interested that the Director
had chosen to wait with the rest of the staff in the
library, and wondered whether this was intended to
demonstrate solidarity with his colleagues, or was a
tactful admission that his office was one of the rooms
which had been due to receive Mrs. Bidwell's early
morning attention, and must, therefore, be of special
interest to Dalgliesh. But that reasoning was surely
too subtle. It was difficult to believe that Howarth
hadn't entered his room since the discovery of the
body. If there were anything to remove, he best of all
must have had the chance to do it.

Dalgliesh had expected the room to be impressive,
but it still surprised him. The plasterwork of the
coved ceiling was splendid, a joyous riot of wreaths,
shells, ribbons and trailing vines, ornate and yet disciplined. The fireplace was of white and mottled
marble with a finely carved frieze of nymphs and pip-
ing shepherds and a classical overmantel with open
pediment. He guessed that the agreeably proportioned
salon, too small to be partitioned and not large
enough for a working laboratory, had escaped the fate
of so much of the house more for administrative and
scientific convenience than from any sensitivity on
Colonel Hoggatt's part to its innate perfection. It was

newly furnished in a style guaranteed not to offend, a nice compromise of bureaucratic orthodoxy and modern functionalism. There was a large glass-fronted bookcase to the left of the fireplace, and a personal locker and a coat-stand to the right. A rectangular conference table and four chairs, of a type provided for senior public servants, stood between the tall windows. Next to it was a steel security cupboard fitted with a combination lock. Howarth's desk, a plain contraption in the same wood as the conference-table, faced the door. Apart from an inkstained blotter and a pen-stand it held a small wooden bookshelf containing the *Shorter Oxford Dictionary*, a dictionary of quotations, *Roget's Thesaurus* and *Fowler's Modern English Usage*. The choice seemed curious for a scientist. There were three metal trays marked 'In,' 'Pending' and 'Out'. The 'Out' tray held two manila files, the top labelled 'Chapel – Proposals for transfer to Department of the Environment', and the second, a large, old and unwieldy file which had been much mended, was marked 'New Laboratory – Commissioning'.

Dalgliesh was struck by the emptiness and impersonality of the whole room. It had obviously been recently decorated for Howarth's arrival, and the pale grey-green carpet, with its matching square under the desk, was as yet unmarked, the curtains hung in pristine folds of dark green. There was only one picture, positioned in the overmantel, but this was an original, an early Stanley Spencer showing the Virgin's Assumption. Plump, foreshortened, varicosed thighs in red bloomers floated upwards from a circle of clutching work-worn hands to a reception committee of gaping cherubim. It was, he thought, an eccentric choice for the room, discordant both in date and style. It was the only object, apart from the books, which reflected a personal taste; Dalgliesh hardly supposed that it had been provided by a Government agency. Otherwise the office had the underfurnished, expectant atmosphere of a room refurbished to receive an unknown occupant, and still awaiting the imprint of his taste and personality. It was hard to believe that Howarth had worked here for almost a year. Mrs. Bidwell, her tight little mouth pursed and eyes narrowed, regarded it with obvious disapproval. Dalgliesh asked:

'Is this how you would have expected to find it?'

'That's right. Every bloody morning. Nothing for me to do here really is there? Mind you, I dusts and polishes around and runs the Hoover over the carpet. But he's neat and tidy, there's no denying it. Not like old Dr. MacIntyre. Oh, he was a lovely man! But messy! You should have seen his desk of a morning. And smoke! You couldn't hardly see across the room sometimes. He had this lovely skull on his desk to keep his pipes in. They dug it up when they was making the trench for the pipes to the new vehicle examination extension. Been in the ground more than two hundred years, Dr. Mac said, and he showed me the crack – just like a cracked cup – where his skull had been bashed in. That's one murder they never solved. I miss that skull. Real lovely that used to look. And he had all these pictures of himself and his friends at university with oars crossed above them, and a coloured one of the Highlands with hairy cattle paddling in a lake, and one of his father with his dogs, and such a lovely picture of his wife – dead she was, poor soul – and another big picture of Venice with gondolas and a lot of foreigners in fancy dress, and a cartoon of Dr. Mac done by one of his friends, showing the friend lying dead, and Dr. Mac in his deerstalker hat looking for clues with his magnifying glass. That was a real laugh that was. Oh, I loved Dr. Mac's pictures!' She looked at the Spencer with a marked lack of enthusiasm.

'And there's nothing unusual about the room this morning?'

'I told you, same as usual. Well, look for yourself.

Clean as a new pin. It looks different in the day, mind you, when he's working here. But he always leaves it as if he isn't expecting to come back in the morning.'

There was nothing else to be learned from Mrs. Bidwell. Dalgliesh thanked her and told her that she could go home as soon as she had checked with Detective-Sergeant Reynolds in the library that he had all the necessary information about where she had spent the previous evening. He explained this with his usual tact, but tact was wasted on Mrs. Bidwell. She said cheerfully and without rancour:

'No use trying to pin this on me, or Bidwell come to that. We was together at the village concert. Sat five rows back between Joe Machin – he's the sexton – and Willie Barnes – he's the rector's warden, and we stayed there until the end of the show. No sneaking out at half time like some I could mention.'

'Who sneaked out, Mrs. Bidwell?'

'Ask him yourself. Sat at the end of the row in front of us, a gentleman whose office we might or might not be standing in at this very moment. Do you want to talk to him? Shall I ask him to step in?' She spoke hopefully and looked towards the door like an eager gun dog, ears pricked for the command to retrieve.

'We'll see to that, thank you, Mrs. Bidwell. And if we want to talk to you again we'll get in touch. You've been very helpful.'

'I thought I might make coffee for them all before I go. No harm in that, I suppose?'

There was no point in warning her not to talk to the Lab staff, or, come to that, the whole village. Dalgliesh had no doubt that his search of the cloakrooms and the missing bloodstained coat would soon be common knowledge. But no great harm would be done. The murderer must know that the police would be immediately alive to the possible significance of that false early morning call to Mrs. Bidwell. He was dealing with intelligent men and women, experienced, even if vicariously, in criminal investigation, know-ledgeable about police procedure, aware of the rules which governed his every move. He had no doubt that, mentally, most of the group now waiting in the library to be interviewed were following his actions almost to the minute.

And among them, or known to them, was a murderer.

9

Superintendent Mercer had selected his two sergeants with an eye to contrast or, perhaps, with a view to satisfying any prejudices which Dalgliesh might harbour about the age and experience of his subordinates. Sergeant Reynolds was near the end of his service, a stolid, broad-shouldered, slow-speaking officer of the old school and a native of the fens. Sergeant Underhill, recently promoted, looked young enough to be his son. His boyish, open face with its look of disciplined idealism was vaguely familiar to Massingham, who suspected that he might have seen it in a police recruitment pamphlet, but decided in the interest of harmonious co-operation to give Underhill the benefit of the doubt.

The four police officers were sitting at the conference table in the Director's office. Dalgliesh was briefing his team before he started on the preliminary interviews. He was, as always, restlessly aware of time passing. It was already after eleven and he was anxious to finish at the Laboratory and see old Mr. Lorrimer. The physical clues to his son's murder might lie in the Laboratory; the clue to the man himself lay elsewhere. But neither his words nor his tone betrayed impatience.

'We start by assuming that the telephone call to Mrs. Bidwell and Lorrimer's death are connected.

That means the call was made by the murderer or an accomplice. We'll keep an open mind about the caller's sex until we get confirmation from Bidwell, but it was probably a woman, probably also someone who knew that old Mr. Lorrimer was expected to be in hospital yesterday, and who didn't know that the appointment had been cancelled. If the old man had been home, the ruse could hardly hope to succeed. As Miss Easterbrook has pointed out, no-one could rely on his going early to bed last night and not realising until after the Lab opened this morning that his son hadn't come home.'

Massingham said:

'The killer would have made it his business to get here early this morning, assuming that he didn't know that his plan had misfired. And assuming, of course, the call wasn't a double bluff. It would be a neat ploy, wasting our time, confusing the investigation and diverting suspicion from everyone except the early arrivals.'

'But for one of the suspects, it could have been an even neater ploy,' thought Dalgliesh. It had been Mrs. Bidwell's arrival at Howarth's house in obedience to the call which had given the Director himself the excuse for arriving so early. He wondered what time Howarth usually put in an appearance. That would be one of the questions to be asked. He said:

'We'll start by assuming that it wasn't a bluff, that the murderer, or his accomplice, made the call to delay Mrs. Bidwell's arrival and the discovery of the body. So what was he hoping to do? Plant evidence or destroy it? Tidy up something which he'd overlooked; wipe the mallet clean; clear up the evidence of whatever it was he was doing here last night; replace the keys on the body? But Blakelock had the best opportunity to do that, and he wouldn't need to have taken them in the first place. The call would have given someone the chance to replace the spare set in the security cupboard here. But that would be perfectly possible without delaying Mrs. Bidwell's arrival. And, of course, it may have been done.'

Underhill said:

'But is it really likely, sir, that the call was intended to delay the finding of the body and to give the killer time to replace the keys? Admittedly Mrs. Bidwell could be expected to be first in the Biology Department this morning when she put out the clean coats. But the murderer couldn't rely on that. Inspector Blakelock or Brenda Pridmore could easily have had occasion to go there.'

Dalgliesh thought it a risk that the murderer might well have thought worth taking. In his experience the early-morning routine in an institution seldom varied. Unless Blakelock had the early-morning job of checking on Lab security – and this was yet another of the questions to be asked – he and Brenda Pridmore would probably have got on with their normal work at the reception desk. In the ordinary course of events Mrs. Bidwell would have been the one to find the body. Any member of staff who went into the Biology Lab before her would have needed a good excuse to explain his presence there, unless, of course, he was a member of the Biology Department.

Massingham said:

'It's odd about the missing white coat, sir. It can hardly have been removed or destroyed to prevent us learning about the fight between Middlemass and Lorrimer. That unedifying but intriguing little episode must have been round the Lab within minutes of its happening. Mrs. Bidwell would see to that.'

Both Dalgliesh and Massingham wondered how far Mrs. Bidwell's description of the quarrel, given with the maximum dramatic effect, had been accurate. It was obvious that she had come into the laboratory after the blow had been struck, and had in fact seen very little. Dalgliesh had recognised, with foreboding, a familiar phenomenon: the desire of a witness, aware of the paucity of her evidence, to make the most of it lest the police be disappointed, while remaining as far as possible within the confines of truth. Stripped of Mrs. Bidwell's embellishments, the core of hard fact had been disappointly small.

'What they was quarrelling about I couldn't take it on myself to say, except that it was about a lady, and that Dr. Lorrimer was upset because she'd telephoned Mr. Middlemass. The door was open and I did hear that much when I passed to go in to the ladies' toilet. I daresay she rang him to arrange a date and Dr. Lorrimer didn't like it. I never saw a man more white. Like death he looked, with a handkerchief held up against his face all bloodied, and his black eyes glaring over the top of it. And Mr. Middlemass was turkey red. Embarrassed, I daresay. Well, it's not what we're used to at Hoggatt's, senior staff knocking each other about. When proper gentlemen start in with the fists there's usually a woman at the bottom of it. Same with this murder if you ask me.'

Dalgliesh said:

'We'll be getting Middlemass's version of the affair. I'd like now to have a word with all the Lab staff in the library and then Inspector Massingham and I will start the preliminary interviews: Howarth, the two women, Angela Foley and Brenda Pridmore, Blakelock, Middlemass and any of the others without a firm alibi. I'd like you, Sergeant, to get on with organising the usual routine. I shall want one of the senior staff in each department while the search is going on. They're the only ones who can tell whether anything in their lab has changed since yesterday. You'll be looking – admittedly without much hope – for the missing page of Lorrimer's notebook, any evidence of what he was doing here last night apart from working on the clunch pit murder, any sign of what happened to the missing coat. I want a thorough search of the whole building, particularly possible means of access and exit. The rain last night is a nuisance. You'll probably find the walls washed clean, but there may be some evidence that he got out through one of the lavatory windows.

'You'll need a couple of men on the grounds. The earth is fairly soft after the rain and if the murderer came by car or motorcycle there could be tyre-marks. Any we find can be checked against the tyre index here; we needn't waste time going to the Met Lab for that. There's a bus-stop immediately opposite the laboratory entrance. Find out what time the buses pass. There's always the possibility that one of the passengers or crew noticed something. I'd like the Laboratory building checked first, and as quickly as possible so that the staff can get back to work. They've a new murder on their hands and we can't keep the place closed longer than is absolutely necessary. I'd like to give them access by tomorrow morning.

'Then there's the smear of what looks like vomit on the first basin in the men's washroom. The smell from the pipe is still fairly distinct. I want a sample of that to go to the Met Lab urgently. You'll probably have to unscrew the joint to get at the basin of the U-bend. We shall need to find out who used the room last yesterday evening and whether he noticed the smear on the basin. If no-one admits to having been sick during the day, or can't produce a witness that he was, we shall want to know what they all ate for the evening meal. It could be Lorrimer's vomit, so we'll need some information on his stomach contents. I'd also like a sample of his blood and hair to be left here at the Lab. But Dr. Blain-Thomson will be seeing to that.'

Reynolds said:

'We take it that the crucial time is from six-fifteen when he was last seen alive in his lab, until midnight?'

'For the present. When I've seen his father and confirmed that he made that call at eight-forty-five we may be able to narrow it down. And we shall get a clearer idea of the time of death when Dr. Blain-Thomson has done the P.M. But judging from the state of rigor, Dr. Kerrison wasn't far out.'

But Kerrison didn't need to be far out, if he were the murderer. Rigor mortis was notoriously unreliable, and if he wanted an alibi for himself, Kerrison could shift the time of death by up to an hour without suspicion. If the timing were tight he might not need even an hour. It had been prudent of him to call in the police surgeon to confirm his estimate of the time of death. But how likely was Dr. Greene, experienced as he might be in viewing bodies, to disagree with the opinion of a consultant forensic pathologist unless the latter's judgment was manifestly perverse? If Kerrison were guilty, he had run little risk by calling in Greene.

Dalgliesh got to his feet.

'Right,' he said. 'Let's get on with it, shall we?'

10

Dalgliesh disliked having more than one other officer present with him at his preliminary and informal interview, so Massingham was taking the notes. They were hardly necessary; Dalgliesh, he knew, had almost total recall. But he still found the practice useful. They were sitting together at the conference table in the Director's office, but Howarth, perhaps because he objected to sitting in his own room other than at his desk, preferred to stand. He was leaning casually against the fireplace. From time to time Massingham lifted an unobtrusive eyebrow to glance at the clear-cut, dominant profile outlined against the classical frieze. There were three bunches of keys on the table; the bunch taken from Lorrimer's body, that handed over by Inspector Blakelock, and the set which Dr. Howarth, manipulating the security lock, had taken from its box in the cupboard. Each set of keys was identical, one Yale key and two security keys to the front door, and one smaller key on a plain metal ring. None was named, presumably for security reasons. Dalgliesh said:

'And these are the only three sets in existence?'

'Except for the set at Guy's Marsh police station, yes. Naturally, I checked earlier this morning that the police still have their set. The keys are kept in the safe under the control of the station officer, and they haven't been touched. They need a set at the police station in case the alarm goes off. There was no alarm last night.'

Dalgliesh already knew from Mercer that the station keys had been checked. He said:

'And the smallest key?'

'That's the one to the Exhibits Store. The system is for all incoming exhibits, after they've been registered, to be stored there until they're issued to the head of the appropriate department. It's his responsibility to allocate them to a specific officer. In addition, we store the exhibits which have been examined and are awaiting collection by the police, and those which have been presented to the court during the case and are returned to us for destruction. Those are mainly drugs. They're destroyed here in the incinerator and the destruction witnessed by one of the Laboratory staff and the officer in charge of the case. The Exhibits Store is also protected by the electronic alarm system, but, obviously, we need a key for internal security when the system hasn't been set.'

'And all the Laboratory internal doors and your office were protected last night once the internal alarm system was set? That means that an intruder could only have got out undetected through the top floor lavatory windows. All the others are either barred or fitted with the electronic alarm?'

'That's right. He could have got in that way too, of course, which was what concerned us most. But it wouldn't have been an easy climb, and the alarm would have gone off as soon as he tried to gain access to any of the main rooms in the Laboratory. We did consider extending the alarm system to the lavatory suite soon after I arrived, but it seemed unnecessary. We haven't had a break-in in the seventy-odd years of the Lab's existence.'

'What are the precise arrangements about locking the Laboratory?'

'Only the two Police Liaison Officers and Lorrimer as the Deputy Security Officer were authorised to lock up. He or the Police Liaison Officer on duty was responsible for ensuring that no staff were left on the premises and that all the internal doors were shut before the alarm was set, and the front door finally locked for the night. The alarm system to Guy's Marsh police station is set whether the door is locked on the inside or the out.'

'And these other keys found on the body, the three in this leather pouch and the single key. Do you recognise any of those?'

'Not the three in the pouch. One is obviously his car keys. But the single one looks very like the key to the Wren chapel. If it is, I didn't know that Lorrimer had it. Not that it's important. But as far as I know, there's only one key to the chapel in existence and that's hanging on the board in the Chief Liaison Officer's room. It isn't a security lock and we're not particularly worried about the chapel. There's nothing left there of real value. But occasionally architects and archaeological societies want to view it, so we let them borrow the key and they sign for it in a book in the office. We don't allow them through the Laboratory grounds to get at it. They have to use the back entrance in Guy's Marsh Road. The contract cleaners take it once every two months to clean and check the heating – we have to keep it reasonably warm in winter because the ceiling and carving are rather fine – and Miss Willard goes there from time to time, to do some dusting. When her father was rector of Chevisham, he used occasionally to hold services in the chapel, and I think she has a sentimental regard for the place.'

Massingham went out to Chief Inspector Martin's office and brought in the chapel key. The two matched. The small notebook which he had found hanging with the key showed that it had last been collected by Miss Willard on Monday the twenty-fifth of October. Howarth said:

'We're thinking of transferring the chapel to the Department of the Environment once we occupy the new Laboratory. It's a constant irritation to the Treasury that our funds are used to heat and maintain it. I've set up a string quartet here, and we held a concert on August the twenty-sixth in the chapel, but otherwise it's completely unused. I expect you will want to take a look at it, and it's worth seeing in its own right. It's a very fine specimen of late seventeenth-century church architecture, although, in fact, it isn't by Wren but by Alexander Fort, who was strongly influenced by him.'

Dalgliesh asked suddenly:

'How well did you get on with Lorrimer?'

Howarth replied calmly:

'Not particularly well. I respected him as a biologist, and I certainly had no complaints either about his work or about his cooperation with me as Director. He wasn't an easy man to know, and I didn't find him particularly sympathetic. But he was probably one of the most respected serologists in the service, and we shall miss him. If he had a fault, it was a reluctance to delegate. He had two scientific officer serologists in his department for the grouping of liquid blood and stains, saliva and semen samples, but he invariably took the murder cases himself. Apart from his casework and attendance at trials and at scenes of crime, he did a considerable amount of lecturing to detective training courses, and police familiarisation courses.'

Lorrimer's rough notebook was on the desk. Dalgliesh pushed it towards Howarth and said:

'Have you seen this before?'

'His rough notebook? Yes, I think I've noticed it in his department, or when he was carrying it with him. He was obsessively tidy and had a dislike of odd scraps of paper. Anything of importance was noted in that book, and subsequently transferred to the files. Claire Easterbrook tells me that the last page is missing.'

'That's why we're particularly anxious to know what he was doing here last night, apart from working on the clunch pit murder. He could have got into any of the other laboratories, of course?'

'If he'd switched off the internal alarm, yes. I believe it was his usual practice, when he was last on the premises, to rely on the Yale lock and the bolt on the front door and only check the internal doors and set the security alarm before he finally left. Obviously it's important not to set off the alarm accidentally.'

'Would he have been competent to undertake an examination in another department?'

'It depends on what he was trying to do. Essentially, of course, he was concerned with the identification and grouping of biological material, blood, body stains and the examination of fibres and animal and plant tissues. But he was a competent general scientist and his interests were wide – his scientific interests. Forensic biologists, particularly in the smaller laboratories, which has been up to now, become pretty versatile. But he wouldn't attempt to use the more sophisticated instruments in the Instrument Section, the mass spectrometer, for example.'

'And you personally have no idea what he could have been doing?'

'None. I do know that he came into this office. I had to look up the name of a consultant surgeon who was giving evidence for the defence in one of our old cases, and I had the medical directory on my desk when I left last night. This morning, it was back in its place in the library. Few things irritated Lorrimer more than people removing books from the library. But if he was in this office last night, I hardly imagine it was merely to check on my carelessness with the reference books.'

Lastly, Dalgliesh asked him about his movements the previous night.

'I played the fiddle at the village concert. The rector had five minutes or so to fill in and asked me if the string quartet would play something which he described as short and cheerful. The players were myself, a chemist, one of the scientific officers from the document examination department, and a typist from the general office. Miss Easterbrook should have been the first 'cello, but she had a dinner engagement which she regarded as important, and couldn't make it. We played the Mozart Divertimento in D major and came third on the programme.'

'And you stayed for the rest of the concert?'

'I intended to. Actually, the hall was incredibly stuffy and just before the interval at eight-thirty I slipped out. I stayed out.'

Dalgliesh asked what precisely he'd done.

'Nothing. I sat on one of those flat tombstones for about twenty minutes, then I left.'

'Did you see anyone, or did anyone see you?'

'I saw a hobby-horse – I know now that it must have been Middlemass deputising for Chief Inspector Martin – come out of the male dressing room. He pranced around rather happily, I thought, and snapped his jaws at an angel on one of the graves. Then he was joined by the troupe of morris-dancers coming through the graveyard form the Moonraker. It was an extraordinary sight. There was the racing moon and these extraordinary figures with their bells jingling and their hats decked with evergreens moving through the swirl of ground mist out of the darkness towards me. It was like an outré film or a ballet. All it needed was second-rate background music, preferably Stravinsky. I was sitting motionless on the gravestone, some distance away, and I don't think they saw me. I certainly didn't make myself known. The hobby-horse joined them, and they went into the hall. Then I heard the fiddle start up. I suppose I stayed sitting there for about another ten minutes, and then I left. I walked for the rest of the evening along Leamings Dyke and got home about ten o'clock. My half-sister Domenica will be able to confirm the time.'

They spent a little time discussing the administrative arrangements for the investigation. Dr. Howarth said that he would move into Miss Foley's room and make his office available to the police. There would be no chance of the Lab opening for the rest of the day, but Dalgliesh said that he hoped it would be possible for work to start again the next morning. Before Howarth left, Dalgliesh said:

'Everyone I've spoken to respected Dr. Lorrimer as a forensic biologist. But what was he like as a man? What, for example, did you know about him except that he was a forensic biologist?'

Dr. Howarth said coldly:

'Nothing. I wasn't aware there was anything to know, except that he was a forensic biologist. And now, if you've no more immediate questions, I must telephone Establishment Department and make sure that, in the excitement of his somewhat spectacular exit, they're not forgetting to send me a replacement.'

11

With the resilience of youth, Brenda Pridmore had re-covered quickly from the shock of finding Lorrimer's body. She had resolutely refused to be taken home and, by the time Dalgliesh was ready to see her she was perfectly calm and, indeed, anxious to tell her story. With her cloud of rich auburn hair and her freckled wind-tanned face she looked the picture of bucolic health. But the grey eyes were intelligent, the mouth sensitive and gentle. She gazed across the desk at Dalgliesh as intently as a docile child and totally without fear. He guessed that all her young life she had been used to receiving an avuncular kindness from men and never doubted that she would receive it, too, from these unknown officers of police. In re-sponse to Dalgliesh's questioning, she described ex-actly what had happened from the moment of her arrival at the Laboratory that morning to the discovery of the body. Dalgliesh asked:

'Did you touch him?'

'Oh no! I knelt down and I think I did put out my hand to feel his cheek. But that was all. I knew that he was dead, you see.'

'And then?'

'I don't remember. I know I rushed downstairs and Inspector Blakelock was standing at the bottom look-ing up at me. I couldn't speak, but I suppose he saw by my face that something was wrong. Then I remem-ber sitting on the chair outside Chief Inspector Mar-tin's office and looking at Colonel Hoggatt's portrait. Then I don't remember anything until Dr. Howarth and Mrs. Bidwell arrived.'

'Do you think anyone could have got out of the building past you while you were sitting there?'

'The murderer, you mean? I don't see how he could have. I know I wasn't very alert, but I hadn't fainted or anything silly like that. I'm sure I would have noticed if anyone had come across the hall. And even if he did manage to slip past me, he would have bumped into Dr. Howarth, wouldn't he?'

Dalgliesh asked her about her job at Hoggatt's, how well she had known Dr. Lorrimer. She prattled away with artless confidence about her life, her colleagues, her fascinating job, Inspector Blakelock who was so good to her and who had lost his own only daughter, telling with every sentence more than she knew. It wasn't that she was stupid, thought Massingham, only honest and ingenuous. For the first time they heard Lorrimer spoken of with affection.

'He was always terribly kind to me, although I didn't work in the Biology Department. Of course, he was a very serious man. He had so many responsibilities. The Biology Department is terribly overworked and he used to work late nearly every night, checking results, catching up with the backlog. I think he was disappointed at not being chosen to succeed Dr. Mac. Not that he ever said so to me – well he wouldn't, would he? – I'm far too junior and he was far too loyal.'

Dalgliesh asked:

'Do you think anyone could have misunderstood his interest in you, might have been a little jealous?'

'Jealous of Dr. Lorrimer because he stopped sometimes at the desk to talk to me about my work and was kind to me? But he was old! That's just silly!'

Suppressing a grin as he bent over his notebook and penned a few staccato outlines, Massingham thought that it probably was.

Dalgliesh asked:

'It seems there was some trouble the day before he died when Dr. Kerrison's children called at the Laboratory. Were you in the hall then?'

'You mean when he pushed Miss Kerrison out of the front hall? Well, he didn't actually push her, but he did speak very sharply. She had come with her small brother and they wanted to wait for Dr. Kerrison. Dr. Lorrimer looked at them, well, really as if he hated them. It wasn't at all like him. I think he's been under some terrible strain. Perhaps he had a premonition of his death. Do you know what he said to me after the clunch pit exhibits came in? He said that the only death we had to fear is our own. Don't you think that was an extraordinary remark?'

'Very strange,' agreed Dalgliesh.

'And that reminds me of another thing. You did say that anything might be important. Well, there was a funny kind of letter arrived for Dr. Lorrimer yesterday morning. That's why he stopped at the desk, so that I could hand over any personal post. There was just this thin brown envelope with the address printed, printed by hand in capital letters, I mean. And it was just his name, no qualifications after it. Odd, wasn't it?'

'Did he receive many private letters here?'

'Oh, no, none really. The Lab writing-paper says that all communications have to be addressed to the Director. We deal at the desk with the exhibits received, but all the correspondence goes to the general office for sorting. We only hand over the personal letters, but there aren't many of those.'

In the quick preliminary examination which he and Massingham had made of Lorrimer's meticulously tidy office, Dalgliesh had found no personal correspondence. He asked whether Miss Pridmore knew if Dr. Lorrimer had gone home for lunch. She said that he had. So it was possible that he had taken the letter home. It could mean anything, or nothing. It was just one more small fact which would have to be investigated.

He thanked Brenda Pridmore, and reminded her

144

again to come back to him if she remembered any-thing which could be of importance, however small. Brenda was not used to dissembling. It was obvious that something had occurred to her. She blushed and dropped her eyes. The metamorphosis from happy confidante to guilty schoolgirl was pathetically comic. Dalgliesh said gently:

'Yes?'

She didn't speak, but made herself meet his eyes and shook her head. He waited for a moment, then said:

'The investigation of murder is never agreeable. Like most unpleasant things in life, it sometimes seems easier not to get involved, to keep oneself un-contaminated. But that isn't possible. In a murder in-vestigation, to suppress a truth is sometimes to tell a lie.'

'But suppose one passes on information. Something private, perhaps, which one hasn't any real right to know – and it throws suspicion on the wrong person?'

Dalgliesh said gently:

'You have to trust us. Will you try to do that?'

She nodded, and whispered 'Yes', but she said noth-ing further. He judged that this was not the time to press her. He let her go, and sent for Angela Foley.

12

In contrast to Brenda Pridmore's artless confiding, Angela Foley presented a bland inscrutable gaze. She was an unusual-looking girl with a heart-shaped face and a wide, exceedingly high forehead from which hair, baby fine, the colour of ripe grain, was strained back and plaited into a tight coil on top of her head. Her eyes were small, slanted, and so deeply set that Dalgliesh found it hard to guess their colour. Her mouth was small, pursed and uncommunicative above the pointed chin. She wore a dress in fine fawn wool, topped with an elaborately patterned, short-sleeved tabard, and short laced boots, a sophisticated and exotic contrast to Brenda's orthodox prettiness and neat- hand-knitted twinset.

If she was distressed by her cousin's violent death, she concealed it admirably. She said that she had worked as Director's secretary for five years, first with Dr. MacIntyre and now with Dr. Howarth. Before that, she had been a shorthand typist in the general office of the Laboratory, having joined Hoggatt's straight from school. She was twenty-seven. Until two years ago, she lived in a bed-sitting-room in Ely, but now shared Sprogg's Cottage with a woman friend. They had spent the whole of the previous evening in each other's company. Edwin Lorrimer and his father had been her only living relatives, but they had seen very little of each other. The family, she explained as if this were the most natural thing in the world, had never been close.

'So you know very little of his private affairs, his will, for example?'

'No, nothing. When my grandmother left him all her money, and we were at the solicitor's office, he said that he would make me his heir. But I think he just felt guilty at the time that I wasn't named in the will. I don't suppose it meant anything. And, of course, he may have changed his mind.'

'Do you remember how much your grandmother left?'

She paused for a moment. Almost, he thought, as if calculating whether ignorance would sound more suspicious than knowledge. Then she said:

'I think about thirty thousand. I don't know how much it is now.'

He took her briefly but carefully through the events of the early morning. She and her friend ran a Mini, but she usually cycled to work. She had done so that morning, arriving at the Laboratory at her usual time, just before nine o'clock, and had been surprised to see Dr. Howarth with Mrs. Bidwell driving in before her. Brenda Pridmore had opened the door. Inspector Blakelock was coming downstairs and he had broken the news of the murder. They had all stayed in the hall together while Dr. Howarth went up to the Biology Lab. Inspector Blakelock had telephoned for the police and for Dr. Kerrison. When Dr. Howarth returned to the hall he had asked her to go with Inspector Blakelock and check on the keys. She and the Director were the only two members of staff who knew the combination of his security cupboard. He had stayed in the hall, she thought talking to Brenda Pridmore. The keys had been in their box in the cupboard, and she and Inspector Blakelock had left them there. She had reset the combination lock and returned to the hall. Dr. Howarth had gone into his office to talk to the Home Office, telling the rest of the staff to wait in the hall. Later, after the police and Dr. Kerrison had arrived, Dr. Howarth had driven her in his car to break the news to old Mr. Lorrimer. Then he had left her with the old man to return to the Laboratory, and she had telephoned for her friend. She and Miss Mawson had been there together until Mrs. Swaffield, the rector's wife, and a constable arrived, about an hour later.

'What did you do at Postmill Cottage?'

'I made tea and took it in to my uncle. Miss Mawson stayed in the kitchen most of the time doing the washing-up for him. The kitchen was in a bit of a mess, mostly dirty crockery from the previous day.'

'How did your uncle seem?'

'Worried, and rather cross about having been left alone. I don't think he quite realised Edwin was dead.'

There seemed little else to be learned from her. As far as she knew, her cousin had had no enemies. She had no idea who could have killed him. Her voice, high, rather monotonous, the voice of a small girl, suggested that it was not a matter of much concern to her. She expressed no regret, advanced no theories, answered all his questions composedly in her high, unemphatic voice. He might have been a casual and unimportant visitor gratifying a curiosity about the routine of the working of the Laboratory. He felt an instinctive antipathy towards her. He had no difficulty in concealing it, but it interested him since it was a long time since a murder suspect had provoked in him so immediate and physical a reaction. But he wondered whether it was prejudice that glimpsed in those deep and secretive eyes a flash of disdain, of contempt even, and he would have given a great deal to know what was going on behind that high, rather bumpy forehead.

When she had left, Massingham said:

'It's odd that Dr. Howarth sent her and Blakelock to check on the keys. He must have immediately realised their importance. Access to the Lab is fundamental to this case. So why didn't he check on them himself? He knew the combination?'

'Too proud to take a witness, and too intelligent to go without one. And he may have thought it more important to supervise things in the hall. But at least he was careful to protect Angela Foley. He didn't send her alone. Well, let's see what Blakelock has to say about it.'

13

Like Dr. Howarth, Inspector Blakelock chose not to sit. He stood at attention, facing Dalgliesh across Howarth's desk like a man on a disciplinary charge. Dalgliesh knew better than to try to get him to relax.

Blakelock had first learned the technique of replying to questions in his detective-constable days in the witness-box. He gave the information he was asked for, no more and no less, his eyes fixed on some spot a foot above Dalgliesh's right shoulder. When he gave his name in a firm expressionless voice, Dalgliesh half expected him to reach out his right hand for the Book and take the oath.

In reply to Dalgliesh's questioning he described his movements since leaving his house in Ely to come to the Laboratory. His account of the finding of the body tallied with that of Brenda Pridmore. As soon as he had seen her face as she came down the stairs he had realised that something was wrong and he dashed up to the Biology Lab without waiting for her to speak. The door had been open and the light on. He described the position of the body as precisely as if its rigid contours were imprinted on the mind's retina. He had known at once that Lorrimer was dead. He hadn't touched the body except, instinctively, to slip his hand into the pocket of the white coat and feel that the keys were there.

Dalgliesh asked:

'When you arrived at the Laboratory this morning you waited for Miss Pridmore to catch you up before coming in. Why was that?'

'I saw her coming round the side of the building after having put her bicycle away, and it seemed courteous to wait, sir. And it saved me having to re-open the door to her.'

'And you found the three locks and the internal security system in good order?'

'Yes, sir.'

'Do you make a routine check of the Laboratory as soon as you arrive?'

'No, sir. Of course if I found that any of the locks or the security panel had been tampered with I should check at once. But everything was in order.'

'You said earlier that the telephone call from Mr. Lorrimer senior was a surprise to you. Didn't you notice Dr. Lorrimer's car when you arrived this morning?'

'No, sir. The senior scientific staff use the end garage.'

'Why did you send Miss Pridmore to see if Dr. Lorrimer was here?'

'I didn't, sir. She slipped under the counter before I could stop her.'

'So you sensed that something was wrong?'

'Not really, sir. I didn't expect her to find him. But I think it did briefly occur to me that he might have been taken ill.'

'What sort of a man was Dr. Lorrimer, Inspector?'

'He was the senior biologist, sir.'

'I know. I'm asking you what he was like as a man and a colleague.'

'I didn't really know him well, sir. He wasn't one for lingering at the reception desk to chat. But I got on all right with him. He was a good forensic scientist.'

'I've been told that he took an interest in Brenda Pridmore. Didn't that mean that he occasionally lingered at the desk?'

'Not for more than a few minutes, sir. He liked to have a word with the girl from time to time. Everyone does. It's nice to have a young thing about the Lab. She's pretty and hard-working and enthusiastic, and I think Dr. Lorrimer wanted to encourage her.'

'No more than that, Inspector?'

Blakelock said stolidly:

'No, sir.'

Dalgliesh then asked him about his movements on the previous evening. He said that he and his wife had bought tickets for the village concert, although his wife was reluctant to go because of a bad headache. She suffered from sinus headaches which were occasionally disabling. But they had attended for the

150

first half of the programme and, because her headache was worse, had left at the interval. He had driven back to Ely, arriving home about a quarter to nine. He and his wife lived in a modern bungalow on the outskirts of the city with no near neighbours and he thought it unlikely that anyone would have noticed their return. Dalgliesh said:

'There seems to have been a general reluctance on the part of everyone to stay for the second part of the programme. Why did you bother to go when you knew your wife was unwell?'

'Dr. MacIntyre – he's the former Director, sir – liked the Laboratory staff to take part in village activities, and Chief Inspector Martin feels the same. So I'd got the tickets and my wife thought we might as well use them. She hoped that the concert might help her to forget her headache. But the first half was rather rowdy and, in fact, it got worse.'

'Did you go home and fetch her, or did she meet you here?'

'She came out earlier in the afternoon by the bus, sir, and spent the afternoon with Mrs. Dean, wife of the Minister at the Chapel. She's an old friend. I went round to collect my wife when I left work at six o'clock. We had a fish and chip supper there before the concert.'

'That's your normal time for leaving?'

'Yes, sir.'

'And who locks up the Laboratory if the scientists are working after your time for leaving?'

'I always check who's left, sir. If there are junior staff working then I have to stay until they're finished. But that isn't usual. Dr. Howarth has a set of keys and would check the alarm system and lock up if he worked late.'

'Did Dr. Lorrimer normally work after you had left?'

'About three or four evenings a week, sir. But I had

no anxiety about Dr. Lorrimer locking up. He was very conscientious.'

'Would he let anyone into the Laboratory if he were alone?'

'No, sir, not unless they were members of the staff, or of the police force, maybe. But it would have to be an officer he knew. He wouldn't let anyone in who hadn't got proper business here. Dr. Lorrimer was very particular about unauthorised people coming into the Laboratory.'

'Was that why he tried forcibly to remove Miss Kerrison the day before yesterday?'

Inspector Blakelock did not lose his composure. He said:

'I wouldn't describe it as a forcible removal, sir. He didn't lay hands on the girl.'

'Would you describe to me exactly what did happen, Inspector?'

'Miss Kerrison and her small brother came to meet their father. Dr. Kerrison was lecturing that morning to the Inspectors' training course. I suggested to Miss Kerrison that she sit down on the chair and wait, but Dr. Lorrimer came down the stairs at that moment to see if the mallet had arrived for examination. He saw the children and asked rather peremptorily what they were doing there. He said that a forensic science lab wasn't a place for children. Miss Kerrison said that she didn't intend to leave, so he walked towards her as if he intended to put her out. He looked very white, very strange, I thought. He didn't lay a hand on her but I think she was frightened that he was going to. I believe she's very highly strung, sir. She started screeching and screaming "I hate you. I hate you." Dr. Lorrimer turned and went back up the stairs and Brenda tried to comfort the girl.'

'And Miss Kerrison and her small brother left without waiting for their father?'

'Yes, sir. Dr. Kerrison came down about fifteen

minutes later and I told him that the children had come for him but had left.'

'You said nothing about the incident?'

'No, sir.'

'Was this typical of Dr. Lorrimer's behaviour?'

'No, sir. But he hadn't been looking well in recent weeks. I think he's been under some strain.'

'And you've no idea what kind of strain?'

'No, sir.'

'Had he enemies?'

'Not to my knowledge, sir.'

'So you've no idea who might have wanted him dead?'

'No, sir.'

'After the discovery of Dr. Lorrimer's body, Dr. Howarth sent you with Miss Foley to check that his bunch of keys were in the security cupboard. Will you describe exactly what you and she did?'

'Miss Foley opened the cupboard. She and the Director are the only two people who know the combination.'

'And you watched?'

'Yes, sir, but I can't remember the figures. I watched her twisting and setting the dial.'

'And then?'

'She took out the metal cash box and opened it. It wasn't locked. The keys were inside.'

'You were watching her closely all the time, Inspector? Are you absolutely sure that Miss Foley couldn't have replaced the keys in the box without your seeing?'

'No, sir. That would have been quite impossible.'

'One last thing, Inspector. When you went up to the body Miss Pridmore was here alone. She told me that she's virtually certain that no-one could have slipped out of the Laboratory during that time. Have you considered that possibility?'

'That he might have been here all night, sir? Yes.

But he wasn't hiding in the Chief Liaison Officer's room because I would have seen him when I went to turn off the internal alarm. That's the room closest to the front door. I suppose he could have been in the Director's Office, but I don't see how he could have crossed the hall and opened the door without Miss Pridmore noticing even if she were in a state of shock. It isn't as if the door were ajar. He'd have had to turn the Yale lock.'

'And you are absolutely certain that your own set of keys never left your possession last night?'

'I'm certain, sir.'

'Thank you, Inspector. That's all for the present. Would you please ask Mr. Middlemass to come in?'

14

The Document Examiner strolled into the office with easy assurance, arranged his long body without invitation in Howarth's armchair, crossed his right ankle over his left knee and raised an interrogatory eyebrow at Dalgliesh like a visitor expecting nothing from his host but boredom, but politely determined not to show it. He was wearing dark brown corduroy slacks, a fawn turtle-necked sweater in fine wool and bright purple socks with leather slip-on shoes. The effect was of a *dégagé* informality, but Dalgliesh noticed that the slacks were tailored, the sweater cashmere, and the shoes hand-made. He glanced down at Middlemass's statement of his movements since seven o'clock the previous evening. Unlike the efforts of his colleagues, it was written with a pen, not a biro, in a fine, high, italic script, which succeeded in being both decorative and virtually illegible. It was not the kind of hand he had expected. He said:

'Before we get down to this, could you tell me about your quarrel with Lorrimer?'

'My version of it, you mean, as opposed to Mrs. Bidwell's?'

'The truth, as opposed to speculation.'

'It wasn't a particular edifying episode, and I can't say I'm proud of it. But it wasn't important. I'd just started on the clunch pit murder case when I heard Lorrimer coming out of the wash-room. I had a private matter I wanted a word about so I called him in. We talked, quarrelled, he struck out at me and I reacted with a punch to his nose. It bled spectacularly over my overall. I apologised. He left.'

'What was the quarrel about? A woman?'

'Well, hardly, Commander, not with Lorrimer. I think Lorrimer knew that there were two sexes but I doubt whether he approved of the arrangement. It was a small private matter, something which happened a couple of years ago. Nothing to do with this Lab.'

'So we have the picture of your settling down to work on an exhibit from a murder case, an important exhibit since you chose to examine it yourself. You are not, however, so absorbed in this task that you can't listen to footsteps passing the door and identify those of Lorrimer. It seems to you a convenient moment to call him in and discuss something which happened two years ago, something which you've apparently been content to forget in the interim, but which now so incenses you both that you end by trying to knock each other down.'

'Put like that, it sounds eccentric.'

'Put like that, it sounds absurd.'

'I suppose it was absurd in a way. It was about a cousin of my wife's, Peter Ennals. He left school with two A-levels in science and seemed keen on coming into the Service. He came to me for advice and I told him how to go about it. He ended up as an S.O. under

Lorrimer in the Southern Lab. It wasn't a success. I don't suppose it was entirely Lorrimer's fault, but he hasn't got the gift of managing young staff. Ennals ended up with a failed career, a broken engagement and what is euphemistically described as a nervous breakdown. He drowned himself. We heard rumours about what had happened at the Southern. It's a small service and these things get around. I didn't really know the boy; my wife was fond of him.

'I'm not blaming Lorrimer for Peter's death. A suicide is always ultimately responsible for his own destruction. But my wife believes that Lorrimer could have done more to help him. I telephoned her after lunch yesterday to explain that I'd be late home and our conversation reminded me that I'd always meant to speak to Lorrimer about Peter. By coincidence I heard his footsteps. So I called him in with the result that Mrs. Bidwell has no doubt graphically described. Mrs. Bidwell, I don't doubt, detects a woman at the bottom of any male quarrel. And if she did talk about a woman or a telephone call, then the woman was my wife and the telephone call was the one I've told you about.'

It sounded plausible, thought Dalgliesh. It might even be the truth. The Peter Ennals story would have to be checked. It was just another chore when they were already hard-pressed and the truth of it was hardly in doubt. But Middlemass had spoken in the present tense: 'Lorrimer hasn't the gift of managing junior staff.' Were there, perhaps, junior staff closer to home who had suffered at his hands? But he decided to leave it for now. Paul Middlemass was an intelligent man. Before he made a more formal statement he would have time to ponder about the effect on his career of putting his signature to a lie. Dalgliesh said:

'According to this statement you were playing the part of a hobby-horse for the morris-dancers at yesterday evening's village concert. Despite this, you say

156

you can't give the name of anyone who could vouch for you. Presumably both the dancers and the audience could see the hobby-horse galumphing around, but not you inside it. But wasn't anyone there when you arrived at the hall, or when you left?'

'No-one who saw me to recognise me. It's a nuisance but it can't be helped. It happened rather oddly. I'm not a morris-dancer. I don't normally go in for these rustic rites and village concerts aren't my idea of entertainment. It was the Senior Liaison Officer's show, Chief Inspector Martin, but he had the chance of this U.S.A. visit unexpectedly and asked me to deputise. We're about the same size and I suppose he thought that the outfit would fit me. He needed someone fairly broad in the shoulders and strong enough to take the weight of the head: I owed him a favour – he had a tactful word with one of his mates on highway patrol when I was caught speeding a month ago – so I couldn't very well not oblige.

'I went to a rehearsal last week and all it amounted to was, as you say, galumphing round the dancers after they'd done their stuff, snapping my jaws at the audience, frisking my tail and generally making a fool of myself. That hardly seemed to matter since no-one could recognise me. I'd no intention of spending the whole evening at the concert, so I asked Bob Gotobed, he's the leader of the troupe, to give me a ring from the hall about fifteen minutes before we were due to go on. We were scheduled to appear after the interval and they reckoned that that would be about eight-thirty. The concert, as you've probably been told, started at seven-thirty.'

'And you stayed working in your Lab until the call came?'

'That's right. My S.O. went out and got me a couple of beef and chutney sandwiches and I ate them at my desk. Bob phoned at eight-fifteen to say that they were running a bit ahead of time and that I'd better come

157

over. The lads were dressed and were proposing to have a beer in the Moonraker. The hall hasn't a licence, so all the audience get in the interval is coffee or tea served by the Mothers' Union. I left the Lab at, I suppose, about eight-twenty.'

'You say here that Lorrimer was alive then as far as you know?'

'We know that he was alive twenty-five minutes later, if his dad is right about the telephone call. But actually I think I saw him. I went out of the front door because that's the only exit but I had to go round the back to the garages to get my car. The light was on then in the Biology Department and I saw a figure in a white coat move briefly across the window. I can't swear that it was Lorrimer. I can only say that it never occurred to me at the time that it wasn't. And I knew, of course, that he must be in the building. He was responsible for locking up and he was excessively tedious about security. He wouldn't have left without checking on all the departments, including Document Examination.'

'How was the front door locked?'

'Only with the Yale and a single bolt. That's what I expected. I let myself out.'

'What happened when you got to the hall?'

'To explain that I'll have to describe the architectural oddities of the place. It was put up cheaply five years ago by the village builder and the committee thought they'd save money by not employing an architect. They merely told the chap that they wanted a rectangular hall with a stage and two dressing-rooms and lavatories at one end, and a reception hall, cloak-room and a room for refreshments at the other. It was built by Harry Gotobed and his sons. Harry is a pillar of the Chapel and a model of Nonconformist rectitude. He doesn't hold with the theatre, amateur or otherwise, and I think they had some difficulty in persuading him even to build a stage. But he certainly didn't intend to have any communicating door between the male and female dressing-rooms. As a result what we've got is a stage with two rooms behind, each with its separate lavatory. There's an exit at each side into the graveyard, and two doors on to the stage, but there's literally no common space behind the stage. As a result the men dress in the right-hand dressing-room and come on to the stage from the prompt side, and the women from the left. Anyone who wants to enter from the opposite side has to leave the dressing-room, scurry in their costume and probably in the rain through the graveyard and, if they don't trip over a gravestone, break their ankle, or fall into an open grave, finally make a triumphant, if damp, appearance on the proper side.'

Suddenly he threw back his head and gave a shout of laughter, then recovered himself and said:

'Sorry, poor taste. It's just that I was remembering last year's performance by the dramatic society. They'd chosen one of those dated domestic comedies where the characters spend most of their time in evening dress making snappy small talk. Young Bridie Corrigan from the general store played the maid. Scurrying through the churchyard she thought she saw old Maggie Gotobed's ghost. She made her entrance screaming, cap awry, but remembered her part sufficiently to gasp: "Holy Mother of God, dinner is served!" Whereat the cast trooped dutifully off stage, the men to one side and the women to the other. Our hall adds considerably to the interest of the performances I can tell you.'

'So you went to the right-hand dressing-room?'

'That's right. It was a complete shambles. The cast have to hang up their outdoor coats as well as keeping the costumes there. There's a row of coat-hooks and a bench down the middle of the room, one rather small mirror and space for two people only to make up simultaneously. The single hand-basin is in the lavatory. Well, no doubt you'll be looking at the place for costumes, boxes and props piled on the bench and yourself. Last night it was chaotic with outdoor coats, overflowing on to the floor. The hobby-horse costume was hanging on one of the pegs, so I put it on.'

'There was no-one there when you arrived?'

'No-one in the room, but I could hear someone in the lavatory. I knew that most of the troupe were over at the Moonraker. When I had got myself into the costume the lavatory door opened and Harry Sprogg, he's a member of the troupe, came out. He was wearing his costume.'

Massingham made a note of the name: Harry Sprogg. Dalgliesh asked:

'Did you speak?'

'I didn't. He said something about being glad I'd made it and that the chaps were over at the Moonraker. He said he was just going to dig them out. He's the only teetotaller of the party so I suppose that's why he didn't go over with them. He left and I followed him out into the cemetery.'

'Without having spoken to him?'

'I can't remember that I said anything. We were only together for about a couple of seconds. I followed him out because the dressing-room was stuffy – actually it stank – and the costume was extraordinarily heavy and hot. I thought I'd wait outside where I could join the boys when they came across from the pub. And that's what I did.'

'Did you see anyone else?'

'No, but that doesn't mean there was no-one there. Vision's a bit restricted through the headpiece. If someone had been standing motionless in the grave-yard I could easily have missed him. I wasn't expecting to see anyone.'

'How long were you there?'

'Less than five minutes. I galumphed around a bit and tried a few trial snaps of the jaw and whisks of

160

the tail. It must have looked daft if anyone was watching. There's a particularly repulsive memorial there, a marble angel with an expression of nauseating piety and a hand pointed upwards. I pranced around that once or twice and snapped my jaws at its asinine face. God knows why! Perhaps it was the joint effect of moonlight and the place itself. Then I saw the chaps coming across the graveyard from the Moonraker and joined up with them.'

'Did you say anything then?'

'I may have said good evening or hello, but I don't think so. They wouldn't have recognised my voice through the headpiece anyway. I raised the front right-hand hoof and made a mock obeisance and then tagged on behind. We went into the dressing-room together. We could hear the audience settling into their seats, and then the stage manager put his head in and said "Right, boys." Then the six dancers went on, and I could hear the violin strike up, the stamping of feet and the jangling of bells. Then the music changed and that was the signal for me to join them and do my bit. Part of the act was to go down the steps from the stage and frolic among the audience. It seemed to go down well enough to judge by the girlish shrieks, but if you're thinking of asking whether anyone recognised me, I shouldn't bother. I don't see how they could have.'

'But after the performance?'

'No-one saw me after the performance. We came tumbling down the steps from the stage into the dressing-room, but the applause went on. Then I realised with considerable horror that some fools in the audience were calling out "encore". The lads in green needed no second invitation and they were up the stairs again like a troop of parched navvies who'd just been told that the bar's open. I took the view that my agreement with Bill Martin covered one performance, not including an encore, and that I'd made enough of a fool of myself for one evening. So when the fiddle struck up and the stamping began I got out of the costume, hung it back on the nail, and made off. As far as I know no-one saw me leave and there was no-one in the car-park when I unlocked my car. I was at home before ten and my wife can vouch for that if you're interested. But I don't suppose you are.'

'It would be more helpful if you could find some-one to vouch for you between eight-forty-five and mid-night.'

'I know. Maddening, isn't it? If I'd known someone was proposing to murder Lorrimer during the even-ing I'd have taken good care not to put the headpiece on until the second before we went on stage. It's a pity the beast's head is so large. It's supported, as you'll discover, from the wearer's shoulders and doesn't actu-ally touch the head or face. If it did you might find a hair or some biological evidence that I'd actually worn the thing. And prints are no good. I handled it at the rehearsals and so did a dozen other people. The whole incident is an example to me of the folly of indulging in good nature. If I'd only told old Bill just what he could do with his blasted hobby-horse I should have been home, and, quite literally, dry before eight o'clock with a nice cosy alibi at the Panton Arms for the rest of the evening.'

Dalgliesh ended the interview by asking about the missing white coat.

'It's a fairly distinctive design. I've got half a dozen of them, all inherited from my father. The other five are in the linen-cupboard here, if you want to have a look at them. They're waisted, in very heavy white linen, buttoning high to the neck with crested Royal Army Dental Corps buttons. Oh, and they've got no pockets. The old man thought pockets were un-hygienic.'

Massingham thought that a coat already stained with Lorrimer's blood might be seen by a murderer as a particularly useful protective garment. Echoing his thought, Middlemass said:

'If it is found again I don't think I could say with certainty exactly what bloodstains resulted from our punch-up. There was one patch about four inches by two on the right shoulder, but there may have been other splashes. But presumably the serologists would be able to give you some idea of the comparative age of the stains.'

If the coat were ever found, thought Dalgliesh. It wouldn't be an easy thing to destroy completely. But the murderer, if he had taken it, would have had all night to dispose of the evidence. He asked:

'And you dropped this particular coat in the soiled-linen-basket in the men's washroom immediately after the quarrel?'

'I meant to, but then I thought better of it. The stain wasn't large and the sleeves were perfectly clean. I put it on again and dropped it in the soiled-linen-basket when I washed before leaving the Lab.'

'Do you remember what wash-basin you used?'

'The first one, nearest the door.'

'Was the basin clean?'

If Middlemass were surprised by the question, he concealed it.

'As clean as it ever is after a day's use. I wash fairly vigorously so it was clean enough when I left. And so was I.'

The picture came into Massingham's mind with startling clarity; Middlemass in his blood-spattered coat bending low over the wash-basin, both taps running full on, the water swirling and gurgling down the waste-pipe, water stained pink with Lorrimer's blood. But what about the timing? If old Lorrimer really had spoken to his son at eight-forty-five then Middlemass must be in the clear, at least for the first part of the evening. And then he pictured another scene; Lorrimer's sprawled body, the raucous ring of

163

the telephone, Middlemass's gloved hand slowly lifting the receiver. But could old Lorrimer really mistake another voice for that of his son?'

When the Document Examiner had left Massingham said:

'At least he has one person to corroborate his story. Dr. Howarth saw the hobby-horse prancing round the angle memorial in the churchyard. They've hardly had opportunity this morning to concoct that story together. And I don't see how else Howarth could have known about it.'

Dalgliesh said:

'Unless they concocted the story in the graveyard last night. Or unless it was Howarth, not Middlemass who was inside that hobby-horse.'

15

'I didn't like him, and I was frightened of him, but I didn't kill him. I know everyone will think that I did, but it's not true. I couldn't kill anyone or anything; not an animal, let alone a man.'

Clifford Bradley had stood up fairly well to the long wait for questioning. He wasn't incoherent. He had tried to behave with dignity. But he had brought into the room with him the sour contagion of fear, that most difficult of all emotions to hide. His whole body twitched with it; the restless hands clasping and un-clasping in his lap, the shuddering mouth, the anxious blinking eyes. He was not an impressive figure, and fear had made him pitiable. He would make an in-effective murderer, thought Massingham. Watching him, he felt some of the instinctive shame of the healthy in the presence of the diseased. It was easy to imagine him retching over that wash-basin, vomiting up his guilt and terror. It was less easy to envisage him tearing out the page of the notebook, destroying the white coat, organising that early morning telephone call to Mrs. Bidwell. Dalgliesh said mildly:

'No-one is accusing you. You're familiar enough with Judge's Rules to know that we wouldn't be talking like this if I were about to caution you. You say that you didn't kill him. Have you any idea who did?'

'No. Why should I have? I don't know anything about him. All I know is that I was at home with my wife last night. My mother-in-law came to supper and I saw her off on the seven-forty-five bus to Ely. Then I went straight home, and I was home all the evening. My mother-in-law telephoned about nine o'clock to say that she'd reached home safely. She didn't speak to me because I was having a bath. My wife told her that. But Sue can confirm that, except for taking her mother to the bus, I was home all the evening.'

Bradley admitted that he hadn't known that old Mr. Lorrimer's hospital admission had been postponed. He thought he had been in the washroom when the old man's call came through. But he knew nothing of the early telephone call to Mrs. Bidwell, the missing page from Lorrimer's notebook, or Paul Middlemass's missing white coat. Asked about his supper on Wednesday night, he said that they had eaten curry made with tinned beef, together with rice and tinned peas. Afterwards there had been a trifle which, he explained defensively, had been made with stale cake and custard. Massingham suppressed a shudder as he made a careful note of these details. He was glad when Dalgliesh said that Bradley could go. There seemed nothing else of importance to be learned from him in his present state; nothing more to be learned, indeed, from anyone at the Laboratory. He was fretting to see Lorrimer's house, Lorrimer's next of kin.

But before they left, Sergeant Reynolds had something to report. He was finding it difficult to keep the excitement from his voice.

'We've found some tyre-marks, sir, about half-way up the drive among the bushes. They look pretty fresh to me. We've got them protected until the photographer arrives and then we'll get a plaster cast made. It's difficult to be sure until we compare them with a tyre index, but it looks to me as if the two back tyres were a Dunlop and a Semperit. That's a pretty odd combination. It should help us to get the car.'

It was a pity, thought Dalgliesh, that Superintendent Mercer had told the photographers they could go. But it wasn't surprising. Given the present pressure of work on the Force, it was difficult to justify keeping men hanging about indefinitely. And at least the fingerprint officers were still here. He said:

'Have you been able to get in touch with Mr. Bidwell yet?'

'Captain Massey says he's up on the five-acre raising sugar beet. He'll tell him you want to see him when he comes in for his dockey.'

'His what?'

'His dockey, sir. That's the meal break which we have in these parts at about half-past ten or eleven.'

'I'm relieved that Captain Massey has a proper sense of priority between agriculture and murder.'

'They're a good bit behind with the five-acre, sir, but Captain Massey will see that he calls in at Guy's Marsh station as soon as they've finished work this afternoon.'

'If he doesn't, you'd better dig him out, even if you have to borrow Captain Massey's tractor to do it. That telephone call is important. I'll have a word with the senior scientists in the library now and explain to them that I want them present in the departments when you do the internal search. The rest of them can go home. I'll tell them that we hope to have finished searching by the end of the day. It should be possible for the Lab to open again tomorrow morning. Inspector Massingham and I will be seeing Dr. Lorrimer's

166

father at Postmill Cottage. If anything breaks, you can contact us there or through the car radio control from Guy's Marsh.'

Less than ten minutes later, with Massingham at the wheel of the police Rover, they were on their way.

Book Three

AN EXPERIMENTAL MAN

1

Postmill Cottage lay two miles to the west of the village at the junction of Stoney Piggott's Road and Tenpenny Lane, where the road curved gently upwards, but so imperceptibly that it was difficult for Dalgliesh to believe that he was on slightly higher ground until the car was parked on the grass verge, and turning to close the door he saw the village strung out along the road below him. Under the turbulent painter's sky, with its changing clusters of white, grey and purple cumulus clouds massing against the pale azure blue of the upper air, and the sunlight moving fitfully across the fields and glittering on roofs and windows, it looked like an isolated frontier outpost, but welcoming, prosperous and secure. Violent death might lurk eastwards in the dark fenlands, but surely not under these neat domestic roofs. Hoggatt's Laboratory was hidden by its belt of trees, but the new building was immediately identifiable, its concrete stumps, ditches and half-built walls looking like the orderly excavation of some long-buried city.

The cottage, a low building of brick with a white wood-cladded front and with the rounded top and sails of the windmill visible behind, was separated from the road by a wide ditch. A wooden plank bridge and white-painted gate led to the front path and the latched door. The first impression of melancholy neglect, induced perhaps by the cottage's isolation and the bareness of outer walls and windows, proved on second glance illusory. The front garden had the dishevelled, overgrown look of autumn, but the roses in the two circular beds, one each side of the path, had been properly tended. The gravel path was clear of weeds, the paintwork on door and windows was shining. Twenty feet farther on two wide and sturdy planks bridged the ditch and led to a flagstoned yard and a brick garage.

There was an old and grubby red Mini already parked next to a police car. Dalgliesh deduced from the bundle of parish magazines, a smaller one of what looked like concert programmes and the bunch of shaggy chrysanthemums and autumn foliage on the back seat, that the rector, or more probably his wife, was already at the cottage, probably on her way to help with the church decorations, although Thursday was an unusual day, surely, for this ecclesiastical chore. He had scarcely turned from this scrutiny of the rectory car when the door of the cottage opened and a woman bustled down the path towards them. No-one who had been born and bred in a rectory could be in any doubt that here was Mrs. Swaffield. She looked indeed like a prototype of a country rector's wife, large-bosomed, cheerful and energetic, exuding the slightly intimidating assurance of a woman adept at recognising authority and competence at a glance, and making immediate use of them. She was wearing a tweed skirt covered with a flowered cotton apron, a hand-knitted twinset, thick brogues and open-work woollen stockings. A felt hat, shaped like a pork pie, its crown stabbed with a steel hatpin, was jammed uncompromisingly over a broad forehead.

'Good morning. Good morning. You're Commander Dalgliesh and Inspector Massingham. Winifred Swaffield. Come in, won't you? The old gentleman is upstairs changing. He insisted on putting on his suit when he heard you were on the way, although I assured him that it wasn't at all necessary. He'll be down in a minute. In the front parlour would be best I think, don't you? This is Constable Davis, but of course you know all about him. He tells me that he's been sent here to see that no-one goes in to Dr. Lorrimer's room and to stop any visitors from bothering the

172

old gentleman. Well, we haven't had any so far except one reporter and I soon got rid of him, so that's all right. But the constable has really been very helpful to me in the kitchen. I've just been getting some lunch for Mr. Lorrimer. It'll only be soup and an omelette, I'm afraid, but there doesn't seem to be much else in the larder except tins and he might be glad of those in the future. One doesn't like to come laden from the rectory like a Victorian do-gooder.

'Simon and I wanted him to come back to the rectory at once but he doesn't seem anxious to leave, and really one mustn't badger people, especially the old. And perhaps it's just as well. Simon's down with this two-day 'flu – that's why he can't be here – and we don't want the old gentleman to catch it. But we can't let him stay here alone tonight. I thought that he might like to have his niece here, Angela Foley, but he says no. So I'm hoping that Millie Gotobed from the Moonraker will be able to sleep here tonight, and we'll have to think again tomorrow. But I mustn't take up your time with my worries.'

At the end of this speech, Dalgliesh and Massingham found themselves ushered into the front living-room. At the sound of their footsteps in the narrow hall Constable Davis had emerged from what was presumably the kitchen, had sprung to attention, saluted, blushed and given Dalgliesh a glance of mingled appeal and slight desperation before disappearing again. The smell of home-made soup had wafted appetisingly through the door.

The sitting-room, which was stuffy and smelt strongly of tobacco, was adequately furnished, yet gave an impression of cheerless discomfort, a cluttered repository of the mementoes of ageing and its sad solaces. The chimney-breast had been boarded up and an old-fashioned gas fire hissed out an uncomfortably fierce heat over a sofa in cut moquette with two greasy circles marking where innumerable heads had once

173

rested. There was a square oak table with bulbous carved legs and four matching chairs with vinyl seats, and a large dresser set against the wall opposite the window, hung with the cracked remnants of long-smashed teasets. On the dresser were two bottles of Guinness and an unwashed glass. To the right of the fire was a high winged armchair and beside it a wicker table with a ramshackle lamp, a tobacco pouch, an ashtray bearing a picture of Brighton pier, and an open draught-board with the pieces set out, crusted with dried food and accumulated grime. The alcove to the left of the fire was filled with a large television set. Above it were a couple of shelves holding a collection of popular novels in identical sizes and bindings, issued by a book club to which Mr. Lorrimer had once apparently briefly belonged. They looked as if they had been gummed together unopened and un-read.

Dalgliesh and Massingham sat on the sofa. Mrs. Swaffield perched upright on the edge of the armchair and smiled across at them encouragingly, bringing into the room's cheerlessness a reassuring ambience of home-made jam, well conducted Sunday schools and massed women's choirs singing Blake's 'Jerusalem'. Both men felt immediately at home with her. Both in their different lives had met her kind before. It was not, thought Dalgliesh, that she was unaware of the frayed and ragged edges of life. She would merely iron them out with a firm hand and neatly hem them down.

Dalgliesh asked:

'How is he, Mrs. Swaffield?'

'Surprisingly well. He keeps talking about his son in the present tense, which is a little disconcerting, but I think he realises all right that Edwin is dead. I don't mean to imply that the old gentleman is senile. Not in the least. But it's difficult to know what the very old are feeling sometimes. It must have been a terrible shock, naturally. Appalling, isn't it? I suppose

174

a criminal from one of those London gangs broke in to get his hands on an exhibit. They're saying in the village that there were no signs of a break-in, but a really determined burglar can get in anywhere, I've always been told. I know Father Gregory has had terrible trouble with break-ins at St. Mary's at Guy's Marsh. The poor-box has been rifled twice and two pews of kneelers stolen, the ones the Mother's Union had specially embroidered to celebrate their fiftieth anniversary. Goodness knows why anyone should want to take those. Luckily we've had no trouble of that kind here. Simon would hate to have to lock the church. Chevisham has always been a most law-abiding village, which is why this murder is so shocking.'

Dalgliesh wasn't surprised that the village already knew that there had been no break-in at the Lab. Presumably one of the staff, on the excuse of needing to telephone home and say that he wouldn't be back for luncheon and avid to break the exciting news, had been less than discreet. But it would be pointless to try to trace the culprit. In his experience news percolated through a village community by a process of verbal osmosis, and it would be a bold man who tried to control or stem that mysterious diffusion. Mrs. Swaffield, like any proper rector's wife, had undoubtedly been one of the first to know. Dalgliesh said:

'It's a pity that Miss Foley and her uncle don't seem to get on. If he could go to stay temporarily with her that would at least solve your immediate problem. She and her friend were here when you arrived this morning, I take it?'

'Yes, both of them. Dr. Howarth came himself with Angela to break the news, which I think was thoughtful of him, then left her here when he went back to the Lab. He wouldn't want to be away for more than a short time, naturally. I think Angela phoned her friend and she came at once. Then the constable arrived and I was here shortly afterwards. There was no point in Angela and Miss Mawson staying on once I'd come, and Dr. Howarth was anxious for most of the staff to be actually in the Lab when you arrived.'

'And there are no other relatives and no close friends, as far as you know?'

'None, I think. They kept themselves very much to themselves. Old Mr. Lorrimer doesn't come to church or take part in village affairs, so that Simon and I never really got to know him. I know that people expect the clergy to come round knocking at doors and rooting people out, but Simon doesn't really believe it does much good, and I must say I think he's right. Dr. Lorrimer, of course, went to St. Mary's at Guy's Marsh. Father Gregory might be able to tell you something about him, although I don't think he took a very active part in church life. He used to pick up Miss Willard from the Old Rectory and drive her over. She might be worth having a word with, although it seems unlikely that they were close. I imagine that he drove her to church because Father Gregory suggested it rather than from inclination. She's an odd woman, not really suitable to look after children, I should have thought. But here comes the one you really want to talk to.'

Death, thought Dalgliesh, obliterates family resemblance as it does personality; there is no affinity between the living and the dead. The man who came into the room, shuffling a little but still upright, had once been as tall as his son, the sparse hair brushed back from a high forehead still showed streaks of the black it had once been; the watery eyes, sunken under the creased lids, were as dark. But there was no kinship with that rigid body on the laboratory floor. Death, in separating them for ever, had robbed them even of their likeness.

Mrs. Swaffield made the introductions in a voice of determined encouragement as if they had all suddenly gone deaf. Then she melted tactfully away, murmuring something about soup in the kitchen. Massingham sprang to help the old man to a chair, but Mr. Lorrimer, with a stiff chopping motion of the hand, gestured him aside. Eventually, after some hesitation, as if the sitting-room were unfamiliar to him, he lowered himself into what was obviously his usual place, the shabby, high-backed armchair to the right of the fire, from which he regarded Dalgliesh steadily.

Sitting there, bolt upright, in his old-fashioned and badly-cut dark blue suit, which smelt strongly of mothballs and now hung loosely on his diminished bones, he looked pathetic, almost grotesque, but not without dignity. Dalgliesh wondered why he had troubled to change. Was it a gesture of respect for his son, the need to formalise grief, a restless urge to find something to do? Or was it some atavistic belief that authority was on its way and should be propitiated by an outward show of deference? Dalgliesh was reminded of the funeral of a young detective constable killed on duty. What he had found almost unbearably pathetic had not been the sonorous beauty of the burial service, or even the young children walking hand in hand with careful solemnity behind their father's coffin. It had been the reception afterwards in the small police house, the carefully planned home-cooked food and the drink, ill-afforded, which the widow had prepared for the refreshment of her husband's colleagues and friends. Perhaps it had comforted her at the time, or solaced her in memory. Perhaps old Mr. Lorrimer, too, felt happier because he had taken trouble.

Settling himself some distance from Dalgliesh on the extraordinarily lumpy sofa, Massingham opened his notebook. Thank God the old man was calm anyway. You could never tell how the relatives were going to take it. Dalgliesh, as he knew, had the reputation of being good with the bereaved. His condolences might be short, almost formal, but at least they sounded sincere. He took it for granted that the family would wish to co-operate with the police, but as a matter of justice, not of retribution. He didn't connive at the extraordinary psychological interdependence by which the detective and the bereaved were often supported, and which it was so fatally easy to exploit. He made no specious promises, never bullied the weak or indulged the sentimental. And yet they seem to like him, thought Massingham. God knows why. At times he's cold enough to be barely human.

He watched Dalgliesh stand up as old Mr. Lorrimer came into the room; but he made no move to help the old man to his chair. Massingham had glanced briefly at his chief's face and seen the familiar look of speculative detached interest. What, if anything, he wondered, would move Dalgliesh to spontaneous pity? He remembered the other case they had worked on together a year previously, when he had been a detective-sergeant; the death of a child. Dalgliesh had regarded the parents with just such a look of calm appraisal. But he had worked eighteen hours a day for a month until the case was solved. And his next book of poems had contained that extraordinary one about a murdered child which no-one at the Yard, even those who professed to understand it, had had the temerity even to mention to its author. He said now:

'As Mrs. Swaffield explained, my name is Dalgliesh and this is Inspector Massingham. I expect Dr. Howarth told you that we would be coming. I'm very sorry about your son. Do you feel able to answer some questions?'

Mr. Lorrimer nodded towards the kitchen.

'What's she doing in there?'

His voice was surprising; high timbred and with a trace of the querulousness of age, but extraordinarily strong for an old man.

'Mrs. Swaffield? Making soup, I think.'

178

'I suppose she's used the onions and carrots we had in the vegetable rack. I thought I could smell carrots. Edwin knows I don't like carrots in soup.'

'Did he usually cook for you?'

'He does all the cooking if he isn't away at a scene of crime. I don't eat much dinner at midday, but he leaves me something to heat up, a stew from the night before or a bit of fish in sauce, maybe. He didn't leave anything this morning because he wasn't at home last night. I had to get my own breakfast. I fancied bacon, but I thought I'd better leave that in case he wants it for tonight. He usually cooks bacon and eggs if he's late home.'

Dalgliesh asked:

'Mr. Lorrimer, have you any idea why anyone should want to murder your son? Had he any enemies?'

'Why should he have enemies? He didn't know anyone except at the Lab. Everyone had a great respect for him at the Lab. He told me so himself. Why would anyone want to harm him? Edwin lived for his work.'

He brought out the last sentence as if it were an original expression of which he was rather proud.

'You telephoned him last night at the Laboratory, didn't you? What time was that?'

'It was a quarter to nine. The telly went blank. It didn't blink and go zig-zag like it sometimes does. Edwin showed me how to adjust the knob at the back for that. It went blank with just one little circle of light and then that failed. I couldn't see the nine o'clock news, so I rang Edwin and asked him to send for the T.V. man. We rent the set, and they're supposed to come at any hour, but there's always some excuse. Last month when I telephoned they didn't come for two days.'

'Can you remember what your son said?'

'He said that it wasn't any use telephoning late at night. He'd do it first thing this morning before he went to work. But, of course, he hasn't. He didn't come home. It's still broken. I don't like to telephone myself. Edwin always sees to everything like that. Do you think Mrs. Swaffield would ring?'

'I'm sure that she would. When you telephoned him did he say anything about expecting a visitor?'

'No. He seemed in a hurry, as if he didn't like it because I phoned. But he always said to ring the Lab up if I was in trouble.'

'And he said nothing else at all except that he'd ring the T.V. mechanic this morning?'

'What else would he say? He wasn't one for chatting over the telephone.'

'Did you ring him at the Laboratory yesterday about your hospital appointment?'

'That's right. I was supposed to go in to Addenbrooke's yesterday afternoon. Edwin was going to drive me in. It's my leg, you see. It's psoriasis. They're going to try a new treatment.'

He made as if to roll up his trouser leg. Dalgliesh said quickly:

'That's all right, Mr. Lorrimer. When did you know the bed wasn't available after all?'

'About nine o'clock they rang. He'd only just left home. So I phoned the Lab. I know the number of the Biology Department, of course. That's where he works – the Biology Department. Miss Easterbrook answered the phone and said that Edwin was at the hospital attending a post-mortem but she would give him the message when she got in. Addenbrooke's said they'd probably send for me next Tuesday. Who's going to take me now?'

'I expect Mrs. Swaffield will arrange something, or perhaps your niece could help. Wouldn't you like her to be here with you?'

'No. What can she do? She was here this morning with that friend of hers, the writing woman. Edwin doesn't like either of them. The friend – Miss Mawson, isn't it? – was rummaging around upstairs. I've got very good ears. I could hear her all right. I went out of the door and there she was coming down. She said she'd been to the bathroom. Why was she wearing washing-up gloves if she was going to the bathroom?'

Why indeed? thought Dalgliesh. He felt a spasm of irritation that Constable Davis hadn't arrived sooner. It was perfectly natural that Howarth should come with Angela Foley to break the news and should leave her with her uncle. Someone had to stay with him, and who more suitable than his only remaining relative? It was probably natural, too, that Angela Foley should send for the support of her friend. Probably both of them were interested in Lorrimer's will. Well, that too was natural enough. Massingham shifted on the sofa. Dalgliesh could sense his anxiety to get upstairs into Lorrimer's room. He shared it. But books and papers, the sad detritus of a dead life, could wait. The living witness might not again be so communicative. He asked:

'What did your son do with himself, Mr. Lorrimer?'

'After work, do you mean? He stays in his room mostly. Reading, I suppose. He's got quite a library of books up there. He's a scholar, is Edwin. He doesn't care much about the television, so I sit down here. Sometimes I can hear the record-player. Then there's the garden most weekends, cleaning the car, cooking and shopping. He has quite a full life. And he doesn't get much time. He's at the Lab until seven o'clock most nights, sometimes later.'

'And friends?'

'No. He doesn't go in for friends. We keep ourselves to ourselves.'

'No weekends away?'

'Where would he want to go? And what would happen to me? Besides, there's the shopping. If he isn't on call for a scene-of-crime visit he drives me into Ely

181

Saturday morning, and we go to the supermarket. Then we have lunch in the city. I enjoy that.'

'What telephone calls did he have?'

'From the Lab? Only when the Police Liaison Officer rings up to say that he's wanted at a murder scene. Sometimes that's in the middle of the night. But he never wakes me. There's a telephone extension in his room. He just leaves me a note and he's usually back in time to bring me a cup of tea at seven o'clock. He didn't do that this morning of course. That's why I rang the Lab. I rang his number first but there wasn't any reply. So then I rang the reception desk. He gave me both numbers in case I couldn't get through to him in an emergency.'

'And no-one else has telephoned him recently, no-one has come to see him?'

'Who would want to come and see him? And no-one has telephoned except that woman.'

Dalgliesh said, very quietly:

'What woman, Mr. Lorrimer?'

'I don't know what woman. I only know she rang. Monday of last week it was. Edwin was having a bath and the phone kept on ringing so I thought I'd better answer it.'

'Can you remember exactly what happened and what was said, Mr. Lorrimer, from the time you lifted the receiver? Take your time, there's no hurry. This may be very important.'

'There wasn't much to remember. I was going to say our number and ask her to hang on, but she didn't give me any time. She started speaking as soon as I lifted the receiver. She said: "We're right, there is something going on." Then she said something about the can being burned and that she'd got the numbers.'

'That the can had been burned and she'd got the numbers?'

'That's right. It doesn't sound sense now, but it was something like that. Then she gave me the numbers.'

182

'Can you remember them, Mr. Lorrimer?'

'Only the last one, which was 1840. Or it may have been two numbers, 18 and 40. I remembered those because the first house we had after I was married was number 18 and the second was 40. It was quite a coincidence, really. Anyway, those numbers stuck in my mind. But I can't remember the others.'

'How many numbers altogether?'

'Three or four altogether, I think. There were two, and then the 18 and the 40.'

'What did the numbers sound like, Mr. Lorrimer? Did you think she was giving you a telephone number or a car registration, for example? Can you remember what impression they made on you at the time?'

'No impression. Why should they? More like a telephone number, I suppose. I don't think it was a car registration. There weren't any letters you see. It sounded like a date; eighteen forty.'

'Have you any idea who was telephoning?'

'No. I don't think it was anyone at the Lab. It didn't sound like one of the Lab staff.'

'How do you mean, Mr. Lorrimer? How did the voice seem?'

The old man sat there, staring straight ahead. His hands, with the long fingers like those of his son, but with their skin dry and stained as withered leaves, hung heavily between his knees, grotesquely large for the brittle wrists. After a moment he spoke. He said:

'Excited.' There was another silence. Both detectives looked at him. Massingham thought that here again was an example of his chief's skill. He would have gone charging upstairs in search of the will and papers. But this evidence, so carefully elicited, was vital. After about a moment the old man spoke again. The word, when it came, was surprising. He said:

'Conspiratorial. That's what she sounded. Conspiratorial.'

They sat, still patiently waiting, but he said nothing else. Then they saw that he was crying. His face didn't change, but a single tear, bright as a pearl, dropped on to the parched hands. He looked at it as if wondering what it could be. Then he said:

'He was a good son to me. Time was, when he first went to College up in London, that we lost touch. He wrote to his mother and me, but he didn't come home. But these last years, since I've been alone, he's taken care of me. I'm not complaining. I daresay he's left me a bit of money, and I've got my pension. But it's hard when the young go first. And who will look after me now?'

Dalgliesh said quietly:

'We need to look at his room, examine his papers. Is the room locked?'

'Locked? Why should it be locked? No-one went into it but Edwin.'

Dalgliesh nodded to Massingham, who went out to call Mrs. Swaffield. Then they made their way upstairs.

2

It was a long, low-ceilinged room with white walls and a casement window which gave a view of a rectangle of unmown grass, a couple of gnarled apple trees heavy with fruit burnished green and gold in the autumn sun, a straggling hedge beaded with berries and beyond it the windmill. Even in the genial light of afternoon the mill looked a melancholy wreck of its former puissance. The paint was peeling from the walls and the great sails, from which the slats had fallen like rotten teeth, hung heavy with inertia in the restless air. Behind the windmill, the acres of black fenland, newly sliced by the autumn ploughing, stretched in glistening clumps between the dykes.

Dalgliesh turned away from this picture of melancholy peace to examine the room. Massingham was already busy at the desk. Finding the lid unlocked, he rolled it back for a few inches, then let it drop again. Then he tried the drawers. Only the top left-hand one was locked. If he were impatient for Dalgliesh to take Lorrimer's keys from his pocket and open it, he concealed his eagerness. It was known that the older man, who could work faster than any of his colleagues, still liked occasionally to take his time. He was taking it now, regarding the room with his dark sombre eyes, standing very still as if he were picking up invisible waves.

The place held a curious peace. The proportions were right and the furniture fitted where it had been placed. A man might have space to think in this uncluttered sanctum. A single bed, neatly covered with a red and brown blanket, stood against the opposite wall. A long wall shelf above the bed held an adjustable reading lamp, a radio, a record-player, a clock, a carafe of water and the Book of Common Prayer. In front of the window stood an oak working-table with a wheel-back chair. On the table was a blotter and a brown and blue pottery mug stacked with pencils and biro pens. The only other items of furniture were a shabby, winged armchair with a low table beside it, a double wardrobe in oak to the left of the door, and to the right an old-fashioned desk with a roll-top. The telephone was fitted to the wall. There were no pictures and no mirror, no masculine impedimenta, no trivia on desk-top or table-ledge. Everything was functional, well-used, unadorned. It was a room a man could be at home in.

Dalgliesh walked over to look at the books. He estimated that there must be about four hundred of them, completely covering the wall. There was little fiction, although the nineteenth-century English and Russian novelists were represented. Most of the books were histories or biographies, but there was a shelf of philosophy; Teilhard de Chardin's *Science and Christ,* Jean Paul-Sartre's *Being and Nothingness: A Humanist Outlook,* Simone Weil's *First and Last,* Plato's *Republic,* the *Cambridge History of Late Greek and Early Medieval Philosophy.* It looked as if Lorrimer had at one time been trying to teach himself Greek. The shelf held a Greek primer and a dictionary.

Massingham had taken down a book on comparative religion. He said:

'It looks as if he was one of those men who torment themselves trying to discover the meaning of existence.'

Dalgliesh replaced the Sartre he had been studying.

'You find that reprehensible?'

'I find it futile. Metaphysical speculation is about as pointless as a discussion on the meaning of one's lungs. They're for breathing.'

'And life is for living. You find that an adequate personal credo.'

'To maximise one's pleasures and minimise one's pain, yes, sir, I do. And, I suppose, to bear with stoicism those miseries I can't avoid. To be human is to ensure enough of those without inventing them. Anyway, I don't believe you can hope to understand what you can't see or touch or measure.'

'A logical positivist. You're in respectable company. But he spent his life examining what he could see or touch or measure. It doesn't seem to have satisfied him. Well, let's see what his personal papers have to tell.'

He turned his attention to the desk, leaving the locked drawer to the last. He rolled back the top to reveal two small drawers and a number of pigeon-holes. And here, neatly docketed and compartmentalised, were the minutiae of Lorrimer's solitary life. A drawer with three bills waiting to be paid, and one for receipts. A labelled envelope containing his parents' marriage lines, his own birth and baptismal certificates. His passport, an anonymous face but with the eyes staring as if hypnotised, the neck muscles taut. The lens of the camera might have been the barrel of a gun. A life assurance certificate. Receipted bills for fuel, electricity and gas. The maintenance agreement for the central heating. The hire-purchase agreement for the television. A wallet with his bank statement. His portfolio of investments, sound, unexciting, orthodox.

There was nothing about his work. Obviously he kept his life as carefully compartmentalised as his filing system. Everything to do with his profession, the journals, the drafts of his scientific papers, were kept in his office at the Lab. They were probably written there. That might account for some of the late hours. It would certainly have been impossible to guess from the contents of his desk what his job had been.

His will was in a separate labelled envelope together with a brief letter from a firm of Ely solicitors, Messrs. Pargeter, Coleby and Hunt. The will was very short and had been made five years earlier. Lorrimer had left Postmill Cottage and £10,000 to his father, and the rest of his estate absolutely to his cousin, Angela Maud Foley. To judge from the portfolio of investments, Miss Foley would inherit a useful capital sum.

Lastly, Dalgliesh took Lorrimer's bunch of keys from his pocket and unlocked the top left-hand drawer. The lock worked very easily. The drawer was crammed with papers covered with Lorrimer's handwriting. Dalgliesh took them over to the table in front of the window and motioned Massingham to draw up the armchair. They sat there together. There were twenty-eight letters in all and they read them through without speaking. Massingham was aware of Dalgliesh's long fingers picking up each sheet, dropping it from his hand then shifting it across the desk towards him, then picking up the next. The clock seemed to him to be ticking unnaturally loudly and his own breathing to have become embarrassingly obtrusive. The letters were a liturgy of the bitter exfoliation of love. It was all here: the inability to accept that desire was no longer returned, the demand for explanations which, if attempted, could only increase the hurt, the excoriating self-pity, the spasms of irrational renewed hope the petulant outbursts at the obtuseness of the lover unable to see where her happiness lay, the humiliating self-abasement.

'I realise that you won't want to live in the fens. But that needn't be a difficulty, darling. I could get a transfer to the Metropolitan Lab if you prefer London. Or we could find a house in Cambridge or Norwich, a choice of two civilised cities. You once said that you liked to live among the spires. Or if you wished, I could stay on here and we could have a flat in London for you, and I'd join you whenever I could. I ought to be able to make it most Sundays. The week without you would be an eternity, but anything would be bearable if I knew that you belonged to me. You do belong to me. All the books, all the seeking and the reading, what does it come to in the end? Until you taught me that the answer was so simple.'

Some of the letters were highly erotic. They were probably the most difficult of all love letters to write successfully, thought Massingham. Didn't the poor devil know that, once desire was dead, they could only disgust? Perhaps those lovers who used a private nursery talk for their most secret acts were the wisest. At least the eroticism was personal. Here the sexual descriptions were either embarrassingly Lawrentian in their intensity, or coldly clinical. He recognised with surprise an emotion that could only be shame. It wasn't just that some of the outpourings were brutally explicit. He was accustomed to perusing the private pornography of murdered lives; but these letters, with their mixture of crude desire and elevated sentiment, were outside his experience. The naked suffering they expressed seemed to him neurotic, irrational. Sex no longer had any power to shock him; love, he decided, obviously could.

He was struck by the contrast between the tranquillity of the man's room and the turbulence of his mind. He thought: at least this job teaches one not to hoard personal débris. Police work was as effective as religion in teaching a man to live each day as if it were his last. And it wasn't only murder that violated privacy. Any sudden death could do as much. If the helicopter had crashed on landing, what sort of a picture would his leavings present to the world? A conformist, right-wing philistine, obsessed with his physical fitness? *Homme moyen sensuel*, and *moyen* everything else for that matter? He thought of Emma, with whom he slept whenever they got the opportunity, and who, he supposed, would eventually become Lady Dungannon unless, as seemed increasingly likely, she found an elder son with better prospects and more time to devote to her. He wondered what Emma, cheerful hedonist with her frank enjoyment of bed, would have made of these self-indulgent, masturbatory fantasies, this humiliating chronicle of the miseries of defeated love.

One half-sheet was covered with a single name. Domenica, Domenica, Domenica. And then Domenica Lorrimer, a clumsy, uneuphonic linking. Perhaps its infelicity had struck him, for he had written it only once. The letters looked laboured, tentative, like those of a young girl practising in secret the hoped-for married name. All the letters were undated, all without superscription and signature. A number were obviously first drafts, a painful seeking after the elusive world, the holograph scored with deletions.

But now Dalgliesh was pushing towards him the final letter. Here there were no alterations, no uncertainties, and if there had been a previous draft, Lorrimer had destroyed it. This was as clear as an affirma-

189

tion. The words, strongly written in Lorrimer's black upright script, were set out in even lines, neatly as an exercise in calligraphy. Perhaps this was one he had intended to post after all.

'I have been seeking for the words to explain what has happened to me, what you have made happen. You know how difficult this is for me. There have been so many years of writing official reports, the same phrases, the same bleak conclusions. My mind was a computer programmed to death. I was like a man born in darkness, living in a deep cave, crouching for comfort by my small inadequate fire, watching the shadows flickering over the cave drawings and trying to find in their crude outlines some significance, a meaning to existence to help me endure the dark. And then you came and took me by the hand and led me out into the sunlight. And there was the real world, dazzling my eyes with its colour and its beauty. And it needed only your hand and the courage to take a few small steps out of the shadows and imaginings into the light. *Ex umbris et imaginibus in veritatem.*'

Dalgliesh laid the letter down. He said:

' "Lord, let me know mine end, and the number of my days: that I may be certified how long I have to live." Given the choice, Lorrimer would probably have preferred his murder to go unavenged than for any eyes but his to have seen these letters. What do you think of them?'

Massingham was uncertain whether he was expected to comment on their subject matter or their style. He said cautiously:

'The passage about the cave is effective. It looks as if he worked over that one.'

'But not entirely original. An echo of Plato's *Republic*. And like Plato's caveman, the brightness dazzled and the light hurt his eyes. George Orwell wrote somewhere that murder, the unique crime, should result only from strong emotions. Well, here is

190

the strong emotion. But we seem to have the wrong body.'

'Do you think Dr. Howarth knew, sir?'

'Almost certainly. The wonder is that no-one at the Lab apparently did. It's not the kind of information that Mrs. Bidwell, for one, would keep to herself. First, I think, we check with the solicitors that this will still stands, and then we see the lady.'

But this programme was to be changed. The wall telephone rang, shattering the peace of the room. Massingham answered. It was Sergeant Underhill trying, but with small success, to keep the excitement out of his voice.

'There's a Major Hunt of Messrs. Pargeter, Coleby and Hunt of Ely wants to see Mr. Dalgliesh. He'd prefer not to talk over the telephone. He says could you ring and say when it would be convenient for Mr. Dalgliesh to call. And sir, we've got a witness! He's over at Guy's Marsh police station now. The name's Alfred Goddard. He was a passenger last night passing the Lab in the nine-ten bus.'

3

'Running down drive he were like the devil out of hell.'

'Can you describe him, Mr. Goddard?'

'Naw. He weren't old.'

'How young?'

'I never said 'e were young. I never seed 'im near enough to tell. But he didn't run like an old 'un.'

'Running for the bus, perhaps.'

'If 'e were 'e never catched it.'

'He wasn't waving?'

''Course he weren't. Driver couldn't see 'im. No point in waving at back of bloody bus.'

191

Guy's Marsh police station was a red-brick Victorian building with a white wooden pediment, which looked so like an early railway station that Dalgliesh suspected that the nineteenth-century police authority had economised by making use of the same architect and the same set of plans.

Mr. Alfred Goddard, waiting comfortably in the interview room with a huge mug of steaming tea before him, looked perfectly at home, neither gratified nor impressed to find himself a key witness in a murder investigation. He was a nut-brown, wrinkled, under-sized countryman who smelt of strong tobacco, alcohol and cow-dung. Dalgliesh recalled that the early fen settlers had been called 'yellow-bellies' by their highland neighbours because they crawled frog-like over their marshy fields, or 'slodgers' splashing web-footed through the mud. Either would have suited Mr. Goddard. Dalgliesh noticed with interest that he was wearing what looked like a leather thong bound round his left wrist, and guessed that this was dried eel-skin, the ancient charm to ward off rheumatism. The mis-shapen fingers stiffly cradling the mug of tea suggested that the talisman had been less than efficacious.

Dalgliesh doubted whether he would have troubled to come forward if Bill Carney, the conductor of the bus, hadn't known him as a regular on the Wednesday evening service travelling from Ely to Stoney Piggott via Chevisham, and had directed the enquiring police to his remote cottage. Having been summarily dug out of his lair, however, he displayed no particular resentment against Bill Carney or the police, and announced that he was prepared to answer questions if, as he explained, they were put to him 'civil-like'. His main grievance in life was the Stoney Piggott bus: its lateness, infrequency, rising fares and, in particular, the stupidity of the recent experiment of using double-deckers on the Stoney Piggott route and his own subsequent banishment each Wednesday to the upper deck because of his pipe.

'But how fortunate for us that you were there,' Massingham had pointed out. Mr. Goddard had merely snorted into his tea.

Dalgliesh continued with the questioning:

'Is there anything at all you can remember about him, Mr. Goddard? His height, his hair, how he was dressed?'

'Naw. Middling tall and wearing a shortish coat, or mac maybe. Flapping open, maybe.'

'Can you remember the colour?'

'Darkish, maybe. I never seed 'im for more'n a second, see. Then trees got in the way. Bus were moving off when I first set eyes on him.'

Massingham interposed:

'The driver didn't see him, nor did the conductor.'

'More than likely. They was on lower deck. Isn't likely they'd notice. And driver were driving bloody bus.'

Dalgliesh said:

'Mr. Goddard, this is very important. Can you remember whether there were any lights on in the Lab?'

'What do you mean, Lab?'

'The house the figure was running from.'

'Lights in the house? If you mean house why not say house?'

Mr. Goddard pantomimed the ardours of intensive thought, pursing his lips into a grimace and half closing his eyes. They waited. After a nicely judged interval he announced:

'Faint lights, maybe. Not blazing out, mind you. I reckon I seed some lights from bottom windows.'

Massingham asked:

'You're quite sure it was a man?'

Mr. Goddard bestowed on him the glance of mingled reproof and chagrin of a viva-voce candidate faced with what he obviously regards as an unfair question.

'Wearing trousers, wasn't he? If he weren't a man then he ought to have been.'

'But you can't be absolutely sure?'

'Can't be sure of nothing these days. Time was when folk dressed in a decent, God-fearing manner. Man or woman, it were human and it were running. That's all I seed.'

'So it could have been a woman in slacks?'

'Never run like a woman. Daft runners women be, keeping their knees tight together and kicking out ankles like bloody ducks. Pity they don't keep their knees together when they ain't running, I say.'

The deduction was fair enough, thought Dalgliesh. No woman ran precisely like a man. Goddard's first impression had been that of a youngish man running, and that was probably exactly what he had seen. Too much questioning now might only confuse him.

The driver and conductor, summoned from the bus depot and still in uniform, were unable to confirm Goddard's story, but what they were able to add was useful. It is not surprising that neither of them had seen the runner, since the six-foot wall and its over-hanging trees cut off a view of the laboratory from the bottom deck and they could only have glimpsed the house when the bus was passing the open drive and slowing down at the stop. But if Mr. Goddard were right and the figure had only appeared when the bus was moving off, they still wouldn't have seen him.

It was helpful that they were both able to confirm that the bus, on that Wednesday evening at least, was running on time. Bill Carney had actually looked at his watch as they moved away. It had shown nine-twelve. The bus had halted at the stop for a couple of seconds. None of the three passengers had made any preliminary moves to get off, but both the driver and the conductor had noticed a woman waiting in the shadows of the bus shelter and had assumed that she would board. However, she hadn't done so, but had turned away and moved back farther into the shadow of the shelter as the bus drew up. The conductor had thought it strange that she was waiting there, since there wasn't another bus that night. But it had been raining slightly and he had assumed, without thinking about it very deeply, that she had been sheltering. It wasn't his job, as he reasonably pointed out, to drag passengers on the bus if they didn't want a ride.

Dalgliesh questioned them both closely about the woman, but there was little firm information they could give. Both agreed that she had been wearing a headscarf and that the collar of her coat had been turned up at her ears. The driver thought that she had been wearing slacks and a belted mackintosh. Bill Carney agreed about the slacks but thought that she had been wearing a duffle coat. Their only reason for assuming that the figure was a woman was the headscarf. Neither of them could describe it. They thought it unlikely that any of the three passengers on the lower deck would be able to help. Two of them were elderly regulars, both apparently asleep. The third was unknown to them.

Dalgliesh knew that all three would have to be traced. This was one of those time-consuming jobs which were necessary but which seldom produced any worthwhile information. But it was astonishing how much the most unlikely people did notice. The sleepers might have been jogged awake by the slowing down of the bus and have had a clearer look at the woman than either the conductor or driver. Mr. Goddard, not surprisingly, hadn't noticed her. He enquired caustically how a chap was expected to see through the roof of a bloody bus shelter and, in any case, he'd been looking the other way hadn't he, and a good job for them that he had. Dalgliesh hastened to propitiate him and, when his statement was at last completed to the old man's satisfaction, watched him driven back to his cottage, siting in some style, like a tiny upright manikin, in the back of the police car.

But it was another ten minutes before Dalgliesh and Massingham could set out for Ely. Albert Bidwell had presented himself conveniently if belatedly at the police station, bringing with him a hefty sample of the mud from the five-acre field and an air of sullen grievance. Massingham wondered how he and his wife had originally met and what had brought together two such dissimilar personalities. She, he felt sure, was born a cockney; he a fenman. He was taciturn where she was avid for gossip and excitement.

He admitted to taking the telephone call. It was a woman and the message was that Mrs. Bidwell was to go to Leamings to give Mrs. Schofield a hand instead of to the Lab. He couldn't remember if the caller had given her name but didn't think so. He had taken calls from Mrs. Schofield once or twice before when she had rung to ask his wife to help with dinner parties or suchlike. Women's business. He couldn't say whether the voice sounded the same. Asked whether he had assumed that the caller was Mrs. Schofield, he said that he hadn't assumed anything.

Dalgliesh asked:

'Can you remember whether the caller said that your wife was to come to Leamings or go to Leamings?'

The significance of this question obviously escaped him but he received it with surly suspicion and, after a long pause, said he didn't know. When Massingham asked whether it was possible that the caller hadn't been a woman but a man disguising his voice, he gave him a look of concentrated disgust as if deploring a mind that could imagine such sophisticated villainy. But the answer provoked his longest response. He said, in a tone of finality, that he didn't know whether it was a woman, or a man pretending to be a woman, or, maybe, a lass. All he knew was that he'd been asked to

196

give his wife a message, and he'd given it to her. And if he'd known it would cause all this botheration he wouldn't have answered the phone.

And with that they had to be content.

4

In Dalgliesh's experience, solicitors who practised in cathedral cities were invariably agreeably housed, and the office of Messrs. Pargeter, Coleby and Hunt was no exception. It was a well preserved and maintained Regency house with a view of the Cathedral Green, an imposing front door whose ebony-black paint gleamed as if it were still wet, and whose brass knocker in the shape of a lion's head had been polished almost to whiteness. The door was opened by an elderly and very thin clerk, Dickensian in his old-fashioned black suit and stiff collar, whose appearance of lugubrious resignation brightened somewhat at seeing them, as if cheered by the prospect of trouble. He bowed slightly when Dalgliesh introduced himself and said:

'Major Hunt is, of course, expecting you, sir. He is just concluding his interview with a client. If you will step this way he won't keep you waiting more than a couple of minutes.'

The waiting room into which they were shown resembled the sitting-room of a man's club in its comfort and air of controlled disorder. The chairs were leather and so wide and deep that it was difficult to imagine anyone over sixty rising from them without difficulty. Despite the heat from two old-fashioned radiators there was a coke fire burning in the grate. The large, circular mahogany table was spread with magazines devoted to the interests of the landed gentry, most of which looked very old. There was a glass-fronted bookcase packed with bound histories of the county and illustrated volumes on architecture and painting. The oil over the mantelpiece of a phaeton with horses and attendant grooms, looked very like a Stubbs, and, thought Dalgliesh, probably was.

He only had time briefly to inspect the room, and had walked over to the window to look out towards the Lady Chapel of the cathedral when the door opened and the clerk reappeared to usher them into Major Hunt's office. The man who rose from behind his desk to receive them was in appearance the opposite of his clerk. He was a stocky, upright man in late middle age, dressed in a shabby but well tailored tweed suit, ruddy-faced and balding, his eyes keen under the spiky, restless eyebrows. He gave Dalgliesh a frankly appraising glance as he shook hands, as if deciding where exactly to place him in some private scheme of things, then nodded as if satisfied. He still looked more like a soldier than a solicitor, and Dalgliesh guessed that the voice with which he greeted them had acquired its loud authoritative bark across the parade-grounds and in the messes of the Second World War.

'Good morning, good morning. Please sit down, Commander. You come on tragic business. I don't think we have ever lost one of our clients by murder before.'

The clerk coughed. It was just such a cough as Dalgliesh would have expected, inoffensive but discreetly minatory and not to be ignored.

'There was Sir James Cummins, sir in 1923. He was shot by his neighbour, Captain Cartwright, because of the seduction of Mrs. Cartwright by Sir James, a grievance aggravated by some unpleasantness over fishing rights.'

'Quite right, Mitching. But that was in my father's time. They hanged poor Cartwright. A pity, my father always thought. He had a good war record – survived the Somme and Arras and ended on the scaffold.

198

Battle-scarred, poor devil. The jury would probably have made a recommendation to mercy if he hadn't cut up the body. He did cut up the body, didn't he, Mitching?'

'Quite right, sir. They found the head buried in the orchard.'

'That's what did for Cartwright. English juries won't stand for cutting up the body. Crippen would be alive today if he'd buried Belle Elmore in one piece.'

'Hardly, sir. Crippen was born in 1860.'

'Well he wouldn't have been long dead. It wouldn't surprise me if he'd reached his century. Only three years older than your father, Mitching, and much the same build, small, pop-eyed and wiry. They live for ever, that type. Ah well, to our muttons. You'll both take coffee, I hope. I can promise you it will be drinkable. Mitching has installed one of those glass retort affairs and we grind our own fresh beans. Coffee then, please Mitching.'

'Miss Makepeace is preparing it now, sir.'

Major Hunt exuded postprandial well being, and Massingham guessed, with some envy, that his business with his last client had been chiefly done over a good lunch. He and Dalgliesh had snatched a hurried sandwich and beer at a pub between Chevisham and Guy's Marsh. Dalgliesh, known to enjoy food and wine, had an inconvenient habit of ignoring mealtimes when in the middle of a case. Massingham wasn't fussy about the quality; it was the quantity he deplored. But, at least, they were to get coffee.

Mitching had stationed himself near the door and showed no inclination to leave. This was apparently perfectly acceptable. Dalgliesh thought that they were like a couple of comedians in the process of perfecting their antiphonal patter, and reluctant to lose any opportunity of practising it. Major Hunt said:

'You want to know about Lorrimer's will, of course.'

'And anything else you can tell us about him.'

'That won't be much, I'm afraid. I've only seen him twice since I dealt with his grandmother's estate. But of course I'll do what I can. When murder comes in at the window privacy goes out of the door. That's so, isn't it Mitching?'

'There are no secrets, sir, in the fierce light that beats upon the scaffold.'

'I'm not sure that you've got that one right, Mitching. And we don't have scaffolds now. Are you an abolutionist, Commander?'

Dalgliesh said:

'I'm bound to be until the day comes when we can be absolutely sure that we could never under any circumstances make a mistake.'

'That's the orthodox answer, but it begs quite a lot of questions, doesn't it? Still you're not here to discuss capital punishment. Mustn't waste time. Now the will. Where did I put Mr. Lorrimer's box, Mitching?'

'It's here, sir.'

'Then bring it over, man. Bring it over.'

The clerk carried the black tin box from a side table and placed it in front of Major Hunt. The Major opened it with some ceremony and took out the will. Dalgliesh said:

'We've found one will in his desk. It's dated the third of May 1971. It looks like the original.'

'So he didn't destroy it? That's interesting. It suggests that he hadn't finally made up his mind.'

'So there's a later will?'

'Oh, indeed there is, Commander. Indeed there is. That's what I wanted to talk to you about. Signed by him only last Friday and both the original and the only copy left here with me. I have them here. Perhaps you'd like to read it yourself.'

He handed over the will. It was very short. Lorrimer, in the accepted form, revoked all previous wills,

200

proclaimed himself to be of sound mind and disposed of all his property in less than a dozen lines. Postmill Cottage was left to his father together with a sum of ten thousand pounds. One thousand pounds was left to Brenda Pridmore 'to enable her to buy any books required to further her scientific education'. All the rest of his estate was left to the Academy of Forensic Science to provide an annual cash prize of such amount as the Academy should see fit for an original essay on any aspect of the scientific investigation of crime, the essay to be judged by three judges selected annually by the Academy. There was no mention of Angela Foley.

Dalgliesh said:

'Did he give you any explanation why he left his cousin, Angela Foley, out of the will?'

'As a matter of fact he did. I thought it right to point out that in the event of his death his cousin, as his only surviving relative apart from his father, might wish to contest the will. If she did, a legal battle would cost money and might seriously deplete the estate. I didn't feel any obligation to press him to alter his decision. I merely thought it right to point out the possible consequences. You heard what he replied, didn't you, Mitching?'

'Yes, indeed, sir. The late Mr. Lorrimer expressed his disapprobation of the way in which his cousin chose to live, in particular he deplored the relationship, which, he alleged, subsisted between his cousin and the lady with whom I understand she makes her home, and said that he did not wish the said companion to benefit from his estate. If his cousin chose to contest the will, he was prepared to leave the matter to the courts. It would no longer be of any concern to himself. He would have made his wishes clear. He also pointed out, if I remember rightly, sir, that the will was intended to be transitional in its nature. He had it in mind to marry and if he did so the will would, of course, become void. In the meantime he wished to guard against what he saw as the remote contingency of his cousin inheriting absolutely should he die unexpectedly before his personal affairs became clearer.'

'That's right, Mitching, that in effect is what he said. I must say that it reconciled me somewhat to the new will. If he were proposing to get married obviously it would no longer stand and he could think again. Not that I thought it necessarily an unjust or unfair will. A man has the right to dispose of his property as he sees fit, if the state leaves him anything to dispose of. It struck me as a bit odd that, if he were engaged to be married, he didn't mention the lady in the interim will. But I suppose the principle's sound enough. If he'd left her a paltry sum she'd hardly have thanked him, and if he'd left her the lot, she'd probably promptly have married another chap and it would all pass to him.'

Dalgliesh asked:

'He didn't tell you anything about the proposed marriage?'

'Not even the lady's name. And naturally I didn't ask. I'm not even sure that he had anyone particular in mind. It could have been only a general intention, or, perhaps, an excuse for altering the will. I merely congratulated him and pointed out that the new will would be void as soon as the marriage took place. He said that he understood that and would be coming to make a new will in due course. In the meantime this was what he wanted and this was what I drew up. Mitching signed it, with my secretary as a second witness. Ah, here she is with the coffee. You remember signing Mr. Lorrimer's will, eh?'

The thin, nervous-looking girl who had brought in the coffee gave a terrified nod in response to the Major's bark and hastened out of the room. Major Hunt said with satisfaction:

'She remembers. She was so terrified that she could

hardly sign. But she did sign. It's all there. All correct and in order. I hope we can draw up a valid will, eh, Mitching? But it will be interesting to see if the little woman makes a fight for it.'

Dalgliesh asked how much Angela Foley would be making a fight for.

'The best part of £50,000, I daresay. Not a fortune these days but useful, useful. The original capital was left to him absolutely by old Annie Lorrimer, his paternal grandmother. An extraordinary old woman. Born and bred in the fens. Kept a village store with her husband over at Low Willow. Tom Lorrimer drank himself into a comparatively early grave – couldn't stand the fen winters – and she carried on alone. Not all the money came from the shop, of course, although she sold out at a good time. No, she had a nose for the horses. Extraordinary thing. God knows where she got it from. Never mounted a horse in her life to my knowledge. Shut up the shop and went to Newmarket three times a year. Never lost a penny, so I've heard, and saved every pound she won.'

'What family had she? Was Lorrimer's father her only son?'

'That's right. She had one son and one daughter, Angela Foley's mother. Couldn't bear the sight of either of them, as far as I can see. The daughter got herself in the family way by the village sexton and the old woman cast her off in approved Victorian style. The marriage turned out badly and I don't think Maud Foley saw her mother again. She died of cancer about five years after the girl was born. The old woman wouldn't have her granddaughter back, so she ended up in local authority care. Most of her life's been spent in foster homes, I believe.'

'And the son?'

'Oh, he married the local schoolmistress, and that turned out reasonably well as far as I know. But the family were never close. The old lady wouldn't leave

203

her money to her son because, she said, it would mean two lots of death duties. She was well over forty when he was born. But I think the real reason was simply that she didn't much like him. I don't think she saw much of the grandson, Edwin, either, but she had to leave the money somewhere and hers was a generation which believes that blood is thicker than charitable soup and male blood thicker than female. Apart from the fact she'd cast off her daughter and never taken any interest in her granddaughter, her generation didn't believe in leaving money outright to women. It only encourages seducers and fortune-hunters. So she left it absolutely to her grandson, Edwin Lorrimer. At the time of her death I think he had qualms of conscience about his cousin. As you know, the first will made her his legatee.'

Dalgliesh said:

'Do you know if Lorrimer told her that he intended to change his will?'

The solicitor looked at him sharply.

'He didn't say. In the circumstances it would be convenient for her if she could prove that he did.'

So convenient, thought Dalgliesh, that she would certainly have mentioned the fact when first interviewed. But even if she had believed herself to be her cousin's heir, that didn't necessarily make her a murderess. If she wanted a share of her grandmother's money, why wait until now to kill for it?

The telephone rang. Major Hunt muttered an apology and reached for the receiver. Holding his palm over the mouthpiece, he said to Dalgliesh:

'It's Miss Foley, ringing from Postmill Cottage. Old Mr. Lorrimer wants to have a word with me about the will. She says he's anxious to know whether the cottage now belongs to him. Do you want me to tell him?'

'That is for you. But he's the next of kin; he may as well know the terms of the will now as later. And so may she.'

Major Hunt hesitated. Then he spoke into the receiver.

'All right, Betty. Put Miss Foley on the line.'

He looked up again at Dalgliesh.

'This piece of news is going to put the cat among the pigeons in Chevisham.'

Dalgliesh had a sudden picture of Brenda Pridmore's eager young face shining across Howarth's desk at him.

'Yes,' he said grimly. 'Yes, I'm afraid it is.'

5

Howarth's house, Leamings, was three miles outside Chevisham village on the Cambridge road, a modern building of concrete, wood and glass cantilevered above the flat fenlands, with two white wings like folded sails. Even in the fading light it was impressive. The house stood in uncompromising and splendid isolation, depending for its effect on nothing but perfection of line and artful simplicity. No other building was in sight except a solitary black wooden cottage on stilts, desolate as an execution shed, and, dramatically, an intricate mirage hung above the eastern skyline, the marvellous single tower and octagon of Ely Cathedral. From the rooms at the back one would see an immensity of sky and look out over vast unhedged fields dissected by Leamings' dyke, changing with the seasons from black scarred earth, through the spring sowing to the harvest; would hear nothing but the wind and, in summer, the ceaseless susurration of the grain.

The site had been small and the architect had needed ingenuity. There was no garden, nothing but a short drive leading to a paved courtyard and the double garage. Outside the garage, a red Jaguar XJS stood beside Howarth's Triumph. Massingham cast envious eyes on the Jaguar and wondered how Mrs. Schofield had managed to get such quick delivery. They drove in and parked beside it. Even before Dalgliesh had switched off the engine, Howarth had strolled out and was quietly waiting for them. He was wearing a butcher's long blue and white striped overall in which he seemed perfectly at ease, evidently seeing no need either to explain or remove it. As they made their way up the open-tread, carved wooden stairs Dalgliesh complimented him on the house. Howarth said:

'It was designed by a Swedish architect who did some of the modern additions at Cambridge. Actually it belongs to a university friend. He and his wife are spending a couple of years' sabbatical at Harvard. If they decide to stay on in the States, they may sell. Anyway, we're settled for the next eighteen months, and can then look around if we have to.'

They were mounting a wide circular wooden staircase rising from the well of the house. Upstairs someone was playing, very loudly, a record of the finale of the third Brandenburg Concerto. The glorious contrapuntal sound beat against the walls and surged through the house; Massingham could almost imagine it taking off on its white wings and rollicking joyously over the fens. Dalgliesh said, above the music:

'Mrs. Schofield likes it here?'

Howarth's voice, carefully casual, came down to talk to them. 'Oh, she may have moved on by then. Domenica likes variety. My half-sister suffers from Baudelaire's *horreur de domicile* – she usually prefers to be elsewhere. Her natural habitat is London, but she's with me now because she's illustrating a new limited edition of Crabbe for the Paradine Press.'

The record came to an end. Howarth paused and said with a kind of roughness, as if regretting an impulse to confide:

'I think I ought to tell you that my sister was widowed just over eighteen months ago. Her husband was killed in a car crash. She was driving at the time but she was lucky. At least, I suppose she was lucky. She was scarcely scratched. Charles Schofield died three days later.'

'I'm sorry,' said Dalgliesh. The cynic in him wondered why he had been told. Howarth had struck him as essentially a private man, one not lightly to confide a personal or family tragedy. Was it an appeal to chivalry, a covert plea for him to treat her with special consideration? Or was Howarth warning him that she was still distraught with grief, unpredictable, unbalanced even? He could hardly be implying that, since the tragedy, she had indulged an irresistible impulse to kill her lovers.

They had reached the top of the stairs and were standing on a wide wooden balcony seemingly hung in space. Howarth pushed open a door and said:

'I'll leave you to it. I'm making an early start on cooking dinner tonight. She's in here.' He called:

'This is Commander Dalgliesh and Detective Inspector Massingham of the Met. The men about the murder. My sister, Domenica Schofield.'

The room was immense, with a triangular window from roof to floor jutting out over the fields like a ship's prow, and a high curved ceiling of pale pine. The furniture was scant and very modern. The room looked, in fact, more like a musician's studio than a sitting-room. Against the wall was a jangle of music stands and violin cases and, mounted above them, a bank of modern and obviously expensive stereo equipment. There was only one picture, a Sidney Nolan oil of Ned Kelly. The faceless metallic mask, with the two anonymous eyes gleaming through the slit, was appropriate to the austerity of the room, the stark blackness of the darkening fens. It was easy to imagine him, a grim latter-day Hereward, striding over the clogging acres.

Domenica Schofield was standing at a drawing desk placed in the middle of the room. She turned, un-smilingly, to look at them with her brother's eyes, and Dalgliesh encountered again those disconcerting pools of blue under the thick, curved brows. As always, in those increasingly rare moments when, unexpectedly, he came face to face with a beautiful woman, his heart jerked. It was a pleasure more sensual than sexual and he was glad that he could still feel it, even in the middle of a murder investigation.

But he wondered how studied was that smooth deli-berate turn, that first gaze, remote yet speculative, from the remarkable eyes. In this light, the irises, like those of her brother, were almost purple, the whites stained with a paler blue. She had a pale, honey-coloured skin, with flaxen hair drawn back from the forehead and tied in a clump at the base of her neck. Her blue jeans were pulled tightly over the strong thighs and were topped with an open-necked shirt of checkered blue and green. Dalgliesh judged her to be about ten years younger than her half-brother. When she spoke, her voice was curiously low for a woman, with a hint of gruffness.

'Sit down.' She waved her right hand vaguely to-wards one of the chrome and leather chairs. 'You don't mind if I go on working?'

'Not if you don't mind being talked to while you do, and if you don't object to my sitting while you stand.'

He swung the chair closer to her easel, from where he could see both her face and her work, and settled himself. The chair was remarkably comfortable. He sensed that already she was regretting her lack of civility. In any confrontation the one standing has a psychological advantage, but not if the adversary is sitting very obviously at ease in a spot he has himself selected. Massingham, with an almost ostentatious quietness, had lifted a second chair for himself and placed it against the wall to the left of the door. She must have been aware of his presence at her back, but she gave no sign. She could hardly object to a situation she had herself contrived, but, as if sensing that the interview had started unpropitiously, she said:

'I'm sorry to seem so obsessively busy, but I have a deadline to meet. My brother's probably told you that I'm illustrating a new edition of Crabbe's poems for the Paradine Press. This drawing is for "Procrastination" – Dinah among her curious trifles.'

Dalgliesh had known that she must be a competent professional artist to have gained the commission, but he was impressed by the sensitivity and assurance of the line-drawing before him. It was remarkably detailed but unfinicky, a highly decorative and beautifully composed balance of the girl's slender figure and Crabbe's carefully enumerated objects of desire. They were all there, meticulously drawn; the figured wallpaper, the rose carpet, the mounted stag's head and the jewelled, enamelled clock. It was, he thought, a very English illustration of the most English of poets. She was taking trouble with the period details. On the right-hand wall was mounted a cork board on which was pinned what were obviously preliminary sketches; a tree, half-finished interiors, articles of furniture, small impressions of landscape. She said:

'It's as well one doesn't have to like a poet's work to illustrate him competently. Who was it called Crabbe "Pope in worsted stockings"? After twenty lines my brain begins to thud in rhymed couplets. But perhaps you're an Augustan. You write verse, don't you?'

She made it sound as if he collected cigarette cards for a hobby.

Dalgliesh said:

'I've respected Crabbe ever since I read as a boy that Jane Austen said she could have fancied being Mrs. Crabbe. When he went to London for the first time

209

he was so poor that he had to pawn all his clothes, and then he spent the money on an edition of Dryden's poems.'

'And you approve of that?'

'I find it appealing.' He quoted:

' "Miseries there were, and woes the world around,
But these had not her pleasant dwelling found;
She knew that mothers grieved and widows wept
And she was sorry, said her prayers and slept:
For she indulged, nor was her heart so small
That one strong passion should engross it all." '

She gave him a swift elliptical glance.

'In this case there is happily no mother to grieve nor widow to weep. And I gave up saying my prayers when I was nine. Or were you only proving that you could quote Crabbe?'

'That, of course,' replied Dalgliesh. 'Actually I came to talk to you about these.'

He took a bundle of the letters out of his coat pocket, opened one of the pages and held it out towards her. He asked:

'This is Lorrimer's handwriting?'

She glanced dismissively at the page.

'Of course. It's a pity he didn't send them. I should have liked to have read them, but not now perhaps.'

'I don't suppose they're so very different from the ones he did post.'

For a moment he thought that she was about to deny receiving any. He thought: 'She's remembered that we can easily check with the postman.' He watched the blue eyes grow wary. She said:

'That's how love ends, not with a bang, but a whimper.'

'Less than a whimper than a cry of pain.'

She wasn't working, but stood still, scrutinising the drawing. She said:

'It's extraordinary how unattractive misery is. He'd

210

have done better to have tried honesty. "It means a lot to me, it doesn't mean very much to you. So why not be generous? It won't cost you anything except an occasional half-hour of your time." I'd have respected him more.'

'But he wasn't asking for a commercial arrangement,' said Dalgliesh. 'He was asking for love.'

'That's something I didn't have to give, and he had no right to expect.'

None of us, thought Dalgliesh, have a right to expect it. But we do. Irrelevantly a phrase of Plutarch fell into his mind. 'Boys throw stones at frogs in sport. But the frogs do not die in sport, they die in earnest.'

'When did you break it off?' he asked.

She looked surprised for a moment.

'I was going to ask you how you knew that I'd done the breaking. But, of course, you've got the letters. I suppose he was whining. I told him that I didn't want to see him again about two months ago. I haven't spoken to him since.'

'Did you give him a reason.'

'No. I'm not sure that there was a reason. Does there have to be?' There wasn't another man if that's what you have in mind. What a beautifully simple view you must have of life. I suppose the police work produces a card-index mentality. Victim – Edwin Lorrimer. Crime – Murder. Accused – Domenica Schofield. Motive – Sex. Verdict – Guilty. What a pity that you can't any longer finish it off neatly with Sentence – Death. Let's say I was tired of him.'

'When you'd exhausted his possibilities, sexual and emotional?'

'Say intellectual, rather, if you'll forgive the arrogance. I find that one exhausts the physical possibilities fairly soon, don't you? But if a man has wit, intelligence, and his own peculiar enthusiasms, then there's some kind of purpose in the relationship. I knew a man once who was an authority on seventeenth-century church architecture. We used to drive for miles looking at churches. It was fascinating while it lasted, and I now know quite a lot about the late seventeenth century. That's something on the credit side.'

'Whereas Lorrimer's only intellectual enthusiasms were popular philosophy and forensic science.'

'Forensic biology. He was curiously inhibited about discussing it. The Official Secrets Act was probably engraved on what he would have described as his soul. Besides, he could be boring even about his job. Scientists invariably are, I've discovered. My brother is the only scientist I've ever met who doesn't bore me after the first ten minutes of his company.'

'Where did you make love?'

'That's impertinent. And is it relevant?'

'It could be – to the number of people who knew that you were lovers.'

'No-one knew. I don't relish my private affairs being giggled over in the women's loo at Hoggatt's.'

'So no-one knew except your brother and yourself?'

They must have decided in advance that it would be stupid and dangerous to deny that Howarth had known. She said:

'I hope you're not going to ask whether he approved.

'No. I took it for granted that he disapproved.'

'Why the hell should you?' The tone was intended to be light, almost bantering, but Dalgliesh could detect the sharp edge of defensive anger. He said mildly:

'I am merely putting myself in his place. If I had just started a new job, and one of some difficulty, my half-sister's affair with a member of my own staff, and one who probably thought he'd been supplanted, would be a complication I'd prefer to do without.'

'Perhaps you lack my brother's confidence. He didn't need Edwin Lorrimer's support to run his Lab effectively.'

'You brought him here?'

'Seducing one of my brother's staff here in his own house? Had I disliked my brother, it might have given the affair extra piquancy. Towards the end I admit it could have done with it. But as I don't, it would merely have been in poor taste. We both have cars, and his is particularly roomy.'

'I thought that was the expedient of randy adolescents. It must have been uncomfortable and cold.'

'Very cold. Which was another reason for deciding to stop it.' She turned to him with sudden vehemence.

'Look, I'm not trying to shock you. I'm trying to be truthful. I hate death and waste and violence. Who doesn't? But I'm not grieving, in case you thought of offering condolences. There's only one man whose death has grieved me, and it isn't Edwin Lorrimer. And I don't feel responsible. Why should I? I'm not responsible. Even if he killed himself I shouldn't feel that it was my fault. As it is, I don't believe his death had anything to do with me. He might, I suppose, have felt like murdering me. I never had the slightest motive for murdering him.'

'Have you any idea who did?'

'A stranger, I imagine. Someone who broke into the Lab either to plant or to destroy some forensic evidence. Perhaps a drunken driver hoping to get his hands on his blood sample. Edwin surprised him and the intruder killed him.'

'The blood alcohol analysis isn't done in the Biology Department.'

'Then it could have been an enemy, someone with a grudge. Someone he'd given evidence against in the past. After all, he's probably well known in the witness box. Death of an expert witness.'

Dalgliesh said:

'There's the difficulty of how his killer got in and out of the Lab.'

'He probably gained entrance during the day and

213

hid after the place was locked up for the night. I leave it to you to discover how he got away. Perhaps he slipped out after the Lab had been opened for the morning during the kerfuffle after that girl – Brenda Pridmore, isn't it? – discovered the body. I don't suppose that anyone was keeping an eye on the front door.'

'And the false telephone call to Mrs. Bidwell?'

'Probably no connection, I'd say. Just someone trying to be funny. She's probably too scared to admit what happened. I should question the junior female staff of the Lab if I were you. It's the kind of joke a rather unintelligent adolescent might find amusing.'

Dalgliesh went on to ask her about her movements on the previous evening. She said that she hadn't accompanied her brother to the concert, having a dislike of rustic junketing, no wish to hear the Mozart indifferently played, and a couple of drawings to complete. They'd had an early supper at about six-forty-five, and Howarth had left home at seven-twenty. She had continued working uninterrupted either by a telephone call or a visitor until her brother returned shortly after ten, when he had told her about his evening over a shared nightcap of hot whisky. Both of them had then gone early to bed.

She volunteered without being asked that her brother had seemed perfectly normal on his return, although both of them had been tired. He had attended a murder scene the night before and had lost some hours' sleep. She did occassionally make use of Mrs. Bidwell, for example before and after a dinner party she and Howarth had given soon after their arrival, but certainly wouldn't call on her on a day when she was due at the Lab.

Dalgliesh asked:

'Did your brother tell you that he left the concert for a time after the interval?'

'He told me that he sat on a tombstone for about

214

half an hour contemplating mortality. I imagine that, at that stage of the proceedings, he found the dead more entertaining than the living.'

Dalgliesh looked up at the immense curved wooden ceiling. He said:

'This place must be expensive to keep warm in winter. How is it heated?'

Again there was that swift elliptical flash of blue.

'By gas central heating. There isn't an open fire. That's one of the things we miss. So we couldn't have burnt Paul Middlemass's white coat. Actually, we'd have been fools to try. The most sensible plan would be to weigh it down with stones in the pockets and sling it into Leamings' sluice. You'd probably dredge it up in the end, but I don't see how that would help you to discover who put it there. That's what I would have done.'

'No, you wouldn't,' said Dalgliesh mildly. 'There weren't any pockets.'

She didn't offer to see them out, but Howarth was waiting for them at the foot of the stairs. Dalgliesh said:

'You didn't tell me that your sister was Lorrimer's mistress. Did you really convince yourself that it wasn't relevant?'

'To his death? Why should it be? It may have been relevant to his life. I very much doubt whether it was to hers. And I'm not my sister's keeper. She's capable of speaking for herself, as you've probably discovered.'

He walked with them out to the car, punctilious as a host speeding a couple of unwelcome guests. Dalgliesh said, his hand on the car door:

'Does the number 1840 mean anything to you?'

'In what context?'

'Any you choose.'

Howarth said calmly:

'Whewell published *Philosophy of the Inductive Sciences*; Tchaikovsky was born; Berlioz composed the

215

Symphonie Funèbre et Triomphale. I think that's the limit of my knowledge of an unremarkable year. Or if you want a different context, the ratio of the mass of the proton to the mass of the electron.'

Massingham called from the other side of the Rover:

'I thought that was 1836, unless you're not fussy about rounding up. Goodnight, sir.'

As they turned out of the drive, Dalgliesh asked:

'How do you come to remember that remarkably irrelevant piece of information?'

'From school. We may have been disadvantaged when it came to social mix, but the teaching wasn't bad. It's a figure which sticks in the mind.'

'Not in mine. What did you think of Mrs. Schofield?'

'I didn't expect her to be like that.'

'As attractive, as talented, or as arrogant?'

'All three. Her face reminds me of someone, an actress. French I think.'

'Simone Signoret when she was young. I'm surprised that you're old enough to remember.'

'I saw a revival last year of *Casque d'Or.*'

Dalgliesh said: 'She told us at least one small lie.'

Apart, thought Massingham, from the one major lie which she may or may not have told. He was experienced enough to know that it was the central lie, the affirmation of innocence, which was the most difficult to detect; and the small, ingenious fabrications, so often unnecessary, which in the end confused and betrayed.

'Sir?'

'About where she and Lorrimer made love, in the back of his car. I don't believe that. Do you?'

It was rare for Dalgliesh to question a subordinate so directly. Massingham disconcertingly felt himself under test. He gave careful thought before replying.

'Psychologically it could be wrong. She's a fastidious, comfort-loving woman with a high opinion of her

216

own dignity. And she must have watched the body of her husband being pulled from the wreckage of their car after that accident when she'd been driving. Somehow I don't think she'd fancy sex in the back of anyone's car. Unless, of course, she's trying to exorcise the memory. It could be that.'

Dalgliesh smiled. 'Actually I was thinking on less esoteric lines. A scarlet Jaguar, and the latest model, is hardly the most inconspicuous vehicle for driving round the country with a lover. And old Mr. Lorrimer said that his son hardly left home in the evenings or at night, unless to a murder scene. These are unpredictable. On the other hand he was frequently late at the Lab. Not all the lateness could have been work. I think that he and Mrs. Schofield had a rendezvous somewhere fairly close.'

'You think it important, sir?'

'Important enough to cause her to lie. Why should she care if we know where they chose to disport themselves? I could understand it if she told us to mind our own business. But why bother to lie? There was another moment, too, when very briefly she lost composure. It was when she talked about seventeenth-century church architecture. I got the impression that there was a small, almost undetectable moment of confusion when she realised that she'd stumbled into saying something indiscreet, or at least something she wished unsaid. When the interviews are out of the way tomorrow, I think we'll take a look at the chapel at Hoggatt's.'

'But Sergeant Reynolds had a look at it this morning, sir, after he'd searched the grounds. It's just a locked, empty chapel. He found nothing.'

'Probably because there's nothing to find. It's just a hunch. Now we'd better get back to Guy's Marsh for that Press conference and then I must have a word with the Chief Constable if he's back. After that I'd like to see Brenda Pridmore again; and I want to call

217

later at the Old Rectory for a word with Dr. Kerrison.
But that can wait until we've seen what Mrs. Gotobed
at the Moonraker can do about dinner.'

6

Twenty minutes later, in the kitchen at Leamings, an
incongruous compromise between a laboratory and
rustic domesticity, Howarth was mixing *sauce vinaigrette*. The sickly, pungent smell of the olive oil,
curving in a thin golden stream from the bottle,
brought back as always, memories of Italy and of his
father, that dilettante collector of trivia, who had
spent most of each year in Tuscany or Venice, and
whose self-indulgent, hypochondriacal, solitary life
had ended, appropriately enough since he affected to
dread old age, on his fiftieth birthday. He had been
less a stranger to his two motherless children than an
enigma, seldom with them in person, always present
mysteriously to their minds.

Maxim recalled a memory of his dressing-gowned
figure, patterned in mauve and gold, standing at the
foot of his bed on that extraordinary night of muted
voices, sudden running footsteps, inexplicable silences,
in which his step-mother had died. He had been home
from prep-school for the holidays, eight years old, ignored in the crisis of the illness, frightened and alone.
He remembered clearly his father's thin, rather weary
voice, already assuming the langours of grief.

'Your step-mother died ten minutes ago, Maxim.
Evidently fate does not intend me to be a husband. I
shall not again risk such grief. You, my boy, must look
after your step-sister. I rely on you.' And then a cold
hand casually laid on his shoulder as if conferring a
burden. He had accepted it, literally, at eight years
old, and had never laid it down. At first the immensity

of the trust had appalled him. He remembered how he had lain there, terrified, staring into the darkness. Look after your sister. Domenica was three months old. How could he look after her? What ought he to feed her on? How dress her? What about his prep-school? They wouldn't let him stay at home to look after his sister. He smiled wryly, remembering his relief at discovering next morning that her nurse was, after all, to remain. He recalled his first efforts to assume responsibility, resolutely seizing the pram handles and straining to push it up the Broad Walk, struggling to lift Domenica into her high chair.

'Give over, Master Maxim, do. You're more of a hindrance than a help.'

But afterwards the nurse had begun to realise that he was becoming more of a help than a nuisance, that the child could safely be left with him while she and the only other servant pursued their own unsupervised devices. Most of his school holidays had been spent helping to look after Domenica. From Rome, Verona, Florence and Venice his father, through his solicitor, sent instructions about allowances and schools. It was he who helped buy the clothes, took her to school, comforted and advised. He had attempted to support her through the agonies and uncertainties of adolescence, even before he had outgrown his own. He had been her champion against the world. He smiled, remembering the telephone call to Cambridge from her boarding school, asking him to fetch her that very night 'outside the hockey pavilion – gruesome torture house – at midnight. I'll climb down the fire escape. Promise.' And then their private code of defiance and allegiance: *'Contra mundum.'*

'Contra mundum.'

His father's arrival from Italy, so little perturbed by the Reverend Mother's insistent summons that it was obvious that he had, in any case, been planning to return.

219

'Your sister's departure was unnecessarily eccentric, surely. Midnight assignation. Dramatic car drive across half England. Mother Superior seemed particularly pained that she had left her trunk behind, although I can appreciate that it would have been an encumbrance on the fire escape. And you must have been out of college all night. Your tutor can't have liked that.'

'I'm post-graduate now, Father. I took my degree eighteen months ago.'

'Indeed. Time passes so quickly at my age. Physics, wasn't it? A curious choice. Couldn't you have called for her after school in the orthodox way?'

'We wanted to get as far away from the place as possible before they noticed she'd gone and started looking.'

'A reasonable strategy, so far as it goes.'

'Dom hates school, Father. She's utterly miserable there.'

'So was I at school, but it never occurred to me to expect otherwise. Reverend Mother seems a charming woman. A tendency to halitosis when under stress, but I shouldn't have thought that would have troubled your sister. They can hardly have come into intimate contact. She isn't prepared to have Domenica back, by the way.'

'Need Dom go anywhere, Father? She's nearly fifteen. She doesn't have to go to school. And she wants to be a painter.'

'I suppose she could stay at home until she's old enough for art college, if that's what you advise. But it's hardly worth opening the London house just for one. I shall return to Venice next week. I'm only here to consult Dr. Mavers-Brown.'

'Perhaps she could go back to Italy with you for a month or so. She'd love to see the Accademia. And she ought to see Florence.'

'Oh, I don't think that would do, my boy. Quite out

of the question. She had much better take a room at Cambridge and you can keep an eye on her. They have some quite agreeable pictures in the Fitzwillian Museum. Oh dear, what a responsibility children are! It's quite wrong that I should be troubled like this in my state of health. Mavers-Brown was insistent that I avoid anxiety.'

And now he lay coffined in his final self-sufficiency, in that most beautiful of burial grounds, the British Cemetery at Rome. He would have liked that, thought Maxim, if he could have borne the thought of his death at all, as much as he would have resented the over-aggressive Italian drivers whose ill-judged acceleration at the junction of the Via Vittoria and the Corso had placed him there.

He heard his sister's steps on the stairs.

'So they've gone.'

'Twenty minutes ago. We had a brief valedictory skirmish. Was Dalgliesh offensive?'

'No more offensive than I to him. Honours even, I should have said. I don't think he liked me.'

'I don't think he likes anyone much. But he's considered highly intelligent. Did you find him attractive?'

She answered the unspoken question.

'It would be like making love to a public hangman.' She dipped her finger in the vinaigrette dressing. 'Too much vinegar. What have you been doing?'

'Apart from cooking? Thinking about father. Do you know, Dom, when I was eleven I became absolutely convinced that he'd murdered our mothers.'

'Both of them? I mean yours and mine? What an odd idea. How could he have? Yours died of cancer and mine of pneumonia. He couldn't have fixed that.'

'I know. It's just that he seemed such a natural widower. I thought at the time that he'd done it to stop them having any more babies.'

221

'Well it would do that all right. Were you wondering whether a tendency to murder is inherited?'

'Not really. But so much is. Father's total inability to make relationships, for example. That incredible self-absorption. Do you know, he'd actually put me down for Stonyhurst before he remembered that it was your mother, not mine, who'd been R.C.'

'A pity he did find out. I should like to have seen what the Jesuits made of you. The trouble with a religious education, if you're a pagan like me, is that you're left all your life feeling that you've lost something, not that it isn't there.'

She walked over to the table and stirred a bowl of mushrooms with her finger.

'I can make relationships. The trouble is that I get bored and they don't last. And I only seem to know one way to be kind. It's as well that we last, isn't it? You'll last for me until the day I die. Shall I change now, or do you want me to see to the wine?'

'You'll last for me until the day I die.' *Contra mundum.* It was too late now to sever that cord even if he wanted to. He remembered Charles Schofield's gauze-cocooned head, the dying eyes still malicious behind two slits in the bandages, the swollen lips painfully moving.

'Congratulations, Giovanni. Remember me in your garden in Parma.'

What had been so astounding was not the lie itself, or that Schofield had believed it, or pretended to believe it, but that he had hated his brother-in-law enough to die with that taunt on his lips. Or had he taken it for granted that a physicist, poor philistine, wouldn't know his Jacobean dramatists? Even his wife, that indefatigable sexual sophisticate, had known better.

'I suppose you'd sleep together if Domenica happened to want it. A spot of incest wouldn't worry her. But you don't need to, do you? You don't need anything as normal as sex to be more to each other than you are. Neither of you wants anyone else. That's why I'm leaving. I'm getting out now while there's still something left of me to get out.'

'Max, what is it?'

Domenica's voice, sharpened with anxiety, recalled him to the present. His mind spun back through a kaleidoscope of spinning years, through superimposed whirling images of childhood and youth, to that last unforgettable image, still, perfectly in focus, patterned for ever in his memory, Lorrimer's dead fingers clawing at the floor of his laboratory, Lorrimer's dull, half-open eye, Lorrimer's blood. He said:

'You get changed. I'll see to the wine.'

7

'What will people say?'

'That's all you ever think of, Mum, what will people say. What does it matter what they say? I haven't done anything to be ashamed of.'

'Of course not. If anyone says different your dad'll soon put them right. But you know what tongues they have in this village. A thousand pounds. I couldn't hardly believe it when that solicitor rang. It's a tidy sum. And by the time Lillie Pearce has passed the news around in the Stars and Plough it'll be ten thousand, more than likely.'

'Who cares about Lillie Pearce, silly old cow.'

'Brenda! I won't have that language. And we have to live in this village.'

'You may have to. I don't. And if that's the kind of minds they've got the sooner I move away the better. Oh, Mum, don't look like that! He only wanted to help me, he wanted to be kind. And he probably did it on impulse.'

'Not very considerate of him, though, was it? He might have talked it over with your dad or me.'

'But he didn't know that he was going to die.'

Brenda and her mother were alone in the farmhouse, Arthur Pridmore having left after supper for the monthly meeting of the Parochial Church Council. The washing-up was finished and the long evening stretched before them. Too restless to settle to the television and too preoccupied with the extraordinary events of the day to take up a book, they sat in the firelight, edgy, half excited and half afraid, missing Arthur Pridmore's reassuring bulk in his high-backed chair. Then Mrs. Pridmore shook herself into normality and reached for her sewing basket.

'Well, at least it will help towards a nice wedding. If you have to take it, better put it in the Post Office. Then it'll add interest and be there when you want it.'

'I want it now. For books and a microscope like Dr. Lorrimer intended. That's why he left it to me and that's what I'm going to do with it. Besides, if people leave money for a special purpose you can't use it for something else. And I don't want to. I'm going to ask Dad to put up a shelf and a work-bench in my bedroom and I'll start working for my science A-levels straight away.'

'He ought not to have thought of you. What about Angela Foley? She's had a terrible life, that girl. She never got a penny from her grandmother's will, and now this.'

'That's not our concern, Mum. It was up to him. Maybe he might have left it to her if they hadn't rowed.'

'How do you mean, rowed? When?'

'Last week sometime. Tuesday it was, I think. It was just before I came home and most of the staff had left. Inspector Blakelock sent me up to Biology with a query on one of the court reports. They were together in Dr. Lorrimer's room and I heard them quarrelling.

224

She was asking him for money and he said he wouldn't give her any and then he said something about changing his will.'

'You mean you stood there listening?'

'Well I couldn't help it, could I? They were talking quite loudly. He was saying terrible things about Stella Mawson, you know, that writer Angela Foley lives with. I wasn't eavesdropping on purpose. I didn't want to hear.'

'You could have gone away.'

'And come up again all the way from the front hall? Anyway, I had to ask him about the report for the Munnings case. I couldn't go back and tell Inspector Blakelock that I hadn't got the answer because Dr. Lorrimer was having a row with his cousin. Besides, we always listened to secrets at school.'

'You're not at school now. Really, Brenda, you worry me sometimes. One moment you behave like a sensible adult, and the next anyone would think you were back in the fourth form. You're eighteen now, an adult. What has school to do with it?'

'I don't know why you're getting so het-up. I didn't tell anyone.'

'Well, you'll have to tell that detective from Scotland Yard.'

'Mum! I can't! It hasn't got anything to do with the murder.'

'Who's to say? You're supposed to tell the police anything that's important. Didn't he tell you that?'

He told her exactly that. Brenda remembered his look, her own guilty blush. He had known that she was keeping something back. She said, with stubborn defiance:

'Well, I can't accuse Angela Foley of murder, or as good as accuse her anyway. Besides,' she proclaimed triumphantly, remembering something Inspector Blakelock had told her, 'it would be hearsay, not proper evidence. He couldn't take any notice of it.

And, Mum, there's another thing. Suppose she didn't really expect him to alter the will so soon? That solicitor told you that Dr. Lorrimer made the new will last Friday, didn't he? Well that was probably because he had to go to a scene of crime in Ely on Friday morning. The police call only came through at ten o'clock. He must have gone into his solicitors then.'

'What do you mean?'

'Nothing. Only if people think that I had a motive, then so did she.'

'Of course you didn't have a motive! That's ridiculous. It's wicked! Oh, Brenda, if only you'd come to the concert with Dad and me.'

'No thank you. Miss Spencer singing "Pale Hands I Loved", and the Sunday School kids doing their boring old Maypole dance, and the W.I. with their hand bells, and old Mr. Matthews bashing away with the acoustic spoons. I've seen it all before.'

'But you'd have had an alibi.'

'So I would if you and Dad had stayed here at home with me.'

'It wouldn't have mattered where you'd been if it weren't for that thousand pounds. Well, let's hope Gerald Bowlem understands.'

'If he doesn't, he knows what he can do! I don't see what it's got to do with Gerald. I'm not married to him, nor engaged for that matter. He'd better not interfere.'

She looked across at her mother and was suddenly appalled. She had only seen her look like this once before, the night when she had had her second miscarriage and had been told by old Dr. Greene that there could never now be another baby. Brenda had only been twelve at the time. But her mother's face, suddenly remembered, had looked exactly as it did now, as if an obliterating hand had passed over it, wiping off brightness, blunting the contours of cheek and

226

brow, dulling the eyes, leaving an amorphous mask of desolation.

She remembered and understood what before she had only felt, the anger and resentment that her mother, indestructible and comforting as a great rock in a weary land, should herself be vulnerable to pain. She was there to soothe Brenda's miseries, not to suffer herself, to comfort, not to seek comfort. But now Brenda was older and she was able to understand. She saw her mother clearly, like a stranger newly met. The cheap crimplene dress, spotlessly clean as always, with the brooch Brenda had given her for her last birthday pinned to the lapel. The ankles thickening above the sensible low-heeled shoes, the pudgy hands speckled with the brown stains of age, the wedding ring of dull gold biting into the flesh, the curly hair that had once been red-gold like her own, still brushed plainly to one side and held in a tortoiseshell slide, the fresh, almost unlined skin. She put her arms round her mother's shoulders.

'Oh, Mum, don't worry. It'll be all right. Commander Dalgliesh will find out who did it and then everything will be back to normal. Look, I'll make you some cocoa. Don't let's wait till Dad's back from the P.C.C. We'll have it now. Mum, it's all right. Really it is. It's all right.'

Simultaneously their ears caught the hum of the approaching car. They gazed at each other, speechless, guilty as conspirators. This wasn't their ancient Morris. And how could it be? The Parochial Church Council never finished their business before half-past eight.

Brenda went to the window and peered out. The car stopped. She turned to her mother, white-faced.

'It's the police! It's Commander Dalgliesh!'

Without a word, Mrs. Pridmore got resolutely to her feet. She placed a hand briefly on her daughter's shoulder, then went out into the passage and opened the door before Massingham had lifted his hand to knock. She said through stiff lips:

'Come in please. I'm glad that you're here. Brenda has something to tell you, something that I think you ought to know.'

8

The day was nearly over. Sitting in his dressing-gown at the small table in front of the window in his bedroom at the Moonraker, Dalgliesh heard the church clock strike half-past eleven. He liked his room. It was the larger of the two which Mrs. Gotobed had been able to offer. The single window looked out over the churchyard towards the village hall and beyond it the clerestory and square flint tower of St. Nicholas's Church. There were only three rooms for guests at the inn. The smallest and noisiest, since it was over the public bar, had fallen to Massingham. The main guest-room had already been taken by an American couple touring East Anglia, perhaps in search of family records. They had sat at their table in the dining-parlour, happily occupied with maps and guidebooks, and if they had been told that their newly arrived fellow guests were police officers investigating a murder, they were too well-bred to betray interest. After a brief smile and a good evening in their soft transatlantic voices they had turned their attention again to Mrs. Gotobed's excellent casserole of hare in cider.

It was very quiet. The muted voices from the bar had long since been silent. It was over an hour since he had heard the last shouted goodbyes. Massingham, he knew, had spent the evening in the public bar hoping, presumably, to pick up scraps of useful information. Dalgliesh hoped that the beer had been good. He had been born close to the fens to know that, otherwise,

Massingham would have found it a frustrating evening.

He got up to stretch his legs and shoulders, looking around with approval at the room. The floor boards were of ancient oak, black and stout as ship's timbers. A fire of wood and turf burned in the iron Victorian grate, the pungent smoke curtseying under a decorated hood of wheat-ears and flower-posies tied with ribbons. The large double bed was of brass, high and ornate with four great knobs, large as polished cannonballs, at the corners. Mrs. Gotobed had earlier folded back the crocheted cover to reveal a feather mattress shaken to an inviting plumpness. In any four-star hotel he might have enjoyed greater luxury, but hardly such comfort.

He returned to his work. It had been a crowded day of interrogation and renewed interrogation, telephone calls to London, a hurriedly arranged and unsatisfactory Press conference, two consultations with the Chief Constable, the gathering of those odd-shaped pieces of information and conjecture which, in the end, would click together to form the completed picture. It might be a trite analogy, this comparison of detection with fitting together a jigsaw. But it was remarkably apt, not least because it was so often that tantalising elusive piece with the vital segment of a human face that made the picture complete.

He turned the page to the last interview of the day, with Henry Kerrison at the Old Rectory. The smell of the house was still in his nostrils, an evocative smell of stale cooking and furniture polish, reminding him of childhood visits with his parents to over-large, ill-heated country vicarages. Kerrison's housekeeper and children had long been in bed and the house had held a melancholy, brooding silence as if all the tragedies and disappointments of its numerous incumbents still hung in the air.

Kerrison had answered the door himself and had

shown him and Massingham into his study where he was occupied in sorting coloured slides of post-mortem injuries to illustrate a lecture he was to give the following week to the detection training school. On the desk was a framed photograph of himself as a boy with an older man, obviously his father. They were standing on a crag, climbing-ropes slung round their shoulders. What interested Dalgliesh as much as the photograph itself was the fact that Kerrison hadn't bothered to remove it.

He hadn't appeared to resent his visitors' late arrival. It was possible to believe that he welcomed their company. He had worked on in the light of his desk-lamp, fitting each slide into his viewer, then sorting it into the appropriate heap, intent as a schoolboy with a hobby. He had answered their questions quietly and precisely, but as if his mind were elsewhere. Dalgliesh asked him whether his daughter had talked to him about the incident with Lorrimer.

'Yes, she did tell me. When I got home for lunch from my lecture I found her crying in her room. It seems that Lorrimer was unnecessarily harsh. But Nell is a sensitive child and it's not always possible to know the precise truth of the matter.'

'You didn't talk to him about it?'

'I didn't talk to anyone. I did wonder whether I ought to, but it would have meant questioning Inspector Blakelock and Miss Pridmore, and I didn't wish to involve them. They had to work with Lorrimer. So, for that matter, did I. The effectiveness of an isolated institution like Hoggatt's largely depends on good relationships between the staff. I thought it was best not to take the matter further. That may have been prudence, or it may have been cowardice. I don't know.'

He had smiled sadly, and added:

'I only know that it wasn't a motive for murder.'

230

A motive for murder. Dalgliesh had discovered enough motives in this crowded but not very satisfactory day. But motive was the least important factor in a murder investigation. He would gladly have exchanged the psychological subtleties of motive for a single, solid, incontrovertible piece of physical evidence linking a suspect with the crime. And, so far, there was none. He still awaited the report from the Mertopolitan Laboratory on the mallet and the vomit. The mysterious figure seen by old Goddard fleeing from Hoggatt's remained mysterious; no other person had yet been traced or had come forward to suggest that he wasn't a figment of the old man's imagination. The tyre-marks near the gate, now definitely identified from the tyre index at the laboratory, still hadn't been linked to a car. Not surprisingly, no trace had been found of Middlemass's white coat and no indication whether or how it had been disposed of. An examination of the village hall and the hobby-horse costumes had produced nothing to disprove Middlemass's account of his evening and it was apparent that the horse, a heavy all-enveloping contraption of canvas and serge, ensured that its wearer would be unidentifiable even, in Middlemass's case, to his elegant hand-made shoes.

The central mysteries of the case remained. Who was it who had telephoned the message to Lorrimer about the can being burned and the number 1840? Was it the same woman who had rung Mrs. Bidwell? What had been written on the missing sheet from Lorrimer's rough notebook? What had prompted Lorrimer to make that extraordinary will?

Lifting his head from the files, he listened. There was a noise, faintly discernible, like the creeping of a myriad insects. He remembered it from his childhood nights, lying awake in the nursery of his father's Norfolk vicarage, a sound he had never heard in the noise of cities, the first gentle sibilant whisper of the night

231

rain. Soon it was followed by a spatter of drops against the window and the rising moan of the wind in the chimney. The fire spluttered and then flared into sudden brightness. There was a violent flurry of rain against the pane and then, as quickly as it had begun, the brief storm was over. He opened the window to savour the smell of the damp night air, and gazed out into a blanket of darkness, black fen earth merging with the paler sky.

As his eyes became accustomed to the night, he could discern the low rectangle of the village hall and, beyond it, the great mediaeval tower of the church. Then the moon sailed out from behind the clouds and the churchyard became visible, the obelisks and gravestones gleaming pale as if they exuded their own mysterious light. Below him, faintly luminous, lay the gravel path along which, the previous night, the morris-dancers, bells jangling, had made their way through the rising mist. Staring out over the churchyard he pictured the hobby-horse pawing the ground to meet them, rearing its grotesque head among the gravestones and snapping the air with its great jaws. And he wondered again who had been inside its skin.

The door beneath his window opened and Mrs. Gotobed appeared and crooned into the darkness, enticing in her cat: 'Snowball! Snowball! Good boy now.' There was a flash of white, and the door was closed. Dalgliesh latched his window and decided that he, too, would call it a day.

1

Sprogg's Cottage, low-built and top heavy under its
low, occluding roof of thatch, wire-netted, strong
against the fen winter gales, was almost invisible from
the road. It lay about three-quarters of a mile north-
east from the village and was fronted by Sprogg's
Green, a wide triangular grass verge planted with
willows. Pushing open the white wicker gate on which
someone had optimistically but fruitlessly substituted
the word 'Lavender' for Sprogg's, Dalgliesh and Massingham stepped into a front garden as brightly
ordered and conventional as that of a suburban villa.
An acacia tree in the middle of the lawn flaunted its
autumn glory of red and gold, the yellow climbing
roses trained over the door still gleamed with a faint
illusion of summer and a massed bed of geraniums,
fuchsia and dahlias, supported by stakes and carefully
tended, flared in discordant glory against the bronze
of the beech hedge. There was a hanging basket of
pink geraniums beside the door, now past their best,
but still bright with a few tattered blooms. The
knocker was a highly polished brass fish, every scale
gleaming.

The door was opened by a slight, almost fragile,
woman, bare-footed and wearing a cotton overblouse,
patterned in greens and brown, above her corduroy
slacks. She had coarse dark hair strongly streaked with
grey and worn in a short bob, with a heavy fringe
which curved low to meet her eyebrows. Her eyes
were her most remarkable feature, immense, the irises
brown speckled with green, translucently clear under
the strongly curved brows. Her face was pale and taut,
deeply etched with lines across the forehead and running from the widely springing nostrils to the corners

of the mouth. It was the face, thought Dalgliesh, of a
tortured masochist in a mediaeval triptych, the
muscles bulging and knotted as if they had been
racked. But no-one coming under the gaze of those
remarkable eyes could call it plain or ordinary. Dalgliesh said:

'Miss Mawson? I'm Adam Dalgliesh. This is Inspector Massingham.'

She gave him a direct, impersonal gaze and said
without smiling:

'Come through into the study, will you? We don't
light the sitting-room fire until the evening. If you
want to speak to Angela, I'm afraid she's not here at
present. She's over at Postmill Cottage with Mrs.
Swaffield meeting the Social Security people. They're
trying to persuade old Lorrimer to go into an old
people's home. Apparently he's being obstinately re-
sistant to the blandishments of bureaucracy. Good
luck to him.'

The front door opened directly into a sitting-room
with a low, oak-beamed ceiling. The room surprised
him. To enter it was like walking into an antique
shop, but one where the proprietor had arranged his
oddly assorted wares with an eye to the general effect.
The mantelshelf and every ledge bore an ornament,
three hanging cupboards held a variety of mugs, tea-
pots, painted jugs and Staffordshire figures, and the
walls were almost covered with prints, framed old
maps, small oil-paintings and Victorian silhouettes in
oval frames. Above the fireplace was the most spectacular object, a curved sword with a finely wrought
scabbard. He wondered whether the room reflected
merely an indiscriminate acquisitiveness, or whether
these carefully disposed objects served as comforting
talismans against the alien, undomesticated spirits of
the encroaching fens. A wood fire was laid but not lit
in the open hearth. Under the window a polished
gate-legged table was already laid for two.

Miss Mawson led the way through to her study. It was a smaller, less cluttered room at the back with a latticed window giving a view of a stone terrace, a lawn with a sundial in the middle, and a wide field of sugar beet, still unharvested. He saw with interest that she wrote by hand. There was a typewriter, but it stood on a table by itself. The working-desk under the window held only a pad of unlined paper, covered with a black upright holograph in an elegant italic. The lines were carefully patterned on the paper, and even the marginal alterations were aligned.

Dalgliesh said:

'I'm sorry if we're interrupting your work.'

'You aren't. Sit down, won't you both. It isn't going well this morning. If it were I should have hung a "don't disturb" notice on the knocker and you wouldn't have got in. Still, it's nearly finished; only one chapter to do now. I suppose you want me to give Angela an alibi. Helping the police, isn't it called? What were we doing on Wednesday night; and when, and why, and where, and with whom?'

'We would like to ask you some questions, certainly.'

'But that one first, presumably. There's no difficulty. We spent the evening and night together from six-fifteen, which was the time she arrived home.'

'Doing what, Miss Mawson?'

'What we normally do. We separated the day from the evening, me with whisky, Angela with sherry. I asked about her day and she enquired about mine. Then she lit the fire and cooked the meal. We had avocado pear with *sauce vinaigrette*, chicken casserole and cheese and biscuits. We washed up together and then Angela typed my manuscript for me until nine. At nine we turned on the television and watched the news, followed by the play. That brought us to ten forty-five, cocoa for Angela, whisky for me, and bed.'

'Neither of you left the cottage?'

'No.'

Dalgliesh asked how long she had lived in the village.

'Me? Eight years. I was born in the fens – at Soham actually – and spent most of my childhood here. But I went up to London University when I was eighteen, took a second-class degree, and then worked, not particularly successfully, at various jobs in journalism and publishing. I came here eight years ago when I heard that the cottage was to let. That's when I first decided to give up my job and become a full-time writer.'

'And Miss Foley?'

'She came to live here two years ago. I advertised locally for a part-time typist and she replied. She was living in lodgings at Ely then and wasn't particularly happy there, so I suggested that she moved in. She had to depend on the bus to get to work. Living here is obviously much more convenient for the Lab.'

'So you've lived long enough in the village to get to know people?'

'As much as one ever does in the fens. But not well enough to point the finger at a murderer for you.'

'How well did you know Dr. Lorrimer?'

'By sight. I wasn't told that Angela was his cousin until she came to live with me. They're not close and he never came here. I've met most of the Lab staff, of course. Dr. Howarth started a string quartet soon after he arrived, and last August they gave a concert in the Wren chapel. Afterwards there was wine and cheese in the vestry. I met a number of the staff then. Actually, I already knew them by sight and name, as one does in a village. We use the same post office and the same pub. But if you're hoping for village and Lab gossip, it's no use coming to me.'

Dalgliesh said:

'Was the concert in the chapel successful?'

'Not particularly. Howarth is a very fine amateur

238

violinist and Claire Easterbrook is a competent cellist, but the other two weren't up to much. He hasn't repeated the experiment. I gather that there was a certain amount of unkind comment about a new arrival who saw it as his duty to civilise the underprivileged natives, and it may have got to his ears. He does rather give the impression that he sees himself as bridging single-handed the culture-gap between the scientist and the artist. Or perhaps he wasn't satisfied with the acoustics. My own view is that the other three didn't want to go on playing with him. As a leader of a quartet he probably behaved with much the same arrogance as he does as Director. The Lab is certainly more efficient; the work output is up twenty per cent. Whether the staff are happy is another matter.'

So she wasn't altogether immune to Lab and village gossip, thought Dalgliesh. He wondered why she was being so frank. Equally frank, he asked bluntly:

'When you were at Postmill Cottage yesterday, did you go upstairs?'

'Fancy the old man telling you that! What did he think I was after, I wonder? I went up to the bathroom to see if there was a tin of scouring powder there to clean the sink. There wasn't.'

'You know about Dr. Lorrimer's will, of course?'

'I imagine the whole village does. Actually I was probably the first to know. The old man was getting agitated to know whether there was any money coming, so Angela rang the solicitor. She'd met him at the time her grandmother's will was read. He told her that the cottage was to go to the old man with £10,000, so she was able to put his mind at rest.'

'And Miss Foley herself gets nothing?'

'That's right. And that a new clerical officer at the Lab, whom Edwin had apparently taken a fancy to, gets a thousand pounds.'

'A not particularly just will.'

'Have you ever known beneficiaries who thought a

239

will was just? His grandmother's will was worse. Angela lost the money then, when it could have made a difference to her life. Now she doesn't need it. We manage perfectly well here.'

'Presumably it wasn't a shock to her. Didn't he tell her of his intentions?'

'If that's meant to be a tactful way of finding out whether she had a motive for murder, you can ask her yourself. Here she is.'

Angela Foley came through the sitting-room, tugging off her head-scarf. Her face darkened at the sight of the visitors and she said with quick defensive annoyance:

'Miss Mawson likes to work in the mornings. You didn't say that you were coming.'

Her friend laughed.

'They haven't worried me. I've been getting a useful insight into police methods. They're effective without being crude. You're back early.'

'The social work department rang to say that they can't get over until after lunch. Uncle doesn't want to see them, but he wants to see me even less. He's having lunch with the Swaffields at the rectory, so I thought I might as well come home.'

Stella Mawson lit a cigarette.

'You've arrived at an opportune time. Mr. Dalgliesh was enquiring tactfully whether you had a motive for murdering your cousin; in other words, did Edwin tell you that he was about to alter his will?'

Angela Foley looked at Dalgliesh and said calmly:

'No. He never discussed his affairs with me and I didn't discuss mine with him. I don't think I've spoken to him during the last two years except about Lab business.'

Dalgliesh said:

'It's surprising, surely, that he should want to change a long-standing will without talking to you about it?'

240

She shrugged, and then explained:

'It was nothing to do with me. He was only my cousin, not my brother. He transferred to Hoggatt's from the Southern Laboratory five years ago to live with his father, not because I was here. He didn't really know me. If he had, I doubt whether he would have liked me. He owed me nothing, not even justice.'

'Did you like him?'

She paused and thought, as if the question was one to which she herself wanted an answer. Stella Mawson, eyes narrowed, regarded her through the cigarette smoke. Then Miss Foley spoke:

'No, I didn't like him. I think I was even a little afraid of him. He was like a man psychologically burdened, unsure of his place in life. Lately the tension and unhappiness were almost palpable. I found it embarrassing and, well, somehow menacing. People who were really secure in their own personalities didn't seem to notice or be bothered by it. But the less secure felt threatened. I think that's why Clifford Bradley was so afraid of him.'

Stella Mawson said:

'Bradley probably reminded Edwin of himself when he was young. He was painfully insecure, even in his job, when he first started. D'you remember how he used to practise his evidence on the night before he went into the box; writing down all the possible questions the opposing counsel might ask, making sure that he was word perfect with the answers, learning all the scientific formulæ by heart to impress the jury? He made a mess of one of his first cases, and never forgave himself.'

There was a strange little silence. Angela Foley seemed about to speak, then changed her mind. Her enigmatic gaze was fixed on her friend. Stella Mawson's eyes shifted. She walked over to her desk and stubbed out her cigarette. She said:

'Your aunt told you. She used to have to read out

241

the questions for him over and over again; an evening of tension and incomprehensible boredom. Don't you remember?'

'Yes,' said Angela in her high, dispassionate voice. 'Yes, I remember.' She turned to Dalgliesh.

'If there's nothing else you want to ask me, there are things I need to get on with. Dr. Howarth isn't expecting me at the Lab until this afternoon. And Stella will want to work.'

Both women showed them out, standing together in the doorway as if politely speeding departing guests. Dalgliesh almost expected them to wave goodbye. He hadn't questioned Miss Foley about the quarrel with her cousin. The time might come for that, but it wasn't yet. It had interested, but not surprised him, that she had lied. But what had interested him more was Stella Mawson's story of Lorrimer rehearsing his evidence on the night before a trial. Whoever had told her this, he was fairly certain that it hadn't been Angela Foley.

As they drove away, Massingham said:

'Fifty thousand pounds could change her whole life, give her some independence, get her away from here. What sort of life is it for a young woman, just the two of them, stuck here in this isolated swamp? And she seems little more than a drudge.'

Dalgliesh, unusually, was driving. Massingham glanced at the sombre eyes in the mirror, the long hands laid lightly on the wheel. Dalgliesh said:

'I'm remembering what old George Greenall, the first detective sergeant I worked under, told me. He'd had twenty-five years in the C.I.D. Nothing about people surprised him, nothing shocked him. He said:

' "They'll tell you that the most destructive force in the world is hate. Don't you believe it, lad. It's love. And if you want to make a detective you'd better learn to recognise it when you meet it." '

242

2

Brenda was over an hour late at the Laboratory on Thursday morning. After the excitement of the previous day she had overslept and her mother had deliberately not called her. She had wanted to go without her breakfast, but Mrs. Pridmore had placed the usual plate of bacon and egg before her, and had said firmly that Brenda wouldn't leave the house until it was eaten. Brenda, only too aware that both her parents would be happier if she never set foot in Hoggatt's again, knew better than to argue.

She arrived, breathless and apologetic, to find Inspector Blakelock trying to cope with a two day's intake of exhibits, a steady stream of arrivals and a constantly ringing telephone. She wondered how he would greet her, whether he had learned about the thousand pounds and, if so, whether it would make any difference. But he seemed his usual stolid self. He said:

'As soon as you've taken off your things, you're to go to the Director. He's in Miss Foley's office. The police are using his. Don't bother about making tea. Miss Foley will be out until after lunch. She has to see someone from the local authority social services about her uncle.'

Brenda was glad that she wouldn't have to face Angela Foley yet. Last night's admission to Commander Dalgliesh was too like betrayal to be comfortable. She said:

'Everyone else is in, then?'

'Clifford Bradley hasn't made it. His wife telephoned to say that he's not well. The police have been here since half-past eight. They've been checking all the exhibits, especially the drugs, and they've

243

made another search of the whole Lab. Apparently they've got the idea that there's something odd going on.'

It was unusual for Inspector Blakelock to be so communicative. Brenda asked:

'What do you mean, something odd?'

'They didn't say. But now they want to see every file in the Lab with a number 18 or 40 or 1840 in the registration.'

Brenda's eyes widened.

'Do you mean for this year only, or do we have to go back to those on microfilm?'

'I've got out this year's and last year's to begin with, and Sergeant Underhill and the constable are working on them now. I don't know what they hope to find, and by the look of them, neither do they. Better look nippy. Dr. Howarth said that you were to go into him as soon as you arrive.'

'But I can't do shorthand and typing! What do you think he wants me for?'

'He didn't say. Mostly getting out files, I imagine. And I daresay there'll be a bit of telephoning and fetching and carrying.'

'Where's Commander Dalgliesh? Isn't he here?'

'He and Inspector Massingham left about ten minutes ago. Off to interview someone, I daresay. Never mind about them. Our job's here, helping to keep this Lab working smoothly.'

It was as close as Inspector Blakelock ever got to a rebuke. Brenda hurried to Miss Foley's office. It was known that the Director didn't like people to knock on his door, so Brenda entered with what confidence she could muster. She thought, 'I can only do my best. If that's not good enough, he'll have to lump it.' He was sitting at the desk apparently studying a file. He looked up without smiling in response to her good morning, and said:

'Inspector Blakelock has explained to you that I

want some help this morning while Miss Foley's away?
You can work with Mrs. Mallett in the general office.'

'Yes, sir.'

'The police will be needing some more files.
They're interested in particular numbers only. But
I expect Inspector Blakelock has explained that.'

'Yes, sir.'

'They're working on the 1976 and '75 registrations
now, so you'd better start getting out the 1974 series
and any earlier years they want.'

He took his eyes from the files and looked directly
at her for the first time.

'Dr. Lorrimer left you some money, didn't he?'

'Yes, sir. One thousand pounds for books and apparatus.'

'You don't need to call me sir, Dr. Howarth will
do. You liked him?'

'Yes. Yes, I did.'

Dr. Howarth had lowered his eyes again and was
turning over the pages of the file.

'Odd, I shouldn't have thought that he would have
appealed to women, or women to him.'

Brenda said resolutely:

'It wasn't like that.'

'What wasn't it like? Do you mean he didn't think
of you as a woman?'

'I don't know. I mean, I didn't think that he was
trying to ...'

Her voice broke off. Dr. Howarth turned a page.
He said:

'To seduce you?'

Brenda took courage, helped by a spurt of anger.
She said:

'Well, he couldn't, could he? Not here in the Lab.
And I never saw him anywhere else. And if you'd
known anything about him at all, you wouldn't talk
like that.'

She was appalled at her own temerity. But the Director only said, rather sadly she thought:

'I expect you're right. I never knew him at all.'

She struggled to explain.

'He explained to me what science is about.'

'And what is science about?'

'He explained that scientists formulate theories about how the physical world works, and then test them out by experiments. As long as the experiments succeed, then the theories hold. If they fail, the scientists have to find another theory to explain the facts. He says that, with science, there's this exciting paradox, that disillusionment needn't be defeat. It's a step forward.'

'Didn't you do science at school? I thought you'd taken physics and chemistry at O-level.'

'No-one ever explained it like that before.'

'No. I suppose they bored you with experiments about magnetism and the properties of carbon dioxide. By the way, Miss Foley has typed a paper on the ratio of staffing to workloads. I want the figures checked – Mrs. Mallett will do it with you – and the paper circulated to all Directors before next week's meeting. She'll give you the list of addresses.'

'Yes, sir. Yes, Dr. Howarth.'

'And I'd like you to take this file to Miss Easterbrook in the Biology Lab.'

He looked up at her, and she thought for the first time that he looked kind. He said, very gently:

'I know how you feel. I felt the same. But there's only a white outline on the floor, just a smudge of chalk. That's all.'

He handed her the file. It was a dismissal. At the door Brenda paused. The Director said:

'Well?'

'I was just thinking that detection must be like science. The detective formulates a theory, then tests it. If the facts he discovers fit, then the theory holds.

If they don't, then he has to find another theory, another suspect.'

Dr. Howarth said drily:

'It's a reasonable analogy. But the temptation to select the right facts is probably greater. And the detective is experimenting with human beings. Their properties are complex and not susceptible to accurate analysis.'

An hour later Brenda took her third set of files into Sergeant Underhill in the director's office. The pleasant-looking detective constable leaped forward to relieve her of her burden. The telephone rang on Dr. Howarth's desk, and Sergeant Underhill went over to answer it. He replaced the receiver and looked across at his companion.

'That's the Met Lab. They've given me the result of the blood analysis. The mallet was the weapon all right. There's Lorrimer's blood on it. And they've analysed the vomit.'

He looked up, suddenly remembering that Brenda was still in the room, and waited until she had left and the door was closed. The detective constable said:

'Well?'

'It's what we thought. Think it out for yourself. A forensic scientist would know that the Lab can't determine a blood group from vomit. The stomach acids destroy the antibodies. What they can hope to say is what was in the food. So all you need to do, if it's your vomit and you're a suspect, is to lie about what you ate for supper. Who could disprove it?'

His companion said:

'Unless . . .'

Sergeant Underhill reached again for the phone.

'Exactly. As I said, think it out for yourself.'

3

After the last few days of intermittent rain and fitful autumn sunlight, the morning was cold but bright, the sun unexpectedly warm against their necks. But even in the mellow light, the Old Rectory, with its bricks the colour of raw liver under the encroaching ivy, and its ponderous porch and carved overhanging eaves, was a depressing house. The open iron gate to the drive, half off its hinges, was embedded in a straggling hedge which bordered the garden. The gravel path needed weeding. The grass of the lawn was pulled and flattened where someone had made an inexpert attempt at mowing it, obviously with a blunt machine, and the two herbaceous borders were a tangle of overgrown chrysanthemums and stunted dahlias half choked with weeds. A child's wooden horse on wheels lay on its side at the edge of the lawn, but this was the only sign of human life.

As they approached the house, however, a girl and a small boy emerged from the porch and stood regarding them. They must, of course, be Kerrison's children, and as Dalgliesh and Massingham approached the likeness became apparent. The girl must, he supposed, be over school age, but she looked barely sixteen except for a certain adult wariness about the eyes. She had straight, dark hair drawn back from a high, spotty forehead into short dishevelled pigtails bound with elastic bands. She wore the ubiquitous faded blue jeans of her generation, topped with a fawn sweater, loose-fitting enough to be her father's. Round her neck Dalgliesh could glimpse what looked like a leather thong. Her grubby feet were bare and palely striped with the pattern of summer sandals.

The child, who moved closer to her at the sight of

strangers, was about three or four years old, a stocky, round-faced boy with a wide nose and a gentle, delicate mouth. His face was a softer miniature model of his father's, the brows straight and dark above the heavily-lidded eyes. He was wearing a pair of tight blue shorts and an inexpertly-knitted jumper against which he was clasping a large ball. His sturdy legs were planted in short, red wellington boots. He tightened his hold on his ball and fixed on Dalgliesh an unblinking disconcertingly judgemental gaze.

Dalgliesh suddenly realised that he knew virtually nothing about children. Most of his friends were childless: those who were not had learned to invite him when their demanding, peace-disturbing, egotistical offspring were away at school. His only son had died, with his mother, just twenty-four hours after birth. Although he could now hardly recall his wife's face except in dreams, the picture of those waxen, doll-like features above the tiny swathed body, the gummed eyelids, the secret look of self-absorbed peace was so clear and immediate that he sometimes wondered whether the image was really that of his child, so briefly but intently regarded, or whether he had taken into himself a prototype of dead childhood. His son would now be older than this child, would be entering the traumatic years of adolescence. He had convinced himself long ago that he was glad to have been spared them.

But now it suddenly occurred to him that there was a whole territory of human experience on which, once repulsed, he had turned his back, and that this rejection somehow diminished him as a man. This transitory ache of loss surprised him by its intensity. He forced himself to consider a sensation so unfamiliar and unwelcome.

Suddenly the child smiled at him and held out the ball. The effect was as disconcertingly flattering as when a stray cat would stalk towards him, tail erect, and condescend to be stroked. They gazed at each other. Dalgliesh smiled back. Then Massingham sprang forward and whipped the ball from the chubby hands.

'Come on. Football!'

He began dribbling the blue and yellow ball across the lawn. Immediately the sturdy legs followed. The two of them disappeared round the side of the house and Dalgliesh could hear the boy's high, cracked laughter. The girl gazed after them, her face suddenly pinched with loving anxiety. She turned to Dalgliesh.

'I hope he knows not to kick it into the bonfire. It's almost out, but the embers are still very hot. I've been burning rubbish.'

'Don't worry. He's a careful chap. And he's got younger brothers.'

She regarded him carefully for the first time.

'You're Commander Dalgliesh, aren't you? We're Nell and William Kerrison. I'm afraid my father isn't here.'

'I know. We've come to see your housekeeper, Miss Willard, isn't it? Is she in?'

'I shouldn't take any notice of anything she says if I were you. She's a dreadful liar. And she steals Daddy's drink. Don't you want to question William and me?'

'A policewoman will be coming with us to talk to you both, sometime, when your father's at home.'

'I won't see her. I don't mind talking to you, but I won't see a policewoman. I don't like social workers.'

'A policewoman isn't a social worker.'

'She's the same. She makes judgements on people, doesn't she? We had a social worker here after my mother left, before the custody case, and she looked at William and me as if we were a public nuisance which someone had left on her doorstep. She went round the house too, poking into things, pretending to admire, making out it was just a social visit.'

250

'Policewomen – and policemen – never pretend that they're just paying a social visit. No-one would believe us, would they?'

They turned and walked together towards the house. The girl said:

'Are you going to discover who killed Dr. Lorrimer?'

'I hope so. I expect so.'

'And then what will happen to him, the murderer, I mean?'

'He'll appear before the magistrates. Then, if they think that the evidence is sufficient, they'll commit him to the Crown Court for trial.'

'And then?'

'If he's found guilty of murder, the judge will pass the statutory penalty, imprisonment for life. That means that he'll be in prison for a long time, perhaps ten years or more.'

'But that's silly. That won't put things right. It won't bring Dr. Lorrimer back.'

'It won't put anything right, but it isn't silly. Life is precious to nearly all of us. Even people who have little more than life still want to live it to the last natural moment. No-one has a right to take it away from them.'

'You talk as if life were like William's ball. If that's taken away he knows what he's lost. Dr. Lorrimer doesn't know that he's lost anything.'

'He's lost the years he might have had.'

'That's like taking away the ball that William might have had. It doesn't mean anything. It's just words. Suppose he was going to die next week anyway. Then he'd only have lost seven days. You don't put someone in prison for ten years to repay seven lost days. They might not even have been happy days.'

'Even if he were a very old man with one day left to him, the law says that he has a right to live it. Wilful killing would still be murder.'

251

The girl said thoughtfully:

'I suppose it was different when people believed in God. Then the murdered person might have died in mortal sin and gone to hell. The seven days could have made a difference then. He might have repented and had time for absolution.'

Dalgliesh said:

'All these problems are easier for people who believe in God. Those of us who don't or can't have to do the best we can. That's what the law is, the best we can do. Human justice is imperfect, but it's the only justice we have.'

'Are you sure you don't want to question me? I know that Daddy didn't kill him. He isn't a murderer. He was at home with William and me when Dr. Lorrimer died. We put William to bed together at half past seven and then we stayed with him for twenty minutes and Daddy read Paddington Bear to him. Then I went to bed because I'd got a headache and wasn't feeling well, and Daddy brought me up a mug of cocoa which he'd made specially for me. He sat by me reading poetry from my school anthology until he thought I'd gone to sleep. But I hadn't really. I was just pretending. He crept away just before nine, but I was still awake then. Shall I tell you how I know?'

'If you want to.'

'Because I heard the church clock strike. Then Daddy left me and I lay there in the dark, just thinking. He came back to look in at me again about half an hour later, but I still pretended to be asleep. So that lets Daddy out, doesn't it?'

'We don't know exactly when Dr. Lorrimer died but, yes, I think it probably does.'

'Unless I'm telling you a lie.'

'People very often do lie to the police. Are you?'

'No. But I expect I would if I thought it would save Daddy. I don't care about Dr. Lorrimer, you see. I'm glad he's dead. He wasn't a nice man. The day before

252

he died William and I went to the Lab to see Daddy. He was lecturing in the morning to the detective training course and we thought we'd call for him before lunch. Inspector Blakelock let us sit in the hall, and that girl who helps him at the desk, the pretty one, smiled at William and offered him an apple from her lunch box. And then Dr. Lorrimer came down the stairs and saw us. I know it was he because the Inspector spoke to him by his name and he said: "What are those children doing in here? A lab isn't a place for children." I said: "I'm not a child. I'm Miss Eleanor Kerrison and this is my brother William, and we're waiting for our father." He stared at us as if he hated us, his face white and twitching. He said: "Well, you can't wait here." Then he spoke very unkindly to Inspector Blakelock. After Dr. Lorrimer had gone, he said we'd better go but he told William not to mind and took a sweet out of his left ear. Did you know that the Inspector was a conjurer?'

'No. I didn't know that.'

'Would you like to see round the house before I take you to Miss Willard? Do you like seeing houses?'

'Very much, but I think perhaps not now.'

'See the drawing-room anyway. It's much the best room. There now, isn't it lovely?'

The drawing-room was in no sense lovely. It was a sombre, oak-panelled, overfurnished room which looked as if little had changed since the days when the bombazine-clad wife and daughters of the Victorian rector sat there piously occupied with their parish sewing. The mullioned windows, framed by dark red, dirt-encrusted curtains, effectively excluded most of the daylight so that Dalgliesh stepped into a sombre chilliness which the sluggish fire did nothing to dispel. An immense mahogany table, bearing a jam-jar of chrysanthemums, stood against the far wall and the fireplace, an ornate edifice of marble, was almost hidden by two immense, saggy armchairs, and a dilapidated sofa. Eleanor said with unexpected formality, as if the room had recalled her to her duty as a hostess:

'I try to keep at least one room nice in case we have visitors. The flowers are pretty, aren't they? William arranged them. Please sit down. Can I get you some coffee?'

'That would be pleasant, but I don't think we ought to wait. We're really here to see Miss Willard.'

Massingham and William appeared in the doorway, flushed with their exercise, William with the ball tucked under his left arm. Eleanor led the way through a brass-studded, green baize door and down a stone passage to the back of the house. William, deserting Massingham, trotted behind her, his plump hand clutching ineffectively at the skin-tight jeans. Pausing outside a door of unpolished oak, she said:

'She's in here. She doesn't like William and me to go in. Anyway, she smells, so we don't.'

And taking William by the hand, she left them.

Dalgliesh knocked. There was a rapid scrabbling noise inside the room, like an animal disturbed in its lair, and then the door was opened slightly and a dark and suspicious eye looked out at them through the narrow aperture. Dalgliesh said:

'Miss Willard? Commander Dalgliesh and Inspector Massingham from the Metropolitan Police. We're investigating Dr. Lorrimer's murder. May we come in?'

The eye softened. She gave a short, embarrassed gasp, rather like a snort, and opened the door wide.

'Of course. Of course. What must you think of me? I'm afraid I'm still in what my dear old nurse used to call my disability. But I wasn't expecting you, and I usually have a quiet moment to myself about this time of the morning.'

Eleanor was right, the room did smell. A smell, Mas-

254

singham diagnosed after a curious sniff, composed of sweet sherry, unfresh body linen and cheap scent. It was very hot. A small blue flame licked the red-hot ovals of coal briquettes banked high in the Victorian grate. The window, which gave a view of the garage and the wilderness which was the back garden, was open for only an inch at the top despite the mildness of the day, and the air in the room pressed down on them, furred and heavy as a soiled blanket. The room itself had a dreadful and perverse femininity. Everything looked moistly soft, the cretonne-covered seats of the two armchairs, the plump row of cushions along the back of a Victorian chaise-longue, the imitation fur rug before the fire. The mantleshelf was cluttered with photographs in silver frames, mostly of a cassocked clergyman and his wife, whom Dalgliesh took to be Miss Willard's parents, standing side by side but oddly dissociated outside a variety of rather dull churches. Pride of place was held by a studio photograph of Miss Willard herself, young, toothily coy, the thick hair in corrugated waves. On a wall shelf to the right of the door was a small woodcarving of an armless Madonna with the laughing Child perched on her shoulder. A night-light in a saucer was burning at her feet, casting a soft glow over the tender drooping head and the sightless eyes. Dalgliesh thought that it was probably a copy, and a good one, of a mediaeval museum piece. Its gentle beauty emphasised the tawdriness of the room, yet dignified it, seeming to say that there was more than one kind of human loneliness, human pain, and that the same mercy embraced them all.

Miss Willard waved them to the chaise-longue.

'My own little den,' she said gaily. 'I like to be private, you know. I explained to Dr. Kerrison that I could only consider coming if I had my privacy. It's a rare and beautiful thing, don't you think? The human spirit wilts without it.'

Looking at her hands, Dalgliesh thought that she was probably in her middle-forties, although her face looked older. The dark hair, dry and coarse and tightly curled, was at odds with her faded complexion. Two sausages of curls over the brow suggested that she had hurriedly snatched out the rollers when she heard their knock. But her face was already made up. There was a circle of rouge under each eye and the lipstick had seeped into the creases pursing her mouth. Her small, square, bony jaw was loose as a marionette's. She was not yet fully dressed and a padded dressing-gown of flowered nylon, stained with tea and what looked like egg, was corded over a nylon nightdress in bright blue with a grubby frill round the neck. Massingham was fascinated by a bulbous fold of limp cotton just above her shoes, from which he found it difficult to avert his eyes, until he realised that she had put on her stockings back to front.

She said:

'You want to talk to me about Dr. Kerrison's alibi, I expect. Of course, it's quite ridiculous that he should have to provide one, a man so gentle, totally incapable of violence. But I can help you, as it happens. He was certainly at home until after nine, and I saw him again less than an hour later. But all this is just a waste of time. You bring a great reputation with you, Commander, but this is one crime which science can't solve. Not for nothing are they called the black fens. All through the centuries, evil has come out of this dank soil. We can fight evil, Commander, but not with your weapons.'

Massingham said:

'Well, suppose we begin by giving our weapons a chance.'

She looked at him and smiled pityingly.

'But all the doors were locked. All your clever scientific aids were intact. No-one broke in, and no-one could have got out. And yet he was struck down. That was no human hand, Inspector.'

Dalgliesh said:

'It was almost certainly a blunt weapon, Miss Willard, and I've no doubt there was a human hand at the end of it. It's our job to find out whose, and I hope that you may be able to help us. You housekeep for Dr. Kerrison and his daughter, I believe?'

Miss Willard disposed on him a glance in which pity at such ignorance was mixed with gentle reproof.

'I'm not a housekeeper, Commander. Certainly not a housekeeper. Shall we say that I'm a working house-guest. Dr. Kerrison needed someone to live in so that the children weren't left alone when he was called out to a murder scene. They're children of a broken marriage, I'm afraid. The old, sad story. You are not married, Commander?'

'No.'

'How wise.' She sighed, conveying in the sibilant release of breath infinite yearning, infinite regret. Dalgliesh persevered:

'So you live completely separately?'

'My own little quarters. This sitting-room and a bedroom next door. My own small kitchenette through this door here. I won't show it to you now because it's not quite as I should like it to be.'

'What precisely are the domestic arrangements, Miss Willard?'

'They get their own breakfast. The Doctor usually lunches at the hospital, of course; Nell and William have something on a tray when she bothers to prepare it, and I look after myself. Then I cook a little something in the evenings, quite simple, we're none of us large eaters. We eat very early because of William. It's more a high tea really. Nell and her father do all the cooking during the weekend. It really works out quite well.'

Quite well for you, thought Massingham. Certainly

William had seemed sturdy and well-nourished enough, but the girl looked as if she ought to be at school, not struggling, almost unaided, with this isolated and cheerless monstrosity of a house. He wondered how she got on with Miss Willard. As if reading his thoughts, Miss Willard said:

'William is a sweet little boy. Absolutely no trouble. I hardly see him really. But Nell is difficult, very difficult. Girls of her age usually are. She needs a mother's hand. You know, of course, that Mrs. Kerrison walked out on her husband a year ago? She ran away with one of his colleagues at the hospital. It broke him up completely. Now she's trying to get the High Court to reverse the custody order and give her the children when the divorce is heard in a month's time, and I'm sure it'll be a good thing if they do. Children ought to be with their mother. Not that Nell's really a child any longer. It's the boy they're fighting over, not Nell. If you ask me, neither of them cares about her. She gives her father a terrible time of it. Nightmares, screaming attacks, asthma. He's going to London next Monday for a three-day conference on forensic pathology. I'm afraid she'll make him pay for that little jaunt when he gets back. Neurotic, you know. Punishing him for loving her brother more, although, of course, he can't see that.'

Dalgliesh wondered by what mental process she had arrived at that glib psychological assessment. Not, he thought, that it was necessarily wrong. He felt profoundly sorry for Kerrison.

Suddenly Massingham felt sick. The warmth and feculent smell of the room overpowered him. A blob of cold sweat dropped on his notebook. Muttering an apology, he strode over to the window and tugged at the frame. It resisted for a moment then slammed down. Great draughts of cool reviving air poured in. The frail light before the carved Madonna flickered and went out.

When he got back to his notebook, Dalgliesh was already asking about the previous evening. Miss Willard said that she had cooked a meal of minced beef, potatoes and frozen peas for supper, with a blancmange to follow. She had washed up alone and had then gone to say goodnight to the family before returning to her sitting-room. They were then in the drawing-room, but Dr. Kerrison and Nell were about to take William up to bed. She had seen and heard nothing else of the family until just after nine o'clock when she had gone to check that the front door was bolted. Dr. Kerrison was sometimes careless about locking up and didn't always appreciate how nervous she felt, sleeping alone and on the ground floor. One read such terrible stories. She had passed the study door, which was ajar, and had heard Dr. Kerrison speaking on the telephone. She had returned to her sitting-room and had switched on the television.

Dr. Kerrison had looked in shortly before ten o'clock to talk to her about a small increase in her salary, but they had been interrupted by a telephone call. He had returned ten minutes or so later and they had been together for about half an hour. It had been pleasant to have the opportunity of a private chat without the children butting in. Then he had said goodnight and left her. She had switched on the television again and had watched it until nearly midnight, when she had gone to bed. If Dr. Kerrison had taken out the car, she felt fairly sure that she would have heard it since her sitting-room window looked out at the garage which was built at the side of the house. Well, they could see that for themselves.

She had overslept the next morning and hadn't breakfasted until after nine. She had been woken by the telephone ringing, but it hadn't been until Dr. Kerrison returned from the Laboratory that she knew about Dr. Lorrimer's murder. Dr. Kerrison had returned briefly to the house shortly after nine o'clock to tell her and Nell what had happened and to ring the hospital to say that any calls for him should be transferred to the reception desk at the Laboratory.

Dalgliesh said:

'I believe Dr. Lorrimer used to drive you to eleven o'clock service at St. Mary's at Guy's Marsh. He seems to have been a solitary and not a very happy man. No-one seems to have known him well. I was wondering whether he found in you the companionship and friendship he seems to have lacked in his working life.'

Massingham looked up, curious to see her response to this blatant invitation to self-revelation. She hooded her eyes like a bird, while a red blotch spread like a contagion over her throat. She said, with an attempt at archness:

'Now I'm afraid you're teasing me, Commander. It is Commander, isn't it? It seems so odd, just like a naval rank. My late brother-in-law was in the navy, so I know a little of these matters. But you were talking of friendship. That implies confidence. I should like to have helped him, but he wasn't easy to know. And there was the age difference. I'm not so very much older, less than five years, I suppose. But it's a great deal to a comparatively young man. No, I'm afraid we were just two reprobate High Anglicans in this Evangelical swampland. We didn't even sit together in church. I've always sat in the third pew down from the pulpit and he liked to be right at the back.'

Dalgliesh persisted:

'But he must have enjoyed your company. He called for you every Sunday, didn't he?'

'Only because Father Gregory asked him. There is a bus to Guy's Marsh, but I have to wait half an hour and, as Dr. Lorrimer drove past the Old Rectory, Father Gregory suggested that it would be a sensible arrangement if we travelled together. He never came in. I was always ready and waiting for him outside the drive. If his father were ill or he himself was out on a

260

case, he'd telephone. Sometimes he wasn't able to let me know, which was inconvenient. But I knew that if he didn't drive up at twenty to eleven he wouldn't be coming, and then I'd set off for the bus. Usually, of course, he came, except during the first six months of this year when he gave up Mass. But he rang early in September to say that he would be stopping for me as he used to. Naturally I never questioned him about the break. One does go through these dark nights of the soul.'

So he had stopped going to Mass when the affair with Domenica Schofield began, and had resumed his churchgoing after the break. Dalgliesh asked:

'Did he take the Sacrament?'

She was unsurprised by the question.

'Not since he started coming to Mass again in mid September. It worried me a little, I confess. I did wonder whether to suggest to him that if anything was troubling him he should have a talk with Father Gregory. But one is on very delicate ground. And it really wasn't any concern of mine.'

And she wouldn't want to offend him, thought Massingham. Those lifts in the car must have been very convenient. Dalgliesh asked:

'So he did very occasionally telephone you. Have you ever rung him?'

She turned away and fussed herself plumping up a cushion.

'Dear me, no! Why should I? I don't even know his number.'

Massingham said:

'It seems odd that he went to church at Guy's Marsh instead of in the village.'

Miss Willard looked at him severely.

'Not at all. Mr. Swaffield is a very worthy man, but he's Low, very Low. The fens have always been strongly Evangelical. When my dear father was rector here, he had constant fights with the Parochial Church Council over Reservation. And then I think that Dr. Lorrimer didn't want to get drawn into church and village activities. It's so difficult not to once you're known as a regular member of the congregation. Father Gregory didn't expect that; he realised that Dr. Lorrimer had his own father to care for and a very demanding job. Incidentally, I was very distressed that the police didn't call for Father Gregory. Someone should have called a priest to the body.'

Dalgliesh said gently:

'He had been dead some hours when the body was discovered, Miss Willard.'

'Even so, he should have had a priest.'

She stood up as if signifying that the interview was at an end. Dalgliesh was glad enough to go. He said his formal thanks and asked Miss Willard to get in touch with him immediately if anything of interest occurred to her. He and Massingham were at the door when she suddenly called out imperiously:

'Young man!'

The two detectives turned to look at her. She spoke directly to Massingham, like an old-fashioned nurse admonishing a child:

'Would you please shut the window which you so inconsiderately opened, and relight the candle.'

Meekly, as if in obedience to long-forgotten nursery commands, Massingham did so. They were left to find their own way out of the house and saw no-one. When they were in the car fastening their seat-belts, Massingham exploded:

'Good God, you'd think Kerrison could find someone more suitable than that old hag to care for his children. She's a slut, a dipsomaniac, and she's half-mad.'

'It's not so simple for Kerrison. A remote village, a large, cold house, and a daughter who can't be easy to cope with. Faced with the choice of that kind of job

262

and the dole, most women today would probably opt for the dole. Did you take a look at the bonfire?'

'Nothing there. It looks as if they're periodically burning a lot of old furniture and garden rubbish which they've got stacked in one of the coach-houses. William said that Nell made a bonfire early this morning.

'William can talk, then?' Dalgliesh asked.

'Oh William can talk. But I'm not sure that you'd be able to understand him, sir. Did you believe Miss Willard when she gave that alibi for Kerrison?'

'I'm as ready to believe her as I am Mrs. Bradley or Mrs. Blakelock when they confirmed Bradley's and Blakelock's alibis. Who can tell? We know that Kerrison did ring Dr. Collingwood at nine and was here to receive his return call at about ten. If Miss Willard sticks to her story, he's in the clear for that hour, and I've a feeling that it's the crucial hour. But how did he know that? And if he did, why suppose that we should be able to pin down the time of death so precisely? Sitting with his daughter until nine and then calling on Miss Willard just before ten looks very like an attempt to establish that he was at home during the whole of that hour.'

Massingham said:

'He must have been, to take that ten o'clock call. And I don't see how he could have got to Hoggatt's, killed Lorrimer and returned home in less than sixty minutes, not if he went on foot. And Miss Willard seems confident that he didn't take the car. I suppose it would just be possible if he took a short cut through the new Laboratory, but it would be a close thing.'

Just then the car radio bleeped. Dalgliesh took the call. It was from the Guy's Marsh control tower to say that Sergeant Reynolds at the Lab wanted to contact them. The Met Lab report had been received.

4

They opened the door together. Mrs. Bradley held a sleeping child in her arms. Bradley said:

'Come in. It's about the vomit, isn't it? I've been expecting you.'

They moved into the sitting-room. He gestured Dalgliesh and Massingham to the two chairs and sat down on the sofa opposite them. His wife moved close to him, shifting the baby's weight against her shoulder. Dalgliesh asked:

'Do you want a solicitor?'

'No. Not yet, anyway. I'm ready to tell the whole truth and it can't hurt me. At least, I suppose it can lose me my job. But that's the worst it can do. And I think I'm almost beyond caring.'

Massingham opened his notebook. Dalgliesh said to Susan Bradley:

'Wouldn't you like to put the baby in her pram, Mrs. Bradley?'

She gazed at Dalgliesh with blazing eyes, and shook her head vehemently, holding the child more tightly as if she expected them to tear her from her arms. Massingham was grateful that, at least, the child was asleep. But he wished that neither she nor her mother were there. He looked at the baby, bunched in her pink sleeping suit against her mother's shoulder, the fringe of longer hair above the tender hollowed neck, the round bare patch at the back of the head, the close shut eyes and ridiculous, snubbed nose. The frail mother with her milky bundle was more inhibiting than a whole firm of recalcitrant anti-police lawyers.

There was a lot to be said for bundling a suspect into the back of a police car and taking him off to the police station to make his statement in the functional anonymity of the interrogation room. Even the Bradleys' sitting-room provoked in him a mixture of irritation and pity. It still smelt new and unfinished. There was no fireplace, and the television held pride of place above the wall-mounted electric heater with, above it, a popular print of waves dashing against a rocky shore. The wall opposite had been papered to match the flowered curtains, but the other three were bare, the plaster already beginning to crack. There was a metal baby's high chair and, underneath it, a spread of plastic sheeting to protect the carpet. Everything looked new, as if they had brought to their marriage no accumulation of small personal impedimenta, had come spiritually naked into possession of this small, characterless room. Dalgliesh said:

'We'll take it that your previous account of your movements on Wednesday night wasn't true, or was incomplete. So what did happen?'

Massingham wondered for a moment why Dalgliesh wasn't cautioning Bradley; then he thought he knew. Bradley might have had the guts to kill if provoked beyond endurance, but he'd never have had the nerve to drop from that third-floor window. And if he didn't, how did he get out of the Laboratory? Lorrimer's killer had either used the keys or he had made that climb. All their investigations, all their careful and repeated examination of the building had confirmed that hypothesis. There was no other way.

Bradley looked at his wife. She gave him a brief, transforming smile and held out her free hand. He clasped it and they edged closer. He moistened his lips, and then began speaking as if the speech had been long rehearsed.

'On Tuesday Dr. Lorrimer finished writing my annual confidential report. He told me he wanted to talk to me about it next day before he passed it to Dr. Howarth, and he called me into his private room soon after he arrived in the Lab. He'd given me an adverse

265

report and, according to the rules, he had to explain why. I wanted to defend myself, but I couldn't. And there wasn't any real privacy. I felt that the whole Laboratory knew what was happening and was listening and waiting. Besides, I was so frightened of him, I don't know why exactly. I can't explain it. He had such an effect on me that he'd only have to be working close to me in the Laboratory and I'd start shaking. When he was away at a scene of crime it was like heaven. I could work perfectly well then. The annual confidential report wasn't unjust. I knew that my work had deteriorated. But he was partly the reason why. He seemed to take my inadequacy as a personal denigration of himself. Poor work was intolerable to him. He was obsessed by mistakes. And because I was so terrified, I made them all the more.'

He paused for a moment. No-one spoke. Then he went on:

'We weren't going to the village concert because we couldn't get a baby-sitter, and, anyway, Sue's mother was coming for supper. I got home just before six. After the meal – the curry and rice and peas – I saw her off on the seven-forty-five bus. I came straight back here. But I kept thinking of the adverse report, what Dr. Howarth would say, what I was going to do if he recommended a move, how we could possibly sell this house. We had to buy when prices were at their peak, and it's almost impossible to find buyers now, except at a loss. Besides, I didn't think another Lab would want me. After a time I thought I'd go back to the Laboratory and confront him. I think I had some idea that we might be able to communicate, that I could speak to him as another human being and make him understand how I felt. Anyway, I felt that I would go mad if I stayed indoors. I had to walk somewhere, and I walked towards Hoggatt's. I didn't tell Sue what I was going to do, and she tried to persuade me not to go out. But I went.'

He looked up at Dalgliesh and said:

'Can I have a drink of water?'

Without a word, Massingham got up and went to find the kitchen. He couldn't see the glasses, but there were two washed cups on the draining-board. He filled one with cold water and brought it back to Bradley. Bradley drained it. He drew his hand over his moist mouth and went on:

'I didn't see anyone on the way to the Laboratory. People don't walk out in this village much after dark, and I suppose most of them were at the concert. There was a light on in the hall of the Laboratory. I rang the bell and Lorrimer came. He seemed surprised to see me but I said I wanted to speak to him. He looked at his watch and said he could only spare me five minutes. I followed him up to the Biology Lab.'

He looked across directly at Dalgliesh. He said:

'It was a strange sort of interview. I sensed that he was impatient and wanted to get rid of me, and part of the time I thought that he hardly listened to what I was saying, or even knew that I was there. I didn't make a good job of it. I tried to explain that I wasn't being careless on purpose, that I really liked the work and wanted to make a success of it and be a credit to the Department. I tried to explain the effect he had on me. I don't know whether he was listening. He stood there with his eyes fixed on the floor.

'And then he looked up and began speaking. He didn't really look at me, he was looking through me, almost as if I wasn't there. And he was saying things, terrible things, as if they were words in a play, nothing to do with me. I kept hearing the same words over and over again. Failure. Useless. Hopeless. Inadequate. He even said something about marriage, as if I were a sexual failure too. I think he was mad. I can't explain what it was like, all this hate pouring out, hate, and misery and despair. I stood there shak-

ing with this stream of words pouring over me as if
. . . as if it were filth. And then his eyes focused on me
and I knew that he was seeing me, me, Clifford Bradley. His voice sounded quite different. He said:

' "You're a third-rate biologist and a fourth-rate
forensic scientist. That's what you were when you
came into this Department and you'll never change.
I have two alternatives, to check every one of your results or to risk the Service and this Laboratory being
discredited in the court. Neither is tolerable. So I suggest that you look for another job. And now I've things
to do, so please leave." '

'He turned his back on me and I went out. I knew
that it was impossible. It would have been better not
to have come. He'd never told me before exactly what
he thought of me, not in those words, anyway. I felt
sick and miserable, and I knew I was crying. That
made me despise myself the more. I stumbled upstairs
to the men's cloakroom and was just able to reach the
first basin before I vomited. I don't remember how
long I stood there, leaning over the basin, half crying
and half vomiting. I suppose it could have been three
or four minutes. After a time I put on the cold tap
and swilled my face. Then I tried to pull myself together. But I was still shaking, and I still felt sick. I
went and sat on one of the lavatory seats and sank my
head in my hands.

'I don't know how long I was there. Ten minutes
perhaps, but it could have been longer. I knew I could
never change his opinion of me, never make him
understand. He wasn't like a human being. I realised
that he hated me. But now I began to hate him and in
a different way. I'd have to leave; I knew he'd see to
that. But at least I could tell him what I thought of
him. I could behave like a man. So I went down the
stairs and into the Biology Laboratory.'

Again he paused. The child stirred in her mother's
arms and gave a little cry in her sleep. Susan Bradley

268

began an automatic jogging and crooning, but kept her eyes on her husband. Then Bradley went on:

'He was lying between the two middle examination tables, face downwards. I didn't wait to see whether he was dead. I know that I ought to feel dreadful about that, about the fact that I left him without getting help. But I don't. I can't make myself feel sorry. But at the time I wasn't glad that he was dead. I wasn't aware of any feeling except terror. I hurled myself downstairs and out of the Laboratory as if his murderer were after me. The door was still on the Yale and I know that I must have drawn back the bottom bolt, but I can't remember. I raced down the drive. I think there was a bus passing, but it had started up before I reached the gate. When I got into the road it was disappearing. Then I saw a car approaching and, instinctively, I stood back into the shadows of the walls. The car slowed down and turned into the Laboratory drive. Then I made myself walk slowly and normally. And the next thing I remember was being home.'

Susan Bradley spoke for the first time:

'Clifford told me all about it. But, of course, he had to. He looked so terrible that I knew something awful must have happened. We decided together what we'd better do. We knew that he'd had nothing to do with what had happened to Dr. Lorrimer. But who would believe Cliff? Everyone in the Department knew what Dr. Lorrimer thought of him. He would be bound to be suspected anyway, and if you found out that he was there, in the Laboratory, and at the very moment it happened, then how could he hope to persuade you that he wasn't guilty? So we decided to say that we'd been together the whole evening. My mother did ring about nine o'clock to say that she'd got safely home, and I told her that Cliff was having a bath. She'd never really liked my marriage and I didn't want to admit to her that he was out. She'd only start criticising him

269

for leaving me and the baby. So we knew that she could confirm what I'd said, and that might be some help, even though she hadn't spoken to him. And then Cliff remembered about the vomit.'

Her husband went on, almost eagerly now, as if willing them to understand and believe:

'I knew I'd swilled cold water over my face, but I couldn't be certain that the bowl was clean. The more I thought about it, the more sure I was that it was stained with vomit. And I knew how much you could learn from that. I'm a secreter, but that didn't worry me. I knew that the stomach acids would destroy the antibodies and that the Lab wouldn't be able to determine my blood group. But there was the curry powder, the dye in the peas. They'd be able to say enough about that last meal to identify me. And I couldn't lie about what we'd had for supper because Sue's mother had been here sharing it with us.

'So we had this idea of trying to stop Mrs. Bidwell going early to the Laboratory. I always get to work before nine, so I would be first on the scene quite naturally. If I went straight to the washroom as I normally would, and cleaned the bowl, then the only evidence that I was in the Lab the previous evening would be gone for ever. No-one would ever know.'

Susan Bradley said:

'It was my idea to phone Mrs. Bidwell, and I was the one who spoke to her husband. We knew that she wouldn't answer the phone. She never did. But Cliff hadn't realised that old Mr. Lorrimer wasn't entering hospital the previous day. He was put out of the Department when old Mr. Lorrimer rang. So the plan went all wrong. Mr. Lorrimer telephoned Inspector Blakelock, and everyone arrived at the Lab almost as soon as Cliff. After that, there was nothing we could do but wait.'

Dalgliesh could imagine how terrible that time of

waiting had been. No wonder that Bradley hadn't been able to face going in to the Lab. He asked:

'When you rang the bell at the Laboratory, how long was it before Dr. Lorrimer answered?'

'Almost immediately. He couldn't have come down from the Biology Department. He must have been somewhere on the ground floor.'

'Did he say anything at all about expecting a visitor?'

The temptation was obvious. But Bradley said:

'No. He talked about having things to do, but I took it that he meant the analysis he was working on.'

'And when you found the body, you saw and heard nothing of the murderer?'

'No. I didn't wait to look, of course. But I'm sure he was there and very close. I don't know why.'

'Did you notice the position of the mallet, the fact that there was a page torn from Lorrimer's notebook?'

'No. Nothing. All I can remember is Lorrimer, the body and the thin stream of blood.'

'When you were in the washroom, did you hear the doorbell?'

'No, but I don't think I could have heard it, not above the first floor. And I'm sure I wouldn't have heard it while I was being sick.'

'When Dr. Lorrimer opened the door to you, did anything strike you as unusual, apart from the fact that he had come so promptly?'

'Nothing, except that he was carrying his notebook.'

'Are you sure?'

'Yes, I'm sure. It was folded back.'

So Bradley's arrival had interrupted whatever it was that Lorrimer had been doing. And he had been on the ground floor, the floor with the Director's office, the Records Department, the Exhibits Store.

Dalgliesh said:

'The car which turned into the drive as you left; what sort of car?'

'I didn't see. All I can remember are the headlights. We don't have a car and I'm not clever at recognising the different models unless I get a clear look.'

'Can you remember how it was driven? Did the driver turn into the drive confidently as if he knew where he was going? Or did he hesitate as if he were looking for a convenient spot to stop and happened to see the open driveway?'

'He just slowed down a little and drove straight in. I think it was someone who knew the place. But I didn't wait to see if he drove up to the Lab. Next day, of course, I knew that it couldn't have been the police from Guy's Marsh or anyone with a key, or the body would have been discovered earlier.'

He looked at Dalgliesh with his anxious eyes.

'What will happen to me now? I can't face them at the Lab.'

'Inspector Massingham will drive you to Guy's Marsh police station so that you can make a formal statement and sign it. I'll explain to Dr. Howarth what has happened. Whether you go back to the Lab and when must be for him and your Establishment Department to say. I imagine they may decide to give you special leave until this affair is settled.'

If it ever were settled. If Bradley were telling the truth, they now knew that Lorrimer had died between eight-forty-five, when his father had telephoned him, and just before nine-eleven when the Guy's Marsh bus had moved away from the Chevisham stop. The clue of the vomit had fixed for them the time of death, had solved the mystery of the call to Mrs. Bidwell. But it hadn't pointed them to a murderer. And if Bradley were innocent, what sort of life would he have, inside or outside the forensic science service, unless the case were solved? He watched Massingham and Bradley on their way, then set out to walk the half-mile back to Hoggatt's, not relishing the prospect of his interview with Howarth. Glancing back, he saw that Susan Bradley was still standing at the doorway looking after him, her baby in her arms.

5

Howarth said:

'I'm not going to trot out the usual platitude about blaming myself. I don't believe in that spurious acceptance of vicarious liability. All the same, I ought to have known that Bradley was near breaking point. I suspect that old Dr. MacIntyre wouldn't have let this happen. And now I'd better telephone the Establishment Department. I expect they'll want him to stay at home for the present. It's particularly inconvenient from the point of view of the work. They need every pair of hands they can get in the Biology Department. Claire Easterbrook is taking on as much of Lorrimer's work as she can manage, but there's a limit to what she can do. At the moment she's busy with the clunch pit analysis. She's insisting on starting the electrophoresis again. I don't blame her; she's the one who'll have to give evidence. She can only speak for her own results.'

Dalgliesh asked what was likely to happen about Clifford Bradley.

'Oh, there'll be a regulation to cover the circumstances somewhere. There always is. He'll be dealt with by the usual compromise between expediency and humanity; unless, of course, you propose to arrest him for murder, in which case, administratively speaking, the problem will solve itself. By the way, the Public Relations Branch have rung. You probably haven't had time to see today's Press. Some of the papers are getting rather agitated about lab security. "Are our blood samples safe?" And one of the Sundays has com-

273

missioned an article on science in the service of crime. They're sending someone to see me at three o'clock. Public Relations would like a word with you, incidentally. They're hoping to lay on another Press conference later this afternoon.'

When Howarth had left, Dalgliesh joined Sergeant Underhill and occupied himself with the four large bundles of files which Brenda Pridmore had provided. It was extraordinary how many of six thousand cases and nearly twenty-five thousand exhibits which the Laboratory dealt with each year, had the numbers 18, 40 or 1840 in their registration. The cases came from all the Departments; Biology, Toxicology, Criminalistics, Document Examination, Blood Alcohol Analysis, Vehicle Examination. Nearly every scientist in the Laboratory above the level of Higher Scientific Officer had been concerned in them. All of them seemed perfectly in order. He was still convinced that the mysterious telephone message to Lorrimer held the clue to the mystery of his death. But it seemed increasingly unlikely that the numbers, if old Mr. Lorrimer had remembered them correctly, bore any reference to a file registration.

By three o'clock he had decided to put the task on one side and see if physical exercise would stimulate his brain. It was time, he thought, to walk through the grounds and take a look at the Wren chapel. He was reaching for his coat when the telephone rang. It was Massingham from Guy's Marsh station. The car which had parked in Hoggatt's drive on Wednesday night had at last been traced. It was a grey Cortina belonging to a Mrs. Maureen Doyle. Mrs. Doyle was at present staying with her parents in Ilford in Essex, but she had confirmed that the car was hers and that on the night of the murder it had been driven by her husband, Detective-Inspector Doyle.

6

The interview room at Guy's Marsh police station was small, stuffy and overcrowded. Superintendent Mercer, with his great bulk, was taking up more than his share of space and, it seemed to Massingham, breathing more than his share of the air. Of the five men present, including the shorthand writer, Doyle himself appeared both the most comfortable and the least concerned. Dalgliesh was questioning him. Mercer stood against the mullioned windows.

'You were at Hoggatt's last night. There are fresh tyre-marks in the earth under the trees to the right of the entrance, your tyre-marks. If you want to waste time for both of us, you can look at the casts.'

'I admit that they're my tyre-marks. I parked there, briefly, on Monday night.'

'Why?'

The question was so quiet, so reasonable, he might have had a genuine, human interest to know.

'I was with someone.' He paused and then added, 'Sir.'

'I hope, for your sake, that you were with someone last night. Even an embarrassing alibi is better than none. You quarralled with Lorrimer. You're one of the few people he would have let into the Lab. And you parked your car under the trees. If you didn't murder him, why are you trying to persuade us that you did?'

'You don't really believe I killed him. Probably you already suspect or know who did. You can't frighten me, because I know you haven't any evidence. There isn't any to get. I was driving the Cortina because the clutch had gone on the Renault, not because I didn't want to be recognised. I was with Sergeant Beale until eight o'clock. We'd been to interview a man called Barry Taylor at Muddington, and then we went on to see one or two other people who'd been at the dance last Tuesday. From eight o'clock I was driving alone, and where I went was my own business.'

'Not when it's a case of murder. Isn't that what you tell your suspects when they come out with that good old bromide about the sanctity of their private lives? You can do better than that, Doyle.'

'I wasn't at the Lab on Wednesday night. Those tyre-marks were made when I parked there last Monday.'

'The Dunlop on the left-hand back wheel is new. It was fitted on Monday afternoon by Gorringe's garage, and your wife didn't collect the Cortina until ten o'clock on Wednesday morning. If you didn't drive to Hoggatt's to see Lorrimer, then what were you doing there? And if your business was legitimate, then why park just inside the entrance and under the trees?'

'If I'd been there to murder Lorrimer, I'd have parked in one of the garages at the back. That would have been safer than leaving the Cortina in the drive. And I didn't get to Hoggatt's until after nine. I knew that Lorrimer would be working late on the clunch pit case, but not that late. The Lab was in darkness. The truth, if you must know, is that I'd picked up a woman at the crossroads just outside Manea. I wasn't in any hurry to get home, and I wanted somewhere quiet and secluded to stop. The Lab seemed as good a place as any. We were there from about nine-fifteen until nine-fifty. No-one left during that time.'

He had taken his time over what was presumably intended to be a quick one-night lay, thought Massingham. Dalgliesh asked:

'Did you trouble to find out who she was, exchange names?'

'I told her I was Ronny McDowell. It seemed as

276

good a name as any. She said she was Dora Meakin. I don't suppose that more than one of us was lying.'

'And that's all, not where she lived or worked?'

'She said she worked at the sugar-beet factory and lived in a cottage near the ruined engine-house on Hunter's Fen. That's about three miles from Manea. She said she was a widow. Like a little gentleman, I dropped her at the bottom of the lane leading to Hunter's Fen. If she wasn't telling me a yarn, that should be enough to find her.'

Chief Superintendent Mercer said grimly:

'I hope for your sake that it is. You know what this means for you, of course?'

Doyle laughed. It was a surprisingly light-hearted sound.

'Oh I know, all right. But don't let that worry you. I'm handing in my resignation, and from now.'

Dalgliesh asked:

'Are you sure about the lights? The Lab was in darkness?'

'I shouldn't have stopped there if it hadn't been. There wasn't a light to be seen. And although I admit I was somewhat preoccupied for a minute or two, I could swear that no-one came down that drive while we were there.'

'Or out of the front door?'

'That would be possible, I suppose. But the drive isn't more than forty yards long, I'd say. I think I'd have noticed, unless he slipped out very quickly. I doubt whether anyone would have risked it, not if he'd seen my headlights and knew that the car was there.'

Dalgliesh looked at Mercer. He said:

'We've got to get back to Chevisham. We'll take in Hunter's Fen on the way.'

7

Leaning over the back of the Victorian chaise-longue, Angela Foley was massaging her friend's neck. The coarse hairs tickled the back of her hands as, firmly and gently, she kneaded the taut muscles, feeling for each separate vertebra under the hot, tense skin. Stella sat, head slumped forward in her hands. Neither spoke. Outside, a light scavenging wind was blowing fitfully over the fens, stirring the fallen leaves on the patio, and gusting the thin, white wood-smoke from the cottage chimney. But inside the sitting-room all was quiet, except for the crackling of the fire, the ticking of the grandfather clock, and the sound of their breathing. The cottage was full of the pungent, resinous aroma of burning apple wood, overlaid with the savoury smell from the kitchen of beef casserole reheated from yesterday's dinner.

After a few minutes Angela Foley said:

'Better? Would you like a cold compress on your forehead?'

'No, that's lovely. Almost gone in fact. Odd that I only get a headache on those days when the book has gone particularly well.'

'Another two minutes, then I'd better see about dinner.'

Angela flexed her fingers and bent again to her task. Stella's voice, muffled in her sweater, suddenly said:

'What was it like as a child, being in local authority care?'

'I'm not sure that I know. I mean, I wasn't in a Home or anything like that. They fostered me most of the time.'

'Well, what was that like? You've never really told me.'

'It was all right. No, that's not true. It was like living in a second-rate boarding house where they don't want you and you know that you won't be able to pay the bill. Until I met you and came here I felt like that all the time, not really at home in the world. I suppose my foster-parents were kind. They meant to be. But I wasn't pretty, and I wasn't grateful. It can't be much fun fostering other people's children, and I suppose one does rather look for gratitude. Looking back, I can't see that I wasn't much joy for them, plain and surly. I once heard a neighbour say to my third foster-mother that I looked just like a foetus with my bulging forehead and tiny features. I resented the other children because they had mothers and I hadn't. I've never really outgrown that. It's despicable, but I even dislike Brenda Pridmore, the new girl on our reception desk, because she's so obviously a loved child, she's got a proper home.'

'So have you now. But I know what you mean. By the age of five you've either learned that the world is good, that everything and everyone in it stretches out towards you with love. Or you know that you're a reject. No-one ever unlearns that first lesson.'

'I have, because of you. Star, don't you think we ought to start looking for another cottage, perhaps nearer Cambridge? There's bound to be a job there for a qualified secretary.'

'We're not going to need another cottage. I telephoned my publishers this afternoon, and I think it's going to be all right.'

'Hearne and Gollingwood? But how can it be all right? I thought you said . . .'

'It's going to be all right.'

Suddenly Stella shook herself free of the ministering hands and stood up. She went into the passage and came back, her duffle-coat over her shoulder, her boots in hand. She moved over to the fireside chair and began to pull them on. Angela Foley watched her without speaking. Then Stella took from her jacket pocket a brown opened envelope and tossed it across. It fell on the velvet of the chaise-longue.

'Oh, I meant to show you this.'

Puzzled, Angela took out the single folded sheet. She said:

'Where did you find this?'

'I took it from Edwin's desk when I was rummaging about for the will. I thought at the time that I might have a use for it. Now I've decided that I haven't.'

'But, Star, you should have left it for the police to find! It's a clue. They'll have to know. This was probably what Edwin was doing that night, checking up. It's important. We can't keep it to ourselves.'

'Then you'd better go back to Postmill Cottage and pretend to find it, otherwise it's going to be a bit embarrassing explaining how we came by it.'

'But the police aren't going to believe that; they wouldn't have missed it. I wonder when it arrived at the Lab. It's odd that he took it home with him and didn't even lock it up.'

'Why should he? There was only the one locked drawer in his desk. And I don't suppose anyone, even his father, ever went into that room.'

'But, Star, this could explain why he was killed! This could be a motive for murder.'

'Oh, I don't think so. It's just a gratuitous bit of spite, anonymous, proving nothing. Edwin's death was both simpler, and more complicated, than that. Murder usually is. But the police might see it as a motive, and that would be convenient for us. I'm beginning to think I should have left it where it was.'

She had pulled on her boots and was ready to go. Angela Foley said:

'You know who killed him, don't you?'

'Does that shock you, that I haven't rushed to confide in that extraordinarily personable Commander?'

Angela whispered:

'What are you going to do?'

'Nothing. I've no proof. Let the police do the work they're paid for. I might have had more public spirit when we had the death penalty. I'm not afraid of the ghosts of hanged men. They can stand at the four corners of my bed and howl all night if it pleases them. But I couldn't go on living – I couldn't go on working, which amounts to the same thing for me – knowing that I'd put another human being in prison, and for life.'

'Not really for life. About ten years.'

'I couldn't stand it for ten days. I'm going out now. I shan't be long.'

'But, Star, it's nearly seven! We were going to eat.'

'The casserole won't spoil.'

Angela Foley watched silently as her friend went to the door. Then she said:

'Star, how did you know about Edwin practising his evidence the night before he had to go into the box?'

'If you didn't tell me, and you say that you didn't, then I must have invented it, I couldn't have learnt it from anyone else. You'd better put it down to creative imagination.'

Her hand was on the door. Angela cried out:

'Star, don't go out tonight. Stay with me. I'm afraid.'

'For yourself, or for me?'

'For both of us. Please don't go. Not tonight.'

Stella turned. She smiled and spread her hands in what could have been a gesture of resignation or a farewell. There was a howl of wind, a rush of cold air as the front door opened. Then the sound of its closing echoed through the cottage, and Stella was gone.

8

'My God, this is a dreary place!'

Massingham slammed the car door and gazed about in disbelief at the prospect before them. The lane, down which they had bumped in the fading light, had at last ended at a narrow iron bridge over a sluice, running grey and sluggish as oil, between high dykes. On the other bank was a derelict Victorian engine-house, the bricks tumbled in a disorderly heap beside the stagnant stream, the great wheel half visible through the ruined wall. Beside it were two cottages lying below water-level. Behind them the scarred and sullen acres of the hedgeless fields stretched to the red and purple of the evening sky. The carcase of a petri-fied tree, a bog-oak, struck by the plough and dredged from the depths of the peat, had been dumped beside the track to dry. It looked like some mutilated pre-historic creature raising its stumps to the uncompre-hending sky. Although the last two days had been dry with some sun, the landscape looked saturated by the weeks of rain, the front gardens sour and waterlogged, the trunks of the few stunted trees sodden as pulp. It looked a country on which the sun could never shine. As their feet rang on the iron bridge a solitary duck rose with an agitated squawking, but otherwise the silence was absolute.

There was a light behind the drawn curtains of only one of the cottages, and they walked between wind-blown clumps of faded Michaelmas daisies to the front door. The paint was peeling, the iron knocker so stiff that Dalgliesh raised it with difficulty. For a few minutes after the dull peremptory thud there was silence. Then the door was opened.

They saw a drab, shallow-faced woman, aged about

forty, with pale anxious eyes and untidy straw-coloured hair strained back under two combs. She was wearing a brown checked crimplene dress topped with a bulky cardigan in a harsh shade of blue. As soon as he saw her, Massingham instinctively drew back with an apology, but Dalgliesh said:

'Mrs. Meakin? We're police officers. May we come in?'

She didn't trouble to look at his proffered identity card. She hardly seemed surprised even. Without speaking she pressed herself against the wall of the passage and they passed before her into the sitting-room. It was small and very plainly furnished, drearily, tidy and uncluttered. The air smelt damp and chill. There was an electric reflector fire with one bar burning, and the single pendant bulb gave a harsh but inadequate light. A plain wooden table stood in the middle of the room, with four chairs. She was obviously about to start her supper. On a tray there was a plate of three fish fingers, a mound of mashed potato and peas. Beside it was an unopened carton containing an apple tart.

Dalgliesh said:

'I'm sorry that we're interrupting your meal. Would you like to take it into the kitchen to keep it warm?' She shook her head and motioned them to sit down. They settled themselves round the table like three card players, the tray of food between them. The peas were exuding a greenish liquid in which the fish fingers were slowly congealing. It was hard to believe that so small a meal could produce so strong a smell. After a few seconds, as if conscious of it, she pushed the tray to one side. Dalgliesh took out Doyle's photograph and passed it across to her. He said:

'I believe you spent some time yesterday evening with this man.'

'Mr. McDowell. He's not in any trouble is he?

You're not private detectives? He was kind, a real gentleman, I wouldn't like to get him into trouble.'

Her voice was low and rather toneless, Dalgliesh thought, a countrywoman's voice. He said:

'No, we're not private detectives. He is in some trouble, but not because of you. We're police officers. You can help him best by telling the truth. What we're really interested in is when you first met him and how long you were together.'

She looked across at him.

'You mean, a sort of alibi?'

'That's right. A sort of alibi.'

'He picked me up where I usually stand, at the crossroads, about half a mile from Manea. That must have been about seven. Then we drove to a pub. They nearly always start off by buying me a drink. That's the part I like, having someone to sit with in the pub, watching the people, hearing the voices and the noise. I usually have a sherry, or a port, maybe. If they ask me, I have a second. I never have more than two drinks. Sometimes they're in a hurry to get away so I only get offered the one.'

Dalgliesh asked quietly:

'Where did he take you?'

'I don't know where it was, but it was about thirty minutes' drive. I could see him thinking where to go before he drove off. That's how I know he lives locally. They like to get clear of the district where they're known. I've noticed that, that and the quick look round it and two vases of artificial roses behind the was called the Plough. I saw that from the illuminated sign outside. We were in the saloon bar, of course, quite nice really. They had a peat fire and there was a high shelf with a lot of different coloured plates round it and two vases of artificial roses behind the bar, and a black cat in front of the fire. The barman was called Joe. He was ginger-haired.'

'How long did you stay there?'

'Not long. I had two ports and he had two doubles of whisky. Then he said we ought to be going.'

'Where did he take you next, Mrs. Meakin?'

'I think it was Chevisham. I glimpsed the signpost at the crossroads just before we got there. We turned in to the drive of this big house and parked under the trees. I asked who lived there, and he said no-one, it was just for Government offices. Then he put out the lights.'

Dalgliesh said gently:

'And you made love in the car. Did you get into the back seat, Mrs. Meakin?'

She was neither surprised nor distressed at the question.

'No, we stayed in the front.'

'Mrs. Meakin, this is very important. Can you remember how long you were there?'

'Oh yes, I could see the clock on the dashboard. It was nearly quarter past nine when we arrived and we stayed there until just before ten. I know because I was a bit worried wondering whether he'd drop me at the end of the lane. That's all I expected. I wouldn't have wanted him to come to the door. But it can be awkward if I'm just left, miles from home. Sometimes it isn't easy to get back.'

She spoke, thought Massingham, as if she were complaining about the local bus service. Dalgliesh said:

'Did anyone leave the house and come down the drive while you were in the car? Would you have noticed if they had?'

'Oh yes, I think   I should have seen if they'd gone out through the space where the gate used to be. There's a street-light opposite and it shines on the drive.'

Massingham asked bluntly:

'But would you have noticed? Weren't you a bit occupied?'

Suddenly she laughed, a hoarse, discordant sound which startled them both.

'Do you think I was enjoying myself? Do you suppose I like it?' Then her voice again became toneless, almost subservient. She said obdurately:

'I should have noticed.'

Dalgliesh asked:

'What did you talk about, Mrs. Meakin?'

The question brightened her. She turned to Dalgliesh almost eagerly.

'Oh, he's got his troubles. Everyone has, haven't they? Sometimes it helps to talk to a stranger, someone you know you won't ever see again. They never do ask to see me again. He didn't. But he was kind, not in a rush to get away. Sometimes they almost push me out of the car. That isn't gentlemanly; it's hurtful. But he seemed glad to talk. It was about his wife really. Not wanting to live in the country. She's a London girl and keeps nagging him to get back there. She wants him to leave his job and go and work for her father. She's at home with her parents now and he doesn't know whether she'll come back.'

'He didn't tell you he was a police officer?'

'Oh no! He said he was a dealer in antiques. He seemed to know quite a lot about them. But I don't take much notice when they tell me about their jobs. Mostly they pretend.'

Dalgliesh said gently:

'Mrs. Meakin, what you are doing is terribly risky. You know that, don't you? Some day a man will stop who wants more than an hour or so of your time, someone dangerous.'

'I know. Sometimes when the car slows down and I'm standing there waiting at the side of the road, wondering what he'll be like, I can hear my heart thudding. I know then that I'm afraid. But at least I'm feeling something. It's better to be afraid than alone.'

Massingham said:

'It's better to be alone than dead.'

She looked at him.

'You think so, sir? But then you don't know anything about it, do you?'

Five minutes later they left, having explained to Mrs. Meakin that a police officer would call for her next day so that she could be taken to make a statement at Guy's Marsh station. She seemed perfectly happy about this, only asking whether anyone at the factory need know. Dalgliesh reassured her.

When they had crossed the bridge, Massingham turned to look back at the cottage. She was still standing at the door, a thin figure silhouetted against the light. He said angrily:

'God, it's all so hopeless. Why doesn't she get out of here, move to a town, Ely or Cambridge, see some life?'

'You sound like one of those professionals whose advice to the lonely is always the same: "Get out and meet people, join a club." Which, come to think of it, is precisely what she's doing.'

'It would help if she got away from this place, found herself a different job.'

'What job? She probably thinks that she's lucky to be employed. And this is at least a home. It takes youth, energy and money to change your whole life. She hasn't any of those. All she can do is to keep sane in the only way she knows.'

'But for what? To end up another corpse dumped in a clunch pit?'

'Perhaps. That's probably what she's subconsciously looking for. There's more than one way of courting death. She would argue that her way at least gives her the consolation of a warm, brightly lit bar and, always, the hope that, next time, it may be different. She isn't going to stop because a couple of intruding

287

policemen tell her that it's dangerous. She knows about that. For God's sake let's get out of here.'

As they buckled their seat belts, Massingham said:

'Who'd have thought that Doyle would have bothered with her. I can imagine him picking her up. As Lord Chesterfield said, all cats are grey in the dark. But to spend the best part of an hour telling her his troubles.'

'They each wanted something from the other. Let's hope they got it.'

'Doyle got something; an alibi. And we haven't done too badly out of their encounter. We know now who killed Lorrimer.'

Dalgliesh said:

'We think we know who and how. We may even think we know why. But we haven't a scintilla of proof and without evidence we can't move another step. At present, we haven't even enough facts to justify applying for a search warrant.'

'What now, sir?'

'Back to Guy's Marsh. When this Doyle affair is settled I want to hear Underhill's report and speak to the Chief Constable. Then back to Hoggatt's. We'll park where Doyle parked. I'd like to check whether it would be possible for someone to sneak down that drive without being seen.'

9

By seven o'clock the work was at last up to date, the last court report had been checked, the last completed exhibit packed for the police to collect, the figures of cases and exhibits received had been calculated and checked. Brenda thought how tired Inspector Blakelock seemed. He had hardly spoken an unnecessary word during the last hour. She didn't feel that he was displeased with her, merely that he hardly knew she was there. She had talked little herself, and then in whispers, afraid to break the silence, eerie and almost palpable, of the empty hall. To her right the great staircase curved upwards into darkness. All day it had echoed to the feet of scientists, policemen, Scene of Crime officers arriving for their lecture. Now it had become as portentous and threatening as the staircase of a haunted house. She tried not to look at it, but it drew her eyes irresistibly. With every fleeting upward glance she half-imagined that she could see Lorrimer's white face forming out of the amorphous shadows to hang imprinted on the still air, Lorrimer's black eyes gazing down at her in entreaty or despair.

At seven o'clock Inspector Blakelock said:

'Well, that's about all then. Your mum won't be best pleased that you've been kept late tonight.'

Brenda said with more confidence than she felt:

'Oh, mum won't mind. She knew I was late starting. I rang her earlier and said not to expect me until half-past.'

They went their separate ways to collect their coats. Then Brenda waited by the door until Inspector Blakelock had set and checked the internal alarm. All the doors of the separate laboratories had been closed and checked earlier in the evening. Lastly they went out by the front door and he turned the two final keys. Brenda's bicycle was kept in a shed by the side of the old stables, where the cars were garaged. Still together, they went round to the back. Inspector Blakelock waited to start his car until she had mounted, then followed her very slowly down the drive. At the gate he gave a valedictory hoot and turned to the left. Brenda waved and set off briskly, pedalling in the opposite direction. She thought she knew why the Inspector had waited so carefully until she was safely off the premises, and she felt grateful. Perhaps, she thought, I remind him of his dead daughter and that's why he's so kind to me.

And then, almost immediately, it happened. The sudden bump and the scrape of metal against tarmac were unmistakable. The bicycle lurched, almost throwing her into the ditch. Squeezing on both brakes she dismounted and examined the tyres by the light of the heavy torch which she always kept in her bicycle saddle-bag. Both were flat. Her immediate reaction was one of intense irritation. This would happen on a late night! She swept the torchlight over the road behind her, trying to identify the source of the mishap. There must be glass or something sharp on the road somewhere. But she could see nothing, and realised that it wouldn't help if she did. There was no hope of repairing the punctures. The next bus home was the one due to pass the Laboratory just after nine o'clock, and there was no-one left at the Lab to give her a lift. She spent very little time in thinking. The best plan was obviously to return the bicycle to its rack and then make her way home through the new Laboratory. It would cut off nearly a couple of miles and, if she walked fast, she could be home just after seven-thirty.

Anger, and ineffective railing against bad luck, is a powerful antidote to fear. So is hunger and the healthy tiredness that longs for its own fireside. Brenda had jerked the bicycle, now reduced to a ridiculously antiquated encumbrance, back into its stand and had walked briskly through the grounds of Hoggatt's and unbolted the wooden gate which led to the new site, before she began to feel afraid. But now, alone in the darkness, the half-superstitious dread which it had seemed safe to stimulate in the Laboratory with Inspector Blakelock so reassuringly by her side, began to prick at her nerves. Before her the black bulk of the half-completed Laboratory loomed like some prehistoric monument, its great slabs bloodstained with ancient sacrifices, rearing upwards towards the implacable gods. The night was fitfully dark with a low ceiling of cloud obscuring the faint stars.

As she hesitated, the clouds parted like ponderous hands to unveil the full moon, frail and transparent as a Communion wafer. Gazing at it she could almost taste the remembered transitory dough, melting against the roof of her mouth. Then the clouds formed again and the darkness closed about her. And the wind was rising.

She held the torch more firmly. It was solidly reassuring and heavy in her hand. Resolutely she picked out her way between the tarpaulin-shrouded piles of bricks, the great girders laid in rows, the two neat huts on stilts which served as the contractor's office, towards the gap in the brickwork which marked the entrance to the main site. Then once again she hesitated. The gap seemed to narrow before her eyes, to become almost symbolically ominous and frightening, an entrance to darkness and the unknown. The fears of a childhood not so far distant reasserted themselves. She was tempted to turn back.

Then she admonished herself sternly not to be stupid. There was nothing strange or sinister about a half-completed building, an artefact of brick, concrete and steel, holding no memories of the past, concealing no secret miseries between ancient walls. Besides, she knew the site quite well. The Laboratory staff weren't supposed to take a short cut through the new buildings — Dr. Howarth had pinned up a notice on the staff notice board pointing out the dangers — but everyone knew that it was done. Before the building had been started there had been a footpath across Hoggatt's field. It was natural for people to behave as if it were still there. And she was tired and hungry. It was ridiculous to hesitate now.

Then she remembered her parents. No-one at home could know about the punctures and her mother would soon begin worrying. She or her father would probably ring the Laboratory and, getting no reply, would know that everyone had left. They would imagine her dead or injured on the road, being lifted unconscious into an ambulance. Worse, they would see her lying crumpled on the floor of the laboratory, a second victim. It had been difficult enough to persuade her parents to let her stay on in the job, and this final anxiety, growing with every minute she was overdue and culminating in the relief and reactive anger of her late appearance, might easily tip them into an unreasoned but obstinate insistence that she should leave. It really was the worst possible time to be late home. She shone her torch steadily on the entrance gap and moved resolutely into the darkness.

She tried to picture the model of the new Laboratory set up in the library. This large vestibule, still unroofed, must be the reception area from which the two main wings diverged. She must bear to the left through what would be the Biology Department for the quickest cut to the Guy's Marsh road. She swept the torch beam over the brick walls, then picked her way carefully across the uneven ground towards the left-hand aperture. The pool of light found another doorway, and then another. The darkness seemed to increase, heavy with the smell of brick dust and pressed earth. And now the pale haze of the night sky was extinguished and she was in the roofed area of the Laboratory. The silence was absolute.

She found herself creeping forward, breath held, eyes fixed in a stare on the small pool of light at her feet. And suddenly there was nothing, no sky above, no doorway, nothing but black blackness. She swept the torch over the walls. They were menacingly close. This room was surely far too small even for an office. She seemed to have stumbled into some kind of cupboard or storeroom. Somewhere, she knew, there must be a gap, the one by which she had entered. But disorientated in the claustrophobic darkness, she could no longer distinguish the ceiling from the walls. With every sweep of the torch the crude bricks seemed to be closing in on her, the ceiling to descend inexorably like the slowly closing lid of a tomb. Fighting for control, she inched gradually along one wall, telling herself that, soon, she must strike the open doorway.

Suddenly the torch jerked in her hand and the pool of light spilt over the floor. She stopped dead, appalled at her peril. In the middle of the room was a square well protected only by two planks thrown across it. One step in panic and she might have kicked them away, stumbled, and dropped into ink nothingness. In her imagination the well was fathomless, her body would never be found. She would lie there in the mud and darkness, too weak to make herself heard. And all she would hear would be the distant voices of the workmen as, brick on brick, they walled her up alive in her black tomb. And then another and more rational horror struck.

She thought about the punctured tyres. Could that really have been an accident? The tyres had been sound when she had parked the bicycle that morning. Perhaps it hadn't been glass on the road after all. Perhaps someone had done it purposely, someone who knew that she would be late leaving the Lab, that there would be no-one left to give her a lift, that she would be bound to walk through the new building. She pictured him in the darkness of the early evening, slipping soundlessly into the bicycle shed, knife in hand, crouching down to the tyres, listening for the hiss of escaping air, calculating how big a rent would cause the tyres to collapse before she had cycled too far on her journey. And now he was waiting for her, knife in hand, somewhere in the darkness. He had smiled, fingering the blade, listening for her every step, watching for the light of her torch. He, too, would have a torch, of course. Soon it would blaze into her face,

293

blinding her eyes, so that she couldn't see the cruel triumphant mouth, the flashing knife. Instinctively she switched off the light and listened, her heart pounding with such a thunder of blood that she felt that even the brick walls must shake.

And then she heard the noise, gentle as a single foot-fall, soft as the brush of a coat-sleeve against wood. He was coming. He was here. And now there was only panic. Sobbing, she threw herself from side to side against the walls, thudding her bruised palms against the gritty, unyielding brick. Suddenly there was a space. She fell through, tripped, and the torch spun out of her hands. Moaning she lay and waited for death. Then terror swooped with a wild screech of exultation and a thrashing of wings which lifted the hair from her scalp. She screamed, a thin wail of sound which was lost in the bird's cry as the owl found the paneless window and soared into the night.

She didn't know how long she lay there, her sore hands clutching the earth, her mouth choked with dust. But after a while she controlled her sobbing and lifted her head. She saw the window plainly, an immense square of luminous light, pricked with stars. And to the right of it gleamed the doorway. She scrambled to her feet. She didn't wait to search for the torch but made straight for that blessed aperture of light. Beyond it was another. And, suddenly, there were no more walls, only the spangled dome of the sky swinging above her.

Still sobbing, but now with relief, she ran unthink-ingly in the moonlight, her hair streaming behind her, her feet hardly seeming to touch the earth. And now there was a belt of trees before her and, gleaming through the autumn branches, the Wren chapel, lit from within, beckoning and holy, shining like a pic-ture on a Christmas card. She ran towards it, palms outstretched, as hundreds of her forebears in the dark fens must have rushed to their altars for sanc-

294

tuary. The door was ajar and a shaft of light lay like an arrow on the path. She threw herself against the oak, and the great door swung inwards into a glory of light.

At first her mind, shocked into stupor, refused to recognise what her dazzled eyes so clearly saw. Uncomprehending, she put up a tentative hand and stroked the soft corduroy of the slacks, the limp moist hand. Slowly, as if by an act of will, her eyes travelled upwards and she both saw and understood. Stella Mawson's face, dreadful in death, drooped above her, the eyes half open, the palms disposed outward as if in a mute appeal for pity or for help. Circling her neck was a double cord of blue silk, its tasselled end tied high to a hook on the wall. Beside it, wound on a second hook, was the single bell-rope. There was a low wooden chair upended close to the dangling feet. Brenda seized it. Moaning, she grasped at the rope and swung on it three times before it slipped from her loosening hands, and she fainted.

10

Less than a mile away across the field and the grounds of Hoggatt's, Massingham drove the Rover into the Laboratory drive and backed into the bushes. He switched off the car lights. The street-lamp opposite the entrance cast a soft glow over the path, and the door of the Laboratory was plainly visible in the moonlight. He said:

'I'd forgotten, sir, that tonight is the night of the full moon. He'd have had to wait until it moved behind a cloud. Even so, he could surely get out of the house and down the drive unseen if he chose a lucky moment. After all, Doyle had his mind – and not only his mind – on other things.'

'But the murderer wasn't to know that. If he saw the car arriving, I doubt whether he would have risked it. Well, we can at least find out if it's possible even without the cooperation of Mrs. Meakin. This reminds me of a childhood game, Grandmother's Footsteps. Will you try first, or shall I?'

But the experiment was destined never to take place. It was at that moment that they heard, faint but unmistakable, the three clear peals of the chapel bell.

11

Massingham drove the car fast on to the grass verge and braked within inches of the hedge. Beyond them the road curved gently between a tattered fringe of windswept bushes, past what looked like a dilapidated barn of blackened wood and on through the naked fens to Guy's Marsh. To the right was the black bulk of the new Laboratory. Massingham's torch picked out a stile, and, beyond it, a footpath leading across the field to the distant circle of trees, now no more than a dark smudge against the night sky. He said:

'Odd how remote from the house it is, and how secluded. You wouldn't know it was there. Anyone would think that the original family built it for some secret, necromantic rite.'

'More probably as a family mausoleum. They didn't plan for extinction.'

Neither of them spoke again. They had instinctively driven the mile and a half to the nearest access to the chapel from the Guy's Marsh road. Although less direct, this was quicker and easier than finding their way by foot through the Laboratory grounds and the new building. Their feet quickened and they found they were almost running, driven by some unacknowledged fear, towards the distant trees.

And now they were in the circle of loosely planted beeches, dipping their heads under the low branches, their feet scuffling noisily through the crackling drifts of fallen leaves, and could see at last the faintly gleaming windows of the chapel. At the half open door Massingham instinctively turned as if to hurl his shoulder against it, then drew back with a grin.

'Sorry, I'm forgetting. No sense in precipitating myself in. It's probably only Miss Willard polishing the brass or the rector saying an obligatory prayer to keep the place sanctified.'

Gently, and with a slight flourish, he pushed open the door and stood aside; and Dalgliesh stepped before him into the lighted antechapel.

After that there was no speech, no conscious thought, only instinctive action. They moved as one. Massingham grasped and lifted the dangling legs and Dalgliesh, seizing the chair upturned by Brenda's slumping body, slipped the double loop of cord from Stella Mawson's neck and lowered her to the floor. Massingham tore at the fastenings of her duffle jacket, forced back her head and, flinging himself beside her, closed his mouth over hers. The bundle huddled against the wall stirred and moaned, and Dalgliesh knelt beside her. At the touch of his arms on her shoulders she struggled madly for a moment, squealing like a kitten, then opened her eyes and recognised him. Her body relaxed against his. She said faintly:

'The murderer. In the new Lab. He was waiting for me. Has he gone?'

There was a panel of light switches to the left of the door. Dalgliesh clicked them on with a single gesture, and the inner chapel blazed into light. He stepped through the carved organ-screen into the chancel. It was empty. The door to the organ loft was ajar. He clattered up the narrow winding stairway into the gallery. It, too, was empty. Then he stood looking down at the quiet emptiness of the chancel, his eyes moving

297

from the exquisite plaster ceiling, the chequered marble floor, the double row of elegantly carved stalls with their high-arched backs set against the north and south walls, the oak table, stripped of its altar-cloth, with their high-arched backs set against the north and dow. All it now held were two silver candlesticks, the tall white candles burnt half down, the wicks blackened. And to the left of the altar, hanging incongruously, was a wooden hymnboard, showing four numbers:

29

10

18

40

He recalled old Mr. Lorrimer's voice, 'She said something about the can being burned and that she'd got the numbers.' The last two numbers had been 18 and 40. And what had been burned was not a can, not cannabis, but two altar candles.

12

Forty minutes later, Dalgliesh was alone in the chapel. Dr. Greene had been sent for, had briefly pronounced Stella Mawson dead, and had departed. Massingham had left with him to take Brenda Pridmore home and to explain to her parents what had happened, to call at Sprogg's Cottage and to summon Dr. Howarth. Dr. Greene had given Brenda a sedative by injection, but had held out no hope that she would be fit to be questioned before morning. The forensic pathologist had been summoned and was on his way. The voices, the questions, the ringing footsteps, all for the moment were stilled.

Dalgliesh felt extraordinarily alone in the silence of of the chapel, more alone because her body lay there, and he had the sense that someone – or something – had recently left, leaving bereft the unencumbered air. This isolation of the spirit was not new to him; he had felt it before in the company of the recently dead. Now he knelt and gazed intently at the dead woman. In life only her eyes had lent distinction to that haggard face. Now they were glazed and gummy as sticky sweetmeats forced under the half-opened lids. It was not a peaceful face. Her features, not yet settled in death, still bore the strain of life's unquietude. He had seen so many dead faces. He had become adept at reading the stigmata of violence. Sometimes they could tell him how, or where, or when. But essentially, as now, they told him nothing.

He lifted the end of the cord still looped loosely around her neck. It was made of woven silk in royal blue, long enough to drape a heavy curtain, and was finished with an ornate silver and blue tassel. There was a five-foot panelled chest against the wall and, putting on his gloves, he lifted the heavy lid. The smell of mothballs came up to him, pungent as an anaesthetic. Inside the chest was a folded pair of faded blue velvet curtains, a starched but crumpled surplice, the black and white of an M.A. hood, and, lying on top of this assorted bundle, a second tasselled cord. Whoever had put that cord round her neck – herself or another – had known in advance where it could be found.

He began to explore the chapel. He walked softly, yet his feet fell with portentous heaviness on the marbled floor. Slowly, he paced between the two rows of splendidly carved stalls towards the altar. In design and furnishing the building reminded him of his college chapel Even the smell was the same, a scholastic smell, cold austere, only faintly ecclesiastical. Now that the altar had been denuded of all its furnishing except the two candlesticks, the chapel looked purely secular, unconsecrated. Perhaps it always had. Its formal classicism rejected emotion. It enshrined man, not God; reason, not mystery. This was a place where certain reassuring rituals had been enacted, reaffirming its proprietor's view of the proper order of the universe and his own place in that order. He looked for some memento of that original owner and found it. To the right of the altar was the chapel's only memorial, a carved bust, half draped with a looped marble curtain, of a bewigged eighteenth-century gentleman, with the inscription:

Dieu aye merci de son ame.

This simple petition, unadorned, so out of period, was singularly inapposite to the formal confidence of the memorial, the proud tilt of the head, the self-satisfied smirk on the opulent marble lips. He had built his chapel and set it in a triple circle of trees, and death had not stayed its hand even long enough to give him time to make his carriage drive.

On either side of the organ-screen and facing the east window were two ornate stalls under carved canopies, each shielded from draughts by a blue velvet curtain similar to those in the chest. The seats were fitted with matching cushions; soft cushions with silver tassels at each corner lay on the book-rests. He climbed into the right-hand stall. On the cushion was a heavy black leather Book of Common Prayer which looked unused. The pages opened stiffly and the bold black and red lettering shone from the page.

'For I am a stranger with thee: and a sojourner, as all my fathers were. O spare me a little, that I may recover my strength: before I go hence, and be no more seen.'

He held the book by its spine and shook it. No paper fluttered from its rigid leaves. But where it had lain, four hairs, one fair and three dark, had adhered to the velvet pile. He took an envelope from his

300

pocket and stuck them to the gummed flap. He knew how little the forensic scientists could hope to do with only four hairs, but it was possible that something could be learned.

The chapel, he thought, must have been ideal for them. Shielded by its trees, isolated, secure, warm even. The fen villagers kept indoors once darkness fell and, even in the evening light, would have a half-superstitious dread of visiting this empty and alien shrine. Even without a key they need fear no casual intruder. She need only watch that she was unobserved when she drove the red Jaguar into Hoggatt's drive to park it out of sight in one of the garages in the stable block. And then what? Wait for the light in the Biology Department to go out at last, for the advancing gleam of light from Lorrimer's torch as he joined her for that walk through the Lab grounds and into the trees. He wondered whether she had dragged the velvet cushions to the sanctuary, whether it had added to the excitement to make love to Lorrimer in front of that denuded altar, the new passion triumphing over the old.

Massingham's flame of hair appeared in the doorway. He said:

'The girl's all right. Her mother got her straight to bed and she's asleep. I called next at Sprogg's Cottage. The door was open and the sitting-room light was on, but there's no-one there. Howarth was at home when I rang, but not Mrs. Schofield. He said he'd be along. Dr. Kerrison is at the hospital at a medical committee meeting. His housekeeper said that he left just after seven. I didn't ring the hospital. If he is there, he'll be able to produce plenty of witnesses.'

'And Middlemass?'

'No answer. Out to dinner, or at the local perhaps. No answer either from the Blakelocks' number. Anything here, sir?'

'Nothing, except what we'd expect to find. You've got a man posted to direct Blain-Thomson when he arrives?'

'Yes, sir. And I think he's arriving now.'

13

Dr. Reginald Blain-Thomson had a curious habit, before beginning his examination, of mincing round the body, eyes fixed on it with wary intensity as if half afraid that the corpse might spring into life and seize him by the throat. He minced now, immaculate in his grey pinstriped suit, the inevitable rose in its silver holder looking as fresh in his lapel as if it were a June blossom, newly plucked. He was a tall, lean-faced, aristocratic looking bachelor with a skin as freshly pink and soft as that of a girl. He was never known to put on protective clothing before examining a body, and reminded Dalgliesh of one of those television cooks who prepare a four-course dinner in full evening dress for the pleasure of demonstrating the essential refinement of their craft. It was even rumoured, unjustly, that Blain-Thomson performed his autopsy in a lounge suit.

But, despite these personal idiosyncrasies, he was an excellent forensic pathologist. Juries loved him. When he stood in the box and recited, with slightly world-weary formality and in his actor's voice, the details of his formidable qualifications and experience, they gazed at him with the respectful admiration of men who know a distinguished consultant when they see one, and have no intention of being so disobliging as to disbelieve what he might choose to tell them.

Now he squatted by the body, listened, smelled and touched. Then he switched off his examination torch and got to his feet. He said:

'Yes, well. Obviously she's dead and it's very recent. Within the last two hours, if you press me. But you must have reached that conclusion yourselves or you wouldn't have cut her down. When did you say you found her? Three minutes after eight. Dead one and a half hours then, say. It's possible. You're going to ask me whether it's suicide or murder. All I can say at the moment is that there's only the double mark encircling the neck and the cord fits. But you can see that for yourselves. There's no sign of manual throttling, and it doesn't look as if the cord were superimposed on a finer ligature. She's a frail woman, little more than seven stone, I'd estimate, so it wouldn't need strength to overpower her. But there's no sign of a struggle and the nails look perfectly clean, so she probably didn't get the chance to scratch. If it is murder, he must have come up behind her very swiftly, dropped the looped cord over her head, and strung her up almost as soon as unconsciousness supervened. As for the cause of death -- whether it's strangulation, broken neck or vagal inhibition -- well, you'll have to wait until I get her on the table. I can take her away now if you're ready.'

'How soon can you do the P.M.?'

'Well, it had better be at once, hadn't it? You're keeping me busy, Commander. No questions about my report on Lorrimer, I suppose?'

Dalgliesh answered:

'None, thank you. I did try to get you on the phone.'

'I'm sorry I've been elusive. I've been incarcerated in committees practically all day. When's the Lorrimer inquest?'

'Tomorrow, at two o'clock.'

'I'll be there. They'll adjourn it, I suppose. And I'll give you a ring and a preliminary report as soon as I've got her sewn up.'

He drew on his gloves carefully, finger by finger, then left. They could hear him exchanging a few words with the constable who was waiting outside to light him across the field to his car. One of them laughed. Then the voices faded.

Massingham put his head outside the door. The two dark-uniformed attendants from the mortuary van, anonymous bureaucrats of death, manœuvred their trolley through the door with nonchalant skill. Stella Mawson's body was lifted with impersonal gentleness. The men turned to trundle the trolley out through the door. But suddenly the way was blocked by two dark shadows, and Howarth and his sister stepped quietly and simultaneously into the light of the chapel. The figures with the trolley paused, stock-still like ancient helots, unseeing, unhearing.

Massingham thought that their entrance seemed as dramatically contrived as that of a couple of film stars arriving at a première. They were dressed identically in slacks and fawn leather jackets, lined with shaggy fur, the collars upturned. And for the first time he was struck by their essential likeness. The impression of a film was reinforced. Gazing at the two pale, arrogant heads framed with fur, he thought that they looked like decadent twins, their fair, handsome profiles theatrically posed against the dark oak panelling. Again simultaneously, their eyes moved to the shrouded lump on the trolley, then fixed themselves on Dalgliesh. He said to Howarth:

'You took your time coming.'

'My sister was out driving and I waited for her to return. You said you wanted both of us. I wasn't given to understand that it was of immediate urgency. What has happened? Inspector Massingham wasn't exactly forthcoming when he so peremptorily summoned us.'

'Stella Mawson is dead by hanging.'

He had no doubt that Howarth appreciated the significance of his careful use of words. Their eyes moved from the two hooks on the chapel wall, one with the bell-rope hitched over it, to the blue cord with its

304

dangling tassel held lightly in Dalgliesh's hand. Howarth said:

'I wonder how she knew how to find the cord. And why choose here?'

'You recognise the cord?'

'Isn't it from the chest? There should be two identical cords. We had an idea of hanging the curtains at the entrance to the chancel when we held our concert on the twenty-sixth of August. As it happens, we decided against it. The evening was too hot to worry about draughts. There were two tasselled cords in the chest then.'

'Who could have seen them?'

'Almost anyone who was helping with the preparations: myself, my sister, Miss Foley, Martin, Blakelock. Middlemass gave a hand arranging the hired chairs, and so did a number of people from the Lab. Some of the women helped with the refreshments after the concert and they were fussing about here during the afternoon. The chest isn't locked. Anyone who felt curious could have looked inside. But I don't see how Miss Mawson could have known about the cord. She was at the concert, but she had no hand in the preparations.'

Dalgliesh nodded to the men with the trolley. They pushed it gently forward, and Howarth and Mrs. Schofield stood aside to let it pass. Then Dalgliesh asked:

'How many keys are there to this place?'

'I told you yesterday. I know of only one. It's kept on a board in the Chief Liaison Officer's room.'

'And that's the one at present in the lock?' Howarth did not turn his head. He said:

'If it's got the Laboratory plastic tab – yes.'

'Do you know if it was handed out to anyone today?'

'No. That's hardly the sort of detail Blakelock would worry me with.'

Dalgliesh turned to Domenica Schofield:

'And that's the one, presumably, that you borrowed to get extra keys cut when you decided to use the chapel for your meetings with Lorrimer. How many keys?'

She said calmly:

'Two. One you found on his body. This is the second.'

She took it from her jacket pocket and held it out in the palm of her hand in a gesture of dismissive contempt. For a moment it appeared that she was about to tilt her palm and let it clatter on the floor.

'You don't deny that you came here?'

'Why should I? It's not illegal. We were both of age, in our right minds, and free. Not even adultery; merely fornication. You seem fascinated by my sex-life, Commander, even in the middle of your more normal preoccupations. Aren't you afraid it's becoming rather an obsession?'

Dalgliesh's voice didn't change. He went on:

'And you didn't ask for the key back when you broke with Lorrimer?'

'Again, why should I? I didn't need it. It wasn't an engagement ring.'

Howarth hadn't looked at his half-sister during this exchange. Suddenly he said harshly:

'Who found her?'

'Brenda Pridmore. She's been taken home. Dr. Greene is with her now.'

Domenica Schofield's voice was surprisingly gentle:

'Poor child. She seems to be making a habit of finding bodies, doesn't she? Now that we've explained to you about the keys, is there anything else you want us for tonight?'

'Only to ask you both where you've been since six o'clock.'

Howarth said:

'I left Hoggatt's at about a quarter to six and I've been at home ever since. My sister's been out driving

306

alone since seven o'clock. She likes to do that occasion-ally.'

Domenica Schofield said:

'I'm not sure if I can give you the precise route, but I did stop at an agreeable pub at Whittlesford for a drink and a meal shortly before eight o'clock. They'll probably remember me. I'm fairly well known there. Why? Are you telling us that this is murder?'

'It's an unexplained death.'

'And a suspicious one, presumably. But haven't you considered that she might have murdered Lorrimer and then taken her own life?'

'Can you give me one good reason why she should have?'

She laughed softly.

'Murdered Edwin? For the best and commonest of reasons, or so I've always read. Because she was once married to him. Hadn't you discovered that for yourself, Commander?'

'How did you know?'

'Because he told me. I'm probably the only person in the world he ever did tell. He said the marriage wasn't consummated and they got an annulment within two years. I suppose that's why he never brought his bride home. It's an embarrassing business, showing off one's new wife to one's parents and the village, particularly when she isn't a wife at all and one suspects that she never will be. I don't think his parents ever did know, so it's really not so surprising if you didn't. But then, one expects you to ferret out everything about people's private concerns.'

Before Dalgliesh could reply, their ears caught, simultaneously, the hurried footfall on the stone step, and Angela Foley stood inside the door. She was flushed with running. Looking wildly from face to face, her body heaving, she gasped:

'Where is she? Where's Star?'

Dalgliesh moved forward, but she backed away as if terrified that he might touch her. She said:

'Those men. Under the trees. Men with a torch. They're wheeling something. What is it? What have you done with Star?'

Without looking at her half-brother, Domenica Schofield put out her hand. His reached out to meet it. They didn't move closer together, but stood, distanced, rigidly linked by those clasped hands. Dalgliesh said:

'I'm sorry, Miss Foley. Your friend is dead.'

Four pairs of eyes watched as her own eyes turned, first to the blue loops of cord dangling from Dalgliesh's hand, then to the twin hooks, lastly to the wooden chair now tidily placed against the wall. She whispered:

'Oh no! Oh no!'

Massingham moved to take her arm, but she shook free. She threw back her head like a howling animal and wailed:

'Star! Star!' Before Massingham could restrain her she had run from the chapel and they could hear her wild, despairing cry borne back to them on the light wind.

Massingham ran after her. She was silent now, weaving through the trees, running fast. But he caught up with her easily before she reached the two distant figures with their dreadful burden. At first she fought madly; but suddenly, she collapsed in his arms and he was able to lift her and carry her to the car.

When he got back to the chapel, thirty minutes later, Dalgliesh was sitting quietly in one of the stalls, apparently engrossed with the Book of Common Prayer. He put it down and said:

'How is she?'

'Dr. Greene's given her a sedative. He's arranged for the district nurse to stay the night. There's no-one else he could think of. It looks as if neither she nor

308

Brenda Pridmore will be fit to be questioned before morning.'

He looked at the small heap of numbered cards on the seat beside Dalgliesh. His chief said:

'I found them at the bottom of the chest. I suppose we can test these and those in the board for finger-prints. But we know what we shall find.'

Massingham asked:

'Did you believe Mrs. Schofield's story that Lorrimer and Stella Mawson were married?'

'Oh yes, I think so. Why lie when the facts can be so easily checked? And it explains so much; that extra-ordinary change of will; even the outburst when he was talking to Bradley. That first sexual failure must have gone deep. Even after all these years he couldn't bear to think that she might benefit even indirectly from his will. Or was it the thought that unlike him, she had found happiness – and found it with a woman – that he found so insupportable?'

Massingham said:

'So she and Angela Foley get nothing. But that's not a reason for killing herself. And why here, of all places?'

Dalgliesh got to his feet.

'I don't think she did kill herself. This was murder.'

BOOK FIVE
THE CLUNCH PIT

1

They were at Bowlem's Farm before first light. Mrs. Pridmore had begun her baking early. Already two large earthenware bowls covered with humped linen stood on the kitchen table, and the whole cottage was redolent with the warm, fecund smell of yeast. When Dalgliesh and Massingham arrived Dr. Greene, a squat broad-shouldered man with the face of a benevolent toad, was folding his stethoscope into the depths of an old-fashioned Gladstone bag. It was less than twelve hours since Dalgliesh and he had last met, since, as police surgeon, he had been the first doctor to be called to Stella Mawson's body. He had examined it briefly and had then pronounced:

'Is she dead? Answer: yes. Cause of death? Answer: hanging. Time of death? About one hour ago. Now you'd better call in the expert and he'll explain to you why the first question is the only one he's at present competent to answer.'

Now he wasted no time on civilities or questions but nodded briefly to the two detectives and continued talking to Mrs. Pridmore.

'The lass is fine. She's had a nasty shock but nothing that a good night's sleep hasn't put right. She's young and healthy, and it'll take more than a couple of corpses to turn her into a neurotic wreck, if that's what you're frightened of. My family has been doctoring yours for three generations and there's none of you gone off your heads yet.' He nodded to Dalgliesh. 'You can go up now.'

Arthur Pridmore was standing beside his wife, his hand gripping her shoulder. No-one had introduced him to Dalgliesh; nor was there need. He said:

'She hasn't faced the worst yet, has she? This is the

second body. What do you think life in this village will be like for her if these two deaths aren't solved?'

Dr. Greene was impatient. He snapped shut his bag.

'Good grief, man, no-one's going to suspect Brenda! She's lived here all her life. I brought her into the world.'

'That's no protection against slander, though, is it? I'm not saying they'll accuse her. But you know the fens. Folk here can be superstitious, unforgetting and unforgiving. There's such a thing as being tainted with bad luck.'

'Not for your pretty Brenda, there isn't. She'll be the local heroine, most likely. Shake off this morbid nonsense, Arthur. And come out to the car with me. I want a word about that business at the Parochial Church Council.' They went out together. Mrs. Pridmore looked up at Dalgliesh. He thought that she had been crying. She said:

'And now you're going to question her, make her talk about it, raking it all up again.'

'Don't worry,' said Dalgliesh gently, 'talking about it will help.'

She made no move to accompany them upstairs, a tact for which Dalgliesh was grateful. He could hardly have objected, particularly as there hadn't been time to get a policewoman, but he had an idea that Brenda would be both more relaxed and more communicative in her mother's absence. She called out happily to his knock. The little bedroom with its low beams and its curtains drawn against the morning darkness was full of light and colour, and she was sitting up in bed fresh and bright-eyed, her aureole of hair tumbling around her shoulders. Dalgliesh wondered anew at the resilience of youth. Massingham, halted suddenly in the doorway, thought that she ought to be in the Uffizi, her feet floating above a meadow of spring flowers, the whole sunlit landscape of Italy stretching behind her into infinity.

It was still very much a schoolgirl's room. There were two shelves of schoolbooks, another with a collection of dolls in national costumes, and a cork board with cut-outs from the Sunday supplements and photographs of her friends. There was a wicker chair beside the bed holding a large teddy bear. Dalgliesh removed it and placed it on the bed beside her, then sat down. He said:

'How are you feeling? Better?'

She leaned impulsively towards him. The sleeve of her cream dressing-jacket fell over the freckled arm. She said:

'I'm so glad you've come. No-one wants to talk about it. They can't realise that I've got to talk about it sometime and it's much better now while it's fresh in my mind. It was you who found me, wasn't it? I remember being picked up – rather like Marianne Dastwood in *Sense and Sensibility* – and the nice tweedy smell of your jacket. But I can't remember anything after that. I do remember ringing the bell, though.'

'That was clever of you. We were parked in Hoggatt's drive and heard it, otherwise it might have been hours before the body was found.'

'It wasn't clever really. It was just panic. I suppose you realise what happened? I got a puncture in my bike and decided to walk home through the new Lab. Then I got rather lost and panicked. I started thinking about Dr. Lorrimer's murderer and imagining that he was lying in wait for me. I even imagined that he might have punctured the tyres on purpose. It seems silly now, but it didn't then.'

Dalgliesh said:

'We've examined the bicycle. There was a lorry-load of grit passing the Lab during the afternoon and some of the load was shed. You had a sharp flint in each tyre. But it was a perfectly natural fear. Can you remember whether there really was someone in the building?'

'Not really. I didn't see anyone and I think I imagined most of the sounds I heard. What really frightened me was an owl. Then I got out of the building and rushed in panic across a field straight towards the chapel.'

'Did you get the impression that anyone might be there alive in the chapel?'

'Well, there aren't any pillars to hide behind. It's a funny chapel, isn't it? Not really a holy place. Perhaps it hasn't been prayed in enough. I've only been there once before when Dr. Howarth and three of the staff from the Lab gave a concert, so I know what it's like. Do you mean he could have been crouched down in one of the stalls watching me? It's a horrible idea.'

'It is rather. But now that you're safe, could you bear to think about it?'

'I can now you're here.' She paused. 'I don't think he was. I didn't see anyone, and I don't think I heard anyone. But I was so terrified that I probably wouldn't have noticed. All I could see was this bundle of clothes strung up on the wall, and then the face drooping down at me.'

He didn't need to warn her of the importance of his next question.

'Can you remember where you found the chair, its exact position?'

'It was lying overturned just to the right of the body as if she had kicked it away. I think it had fallen backwards, but it might have been on its side.'

'But you're quite sure that it had fallen?'

'Quite sure. I remember turning it upright so that I could stand on it to reach the bell rope.' She looked at him, bright-eyed.

'I shouldn't have done that, should I? Now you won't be able to tell whether any marks or soil on the seat came from my shoes or hers. Was that why Inspector Massingham took away my shoes last night? Mummy told me.'

'Yes, that's why.'

The chair would be tested for prints, then sent for examination to the Metropolitan Laboratory. But this murder, if it were murder, had been premeditated. Dalgliesh doubted whether, this time, the killer would have made any mistakes.

Brenda said:

'One thing has struck me, though. It's odd, isn't it, that the light was on?'

'That's another thing that I wanted to ask you. You're quite sure that the chapel was lit? You didn't switch on the light yourself?'

'I'm quite sure I didn't. I saw the lights gleaming through the trees. Rather like the City of God, you know. It would have been more sensible to have run for the road once I'd got clear of the new building. But suddenly I saw the shape of the chapel and the light shining faintly through the windows, and I ran towards it almost by instinct.'

'I expect it was by instinct. Your ancestors did the same. Only they would have run for sanctuary to St. Nicholas's.'

'I've been thinking about the lights ever since I woke up. It looks like suicide, doesn't it? I don't suppose people kill themselves in the dark. I know I wouldn't. I can't imagine killing myself at all unless I was desperately ill and lonely and in terrible pain, or someone was torturing me to make me give them vital information. But if I did, I wouldn't switch the lights off. I'd want to see my last of the light before I went into the darkness, wouldn't you? But murderers always want to delay discovery of the body, don't they? So why didn't he turn off the light and lock the door?'

She spoke with happy unconcern. The illness, the loneliness and the pain were as unreal and remote as was the torture. Dalgliesh said:

'Perhaps because he wanted it to look like suicide. Was that your first thought when you found the body, that she'd killed herself?'

'Not at the time. I was too frightened to think at all. But since I've woken up and started considering it all – yes, I suppose I do think it was suicide.'

'But you're not sure why you think that?'

'Perhaps because hanging is such a strange way of killing someone. But suicides often do hang themselves, don't they? Mr. Bowlem's previous pigman did – in the tithe-barn. And old Annie Makepeace. I've noticed that, in the fens, people usually shoot themselves or hang themslves. You see, on a farm, there's always a gun or a rope.'

She spoke simply and without fear. She had lived on a farm all her life. There was always birth and death, the birth and death of animals and of humans too. And the long nights of the fen winters would bring their own miasma of madness or despair. But not to her. He said:

'You appal me. It sounds like a holocaust.'

'It doesn't happen often, but one remembers when it does. I just associate hanging with suicide. Do you think this time I'm wrong?'

'I think you could be. But we shall find out. You've been very helpful.'

He spent another five minutes talking to her, but there was nothing that she could add. She hadn't gone with Inspector Blakelock to Chief Inspector Martin's office when he set the night alarms, so couldn't say whether or not the key to the chapel was still on its hook. She had only met Stella Mawson once before at the concert in the chapel, when she had sat in the same row as Angela Foley, Stella Mawson, Mrs. Schofield and Dr. Kerrison and his children.

As Dalgliesh and Massingham were leaving, she said:

'I don't think Mum and Dad will let me go back to the Lab now. In fact I'm sure they won't. They want me to marry Gerald Bowlem. I think I would like to marry Gerald, at least, I've never thought of marrying anyone else, but not just yet. It would be nice to be a scientist and have a proper career first. But Mum won't have an easy moment if I stay at the Lab. She loves me, and I'm all she's got. You can't hurt people when they love you.'

Dalgliesh recognised an appeal for help. He went back and sat again in the chair. Massingham, pretending to look out of the window, was intrigued. He wondered what they would think at the Yard if they could see the old man taking time from a murder investigation to advise on the moral ambiguities of Women's Lib. But he rather wished that she had asked him. Since they had come into the room she had looked only at Dalgliesh. Now he heard him say:

'I suppose a scientific job isn't easy to combine with being a farmer's wife.'

'I don't think it would be very fair to Gerald.'

'I used to think that we can have almost anything we want from life, that it's just a question of organisation. But now I'm beginning to think that we have to make a choice more often than we'd like. The important thing is to make sure that it's our choice, no-one else's, and that we make it honestly. But one thing I'm sure of is that it's never a good thing to make a decision when you're not absolutely well. Why not wait a little time, until we've solved Dr. Lorrimer's murder anyway. Your mother may feel differently then.'

She said:

'I suppose this is what murder does, changes people's lives and spoils them.'

'Changes, yes. But it needn't spoil. You're young and intelligent and brave, so you won't let it spoil yours.'

Downstairs, in the farmhouse kitchen, Mrs. Pridmore was sandwiching fried rashers of bacon between generous slices of crusty bread. She said gruffly:

'You both look as if you could do with some breakfast. Up all night, I daresay. It won't hurt you to sit down and take a couple of minutes to eat these. And I've made fresh tea.'

Supper the previous night had been a couple of sandwiches fetched by a constable from the Moonraker and eaten in the antechapel. Not until he smelt the bacon did Massingham realise how hungry he was. He bit gratefully into the warm bread to the oozing saltiness of home-cured bacon, and washed it down with strong, hot tea. He felt cosseted by the warmth and friendliness of the kitchen, this cosy womb-like shelter from the dark fens. Then the telephone rang. Mrs. Pridmore went to answer it. She said:

'That was Dr. Greene ringing from Sprogg's Cottage. He says to tell you that Angela Foley is well enough to speak to you now.'

2

Angela Foley came slowly into the room. She was fully dressed and perfectly calm, but both men were shocked by the change in her. She walked stiffly, and her face looked aged and bruised as if she had suffered all night a physical assault of grief. Her small eyes were pale and sunken behind the jutting bones, her cheeks were unhealthily mottled, the delicate mouth was swollen and there was a herpes on the upper lip. Only her voice was unchanged; the childish, unemphatic voice with which she had answered their first questions.

The district nurse, who had spent the night at

Sprogg's Cottage, had lit the fire. Angela looked at the crackling wood and said:

'Stella never lit the fire until late in the afternoon. I used to lay it in the morning before I went to the Lab, and she'd put a match to it about half an hour before I was due home.'

Dalgliesh said:

'We found Miss Mawson's house-keys on her body. I'm afraid we had to unlock her desk to examine her papers. You were asleep, so we weren't able to ask you.'

She said, dully:

'It wouldn't have made any difference, would it? You would have looked just the same. You had to.'

'Did you know that your friend once went through a form of marriage with Edwin Lorrimer? There wasn't a divorce; the marriage was annulled after two years because of non-consummation. Did she tell you?'

She turned to look at him, but it was impossible to gauge the expression in those small, pig-like eyes. If her voice held any emotion, it was closer to wry amusement than to surprise.

'Married? She and Edwin? So that's how she knew . . .' She broke off. 'No, she didn't tell me. When I came to live here it was a new beginning for both of us. I didn't want to talk about the past and I don't think she did either. She did sometimes tell me things, about her life at university, her job, odd people she knew. But that was one thing she didn't tell me.'

Dalgliesh asked gently:

'Do you feel able to tell me what happened last night?'

'She said that she was going for a walk. She often did, but usually after supper That's when she thought about her books, worked out the plot and dialogue, striding along in the darkness on her own.'

'What time did she go?'

'Just before seven.'

'Did she have the key of the chapel with her?'

'She asked me for it yesterday, after lunch, just before I went back to the Lab. She said she wanted to describe a seventeenth-century family chapel for the book, but I didn't know that she meant to visit it so soon. When she hadn't come home at half-past ten, I got worried and went to look for her. I walked for nearly an hour before I thought of looking in the chapel.'

Then she spoke directly to Dalgliesh, patiently, as if explaining something to an obtuse child:

'She did it for me. She killed herself so that I could have the money from her life assurance. She told me that I was her only legatee. You see, the owner wants to sell this cottage in a hurry; he needs the cash. We wanted to buy it, but we hadn't enough money for the deposit. Just before she went out, she asked me what it was like to be in local authority care, what it meant to have no real home. When Edwin was killed, we thought that there might be something for me in his will. But there wasn't. That's why she asked me for the key. It wasn't true that she needed to include a description of the chapel in her book, not this book anyway. It's set in London, and it's nearly finished. I know. I've been typing it. I thought at the time that it was odd that she wanted the key, but I learned never to ask Stella questions.

'But now I understand. She wanted to make life safe for me here, where we'd been happy, safe for ever. She knew what she was going to do. She knew she'd never come back. When I was massaging her neck to make her headache better, she knew that I should never touch her again.'

Dalgliesh asked:

'Would any writer, any writer who wasn't mentally

ill, choose to kill herself just before a book was finished?'

She said dully:

'I don't know. I don't understand how a writer feels.'

Dalgliesh said:

'Well, I do. And she wouldn't.'

She didn't reply. He went on gently:

'Was she happy, living here with you?'

She looked up at him eagerly, and, for the first time, her voice became animated, as if she were willing him to understand.

'She said that she had never been as happy in all her life. She said that was what love is, knowing that you can make just one other person happy, and be made happy by them in return.'

'So why should she kill herself? Could she really have believed that you'd rather have her money than herself? Why should she think that?'

'Stella always underrated herself. She may have thought that I'd forget her in time, but the money and the security would go on for ever. She may even have thought that it was bad for me to be living with her – that the money would somehow set me free. She once said something very like that.'

Dalgliesh looked across at the slim, upright figure, sitting, hands folded in her lap, opposite to him in the high winged chair. He fixed his eyes on her face. Then he said quietly:

'But there isn't going to be any money. The life assurance policy had a suicide clause. If Miss Mawson did kill herself, then you get nothing.'

She hadn't known. He could be certain of that at least. The news surprised her, but it didn't shock. This was no murderess balked of her spoils.

She smiled and said gently:

'It doesn't matter.'

'It matters to this investigation. I've read one of

your friend's novels. Miss Mawson was a highly intelligent writer, which means that she was an intelligent woman. Her heart wasn't strong and her life assurance premiums weren't cheap. It can't have been easy to meet them. Do you really think that she didn't know the terms of her policy?'

'What are you trying to tell me?'

'Miss Mawson knew, or thought she knew, who had killed Dr. Lorrimer, didn't she?'

'Yes. She said so. But she didn't tell me who it was.'

'Not even whether it were a man or a woman?'

She thought:

'No, nothing. Only that she knew. I'm not sure that she said that, not in so many words. But when I asked her, she didn't deny it.'

She paused, and then went on with more animation:

'You're thinking that she went out to meet the murderer, aren't you? That she tried to blackmail him? But Stella wouldn't do that! Only a fool would run into that kind of danger, and she wasn't a fool. You said so yourself. She wouldn't voluntarily have gone alone to face a killer, not for any money. No sane woman would.'

'Even if the murderer were a woman?'

'Not alone and at night. Star was so small and fraggile, and her heart wasn't strong. When I put my arms round her it was like holding a bird.' She looked into the fire and said, almost wonderingly:

'I shall never see her again. Never. She sat in this chair and pulled on her boots, just as she always did. I never offered to go with her in the evenings. I knew that she needed to be alone. It was all so ordinary, until she got to the door. And then I was frightened. I begged her not to go. And I shall never see her again. She won't ever speak again, not to me, not to anyone. She'll never write another word. I don't believe it yet.

324

I know that it must be true or you wouldn't be here, but I still don't believe it. How shall I bear it when I do?'

Dalgliesh said:

'Miss Foley, we have to know if she went out on the night Dr. Lorrimer was killed.'

She looked up at him.

'I know what you're trying to make me do. If I say that she did go out, then the case is finished for you, isn't it? It's all nicely tied up; means, motive, opportunity. He was her ex-husband and she hated him because of the will. She went to try and persuade him to help us with money. When he refused, she seized the first weapon to hand and struck him down.'

Dalgliesh said:

'He may have let her into the Laboratory, although it's unlikely. But how did she get out?'

'You'll say that I took the keys from Dr. Howarth's security safe and lent them to her. Then I put them back next morning.'

'Did you?'

She shook her head.

'You could only have done that if you and Inspector Blakelock were in this together. And what reason has he for wishing Dr. Lorrimer dead? When his only child was killed by a hit-and-run driver, the evidence of the forensic scientist helped secure an acquittal. But that was ten years ago, and the scientist wasn't Dr. Lorrimer. When Miss Pridmore told me about the child we checked. That evidence was to do with paint particles, the job of a forensic chemist, not a biologist. Are you telling me that Inspector Blakelock lied when he said that the keys were in the security cupboard?'

'He didn't lie. The keys were there.'

'Then any case we might seek to build against Miss Mawson weakens, doesn't it? Could anyone really believe that she climbed out of a third-floor window?

You must believe that we're here to find the truth, not to fabricate an easy solution.'

But she was right, thought Massingham. Once Angela Foley had admitted that her friend had left Sprogg's Cottage that night, it would be difficult to bring home the crime to anyone else. The solution she had propounded was neat enough and, whoever was brought to trial for Lorrimer's murder, the defence would make the most of it. He watched his chief's face. Dalgliesh said:

'I agree that no sane woman would go out alone at night to meet a murderer. That's why I don't think she did. She thought she knew who had killed Edwin Lorrimer, and if she did have an assignation last night, it wasn't with him. Miss Foley, please look at me. You must trust me. I don't know yet whether your friend killed herself or was killed. But if I'm to discover the truth, I'll have to know whether she went out the night Dr. Lorrimer died.'

She said dully:

'We were together all the evening. We told you.'

There was a silence. It seemed to Massingham to last for minutes. Then the wood fire flared and there was a crack like a pistol shot. A log rolled out on the hearth. Dalgliesh knelt and with the tongs eased it back into place. The silence went on. Then she said:

'Please tell me the truth first. Do you think Star was murdered?'

'I can't be sure. I may never be able to prove it. But yes, I do.'

She said:

'Star did go out that night. She was out from half past eight until about half past nine. She didn't tell me where she'd been, and she was perfectly ordinary, perfectly composed, when she got home. She said nothing, but she did go out.'

She said at last:

326

'I'd like you to go now, please.'

'I think you should have someone with you.'

'I'm not a child. I don't want Mrs. Swaffield or the district nurse or any of the village do-gooders. And I don't need a policewoman. I haven't committed a crime, so you've no right to force yourselves on me. I've told you everything I know. You've locked her desk, so no-one can get at Stella's things. I shan't do anything foolish – that's the expression people use when they're trying to ask tactfully if you're planning to kill yourself, isn't it? Well, I'm not. I'm all right now. I just want to be left alone.'

Dalgliesh said:

'I'm afraid we shall need to force ourselves on you later again.'

'Later is better than now.'

She wasn't trying to be offensive. It was a simple statement of fact. She got up stiffly and walked towards the door, her head held rigidly high as if only the body's discipline could hold intact the fragile integrity of the mind. Dalgliesh and Massingham exchanged glances. She was right. They couldn't force comfort or company where neither was wanted. They had no legal authority either to stay or to compel her to leave. And there were things to do.

She went over to the window and watched from behind the curtains as the car rounded Sprogg's Green and accelerated towards the village. Then she ran into the hall and dragged out the telephone directory from its shelf. It took only a few seconds of feverishly leafing to find the number she wanted. She dialled, waited and then spoke. Replacing the receiver she went back into the sitting-room. Slowly, with ceremony, she lifted the French sword from the wall and stood very still, holding out her arms, the weapon resting across her palms. After a few seconds she curled her left hand round the scabbard, and with her right slowly and deliberately withdrew the blade. Then she took her

327

stand just inside the sitting-room door, naked sword in her hand, and measured the room with her eyes, regarding the disposition of furniture and objects, intent as a stranger calculating her chances in some coming trial.

After a few minutes she moved into the study, and again stood silently surveying the room. There was a Victorian button-backed chair beside the fireplace. She dragged it to the study door and hid the naked sword behind it, the tip resting against the floor; then slid the scabbard under the chair. Satisfied that neither could be seen she returned to the sitting-room. She took her seat beside the fire and sat motionless, waiting for the sound of the approaching car.

3

If Claire Easterbrook was surprised, on her arrival at the Laboratory just before nine o'clock, to be asked by Inspector Blakelock to see Commander Dalgliesh immediately, she concealed it. She changed first into her white coat, but otherwise did not delay in obeying the summons more than was strictly necessary to assert her independence. When she went into the Director's office, she saw the two detectives, the dark head and the red, quietly conferring together at the window almost, she thought, as if their business was ordinary, their presence unremarkable. There was an alien file on Dr. Howarth's desk, and a plan of the Laboratory and an Ordnance Survey map of the village laid open on the conference table, but otherwise the room seemed unchangd. Dalgliesh moved to the desk and said:

'Good morning, Miss Easterbrook. You heard what happened last night?'

'No. Should I have? I was at the theatre after

dinner, so people couldn't reach me, and I've spoken to no-one but Inspector Blakelock. He hasn't told me anything.'

'Stella Mawson, Miss Foley's friend, was found hanged in the chapel.'

She frowned as if the news were personally offensive, and said with no more than polite interest:

'I see. I don't think I've met her. Oh yes, I remember. She was at the concert in the chapel. Grey-haired, with remarkable eyes. What happened? Did she kill herself?'

'That's one of two possibilities. It's unlikely to have been an accident.'

'Who found her?'

'Miss Pridmore.'

She said with suprising gentleness:

'Poor child.'

Dalgliesh opened the file, picked up two transparent exhibit envelopes, and said:

'I'd like you to have a look at these four hairs urgently for me. There's no time to get them to the Met Lab. I want to know, if possible, if the dark hairs came from the same head.'

'It's easier to say whether they don't. I can have a look under the microscope but I doubt whether I can help you. Hair identification is never easy, and I can't . hope to do much with only three samples. Apart from microscopic examination, we'd normally use mass spectrometry to try to identify differences in the trace elements, but even that isn't possible with three hairs. If these were submitted to me, I'd have to say that I couldn't give an opinion.'

Dalgliesh said:

'I'd be grateful, all the same, if you'd take a look. It's just a hunch and I want to know whether it's worth following up.'

Massingham said:

'I'd like to watch, if you don't mind.'

She gazed at him.

'Would it make any difference if I did?'

Ten minutes later she lifted her head from the comparison microscope and said:

'If we're talking of hunches, mine, for what it's worth, is that they came from different heads. The cuticle, cortex and medulla are all significantly different. But I think they're both male. Look for yourself.'

Massingham bent his head to the eyepiece. He saw what looked like the sections of two logs, patterned and grained. And beside them were two other logs, their barks shredded. But he could see that they were different logs, and that they came from different trees. He said:

'Thank you. I'll let Mr. Dalgliesh know.'

4

There was nothing he could put between himself and that shining, razor-sharp blade. He thought wryly that a bullet would have been worse; but then he wondered. To use a gun at least required some skill, a preliminary aim. A bullet could go anywhere, and if her first shot was wide he could at least have ensured that she got no second chance. But she had three feet of cold steel in her hand and, in this confined space, she had only to lunge or slash and he would be cut to the bone. He knew now why she had shown him into the study. There was no room here to manœuvre; no object within his range of sight which he could seize and hurl. And he knew that he mustn't look round, must keep his eyes firmly and without fear on her face. He tried to keep his voice calm, reasonable; one nervous smile, one hint of hostility or provocation and it might be too late to argue. He said:

'Look, don't you think we ought to talk about this? You've got the wrong man, believe me.'

She said:

'Read that note. The one on the desk behind you. Read it out loud.'

He didn't dare turn his head, but reached back and fumbled on the desk. His hand encountered a single sheet of paper. He read:

'You'd better check on the cannabis exhibits when Detective Inspector Doyle's around. How do you think he managed to afford his house?'

'Well?'

'Where did you get this?'

'From Edwin Lorrimer's desk. Stella found it and gave it to me. You killed her because she knew, because she tried to blackmail you. She arranged to meet you last night in the Wren chapel and you strangled her.'

He could have laughed at the irony of it, but he knew that laughter would be fatal. And at least they were talking. The longer she waited, the greater his chances.

'Are you saying that your friend thought that I killed Edwin Lorrimer?'

'She knew you didn't. She was out walking the night he died and I think she saw someone she recognised leaving the Laboratory. She knew that it wasn't you. She wouldn't have risked meeting you alone if she'd thought that you were the murderer. Mr. Dalgliesh explained that to me. She went to the chapel thinking that she was safe, that she could come to some arrangement with you. But you killed her. That's why I'm going to kill you. Stella hated the thought of shutting people away in prison. I can't bear the thought of her murderer ever being free. Ten years in exchange for Stella's life. Why should you be alive when she's dead?'

He had no doubt that she meant what she said. He had dealt before with people pushed over the brink

331

of endurance into madness, had seen before that look of dedicated fanaticism. He stood very still, poised on the soles of his feet, waiting for that first instinctive tightening of the muscles before she struck. He tried to keep his voice low, calm, with no trace of facetiousness.

'That's a reasonable point of view. Don't think that I'm against it. I've never understood why people are squeamish about killing a convicted murderer instantaneously and resigned to killing him slowly over twenty years. But at least they have been convicted. There's the little matter of a trial. No execution without due process. And believe me, Miss Foley, you've got the wrong man. I didn't kill Lorrimer, and luckily for me I can prove it.'

'I don't care about Edwin Lorrimer. I only care about Stella. And you killed her.'

'I didn't even know that she was dead. But if she was killed yesterday any time between half past three and half past seven, then I'm in the clear. I've got the best possible alibi. I was at Guy's Marsh police station most of the time being interrogated by the Yard. And when Dalgliesh and Massingham left, I was there for another two hours. Ring them. Ask anyone. Look, you can lock me away in a cupboard – somewhere I can't escape – while you telephone Guy's Marsh. For God's sake, you don't want to make a mistake, do you? You know me. Do you want to kill me, messily, horribly, while the real murderer escapes? An unofficial execution is one thing; murder's another.'

He thought that the hand holding the sword lost some of its tension. But there was no change in the taut, white face. She said:

'And the note.'

'I know who sent the note – my wife. She wanted me to leave the Force, and she knew that there'd be nothing like a little official harassment to push me into resigning. I had a spot of trouble with the Force about two years ago. The disciplinary committee exonerated me, but I damn nearly resigned then. Can't you recognise feminine spite when you see it? That note proves nothing except that she wanted me disgraced and out of the Force.'

'But you have been stealing cannabis, substituting an inert substance?'

'Ah, that's a different question. But you're not killing me for that. You won't be able to prove it, you know. The last batch of cannabis exhibits I was concerned with had a destruction authorisation from the court. I helped burn them myself. Just in time, luckily; the incinerator broke down immediately afterwards.'

'And the court exhibits you burned, were they cannabis?'

'Some of them were. But you'll never prove I made the substitution, even if you decide to make use of that note, not now. But what does it matter? I'm out of the Force. Look, you know that I've been working on the clunch pit murder. Do you really suppose that I'd have been sitting at home at this time of day, free to drive over here as soon as you rang me merely to satisfy my curiosity, if I were on a murder case, if I hadn't been suspended or resigned? I may not be a shining example of probity to the Force, but I'm not a murderer, and I can prove it. Ring Dalgliesh and ask him.'

There was no doubt about it now, her grip on the sword had relaxed. She stood there, very still, no longer looking at him, but with her gaze fixed out of the window. Her face didn't change, but he saw that she was crying. The tears were streaming out of the tight little eyes to roll unimpeded down her cheeks. He moved quietly forward and took the sword from her unresisting hand. He placed an arm on her shoulders. She didn't flinch. He said:

'Look, you've had a shock. You shouldn't have been

333

left here on your own. Isn't it time we had a cup of tea? Show me where the kitchen is and I'll make it. Or better still, have you anything stronger?'

She said dully:

'There's whisky, but we keep that for Stella. I don't drink it.'

'Well, you're going to drink it now. It'll do you good. And, by God, I need it. And then you'd better sit down quietly and tell me all about it.'

She said:

'But if it wasn't you, who did kill Stella?'

'My guess is, the same person who killed Lorrimer. A couple of murderers loose in one small community is too much of a coincidence. But look, you've got to let the police know about that note. It can't hurt me, not now, and it might help them. If your friend found one incriminating piece of information in Lorrimer's desk, then she may have found another. She didn't use that note. She probably knew how little it was worth. But what about the information she did use?'

She said dully:

'You tell them, if you want to. It doesn't matter now.'

But he waited until he had made the tea. The tidiness and good order of the kitchen pleased him, and he took trouble over the tray, setting it in front of her on a low table which he drew up before the fire. He replaced the sword above the fireplace, standing back to make sure that it hung correctly. Then he made up the fire. She had shaken her head when he had offered her the whisky, but he poured himself a generous measure and sat opposite to her on the other side of the fire. She didn't attract him. Even in their brief encounters at the Laboratory he had given her no more than a passing dismissive glance. It was unusual for him to put himself out for a woman from whom he wanted nothing, and the sensation of disinterested kindness was unfamiliar but agreeable. Sitting opposite to her in silence, the traumas of the day faded, and he felt a curious peace. They had some quite decent stuff in the cottage, he decided, looking around at the cosy, cluttered sitting-room. He wondered whether it was all coming to her.

It was ten minutes before he went out to telephone. When he returned the sight of his face roused her from her benumbed misery. She said:

'What is it? What did he say?'

He moved into the room, frowning. He said:

'He wasn't there. He and Massingham weren't at Guy's Marsh or at the Lab. They're at Muddington. They've gone to the clunch pit.'

5

They drove again over the route they had followed the previous night when they had heard those three clangs from the chapel bell, the mile-and-a-half to the junction of Guy's Marsh road and then right through the main street of the village. Neither spoke. Massingham had taken one look at his chief's face and had decided that silence would be prudent. And it was certainly no time for self-congratulation. They still lacked proof, the one clinching fact that would break the case open. And Massingham wondered if they would ever get it. They were dealing with intelligent men and women who must know that they had only to keep their mouths shut and nothing could be proved.

In the village street, the first Saturday-morning shoppers were making their appearance. The gossiping groups of women turned their heads to glance briefly at the car as it passed. And now the houses were thinning and Hoggatt's field, with the new building, was on their right. Massingham had changed down to turn into the drive of the Old Rectory when it happened. The blue and yellow ball bounced out into the road in front of them, and after it, red wellingtons flashing, ran William. They were driving too slowly for danger, but Massingham cursed as he swerved and braked. And then came two seconds of horror.

Afterwards it seemed to Dalgliesh that time was suspended so that he saw in memory the whole accident like a film run slowly. The red Jaguar leaping and held suspended in the air; a blaze of blue from the terrified eyes; the mouth gaping in a soundless scream; the white knuckles wrenching at the wheel. Instinctively he cradled his head and braced himself for the impact. The Jaguar crashed the rear bumper of the Rover, ripping it away in a scream of torn metal. The car rocked wildly and spun round. There was a second of absolute silence. Then he and Massingham were out of their seat-belts and rushing across to the opposite verge to that small, motionless body. One boot lay in the road, and the ball trickled slowly towards the grass verge.

William had been tossed into a heap of hay left on the verge after the late summer scything. He lay spreadeagled, so relaxed in his perfect stillness that Massingham's first horrified thought was that his neck was broken. In the couple of seconds in which he was resisting the impulse to sweep the boy into his arms, and turning instead to telephone from the car for an ambulance, William recovered his wind and began struggling against the prickling dampness of the straw. Bereft both of dignity and his ball he began to cry. Domenica Schofield, hair streaming across her bleached face, stumbled up to them.

'Is he all right?'

Massingham ran his hands over William's body, then took the boy in his arms.

'I think so. He sounds all right.'

They had reached the drive of the Old Rectory when Eleanor Kerrison came running down the path

336

towards them. She had obviously been washing her hair. It lay now in dank, dripping swathes across her shoulders. William, seeing her, redoubled his crying. As Massingham strode towards the house she ran clumsily beside him, clutching his arm. Drops of water sprayed from her hair to lie like pearls on William's face.

'Daddy's been called to a body. He said he'd take William and me to lunch at Cambridge when he got back. We were going to buy a grown-up bed for William. I was washing my hair specially. I left William with Miss Willard. He's all right, isn't he? Are you sure he's all right? Oughtn't we to take him to the hospital? What happened?'

'We didn't see. I think he was caught and tossed by the front bumper of the Jaguar. Luckily he landed on a heap of straw.'

'He could have been killed. I warned her about the road. He isn't supposed to play in the garden on his own. Are you sure we oughtn't to get Dr. Greene?'

Massingham went straight through the house to the drawing-room and laid William on the sofa. He said:

'It might be as well, but I'm sure he's all right. Just listen to him.'

William, as if he understood, cut off his bawling instantaneously and struggled upright on the couch. He began hiccuping loudly but, apparently undistressed by the paroxysms which were jerking his body, he regarded the company with interest, then fixed his stare consideringly on his bootless left foot. Looking up at Dalgliesh he asked sternly:

'Where's Willum's ball?'

'At the edge of the road, presumably,' said Massingham. 'I'll fetch it. And you'll have to do something about fixing a gate for that drive.'

They heard footsteps in the hall, and Miss Willard stood, fluttering uneasily in the doorway. Eleanor had been sitting beside her brother on the sofa. Now she stood up and confronted the woman with a silent contempt so unmistakable that Miss Willard blushed. She glanced round the watching faces and said defensively:

'Quite a little party. I thought I heard voices.'

Then the girl spoke. The voice, thought Massingham, was as arrogant and cruel as that of a Victorian matron dismissing a kitchen maid. The confrontation would have been almost comic if it hadn't been at once pathetic and horrible.

'You can pack up your bags and get out. You're dismissed. I only asked you to watch William while I washed my hair. You couldn't even do that. He might have been killed. You're a useless, ugly stupid old woman. You drink and you smell and we all hate you. We don't need you any more. So get out. Pack your beastly, horrible things and go. I can look after William and Daddy. He doesn't need anyone but me.'

The silly, ingratiating smile faded on Miss Willard's face. Two red weals appeared across her cheeks and forehead as if the words had been a physical whiplash. Then she was suddenly pale, her whole body shaking. She reached for the back of a chair for support and said, her voice high and distorted with pain:

'You! Do you think he needs you? I may be middle-aged and past my best but at least I'm not half-mad. And if I'm ugly, look at yourself! He only puts up with you because of William. You could leave tomorrow and he wouldn't care. He'd be glad. It's William he loves, not you. I've seen his face, I've heard him and I know. He's thinking of letting you go to your mother. You didn't know that, did you? And there's something else you don't know. What do you think your precious daddy gets up to when he's drugged you into sleep? He sneaks off to the Wren chapel and makes love to her.'

Eleanor turned and looked at Domenica Schofield. Then she spun round and spoke directly to Dalgliesh.

'She's lying! Tell me she's lying! It isn't true.'

There was a silence. It could only have lasted a couple of seconds while Dalgliesh's mind phased the careful answer. Then, as if impatient to forestall him, not looking at his chief's face, Massingham said clearly:

'Yes, it's true.'

She looked from Dalgliesh to Domenica Schofield. Then she swayed as if she were about to faint. Dalgliesh went towards her, but she backed away. She said in a voice of dull calm:

'I thought he did it for me. I didn't drink the cocoa he made for me. I wasn't asleep when he came back. I went out and watched him in the garden, burning the white coat on the bonfire. I knew that there was blood on it. I thought he'd been to see Dr. Lorrimer because he was unkind to William and me. I thought he did it for me, because he loves me.'

Suddenly she gave a high despairing wail like an animal in torment, and yet so human and so adult that Dalgliesh felt his blood run cold.

'Daddy! Daddy! Oh no!'

She put her hands to her throat and pulling the leather thong from beneath her sweater, struggled with it, twisting like a creature in a trap. And then the knot broke. Over the dark carpet they scattered and rolled, six newly-polished brass buttons, bright as crested jewels.

Massingham stooped and carefully gathered them up into his handkerchief. Still no-one spoke. William propelled himself off the sofa, trotted over to his sister and fastened his arms around her leg. His lip trembled. Domenica Schofield spoke directly to Dalgliesh.

'My God, yours is a filthy trade.'

Dalgliesh ignored her. He said to Massingham:

'Look after the children. I'll ring for a W.P.C. and we'd better get Mrs. Swaffield. There's no-one else I can think of. Don't leave her until they both arrive. I'll see to things here.'

Massingham turned to Domenica Schofield.

'Not a trade. Just a job. And are you saying that it's one you don't want done?'

He went up to the girl. She was trembling violently. Dalgliesh thought that she would cringe away from him. But she stood perfectly still. With three words he had destroyed her. But who else had she to turn to? Massingham took off his tweed coat and wrapped it round her. He said gently without touching her:

'Come with me. You show me where we can make some tea. And then you'll have a lie down and William and I will stay with you. I'll read to William.'

She went with him as meekly as a prisoner with a gaoler, without looking at him, the long coat trailing on the floor. Massingham took William's hand. The door closed after them. Dalgliesh wished never to see Massingham again. But he would see him again and, in time, without even caring or remembering. He never wanted to work with him again; but he knew that he would. He wasn't the man to destroy a subordinate's career simply because he had outraged susceptibilities to which he, Dalgliesh, had no right. What Massingham had done seemed to him now unforgivable. But life had taught him that the unforgivable was usually the most easily forgiven. It was possible to do police work honestly; there was, indeed, no other safe way to do it. But it wasn't possible to do it without giving pain.

Miss Willard had groped her way to the sofa. She muttered, as if trying to explain it to herself:

'I didn't mean it. She made me say it. I didn't mean it. I didn't want to hurt him.'

Domenica Schofield turned to go.

'No, one seldom does.' She said to Dalgliesh:

'If you want me, you know where I'll be.'

'We shall want a statement.'

'Of course. Don't you always? Longing and loneliness, terror and despair, all the human muddle, neatly

340

documented, on one-and-a-half sheets of official paper.'

'No, just the facts.'

He didn't ask her when it had begun. That wasn't really important; and he thought that he didn't need to ask. Brenda Pridmore had told him that she had sat in the same row as Mrs. Schofield and Dr. Kerrison and his children at the concert in the chapel. That had been held on Thursday the twenty-sixth of August. And early in September, Domenica had broken with Edwin Lorrimer.

At the door she hesitated and turned. Dalgliesh asked:

'Did he telephone you the morning after the murder to let you know that he'd replaced the key on Lorrimer's body?'

'He never telephoned me. Neither of them did, ever. That was our arrangement. And I never rang him.' She paused and then said gruffly:

'I didn't know. I may have suspected, but I didn't know. We weren't – what's your expression? – in it together. I'm not responsible. It wasn't because of me.'

'No,' said Dalgliesh. 'I didn't suppose it was. A motive for murder is seldom so unimportant.'

She fixed on him her unforgettable eyes. She said:

'Why do you dislike me?'

The egotism which could ask such a question, and at such a time, astounded him. But it was his own self-knowledge which disgusted him more. He understood only too well what had driven those two men to creep guiltily like randy schoolboys to that rendezvous, to make themselves partners in her erotic, esoteric game. Given the opportunity, he would, he thought bitterly, have done the same.

She was gone. He went over to Miss Willard.

'Did you telephone Dr. Lorrimer to tell him about the burnt candles, the numbers on the hymn-board?'

'I chatted to him when he drove me to Mass the Sunday before last. I had to talk about something on

341

the journey; he never did. And I was worried about the altar candles. I first noticed that someone had lit them when I went to the chapel at the end of September. On my last visit they were burnt even lower. I thought that the chapel might be being used by devil-worshippers. I know it's been deconsecrated, but it's still a holy place. And it's so secluded. No-one goes there. The fen people don't like to walk out after dark. I wondered if I ought to talk to the Rector or consult Father Gregory. Dr. Lorrimer asked me to go to the chapel again next day and let him know the numbers on the hymn-board. I thought it was an odd thing to ask, but he seemed to think that it was important. I hadn't even noticed that they'd been altered. I could ask for the key, you see. He didn't like to.'

But he could have taken it without signing for it, thought Dalgliesh. So why hadn't he? Because of the risk that he might be seen? Because it was repugnant to his obsessional, conformist personality to break a Laboratory rule? Or, more likely, because he couldn't bear to enter the chapel again, to see with his own eyes the evidence of betrayal? She hadn't even bothered to change their meeting-place. She had still used the same ingenious code to fix the date of the next assignation. Even the key she had handed to Kerrison had been Lorrimer's key. And none better than he had known the significance of those four numbers. The twenty-ninth day of the tenth month at six-forty. He said:

'And you waited together last Friday in the shelter of the trees?'

'That was his idea. He needed a witness, you see. Oh, he was quite right to be worried. A woman like that, quite unsuitable to be a stepmother to William. One man after another, Dr. Lorrimer said. That's why she had to leave London. She couldn't leave men alone. Any man would do. He knew about her, you

342

see. He said the whole Lab knew. She'd even made advances to him once. Horrible. He was going to write to Mrs. Kerrison and put a stop to it. I couldn't tell him the address. Dr. Kerrison's so secretive about his letters, and I'm not sure that even he knows exactly where his wife is. But we knew that she'd run away with a doctor, and we knew his name. It's quite a common name, but Dr. Lorrimer said he could trace them from the Medical Directory.'

The Medical Directory. So that was why he had wanted to consult it, why he had opened the door so quickly when Bradley rang. He had only had to come from the Director's office on the ground floor. And he had been carrying his notebook. What was it that Howarth had said? He hated scraps of paper. He used the book to note down anything of importance. And this had been important. The names and addresses of Mrs. Kerrison's possible lovers.

Miss Willard looked up at him. Dalgliesh saw that she was crying, the tears streaking her face and dropping unimpeded over the twisting hands. She said:

'What will happen to him? What will you do to him?'

The telephone rang. Dalgliesh strode across the hall and into the study and lifted the receiver. It was Clifford Bradley. His voice sounded as high and excited as a young girl's. He said:

'Commander Dalgliesh? They said at the police station you might be there. I have to tell you at once. It's important. I've just remembered how I knew that the murderer was still in the Lab. I heard a sound as I got to the Lab door. I heard the same sound again two minutes ago coming downstairs from the bathroom. Sue had just finished telephoning her mother. What I heard was someone replacing the telephone receiver.'

It was no more than confirmation of what he had long ago suspected He returned to the drawing-room and said to Miss Willard:

343

'Why did you tell us that you overheard Dr. Kerrison making that nine o'clock telephone call from his study? Did he ask you to lie for him?'

The blotched face, the tear-stained eyes looked up at him.

'Oh, no, he'd never do that! All he asked was whether I'd happened to hear him. It was when he came back to the house after he'd been called to the body. I wanted to help him, to make him pleased with me. It was such a little, unimportant lie. And it wasn't really a lie. I thought that perhaps I did hear him. You might have suspected him, and I knew that he couldn't have done it. He's kind, and good and gentle. It seems such a venial sin to protect the innocent. That woman had got him into her clutches, but I knew he could never kill.'

He had probably always intended to telephone the hospital from the Laboratory if he wasn't back home in time. But, with Lorrimer lying dead, it must have taken nerve. He could hardly have put down the receiver before he heard the approaching footsteps. And what then? Into the darkroom to watch and wait? That must have been one of his worst moments, standing there rigidly in the darkness, breath held, his heart thudding, wondering who could be arriving at this late hour, how they could have got in. And it could have been Blakelock; Blakelock who would have rung at once for the police, who would have made an immediate search of the Lab.

But it had only been a terrified Bradley. There had been no telephone call, no summons for help, only the echo of panicking feet down the corridor. And now all he had to do was to follow, make his way quietly out of the Lab and home through the new Lab the way he had come. He had put out the light and reached the front door. And then he had seen the headlights of Doyle's car swinging into the drive and backing to park among the bushes. He no longer dared leave by that door. The way was barred. And he couldn't wait for them to drive off. There was Nell at home who might wake and ask for him. There was the return telephone call at ten o'clock. He had to get back.

But he had still kept his head. It had been a clever move to take Lorrimer's keys and lock the Laboratory. The police investigation would inevitably concentrate on the four sets of keys and the limited number of people who had access to them. And he knew the one way he could get out and had the skill and nerve to do it. He had put on Middlemass's jacket to protect his clothes; he knew how fatal a torn thread of cloth could be. But there had been no tear. And in the early hours of the morning a light rain had washed away any evidence on walls or windows which could have betrayed him.

He had reached home safely and made an excuse to call in on Miss Willard, establishing his alibi more firmly. No-one had telephoned for him; no-one had called. And he knew that, next day, he would be among the first to examine the body. Howarth had said that he had stood by the door while Kerrison made his examination. It must have been then that he had slipped the key into Lorrimer's pocket. But that had been one of his mistakes. Lorrimer carried his keys in a leather pouch, not loose in his pocket.

There was the crunch of tyres on the gravel of the drive. He looked out of the window and saw the police car with Detective Sergeant Reynolds and two women police constables in the back. The case had broken; except that it was never the case that broke, only the people. And now he and Massingham were free for the last interview, the most difficult of all.

At the edge of the clunch field a boy was flying a red kite. Tugged by the freshening wind it soared and dipped, weaving its convoluted tail against an azure sky as clear and bright as on a summer day. The clunch field was alive with voices and laughter. Even the discarded beer-cans glinted like bright toys and the waste paper bowled along merrily in the wind. The air was keen and smelt of the sea. It was possible to believe that the Saturday shoppers trailing with their children across the scrubland were carrying their picnics to the beach, that the clunch field led on to dunes and marram grass, to the child-loud fringes of the sea. Even the screen, which the police were fighting to erect against the wind, looked no more frightening than a Punch-and-Judy stand with a little group of curious people standing patiently at a distance, waiting for the show to begin.

It was Superintendent Mercer who came first up the slope of the clunch pit towards them. He said:

'It's a messy business; the husband of the girl who was found here on Wednesday. He's a butcher's assistant. Yesterday he took home one of the knives and came here last night to cut his throat. He left a note confessing to her murder, poor devil. It wouldn't have happened if we'd been able to arrest him yesterday. But Lorrimer's death and Doyle's suspension held us up. We only got the blood result late last night. Who is it you want to see?'

Mercer looked at Dalgliesh keenly, but said only:

'Dr. Kerrison.'

'He's finished here now. I'll let him know.'

Three minutes later Kerrison's figure appeared over the rim of the clunch pit and he walked towards them. He said:

'It was Nell, wasn't it?'

'Yes.'

He didn't ask how or when. He listened intently as Dalgliesh spoke the words of the caution, as if he hadn't heard them before and wanted to commit them to memory. Then he said, looking at Dalgliesh:

'I'd rather not go to Guy's Marsh police station, not yet. I want to tell you about it now, just you, no-one else. There won't be any difficulty. I'll make a full confession. Whatever happens, I don't want Nell to have to give evidence. Can you promise me that?'

'You must know that I can't. But there's no reason why the Crown should call her if you intend to plead guilty.'

Dalgliesh opened the door of the car, but Kerrison shook his head. He said without a trace of self-pity:

'I'd rather stay outside. There'll be so many years of sitting when I shan't be able to walk under the sky. Perhaps for the rest of my life. If it were only Lorrimer's death, I might have hoped for a verdict of manslaughter. His killing wasn't premeditated. But the other was murder.'

Massingham stayed by the car while Dalgliesh and Kerrison walked together round the clunch pit. Kerrison said:

'It started here, at this very spot, only four days ago. It feels like an eternity. Another life, another time. We'd both been called to the clunch pit murder, and afterwards he drew me to one side and told me to meet him that evening at eight-thirty at the Laboratory. Not asked; told. And he told me, too, what he wanted to talk about. Domenica.'

Dalgliesh asked:

'Did you know that he was her lover before you?'

'Not until I met him that night. She had never talked about him to me, never once mentioned his name. But when he poured out his stream of hate and envy and jealousy, then, of course, I knew. I didn't ask him how he'd found out about me. I think he was mad. Perhaps we were both mad.'

'And he threatened to write to your wife and prevent your getting custody of the children unless you gave her up.'

347

'He was going to write anyway. He wanted her back, and I think, poor devil, that he actually believed that it might be possible. But he still wanted to punish me. I've only once before known such hate. He was standing there, white-faced, railing at me, taunting me, telling me that I'd lose the children, that I wasn't fit to be a father, that I'd never see them again. And suddenly it wasn't Lorrimer speaking. You see, I'd heard it all before from my wife. It was his voice, but her words. And I knew that I couldn't take any more. I'd been up for most of the night; I'd had a terrible scene with Nell when I got home; and I'd spent the day worrying what Lorrimer might have to tell me.

'It was then that the telephone rang. It was his father complaining about the television. He only spoke briefly, then he put down the receiver. But when he was speaking I saw the mallet. And I knew that I had gloves in my coat pocket. The call to his father seemed to have sobered him. He told me there was nothing else he wanted to say. It was when he turned his back on me dismissively that I seized the mallet and struck. He fell without a sound. I put the mallet back on the table, and it was then I saw the open notebook with the names and addresses of three doctors. One of them was my wife's lover. I tore out the page and crumpled it in my pocket. Then I went to the telephone and made my call. It was just nine o'clock. The rest, I think, you know.'

They had circled the clunch pit, pacing together, their eyes fixed on the bright grass. Now they turned and retraced their steps. Dalgliesh said:

'I think you'd better tell me.'

But there was nothing new to learn. It had happened just as Dalgliesh had reasoned. When Kerrison had finished describing the burning of the coat and the page from the notebook, Dalgliesh asked:

'And Stella Mawson?'

'She rang me at the hospital and asked me to meet her in the chapel at half-past seven yesterday. She gave me an idea what it was about. She said that she had a draft letter which she wanted to discuss with me, one she'd found in a certain desk. I knew what it would say.'

She must have taken it with her to the chapel, thought Dalgliesh. It hadn't been found in her desk, neither the original nor the copy. It seemed to him extraordinary that she had actually risked letting Kerrison know that she had the letter on her. How could he be sure, when he killed her, that she hadn't left a copy? And how could she be sure that he wouldn't overpower her and take it?

Almost as if he knew what was going through Dalgliesh's mind, Kerrison said:

'It wasn't what you're thinking. She wasn't trying to sell me the letter. She wasn't selling anything. She told me that she'd taken it from Lorrimer's desk almost on impulse because she didn't want the police to find it. For some reason which she didn't explain, she hated Lorrimer, and she bore me no ill will. What she said was: "He caused enough misery in his life. Why should he cause misery after his death?" She said another extraordinary thing. "I was his victim once. I don't see why you should be his victim now." She saw herself as on my side, someone who'd done me a service. And now she was asking me for something in return, something quite simple and ordinary. Something she knew that I'd be able to afford.'

Dalgliesh said:

'The cash to buy Sprogg's Cottage, security for herself and Angela Foley.'

'Not even a gift, merely a loan. She wanted four thousand pounds over five years at a rate of interest she could afford. She needed the money desperately, and she had to find it quickly. She explained to me that

349

there was no-one else she could ask. She was perfectly ready to have a legal agreement drawn up. She was the gentlest, most reasonable of blackmailers.'

And she thought that she was dealing with the gentlest, most reasonable of men. She had been totally without fear, until that last hideous moment when he had drawn the cord from his coat pocket and she had realised that she was facing, not a fellow victim, but her murderer. Dalgliesh said:

'You must have had the cord ready. When did you decide she had to die?'

'Even that, like Lorrimer's death, was almost chance. She had got the key from Angela Foley and she arrived at the chapel first. She was sitting in the chancel, in one of the stalls. She had left the door open, and when I went into the antechapel I saw the chest. I knew the cord was inside it. I'd had plenty of time to explore the chapel when I'd been waiting for Domenica. So I took it out and put it in my pocket. Then I went through to her, and we talked. She had the letter with her, in her pocket. She took it out and showed it to me without the least fear. It wasn't the finished letter; just a draft that he'd been working on. He must have enjoyed writing it, must have taken a lot of trouble getting it right.

'She was an extraordinary woman. I said that I'd lend her the money, that I'd have a proper agreement drawn up by my solicitor. There was a Prayer Book in the chapel, and she made me put my hand on it and swear that I'd never tell anyone what had happened between us. I think she was terrified that Angela Foley would get to know. It was when I realised that she, and only she, held this dangerous knowledge, that I decided that she must die.'

He stopped walking. He turned to Dalgliesh and said:

'You see, I couldn't take a chance on her. I'm not trying to justify myself. I'm not even trying to make

350

you understand. You aren't a father, so you never could understand. I couldn't risk giving my wife such a weapon against me when the custody case comes before the high court. They probably wouldn't worry overmuch that I had a mistress; that wouldn't make me unfit to care for my children. If it did, what chance would most parents have of getting custody? But a secret affair which I'd concealed from the police with a woman whose previous lover was murdered, a murder for which I had only a weak alibi and a strong motive. Wouldn't that tip the balance? My wife is attractive and plausible, outwardly perfectly sane. That's what makes it so impossible. Madness isn't so very difficult to diagnose, neurosis is less dramatic but just as lethal if you have to live with it. She tore us apart, Nell and me. I couldn't let her have William and Nell. When I stood in the chapel and faced Stella Mawson, I knew it was their lives against hers.

'And it was so easy. I slipped the double cord round her neck and pulled tight. She must have died at once. Then I carried her into the antechapel and strung her up on the hook. I remembered to scrape her boots on the chair seat and leave the chair overturned. I walked back across the field to where I'd left my car. I'd parked it where Domenica parks hers when we meet, in the shadow of an old barn on the edge of Guy's Marsh Road. Even the timing was right for me. I was due at the hospital for a medical committee meeting, but I'd planned to go into my laboratory first and do some work. Even if someone at the hospital noted the time when I arrived, there was only about twenty minutes unaccounted for. And I could easily have spent an extra twenty minutes on the drive.'

They walked on in silence towards the car. Then Kerrison began speaking again:

'I still don't understand it. She's so beautiful. And it isn't only her beauty. She could have had any man she wanted. It was amazing that, for some extraordinary reason, she wanted me. When we were together, lying by candlelight in the quietness of the chapel after we'd made love, all the anxieties, all the tensions, all the responsibilities were forgotten. It was easy for us, because of the dark evenings. She could park her car by the barn in safety. No-one walks on the Guy's Marsh road at night, and there are only a few cars. I knew it would be more difficult in the spring with the long evenings. But then, I didn't expect she would want me that long. It was a miracle that she wanted me at all. I never thought beyond the next meeting, the next date on the hymn-board. She wouldn't let me telephone her. I never saw or spoke to her except when we were alone in the chapel. I knew that she didn't love me, but that wasn't important. She gave what she could, and it was enough for me.'

They were back at the car now. Massingham was holding open the door. Kerrison turned to Dalgliesh and said:

'It wasn't love, but it was in its own way a kind of loving. And it was such peace. This is peace, too, knowing that there's nothing else I need do. There's an end of responsibility, an end of worry. A murderer sets himself aside from the whole of humanity for ever. It's a kind of death. I'm like a dying man now, the problems are still there, but I'm moving away from them into a new dimension. I forfeited so many things when I killed Stella Mawson, even the right to feel pain.'

He got into the back of the car without another word. Dalgliesh closed the door. Then his heart lurched. The blue and yellow ball came bounding across the clunch field towards him and after it, shouting with laughter, his mother calling after him, ran the child. For one dreadful second, Dalgliesh thought that it was William, William's dark fringe of hair, William's red wellingtons flashing in the sun.